"Harsh, sometimes grotesque, strongly compelling – a classical journey told in a new, uncompromising voice."

John Meaney

"Harvey paints a grimly convincing portrait of a subsistence existence on the inhospitable world. Harvey's novel depicts a fascinating universe of want and plenitude, to which he will hopefully return in future novels."

The Guardian

"An entertaining read in an unforgiving environment. *Winter Song* is a novel that has more than a few surprises up its sleeve… a story focused on human characters who developed and grew with each situation they faced. Highly recommended."

Walker of Worlds

"This is a tale about personal struggle and will leave you thinking about it weeks later. [Colin Harvey] deserves a place on your shelf along with Asher, Reynolds, Hamilton and Stross."

Deadwood Reviews

"A believably harsh tale of survival in bleak and unforgiving environments. Karl and Bera make an interesting, unusual pair, and the terrible conditions of Isheimur are conveyed matter-of-factly. This is a yarn with brawn and brains."

SFX

COLIN HARVEY

Winter Song

ANGRY ROBOT

ANGRY ROBOT
A member of the Osprey Group
Lace Market House,
54-56 High Pavement,
Nottingham
NG1 1HW, UK

www.angryrobotbooks.com
Whiteout conditions

Originally published in the UK by Angry Robot 2009
First American paperback printing 2010

Distributed in the United States by Random House, Inc., New York.

ISBN 978-0-85766-025-1

Printed in the United States of America

9 8 7 6 5 4 3 2 1

To Kate,
for shielding me from too
much reality at home.

PART ONE

ONE
Karl

Karl was dreaming of his clone-wife, far away on distant Avalon, when the plasma bolt slammed into Ship's engines.

One moment he was bathing with Karla in iodised springs beneath Jodi's Falls, soaping her up-tilted breasts in the warm sunlight of Delta Pavonis, the next a giant was sitting on his chest while alarms screeched in the emergency lighting.

The pressure lifted and he floated naked in his bed-web on the bridge, a voice calling ever louder, "Karl, we are under attack." That Ship's too-perfect alto was gravelled by static showed how mortal the blow might be. His interface wasn't working; none of the usual displays were scrolling down his field of vision, and with no data feeding directly into his brain he was forced to use archaic Voice. "What – what's the damage?" He smelled the acrid tang of smoke and the monitors – used only by passengers – were blank.

He coughed, his eyes stinging, and a smooth wall opened and out popped a freshly grown mask connected to an air-pack.

"I'm not wearing that," Karl muttered between coughs. "I hate putting things on my face."

"You're enhanced, not invulnerable," Ship snapped. "Put it on!"

Muttering, Karl complied.

"Thank you," Ship said. "We have lost all but emergency power in this third. In the central third we have intermittent power. The rest is undamaged. When waves from the gravity generator threatened to crush you, I had to take the engines down, and can't restart them. I'm attempting to dodge a second incoming bolt with lateral power, but it's already expanded, and complete evasion is unlikely. Time to impact is four minutes."

Karl tried to digest the news that he was probably dead. "They must have fired as soon as they dropped out of fold-space."

Ship didn't answer directly. "The second bolt came from different co-ordinates, indicating another ship, though it's difficult to scan through the asteroid belt. I've registered a third ship nearby." It sounded sheepish; "They must have identified us before I could see them. The first I knew was their plasma bolt coming at point-nine-cee. I had barely three minutes' warning. I'm sorry, Karl."

"Forget it," Karl said.

That meant there would be no respite while the others re-charged their capacitors. Even if by a miracle they dodged this second bolt, and one from the third ship, the first would have recharged and be ready to fire.

He slipped free of the amniotic safety of the bed-web. "Are they the Aye ships we spotted earlier?" Unlikely, he knew. The ships that were each individual Artificial Intelligences rarely interacted with the Flesh-bound, who held little interest for them. He floated over to one of the screens. "Can you get this working?"

Ship paused for so long that Karl wondered if it had died.

"Yes," it said.

A schematic appeared, of Ship at less than three Standard AUs from Mizar B2. Karl had thought that here on the sunward edge of the system's asteroid belt, surrounded by the myriad dots among which Ship and he had lurked, they would be safe to spy upon the Ayes. There *they* were, the symbols denoting the Ayes around the nearest of the four stars – the double pair that had so attracted astrophysicists ever since their nature had been discovered – in close orbit around the upper chromosphere of Mizar B2, doing whatever incomprehensible things Ayes did.

Scattered among the debris of the outer belt were three perfectly spherical ships, their regularity a defiant cry to the universe. "Their signatures indicate that they're Traditionals. I'm sorry, Karl. You've been fired upon by your own species."

Though it was debatable whether their assailants would consider Karl human, it was no surprise – Ship's design was clearly the angular asymmetry of the Radicals; the Pures, the most likely suspects among the Traditionals, would have guessed that he had man-machine interfaces, and was therefore to be despised even more than the Ayes they hated. Like all bullies they picked on him, a single target, rather than five Aye ships.

Between the symbols denoting Ship and their assailants was the pulsing sphere of a plasma bolt, the enemy's fuel hawked up from their engine and spat out of a tube.

"How far away are they?"

"Two AUs spaceward."

"Recommendations?"

"With five… four minutes to impact, your logical course is to abandon ship."

"Stitch that." He gazed at the monitor. "Let's see how far lateral power gets us. Are we dead centre of the bolt?"

"Slightly to starboard, so I have already set course in that direction."

"Good girl. What else can we do?"

"I can get no more power through the vents." As always, Ship ignored his anthropomorphising.

He thought. "What if we vented atmosphere from the hold?"

Ship paused so long that Karl thought he would have to prompt it. "It'd increase velocity by an additional one per cent. Not enough. We need seven."

"Vent the airlocks as well. Take the air pressure as low as possible, then drop it another per cent."

"I can't do that, Karl. I'm programmed to protect you. It's an unacceptable risk."

"And being blown up isn't?"

"That's why I recommended that you abandon ship. You have two minutes to decide. You should leave two minutes earlier not to be caught by debris and radiation. That's now, by the way."

"Jack it, I'm not leaving you!" Or the lump of neutronium locked in a stasis field in the corner of the hold. If the field failed the cargo would devour the ship in less time than it took to scarf down one of the tasteless protein-burgers he'd lived on for a month.

"Karl, that's sentimental nonsense," Ship said. "The major risk to you is from exposure, but I've sent a tight-beam Mayday toward the Hanghzou Relay, which I estimate the nearest one sympathetic. It's about four light-months away. They can jump here in days once they have the signal, and the lifegel will keep you safe – even in vacuum – until then."

"I'm glad you haven't suggested I let our attackers pick me up," Karl said.

Ship ignored his feeble humour. "You have many months of power in your companion, which will kick in as soon as I am out of range. But before the power fails, the lifegel will need fuel, and will slowly consume your body. Even before that, there will be side-effects – weight loss, anaemia, eczema. Such skinsuits are only designed as a short-term measure."

Karl nodded, clenching and unclenching his fists. "I wish I had these bastards in reach."

"Adrenaline has that effect," Ship said. It added, "I am an object; you can replace me, probably even approximate my programming. But I am no more a person than any other vehicle. I am expendable. You are not. You should leave now, from Bay Eight."

Karl slapped the wall, but it didn't make him feel any better. "Bay Eight, then. Keep talking while I'm en route."

"Karl," Ship said. "There's something else you should know."

"Go on."

"I've found some data that was previously misfiled. This system was settled over four centuries ago."

"These bastards are local?"

"I believe not. There's no other indication of local traffic. The last records are over two centuries ago, from just before the onset of the Long Night. If the colony survived, they probably slipped back during the conflict.

"It's unlikely that they did survive. If the war didn't get them, the planet's orbit is elliptical. During summer it would just be habitable, but its winters too cold to survive."

"Which star is it orbiting?"

"It appears to be orbiting both of the Mizar B pairing, at a distance that would give it a sub-Martian climate."

"Can I reach it from here?"

Ship said, "It's about eighteen million kilometres from here, so it will take…"

There was a perceptible pause, which told Karl how terribly, terribly wrong things were – Ship should have been able to calculate the numbers instantly, as well as simultaneously managing a multiplicity of other tasks. "Three standard weeks."

It added, "I will get you there. And I will download all the information I have to you. Plug in."

Gritting his teeth, Karl wiped the dust from the jack that hung beside the monitor screen for emergencies, and inserted it in the socket behind his right ear. "Aagh! That's horrible!" he cried. "It's like someone running claws down a stone wall, really, *really* loudly."

"I'm sorry," Ship said. "If so many of my systems weren't down…"

"Doesn't matter," he said, blinking a lie to the two words. The symbols flashed in front of his eyes, too fast to comprehend; he would review the data later, while he drifted in space.

Then he was pulling himself hand-over-hand down the corridor. As he rounded the first bend, Ship said, "The Ayes' behaviour is curious."

"How… so?" He was panting from the effort as he passed the hold, with the lump of super-heavy cargo that would have paid for the trip. Particularly if he could have traded it for information on the next leg.

"If I were to assume that they are going to continue with their actions, what the Ayes are doing to the star's upper chromosphere could have the effect of making the stars burn hotter."

"Why would they do that?"

"I don't know. They have never attempted to modify a star before, as far as we know."

Karl reached Bay Eight, and paused.

Before he could speak, Ship said. "You must go now."

Karl ripped off the mask, sighing with relief. He nodded, thin-lipped, and patted the wall. "Thanks... uh, you know–"

"No time," Ship said. "Go now."

The door irised slowly, revealing a wall of quivering blue jelly, three metres high and stuffed full of nanos. He paused, steeled himself, then pushed into the gel, which gave against him. He felt the stupid-smart goo hook into his skin and poke squidgy fingers into his nostrils, ears and even up his anus and urethra. It had little more intellect than an amoeba but was hardwired to climb into him and form a second skin, and did so relentlessly. He'd done this a hundred times, but every time it felt deeply unpleasant.

"Why would Terraformers pick a planet with such an unorthodox primary?" Karl wasn't really that interested, but it was better than thinking about the gel, or worse, the boiling mass of superheated plasma hurtling toward them at a quarter of a million kilometres a second. He fought down a rising tide of panic as the gel pushed deeper. It took a mighty effort of will to open his mouth and let it flow down into his lungs. It formed an impenetrable skin over the vitreous liquid of his eyes: when it transluced so he could see the exit button, he knew that the covering was complete, and it had formed a tasteless, odourless emulsion between his frail flesh and the vacuum of space.

"With high maintenance, it would have been a viable project," Ship said. "What they didn't foresee was the coming war. They never do. That changed everything."

Karl felt, rather than heard, the deep groan in the bowels of the ship as the containment fields around the neutronium weakened, and began to tear Ship apart.

"Got to go now!" he shouted to Ship by way of farewell.

"I have been squeezing all the lifegel into Bay Eight," Ship said.

Before he could ask why, because the extra gel would do him no good, the closet-sized airlock opened onto space. The depressurising atmosphere fired him clear, and he understood then. The extra gel was propellant, and as he tumbled head over heels, he blessed his clever, dependable Ship.

Counting showed that he was rotating head over heels every six seconds. The lifegel opaqued to protect his eyes – leaving him with only turquoise-blue to stare at – every time he faced the eye-meltingly fierce glare of the Mizar quartet. As he turned to face shadow, it cleared again.

The lifegel formed a perfect seal around him, but he couldn't stop his chest from rising and falling; the carbon dioxide he breathed out was absorbed by the goo and gradually converted back into an oxygen and nitrogen mix a few microns thick, between him and the membrane.

He hadn't counted how long he had been accelerating when Ship said, "Karl, there's something else that I should tell you. The colonised planet's ozone layer appears–" and broke off.

Despite the fact that Karl was facing away from the suns, the membrane opaqued. Then – even though it was supposed to absorb all kinetic energy – he felt a punch in his back that would have been a fragment of Ship, blown to pieces.

Although it had only been a semi-organic machine, Ship had been closer to him at times than any lover, and he wept for his loss.

Later, after he had exhausted his tears, he slept. It was a fitful doze, more to process everything that had happened since his rude awakening than from exhaustion.

When he awoke, he held himself in as long as possible until there was no evading the unpleasant sensation of voiding himself into the membrane and allowing it to absorb the deposit. If it had not been for his circumstances, hanging in space would have been enjoyable. He even wondered why no one had used the lifegel at home to sight-see Avalon's neighbour worlds.

Astronomers on Ancient Earth had thought Mizar was one star. When they made the first telescopes, they realised that "it" was a pair. Still later, they finally understood that each pair – Mizar A and B – was in turn a pair.

Using the info that Ship had fired into him he went through the seven worlds orbiting the smaller pair that was Mizar B and the centuries-old ruin of the semi-mythical Mizar B3, glimpsed only briefly before it flared and died again.

Farthest away from the stars that the settlers had named Alfasol, Betasol, Gamasol and Deltasol was tiny Asgard, a ball of ice and methane around a rocky core. Next was Valhalla, a blue hydrogen, helium and methane giant like Neptune. Moving inward past green Midgard – Mizar B's Uranus – Vanaheim was the largest world, though only slightly bigger than many-mooned Asagarth, next to it and closest to the asteroid belt dubbed Bifrost. While sunward little Ragnarok was scorched to sterility. What this system lacked, Karl realised, was an equivalent to Earth and Venus; it would have made the Terraformers' choices much easier.

And ahead of him was the other world, his destination. Isheimur, the settlers had named it – *ice world*.

The colony would have faded with the curtain-like falling of the Long Night, when the two types of humans, the Terraformers who wanted to shape worlds to fit humans, clashed with those Pantropists who rather wished to change humanity, to fit the worlds they settled. It had been a war that raged for decades, across only a few disputed systems to start with, but spreading like a virus.

Two centuries on, he had no idea whether there were survivors here or he was falling toward a dead world. The thought of re-entry made his mouth go dry, but at least the interminable waiting would be over – if he didn't miss altogether and spin onward until the lifegel ate him alive.

Days, weeks, perhaps months passed. He had no way of telling one day from the next. He could have switched his companion on, but the semi-idiot objects reminded him too much of Ship, and he needed to save the power for more important things, like conserving the lifegel.

Isheimur crept closer until it filled his whole sky and he saw patches of blue and grey toward the equator. Sometimes it even eclipsed Mizar B – or Gamasol and Deltasol, as he should now call them, he decided.

He'd never heard of anyone trying what he was about to do, and he was sure that Ship would have told him if there was a precedent. No, this was the first attempt to confirm something that existed only as theory.

He was desperate to test the theory, for he still hadn't got used to the gel taking care of his bodily functions; as well as the waste, it fed him through intravenous drips of nutrient-rich saline. Worse, he felt at times as if he was starting to lose his mind.

If he had switched it on, his sub-moronic companion would have fed basic data directly into his cortex. But it would have been nothing compared to what sounded like Ship haunting him; he awoke from fragmented dreams with whispers still pulsing in his ears. Sometimes he woke crying. It seemed wrong that he should miss an artificial construct more than his own partners, but he'd spent more time with Ship than with them.

He wondered what Karla was doing, where she was, who she was with. More mercurial than he, though they were supposedly the same, would she and the others wait for him, or would they decant a replacement?

At last, he felt the drag of atmosphere. He swung his feet around so that he seemed to be standing on the still near-vacuum, but what air there was began to glow as he cut through it. He opened his arms to create drag, spreading himself as wide as he could. The gel rushed to insulate his feet and under his arms, but even so, some of the heat began to seep through.

He doubted that anyone had ever tried to dive feet-first into atmosphere, to fall all the way to the ground, and actually survived. Even with the lifegel, it felt as though giant hands squeezed him, and someone was applying a blow-torch to the soles of his feet.

The roaring grew louder, louder, louder, louder – until it filled his whole world. It drilled into his ears and the hands around him squeezed ever harder and each breath was an effort. When oblivion came it was a merciful release.

TWO
Bera

Bera wanted to scream her grief at the night, but that would rouse the farmyard dogs. That would in turn wake the sleepers. She already felt so raw that she might as well have been scoured by sandpaper, and a public lecture from Hilda was more than she could face, so she clamped her jaw shut until it ached.

The farmyard was so cold that her breath threatened to freeze solid in the midnight air – not that Isheimur's midnight sky was like other worlds, she gathered. It would be another five weeks until the equinox, when the Mizar quartet would line up together on Isheimur's far side, with only the twin moons, Stor and Litid, to illuminate the true-dark for a few hours. Until then, though Gamasol and Deltasol had set within a few hours of one another, the further pair was still high in the sky.

That she could see where to put her feet on the rocky slope up to the grave made the act of mourning her dead son easier, and at least Ragnar had allowed her to bury Palli here, rather than in open ground. The graveyard was in a pocket of such boulder-strewn land that it was good for nothing else, unlike the rest of the valley. Its rocky border at least protected the bodies from burrowing marauders. Snolfurs were another matter – only a precious bullet or arrow would deter one of them.

She clambered past a tapped-out steam-vent which no longer gave its energy to the generator, the metre-wide pipe to the water tank down the hill now disconnected. Putting the sprig of lavender on the unmarked cairn was a pathetic little token, but it was all she had. At the thought of Palli's little face turning blue, the tears started up again, half-blinding her, freezing on her face as they trickled down.

She crouched, offering prayers, to Wotan, Yahweh – any of the old ones who might exist, just in case – to take care of Palli. Assuming that there was an afterlife, rather than just mouldering in the dirt.

Wiping her eyes, she glimpsed something streak above the top of the Reykleif hills in a flat curve, so it couldn't be a shapeshifter; nor did any troll ever move that fast. It was fiery bright, so it was most likely a meteor, she decided.

Standing again, she winced. Moving sent slivers of pain shooting through her cramped-up feet, numb even through the fur-lined house-shoes. Taking outside boots would have meant stumbling around in the boot-room, perhaps falling over one of the sleeping farmhands. She didn't want that. Better her feet froze than to admit to the other women that she still grieved for her beloved bastard.

If her body didn't give her away: ten days after burying him, her breasts were still swollen and sore, her blouses sodden even through the wadding that she'd shoved into her bra. The others must have noticed, but if they had, for once – in a rare show of restraint – they had said nothing.

Bera turned back, looking down the slope to face Skorradalur. Farmhouses crouching into the hillside formed three sides of a square round a courtyard, with the lake Skorravatn beyond the barn the fourth side. On the far side of the lake, antique wind-turbines hunched in the lee of the valley slope, their blades turning slowly in the incessant wind, the open grassland between them peppered with sheep, grazing on the last of the late-summer long grass.

She descended the stony, treacherous slope to Ragnarholt, the biggest farmhouse, passing the water-tank which took the excess steam from the newer geo-thermal vent; what wasn't needed to heat the house was allowed to condense inside its bulk to provide fresh water, so that the settlers didn't need to venture down to Skorravatn in winter and risk ambush from lurking creatures. It wasn't the halcyon days of when the farm had fusion power, but it was better than nothing.

Even in the thickening twilight she had to be careful not to turn an ankle on the stony ground. But if its aid in finding her way was a blessing, when the deep boom echoed from the west, waking the farm-dogs into a barrage of barking, it was a curse. Any onlooker could see her picking her way back. She speeded up, and twice nearly fell in hidden dips in the grass. Looking up, the shadowy bulk of Thorir perched in the watch-tower atop the farmhouse hadn't moved. Hopefully, he was asleep. Thorir was good at that, even though, if he were caught, it would mean a flogging.

The breeze strengthened, the wind-turbines' blades speeding up.

Brynja caught Bera's scent and yapped.

"Hush!" Bera hissed.

But instead the puppy redoubled her efforts to slip the leash, where she was tied to the courtyard water tap. Droplets from the tap had frozen so that Brynja's feet slipped and skidded on them.

Reluctantly, Bera fondled the little dog's ears. She was as white and fluffy as the rest of the litter, but they'd all found homes. No one wanted the little runt, though, so Ragnar had banished her to the courtyard, saying, "We can't afford to throw away what resources we have on animals that aren't viable, however cute they look now." If Brynja survived on the scraps that she could scavenge, she would live, but she was already skin and bone.

Desperately, shivering, Brynja tried to climb inside Bera's coat and nuzzled her blouse.

Still thinking of Palli, and of Ragnar's ruthlessness, Bera undid the leash, her jaw clamped. Freed, the puppy scrambled inside her coat in a flurry of paws. Brynja nuzzled and nuzzled at her blouse, until Bera sighed. She reached in and undid her bra.

Teeth like needles clamped onto her nipple. The pain made Bera draw her lips back from her teeth in a silent scream, but in a perverse way she welcomed it. However bad it was, it was real, and for a few too-short moments it obliterated memories of a tiny face turning blue and silent.

Finally, the needles grew too fierce, and she prised her bloodied breast away from the seeking mouth. Rocking her furry cargo, humming an almost soundless lullaby, she crept across the farmyard to the back door.

Looking up again, she saw a faint glow to the northwest between the hills.

It's not any of the suns, she thought, and if that's a fire, then someone's farmstead is burning.

But she couldn't think of any farmhouses in that direction. Too many trolls likely to midnight-raid the settlements, if the old records were true. And if it

23

were a fire, then Hilda and the others would already be spilling into the courtyard to answer the distress calls.

She lifted the latch carefully, and ducking to step down into the lobby shut the door behind her.

A light snapping on blinded her, though it was only dim. Her vision cleared to reveal Thorir standing with sword in hand and an evil grin on his face at his cleverness in sneaking down from the watch-tower.

Behind him, his wife Hilda stood with folded arms and bulging eyes: "Bera Sigurdsdottir! What on Isheimur are you doing? Have you lost your wits?"

Nothing Bera could say would spare her from a scolding, so she just slumped.

Hilda said, "Go back on watch, darling, while I sort this out." She snapped off the light. There were the noises of Thorir leaving, then Hilda hissed, "Stupid girl!"

"Sorry," Bera said quietly.

"Pappi took you in when his old friend died – you repay us by disturbing our sleep while he's away?"

Even after six years, you haven't forgiven me? Bera thought. I don't want his attention!

As self-appointed surrogate mother, Hilda didn't hesitate to "correct" Bera whenever Hilda felt it necessary, which was frequently. "We thought you were an outlaw – or worse."

"Did you hear the sound?" Bera said, in a desperate attempt to distract her foster-sister. "Like muffled thunder."

"Never mind that," Hilda said. Although she hadn't distracted Hilda, Bera's trick had at least robbed her rant of momentum. "Go back to bed. Try not to fall over the others on the way through."

Bera wondered how much of Hilda's anger was that Bera had shown her husband, and therefore Hilda, for the fool he was. If Bera could slip out without him noticing, then raiders could do the same in the opposite direction.

Or whether Hilda thought he hadn't been sleeping, but that Bera had paid him in kind to look away. Bera couldn't tell Hilda that she'd sooner drink acid than go with Thorin. Hilda wouldn't believe her, would instead point to the cairn as proof that Bera would go with anyone.

Next day in the kitchen no one spoke to Bera over breakfast, but that wasn't unusual. She had managed not to bump into the cots of the sleeping children and farm hands, so no one was angry with her – at least, no more than usual.

All ten of Ragnar's grandchildren, from the youngest toddler to eight year-old Toti, Hilda's eldest, sat around the vast table, assembled by nanobots centuries earlier to resemble oak, now stained and pitted with age.

Bera and the other women shuttled pots and plates to and from the vast stove, while the men were out checking the flocks as always.

Except Yngi, of course. Bera had seen him at first sunrise, as Gamasol stained the horizon with its searchlight glare. She had snuck out again and clipped Brynja back to the water-tap, where a few shards of ice had half-melted in the direct sunlight, staining Brynja's white fur with muddy streaks. The puppy yapped as Bera walked away, but she hurried and was back indoors before anyone noticed... she hoped.

Now she waited her turn for the porridge bowl, and when the others had taken their fill, scraped out the dregs of the weak, watery liquid. She got the last few bits when Thorbjorg said, "Why don't you lick the pattern off the plate?"

Her face burned, but she didn't answer Ragnar's younger daughter-in-law. Thorbjorg was only four years older than Bera, but she was as pretty as Bera was plain, and used her voluptuousness like a weapon on the men. And besides, she was married, so respectable.

"Well?" Thorbjorg challenged.

"There is no pattern," Bera mumbled.

Thorbjorg's laugh was a caw. "No there isn't, is there? You must have licked it off yesterday. Maybe if you weren't such a greedy pig, your teats would dry up – it's not as if you need the milk."

Bera shut her eyes, dug her fingers into her palms.

Hilda must have seen how intense the pain was, and if any of them would understand, she would – now the medic had said that any more pregnancies would pose a life-threatening risk. "That's enough," Hilda said. "Save your wit for later, Thorbjorg."

Bera slid into daydream, her usual refuge. Maybe there was some kind of payback. Bera had felt sorry for Hilda when she'd heard the others talking about it: barren at twenty-seven, with only two children to her name.

"How will we fill this big empty world if we can only have two children?" Thorbjorg had asked, smug in her brood-cow status. Bera had hated her for Hilda then: five children at twenty-one. Yngi might have been addled in the head, but his seed was potent – if it was his. Thorbjorg was always flirting with old Ragnar, always possessive with her hugs and touches.

Bera had wished that it was Thorbjorg who had miscarried instead of Hilda. When the others had gone, she had slipped into Hilda's room and asked, "Is there anything I can do, Hilda? I'm so sorry to hear about..." and trailed off, not sure what to call it. Loss? Too tame. Miscarriage? Too clinical. So she had left the sentence unfinished.

But Hilda had seemed to understand. She shook her head. "I just want to be alone."

That had been the last half-civilised conversation between them. They had never been friends, but as long as Bera was duly deferential to Ragnar's eldest child, they had been civil. But a month later, two months after the Spring Fair, Bera had missed her period, and soon after, she knew that she was pregnant. Refusing to name the father meant that no bill of settlement could be made to another house, and as good as admitted that Bera would sleep with any man.

"Bera!" Hilda's cry snatched her back, to the other's amusement.

"Daydreaming again," Toti said. Like most children, he could spot a legitimate target for teasing. "Bera's daydreaming, Bera's dreaming of her boyfriend!" he sang.

"That'll do, young man!" Hilda said. "Enough of that or you lose your time at the Oracle!"

"Sorry." Bera went without prompting to the sink to rinse the pots.

"You're washing clothes today." Hilda lowered her voice, "I've not said anything to the others about your star-gazing, but I will if it happens again. We can't afford to heat the countryside."

"But I closed the doors straight away!"

"And we'd have to send out search parties if raiders spirited you off. Bera, you're so selfish!"

Bera managed not to snap back that she'd be the last person they'd send out rescue parties for, if outlaws, trolls or shapeshifters struck.

Later, as Bera loaded up the vast tin bath with clothes and ran water from the hot tap into it, it struck her as odd that shapeshifters were always lumped into the

27

same category as trolls and outlaws, snolfurs and other predators. But shapeshifters were so rare that no one – as far as she knew – had ever definitely been attacked by one. Maybe, if she could snatch five minutes on the Oracle later, she'd search.

She managed to turn the tap off before boiling water ran over the pan's lip; at least – for all Hilda's carping – there was no shortage of heat and hot water. It was a shame that, according to the Oracle, there was no longer the resource to tip Isheimur's boundless low-level geo-thermal energy into full-scale vulcanism.

She was used to washing by hand. The farm had finally run out of parts for the antique washing machine when Bera had first arrived from the North, and the Norns refused to consider such parts life-saving, so their petitions via the Oracle for replacements had been useless. But she hated the way it chapped her hands, and the effort required to wring out the sopping clothes left her hands and shoulders aching. Still, she managed to wrestle the sodden blouses and shirts into the mangle, bolt the rollers into place and then turn the handle against a wall of inertia.

She jumped at the voice; "You want help?"

She turned. "Oh, Yngi, you startled me." Isheimur only knew how Yngi the Halt with his club foot had managed to creep up on her.

His freckled face was as transparent as any window, so she saw his disappointment. She added hastily, "I know you didn't mean to, but you should cough or clear your throat, or–"

"OK, Bera," he said. Ruddy features lit up: "You need help with that? I'm stronger than you are, even if I'm not as clever."

She shook her head. "No thanks, Yngi. I'm almost done."

He turned to go, just as Thorbjorg's voice cut across them: "Yngvar Ragnarsson, get away from that whore!"

Yngi cringed, and Bera swung round at his wife, anger at one humiliation too many finally breaking her self-control. Before she could speak, a shriek from the courtyard interrupted them: "Grandpappi! Grandpappi's coming!"

Bera and Thorbjorg rushed out into the courtyard, Yngi hobbling behind. Both suns were now high in the sky, and Bera had to blink to focus. She followed the other's gaze down the valley to the west, and the men returning from a week at the Summer Fair.

The two men at the front of the group rode shaggy Isheimuri horses, which stood only chest-high to a tall man, but were formidably strong. Ragnar liked to brag that his was the strongest horse on Isheimur, and the chunky buttermilk-coloured stallion needed to be to carry his owner and his belongings, which between them probably massed over a hundred and fifty kilos. Arnbjorn rode a slightly smaller horse alongside him.

Surprisingly the other two horses were riderless, and Ragnar's tenant farmers walked beside their mounts, which were dragging something, but Bera couldn't make out what it was. Bringing up the rear of the procession were the farmer's eldest sons. Both had been unbearable ever since Ragnar had agreed to take them to the Summer Fair, and Bera suspected that they would be even more conceited now they had been, and would consider themselves too grand to mix with children. One had been flirting with Bera before she'd become pregnant, but had quickly lost interest when he learned of her condition, and probably wouldn't even speak to her now.

"Come on, Bera!" Hilda interrupted her daydreaming. "They're ten minutes away yet, so back to work for a little while."

Bera resisted the urge to say "Yes, boss." Sarcasm would only earn her a lecture.

Instead she returned to grappling with the sopping wet clothes until shrieks from her foster-nephews and nieces announced Ragnar's arrival. His gravelly voice boomed, "What? No hug for your Grandpappi, then?"

She felt the puppy stir beneath her bulky jacket, then return to sleep, and prayed that Brynja would sleep a while longer.

By the time Bera had joined the others but watching from the sidelines, women and children were hugging men, the tenant farmer's mousey wives had erupted from their own dwellings, and the whole group had aggregated into one swarming, shapeless mass. Only Ragnar stood slightly apart from the reunions, a sad smile on his face.

Then Yngi's wife Thorbjorg threw her arms around him. "Welcome back, Pappi!" It might have been Bera's imagination, but she thought she saw him grimace, before he made his dark, brooding features as impassive as before.

He looked across at Bera. She gave him a little smile which she tried to make welcoming, but he only scowled, and she looked away so that he wouldn't see how hurt she was. *All you have to do is give him the name of the father. Make one up if need be.*

Except that whichever name she gave Ragnar would be signing a man's death warrant, if such a name existed – and names were strictly bound by custom, like everything else here. Bera wondered how it would be to grow up on a world that had never splintered away from the rest of humanity, never been driven apart by a seemingly – to the rest of the Galaxy – insane urge to speak a different tongue and adhere to old ways. To call oneself what one liked, to dress how one liked, do what one liked…

"What's this?" Hilda pointed to a travois, which was hitched to the two horses belonging to the tenant-farmers.

"You heard the noise last night?" Ragnar said. "A meteorite crashed near where we'd camped." He continued, "We heard what we thought was a small volcano where it fell, so we rushed toward it for a look. It took us a half-hour. When we got there, we found only this character," Ragnar pointed at the travois, "lying in the snow."

Bera eased around for a look, and gasped. The man lying unmoving in the travois was stark naked, his skin a copper so dark as to be almost purple. His massive chest rose and fell irregularly, but apart from that he didn't move. His eyes were closed. Bera had never seen such muscle definition on a man; corded, sinewy, he took her breath away. The face below the shaven skull was equally striking, with its chiselled zygomatic bones and almost inhuman symmetry. Bera looked down, then away, blushing, then glanced at him again. He was certainly impressive. She made her self focus instead on the splints on his legs.

"Cover him up!" Asgerd said, Ragnar's older daughter-in-law reaching for a blanket from one of the horses. "He'll scare the children!"

Ragnar reached out, and his daughter grew still. "You don't cover burns like that." He pointed to the man's lower torso, and clearly broken legs. His legs would have been long, strong and muscular before they were broken.

Bera dragged her attention back to Ragnar, who said, "He was screaming, rolling around in the snow. We

31

couldn't leave him like that. Either I killed him, and I'd no stomach for cold-blooded neck-snapping, or we brought him home."

"Can we spare the food?" Asgerd said, her thin lips when she closed them giving her opinion: No, we can't.

"You tell me, ladies." Ragnar opened his arms to include Hilda and Thorbjorg in the question. "The management of the household is your responsibility, after all. I wouldn't dream of interfering in your demesne."

Not much, Bera thought. Ragnar didn't hesitate when he felt it necessary.

"Of course we can, my lord." Thorbjorg sensed as always which way the wind was blowing, and said what she guessed he wanted to hear.

Ragnar's face split with a grin. "Then that's settled." He rubbed his hands together.

"How do you know that he's not a vagrant?" Asgerd said.

"We thought that initially," Ragnar said. "We were ready to leave him to die, until Bjarney pointed out that a trespassing vagrant can be indentured, if he recovers." He shrugged. "If he doesn't recover, he won't eat, anyway."

"Hmmph," Hilda said, but didn't argue.

"Funny," Ragnar said, "the snow was stained blue." Whether it was the colour or simply the fact that the snow was dyed, it seemed to Bera that Ragnar sounded uneasy. It was so rare that Bera couldn't help staring.

He caught her looking and straightened, returning to his normal forceful manner. "Here's someone who can help. Bera, I need someone to safeguard our new investment. You can nurse our new worker."

Bera looked down, bobbing her head in assent.

Ragnar must have mistaken her shyness for reluctance, or his next words would surely never have been so cruel (at least, she thought, not before you got pregnant): "Well, come on girl! Look to it! You should be grateful – it'll give you something to think about, take your mind off that dead bastard of yours."

She felt tears sting her eyes, and lunged toward the travois.

But Ragnar must have seen her well up, for she heard him half-groan, and mutter, "Well, you shouldn't have brought shame on my house by opening your legs to the first man who ignored your plainness. My darling Gunnhild would spin in her grave if she could see what you've turned into."

Bera wanted to shout that, but for the eruption on Surtsey, she would have gone home as soon as she was pregnant, but that was pointless. Her family was dead, and now she just had to get on with living.

So she didn't answer, but instead wrestled the stranger off the travois. But in so doing, Bera scraped the stranger's back on the stones, and he roused screaming from his near-coma. Ragnar shouted, "Yngi! Thorir! Give her a hand with that!"

The two men helped ease the stranger back into the travois and unhitch it. Thorir called, "Where do you want it?" He stood far too close to Bera for her liking.

"Put it in with the animals," Ragnar said.

Grunting with effort the men picked him up, and staggered toward the stables. Bera shadowed them into the warm, odorous darkness. She gazed at the horses, three of which were hers. But the web of debts incurred had bound her too tight to indulge any fantasies of flight while she was pregnant.

Ragnar appeared in the doorway. "Mind you take good care of him."

Bera didn't answer.

When she was sure that Ragnar had gone, she took Brynja from under her furs. Weeping quietly, she let the puppy nuzzle the other nipple from the one she had suckled the night before. "Like Romulus and Remus," she said, "but in reverse."

"Let's hope it doesn't end in tears," Ragnar said, making her jump at his unexpected return. Luckily, he was so busy staring at the stranger lying on the hay that he didn't notice the puppy, instead assuming her reference was to the man. He kept staring at the man, barely able to conceal his repugnance. "It's an Icelandic tradition, to fear the stranger, but even so, this hairless stranger bothers me. His presence means trouble... we'll call him Loki. It seems fitting."

"I'll do my best for you," Bera said, shielding Brynja by turning away slightly.

Ragnar roused himself. "You will," he said. "We've a critical time coming. Once the crops ripen fully, it's a race to get them in. We'll need every able-bodied hand we can get. He can repay us our hospitality – if he recovers."

"If he doesn't? Or he recovers, but stays an invalid?"

"That won't happen," Ragnar said. The feral look on his face chilled Bera. "He'll have an accident before that happens. Clear?"

Bera nodded, swallowing.

THREE
Loki

The world through your eyes is full of pain and wonder, made even stranger by the whirlwind of voices shrieking for your attention:

"The Mizar Quartet are Sol-type hydrogen-fusing dwarf stars—"

"Isheimuri lingua confirmed as mix of Standard and Icelandic—"

Some voices verge on making sense, but most babble gibberish. Each is accompanied by a dizzying sense of vertigo, and little shocks deep inside your body. Occasionally you smell burning. Sometimes you taste colours, can hear, flickering jeering shadows behind your eyelids.

"Absolute magnitude uses the same convention as visual—"

You are dimly aware that the nanophytes within you that keep your muscle tone even as you waste away are locked in a desperate fight against the cannibal predations of the remaining lifegel in a near sub-atomic battle of the idiots. Either through accident or a design flaw, the inhibitors appear to have failed, and if left to themselves will eat you alive.

"The Long Night was the longest conflict since the Hundred Years War–"

A strangely familiar voice cries out, "I won't lie down and die!"

"The Isheimur populace is likely to suffer genetic drift and disease–"

The man Ragnar's voice is a rumble from a mouth full of misshapen teeth, his words unintelligible.

"Pappi: estimated height one-metre-eighty, mass eighty kilos–"

The woman beside him answers, her voice lower. Her hair is lighter, but her features equally mismatched, one shoulder slightly higher than the other.

"Oedipus: son of King Laius and Jocasta of Thebes–"

You realise that the voice refusing to die was your own, but it sounds strange. It should be alto but is tenor instead. Perhaps your voice-box was damaged in the accident?

"Pantropy lost favour as Terraforming grew easier–"

The accident. The pain increases as a shard of memory brings with its suddenly perfect recall the accompanying agony: the smell of burning dust, the isolation, the heat. After a while your throat hurts with the scream – which tails off into a whimper.

"A quasar at absolute magnitude −25.5 is 100 times brighter than our galaxy–"

The girl – barely a woman – Bera strokes your head. "Hush, Pappi, he kannske skilja you," she says. Her breasts ooze milk, and a part of you realises that while she has given birth in the last three weeks for there to be lactation, there is no sound of a baby. The rational corner of your mind tucks this away for later, but the animal part that has control has you lunging forward on all fours, scrabbling at her clothes.

"Humanity only found other sentient life after four centuries of spaceflight–"

"Neh!" The sting of her palms raining down on your face and head are microscopic compared to the waves of agony that ripple across you, but still they are enough to make you pause. You stare up at her dark hair, wide-set eyes and full mouth and wonder what her lips would taste like if you ripped them from her face.

"Oedipus left for dead with a shepherd but adopted–"

"He eats like an hungradur dyr," Bera says, becoming more understandable with each sentence, as the lingua-weave begins to take effect. "He almost choked on that meat we fed him before. But he can eat elda food now. No more breastfeeding–"

"An Icelandic chieftain was politician, lawyer, and police-man combined–"

Some residual decorum makes you lurch away from her into a corner.

"Grain was only grown in limited quantities in Iceland–"

"Agh, he's vomiting! He splashed my best boots!" Pappi kicks you. You growl, but you are too busy gazing at the pool of vomit to attack.

"The Mizar B pair mass approximately 1.6 times that of Sol–"

"No, Pappi! He doesn't know what he's doing. The horsemeat was too much for him to digest at this stage of his bati."

"In Iceland, the chieftain's position could be bought or sold–"

"Well, keep him away. Oh, what's he doing now? He's eating his own puke!"

"Nanotechnology requires vast consumption of energy–"

The undigested horsemeat still tastes much as it did before, though now with a rancid flavour that may be the bile that you've brought up with it, but there are also others: salt and a metallic taste. By squinting you can zoom right in and see shapes invisible to an unen-hanced human eye crawling among the chunks of meat. You have vomited up nanophytes with the food. From somewhere comes the knowledge that vomit is as corrosive as battery acid – their tiny carapaces must be almost indestructible to withstand it.

"Sheep farming was the most common type in Iceland–"

You know you must eat it to get the nanophytes back into your system, but Bera clings onto you, trying to pull you away as you gobble the vomited meat.

"Isheimur has a lower water content than Terra–"

"No, no, Loki! Don't eat that! Here!" She undoes her blouse but you ignore her, concentrating on re-ingest-ing the refugee nanophytes. You don't know whether they're still locked onto you as their source/target, but you can't risk them eating the planet in some long-term runaway disaster. You brush against her face; you feel wetness, and note that she is weeping, and another cor-ner of your broken mind wonders why.

Finally, when you've eaten all the meat and licked up the liquid, you allow her to guide you to her breast. "It'd give Palli's death meaning if his milk were to save another's life," she whispers.

"Isheimur's mass is 0.80 of Terra, but its gravity is only 0.67 – sub-optimal for atmospheric retention–"

"Jao," Pappi growls assent.

"At 1.7 AUs, its year is 2.85 Terran years–"

She sobs, even as she strokes your head. "This is the last time I'll do this," she says to the Ragnar-man as you nuzzle her nipple. "I wasn't going to let him feed today, but if it stops him eating his own puke, then I'll make an exception. But after this, no more breastfeeding: you can whip me or starve me, but I'll not do it again. I can't cope with this. It's like an eighty kilo baby with the habits of a wild animal."

"Isheimur's year comprises 1096 days of 22 hours 37 minutes–"

"Agreed," Ragnar says, and you see the surprise dart across her face. He turns to go. "I've no desire to see any more of this sick, feral creature, anyway, even if he has displayed almost superhuman powers of recovery. Odin's Beard – to think that he only came out of his stupor yesterday!"

"Hunger is my friend." The words echo through your mind as you swallow the warm, rich milk. "When I'm trying to lose weight, I embrace my hunger–"

You release her nipple, which she rubs.

The fool that said that clearly never had hunger eating them from within like a black hole, sucking everything into it, consuming it yet still wanting more more more–

"Isheimur is so cold, its air so thin that the colony's long-term survival is marginal–"

"Stop it!" you scream, clutching your head. Bera frantically hushes you, tries to pour sugared water into your mouth, but you gag.

For a while, as if taking pity, the voices fade away almost to nothing…

"We'll feed him from our stores for another few days," Ragnar says.

"You still here?" Bera says. "I thought you'd seen enough of him?"

His laugh is bitter and mocking, devoid of humour. "I can't help it. I get no pleasure from watching him, but there is a sort of horrible fascination." Ragnar sighs. "If he keeps this up, we won't be able to put him to work." He says, "Just my luck that I've probably saved someone with an advanced psychosis. If it's schizophrenia, that would explain why he was wandering."

"Schizo–" Bera tries to wrap her lips around the word, which is clearly unfamiliar. Part of you would like to plunge your rigid member into her, but you have suckled at her breast, and another part of you analyses your memory of mores to determine why this is wrong.

"Schizophrenics," Ragnar says, "were often considered possessed in the olden days, before people understood personality disorders. Most likely that his family tried to care for him, but finally gave up when he became too much trouble." When he continues, he seems to be talking to himself. "Food's always so scarce even at the end of a good summer that we can't afford to pour it down an invalid's throat if there's no chance of recovery."

"What are you going to do?" Bera asks, moving between you and the Ragnar-man.

But he doesn't seem to have heard her, instead saying, "The climate, even down here in the tropics, is so harsh that still the toughest Terran-descended crops grow poorly, and we live on the very edge of survival."

"What are you saying?" Bera says. The fear in her voice hooks your attention away from the pain and the whirling madness of the world.

Ragnar shrugs. "What if we had left him where he lay? No one would have blamed us, leaving an outlaw to die at the teeth of trolls or snolfurs."

"But you didn't leave him, did you?" Bera says. "When you brought him here, you made him your responsibility."

"Aye," Ragnar says. "No good deed goes unpunished."

"So what are you going to do now?" Bera says. "Take him back up into the hills? Murder him and toss his body into a geysir? Eat him, if we get hungry enough?"

"Don't be silly, girl," Ragnar says. "Remember who you're talking to."

"I know who I'm talking to, my lord," the girl says. You hear the wobble of fear in her voice, but she ploughs on. "A man who's sworn to uphold the law and customs our forefathers embraced. And now talks of leaving a sick man in the snow?"

"I can remember who I am without needing your reminding." He leans into her face; you see her swallow, but she doesn't flinch. "I've worked long and hard to earn and keep my people's respect. *I* fought off three tribes of trolls at the Battle of Giri Pass. I've won the Silver Shield for my verse from the Althing, and been compared with the legendary Egil Skalla-grimsson." He bangs the wooden pillar supporting the barn's roof as if he is one of the Viking warriors of Old Earth beating out his defiance on his shield. "What have you ever done, girly? Apart from open your legs the minute a man looks at you. Bringing shame on yourself and I, who was foolish enough to take you in! That'll teach me to think out loud in front of a chit of a girl who misunderstands the processes of thought! I know who I am, girly – remember who you are!"

He stalks from the barn, leaving her shivering, but when she looks up at you, her eyes blaze with triumph. "The danger with myths and heroes, Loki, is that sometimes the myth starts to become more real to the heroes than the truth."

When she leaves you alone for a little while, you taste the straw that is your bedding. It's almost inedible, but overwhelmed by hunger you force it down. When she returns and catches you, she scolds you. "I've bought you extra gruel," she adds. "It's all there is."

You get most of it in your mouth, finishing it within seconds. You lick the plate clean with what the rational part of your mind flags with inappropriate haste (inappropriate to what?), then you nuzzle amongst the straw and lick it clean.

"Oh, Loki." Bera gently touches your arm. "You have to start behaving more like a man, and less an animal, or Ragnar will have all the excuse he needs to get rid of you." You look up at her, drinking in her features. She says, "Do my looks repel even you, my child-man? Or do you not care? He didn't."

Then, as if the food has awoken some animal from its slumbers, the world is again full of voices shouting mostly meaningless words:

"Iceland had no fruit-bearing trees–"

"Humanity has split into a myriad of factions–"

"Isheimur's low gravity and inability to generate carbon dioxide through vulcanism render the colony sub-optimal, unlikely to return the company's investment–"

People behave as if you're a zoo exhibit. Like the tides the pain that accompanies the strangeness (and yes, the terrible beauty) recedes for a while, before sweeping in to the shoreline of your mind and you start gibbering again.

One of the gawpers is a pregnant woman who nudges her friend, an older woman. "See? He's possessed: jabbering like he's got a head full of spirits. I reckon that he's a seidr."

"Don't let our Gothi hear you talk like that," Bera says from the doorway. Even though part of your mind is still in the here-and-now and you're aware of your surroundings, you hadn't noticed her arrive. "He'll flay you alive if he hears you talking about warlocks and spirits. You know how he is."

"Who are you to tell us what we should talk about, girl?" The pregnant woman backs toward the doorway. "His science is failing. Our founders wanted us to keep to the old ways. Well, the Norse gods and magic are among the old ways."

"The old ways included birth without anaesthetic, Salbjerg," Bera says. "Think that that's one old way we should return to? Our founders wanted us to cherry-pick the best of the old ways, not embrace every superstition."

"Perhaps Pappi's grown tolerant in his old age?" Salbjerg says to her friend. "I remember a time when a chit of a girl who got herself knocked up without keeping hold of the man's dick would have had the skin peeled from her back one layer at a time."

"Or maybe Pappi *is* the Pappi," the older woman says, leering.

Bera doesn't answer at first. Then she looks up. "Do you fear that I lay with your Bjarney, Salbjerg? You've nothing to worry about. He's never even glanced at me. I promise you that."

"Of course I wasn't worried, you little slut." The flush rising to Salbjerg's face gives the lie to that. "Why would my man want a nothing like you?"

You watch Bera's jaw work, and a part of you feels a surge of protectiveness toward her. She shouldn't have to take such abuse. Ignoring the voices momentarily, you let out a low growl and both the women step back.

"You should go now," Bera says. "Before Loki decides that he prefers cannibalism to starving to death. He might take a chunk out of you, Salbjerg."

The women back away, muttering, and when they've gone, Bera laughs softly to herself. "Quite the lioness defending her cub, aren't I, Loki? Who'd have thought milk-and-water Bera would bare her teeth so?"

But you arch to let the voices out, and clutch at your head; she holds you, shushing you.

Later, when the smell of burning has faded away, and the pain has receded to a level that's almost bearable, you fall silent.

Bera is joined by a ruddy-faced giant. She says to him, "Help me get him into the wheelbarrow, Yngi."

You whimper when you try to stand, but when they ease their grip, you grab a pillar, and hold yourself up with it. They grip you under an arm each, and Bera nudges you toward the wheelbarrow, where they settle you into it.

"Thanks, Yngi," she says.

"What are you going to do with him?" Yngi says.

"I'm going to wheel him outside," Bera says.

The Other is pushing at you, pushing you down into a pit of blackness. Your skull isn't large enough to contain both of you. You moan and clutch the sides of your head. The Other has awoken, and his voice is the loudest of them all, begging to be allowed his body back – as if it is his, the madman.

"Hush, now," Bera croons. She pushes the wheelbarrow, grunting with the effort, and the world tilts alarmingly. You would get out, but the effort makes the barrow lurch, and at her urging you sit still.

"Ooh, look!" calls out the woman Thorbjorg who visited the barn earlier. "Bera's got herself a pram! Taking baby for a walk?"

There are subdued laughs at this, but Hilda says fiercely, "Thorbjorg! She may have lapsed, but no woman deserves mockery after losing a child!"

Thorbjorg looks sulky.

"What are you doing, Bera?" Hilda says.

"He's permanently hungry," Bera says. "And then I realised there are lichens he can eat." Your world tips and

44

she half-laughs, half-cries, "Aagh! He's falling!"

The grass is sweet and juicy, and as you lie prone on the ground you tear at it with your teeth, feeling some trickle down your chin. "Don't eat that, Loki," Bera says. "You can't digest grass. Come on now, leave it!"

A noise catches your attention, just for a moment. A man whose name you don't know – he has never been into the barn – dances on stilt-like legs. "Bera haad a little lamb," he sings as he stops. "Baa, baa," he bleats in that thin little voice that disrupted your eating.

A part of you notes, *The young of all species share common characteristics: large eyes, small, thin voices. Although from his size he's merely mimicking a cub, what's more interesting is that you responded to the stimulus of what you thought was a youngster in distress. Maybe that's a sign that this pseudo-autism is losing its grip.*

You ignore the voice, and return to chewing the grass. At the same time the man stops his little dance and stands normally as Bera shouts, "Stop it, Thorir!"

Your chewing is again interrupted, by the man bleating, "I'm another of Ra-a-gn-a-ar's little lost lambs; please let me suck on your titties, Bera-a-a–" His bleating is cut short by a thud, and he topples forward.

Ragnar stands over him, opening and closing his right hand, rubbing at its knuckles. "If you weren't my son-in-law, Thorir, we'd be duelling at dawn tomorrow for that insult."

"I– I didn't mean to insult you," Thorir says. "I was merely teasing Bera."

"Even if what you say is true," Ragnar says. "Your insult of my foster-daughter is an implicit slur of me. Though I would expect nothing more of Thorir the Stupid. How did you persuade Hilda you were worthy of her at the Spring Fair? Ye gods, you must be good at shagging, because you're good for nothing else. Get up, you cur!"

Thorir drags his knees toward his head, and pushes himself upright.

Your head is yanked back, the pain so excruciating that your fugue is broken. Bera shrieks, "Don't hurt him!"

"You were eating grass?" the red-faced chieftain bellows over background laughter that subsides instantly at his glare.

"It's the nanophytes," you say, though you don't understand half of the words that the Other pushes out of your mouth; he's wresting control from you. "I've lost so much weight to the lifegel that the nanophytes have taken control. They're assimilating them, but that requires energy. I'd need to eat a lot anyway to regain the lost mass, but on top of that I need thousands of calories a day. Every day. I'm so hungry, I'll eat anything – even if I can't digest it the nanophytes are swarming up into my gullet and converting the fuel directly."

Ragnar is staring at you with both pity and revulsion. "You can talk. Even if half is gibberish."

"The lingua-weave," you say. "It intercepts what you say in your tongue while it's still in my auditory nerves. That's why I can't watch your lips – it confuses the signals. When I reply in Anglish, it intercepts the signal again, takes control of the mouth and vocal cords, and turns it into Isheimuri."

Ragnar clearly doesn't understand. "Stop. Prattling." He separates the words for emphasis. "Do something useful. Help the women work."

You stare at him, still chewing on a mouthful of cud, as he stomps away.

"The AIs' presence is probably the one unifying thing that stops humanity from exterminating itself–"

"Come and help us pick lichens, Bera," a woman says, baring her teeth in a rictus that you catalogue as a smile. Her teeth are crooked and irregular, but her lips are full, and again you feel a surge of desire for her.

"This report's conclusion is that without constant access to technology the Isheimur colony's long-term survival is unlikely—"

She looks down at the gown that Bera draped over you, and her face is red, but she smiles. "My," she says, "he certainly is a big boy, isn't he, Bera?" You interpret this as reciprocatory interest, but before you can reach for her, Bera pushes you back into the wheeled device.

"Hormonal imbalance," the Other says in that too-deep voice. "Testosterone and adrenaline will be re-absorbed into the bloodstream."

You find it difficult to concentrate on anything. The sky is too big, the suns too bright, the wind too chill. Absently, the cataloguing part of you notices the absence of odours, as if the weather is so cold that it's frozen them. You rotate your head around, staring at the sky and grassy hillocks that lead up to hills dotted with white blobs, that the cataloguing part identifies as *sheep*, domestic animals kept for meat and wool.

"Sheep," you say, tasting the word.

Bera laughs. "You're getting better!" Her words turn into a sob.

"You see this?" Bera says, pointing to a plant that covers several nearby rocks. "It's edible moss, called lichens. We're going to pick it, and you eat what you want, Loki, and we put the rest into this bag, here. You see?" She crouches on all fours, and you notice her haunches straining against her dress. She picks some of the plant, shows you, then loads it into the canvas bag that she is carrying. "OK?"

You don't answer, but pick at the lichen. However, it all goes into your mouth, and none of it into the bag.

Suddenly Bera stiffens. "Loki, do not move – not if you want to live."

You stiffen, and watch her climb slowly to her feet. She calls out, "Asgerd, there's a snolfur here. Can you make some noise?"

On cue, the others let out whoops and shrieks and yells, and stomp toward them in a long straight line. Bera nods, and you slowly turn your head, and follow her gaze to where something like a metre and a half-high weasel is backing away, baring sabre teeth. It turns and speeds away with a liquid, rippling motion belying its stocky frame.

"That," Bera says to you, and lets out a long sigh, "was a snolfur. It probably wouldn't have attacked you. They prefer to feed on carrion. But then again, they're not usually this far north so early in the fall. So maybe things are changing."

"It's likely to be a sign of a hard winter," the woman Asgerd explains. "The longer the snolfurs stay toward the South Pole before venturing north the better."

She seems one of only a few people, with Bera and the man Yngi, to be friendly.

You sketch a smile, and return to picking the lichens. They are dark green, with a curious musty odour.

Most of the lichens end up in your belly rather than in the sack, but no one seems to mind. The others seem content to ignore you as long as you do not eat grass. The cataloguing part of your mind describes this as appropriate behaviour.

Eating grass is clearly not appropriate behaviour.

There are days of this routine. Some days you have pangs of hunger, and you eat straw or rip bits of wood from the beams if you are indoors, or if you are outside, grass or even earth (the grubs in it are tasty). Little by little you totter around the barn. Your legs are still unsteady, but your body grow stronger every day. Your mind, however, is still fragmented. There is the cataloguing part, there is you, and there is the Other.

Then one morning you awaken, and you feel completely different. The pain has gone. Your head feels clearer than – you don't know when, because one moment your feet were on fire, and the next you're here. Wherever here is. You're lying on straw in a dark building that smells faintly of animals. The smells seem as ingrained as the stains on the dark wooden beams.

A woman, barely a girl enters. Her name is Bera, you realise, although you don't know how you know. You suspect that your companion has been assimilating data while you've been – where?

"*Gon t'ayn*," she mouths before you can look away, and her voice in your head says "Good morning." The translation module will soon synchronise – you hope – but in the meantime you're careful not to look at her lips, which will be moving in the local dialect.

"Gon t'ayn," you say back, in your too-deep voice, in what you hope is a serviceable accent, and her eyes widen, and slowly, shyly, she starts to smile.

"Well, well, this is progress, indeed," she says. "Ragnar will be delighted with this, Loki."

"Who's Loki?" you say, wondering whether you've misunderstood something. "My name's Karl. Karl Allman."

FOUR
Ragnar

Ragnar cradled the lamb in his arms as he surveyed the long thin valley that was Skorradalur. On the far side the shallow hills were already dusted with early snow, a harbinger of the winter to come. "Sometimes, Grensosa, I wonder about these damned fools."

He watched Bera leading Loki – or Karl, as the stranger now insisted they call him – across the courtyard to the kitchen, walking close together, but without – as far as Ragnar could see – touching.

Only two days since Bera had run shrieking from the barn that Loki was awake, and talking. Ragnar scowled at the memory of his first encounter with Allman. He had walked into the barn to find the man staring into space, frowning in evident puzzlement. When he looked up at Ragnar he had recoiled as though someone had waved a shit-stained rag under his nose.

Ragnar had a long memory, and though the man had pulled himself together quickly and hidden his true feelings, the Isheimuri would neither forgive nor forget that look in a hurry.

Two days, and the stranger was walking more strongly every day. Ragnar rubbed his hands. He already had Allman helping Bera with the women's work, but the man should be fit enough in time to help move the flocks from the furthest slopes down to the farm.

Meanwhile Allman and Bera did the lighter work that allowed the women to come and scythe the corn. It grew stunted and feeble, but it was better than nothing, and crucial to their survival. If the Norns would grant them harvesting machines, they could do it in a fraction of the time, but their requests had never yielded a single harvester.

Orn the Strong emerged from the barn he used to repair their equipment, and Ragnar hastily put the lamb down. He had a reputation for fierceness to maintain, and cuddling a six month-old lamb would soften it, naming it "Green Sauce" or not. When the time came, of course Grensosa was destined for the table – but as mutton, rather than lamb. He wasn't the first farmer to name his future dinner, nor would he be the last.

Ragnar strolled down to the lake, where he threw skipping stones across the water. He had things to do. More than usual, as he'd lost most of the last month preparing for the Summer Fair, spending the week there dispensing justice, and returning to a mountain of pending claims on his time. He just wasn't ready to face them yet. What was the point of his being Gothi, if he wasn't able to choose when he worked?

Instead his thoughts kept sliding away: to the Widow Helga, now past childbearing, but still with an appetite to match his, as she'd shown at the fair – but marrying as she'd suggested wasn't something he would consider. His widower status enabled him to play the women around him against one another.

Thinking of women, his thoughts turned to Bera. But he could feel his blood rising at her betrayal of their reputation, and tried to think of something else, but his thoughts wouldn't settle.

The stranger, Allman, was the true source of Ragnar's restlessness – or rather the unsettling effect of his arrival on the fragile equilibrium of the farm.

Strolling around the lake-shore, he allowed Orn's path to cross his. Ragnar's older tenant rubbed his bald head, squinting into the suns, one of which was momentarily obscured by grey clouds as often happened as the day wore on. "We've managed to make a replacement pin for the gun without cannibalising the other one."

"So we eke out another week, or month, or year of life," Ragnar said. Orn looked shocked, disappointed, and angry in such quick succession that Ragnar almost laughed. Instead he said, "Sorry, didn't mean to mock your efforts. You did well, fixing it without wrecking anything else for the part."

Orn nodded, mollified. "We do what we can. If it means the difference between the Formers returning to a dead colony or a live one, then it's worth it."

But they aren't coming back! Ragnar wanted to shout, but bit his tongue. They'd had this argument too many times in the past. It was what marked Ragnar as eccentric, though his fists and his sword meant no one dared call him Ragnar the Mad to his face if they wanted to live.

No one else believed that the colony had been abandoned. They couldn't without facing the almost unbearable thought that they had to tame an only half-finished world alone but for the Norns and whatever they could scratch out from the soil. Ragnar had kept his counsel as best he could, but still word of his near-heresy had spread.

Orn seemed to read his mind. "I know, we're wasting our time, trying to drag it out," he said, half-mockingly. "I want to make it work, even if it's just for now."

"That's my view of life," Ragnar said, almost mocking himself. "Make it work." He was self-aware enough to know that he was the kind of man who believed that his world should fit itself to him, rather than vice versa. "If the colony's been abandoned, then there's no point rationing our limited tech until such times as the others return, but we should instead take apart everything they have to find out how it works – *make* it work, rather than relying on the hand-outs from the Norns. They have their own priorities. Self-repair, stabilise the climate as best they can, then let us have whatever tools they can spare enough nanos to facture." He didn't know that, of course. The nano-factories weren't communicative; they just provided what they chose to, or refused a request.

"I bet you're the high-roller at backgammon," Orn said. "Not for you the half-kronur housewives' bets."

"Damn right." Ragnar grinned, and punched Orn's arm, hard enough to make any other man wince, but the farmer hadn't earned his nickname for nothing. "What's on your mind, old friend? You didn't come out here just to tell me they've fixed the gun."

Orn nodded, looking sheepish. He knew he wasn't the brightest light bulb in the house, but he wouldn't like to think he could be read so easily. "I threw the kids off the Oracle last night," he said. "And went over the readings from the Urdrs." Orn was referring to the automated weather stations seeded across Isheimur. "Those that haven't broken down altogether."

"Go on."

"Temperatures are down year on year over the last decade," Orn said, "but the forecast is more worrying.

There's a high probability of a hard winter, one that'll come early."

"How reliable is the data?" Ragnar knew that the stations that were malfunctioning but hadn't completely failed were the biggest problem; their data would skew the readings. There was no point in reopening that old discussion.

Orn shrugged. "Dunno. But you want to risk it? We're going to have to move in the flocks in a couple of months, anyway. Why not bring the migration forward, start moving them down from the Seterfjell now?"

What about the harvest?" Ragnar said.

"Put Bera and the man on harvesting as well. I'll take two of the Thralls, and go with them."

Ragnar frowned at losing two of the indentured farm hands. "Lose valuable grazing time? Fodder stocks are problematic at best. We lose two months, plus bringing them in means we lose time from the hay-making, so we lose doubly."

"But we can't risk it, Ragnar!" Orn's fists balled, though Ragnar knew it was frustration.

Nonetheless, Ragnar gripped Orn's upper arm. "We'll compromise: half the men – including Allman – will start in a month. Agreed?" It was a rhetorical question; they both knew it. Orn knew from experience that to keep arguing when Ragnar had made his decision would only provoke the Gothi, and Orn knew what happened when Ragnar lost his temper.

So the farmer nodded. "About our... guest..." He wrung his hands, and looked away.

"What?" They were walking back toward the farms now anyway, so Ragnar decided that he might as well look in on Bera and her surrogate child.

Orn shook his head. "The others..." His next words came in a rush. "You know that some of Bjarney's kids are a bit superstitious. Some of the others too – as our science fails, so their belief in it starts to fail as well."

"What do you mean?" Ragnar said. "We've always had nonsense about shapeshifters and wraiths, but no one seriously thinks that 'cause we've named the locals for trolls, and called the lizards 'dragons', that they're from Old Earth. What are you getting at, Orn?"

Orn looked even more uncomfortable. "You know that the stranger talks to himself?"

"So? That's common in delirium."

"His voice changes," Orn said. "It gets deeper, rougher. Some of the kids think that he's possessed. Or that he's a seidr, with the gift of second-sight."

Ragnar made a great show of laughing. "Possession? What sort of rubbish is that? Next you'll be telling me that the Yule Lads will be calling this winter, and ghosts are rising from the graveyard. Pull yourself together!" Laughing, he clapped Orn on the shoulder, and the big man smiled, looking embarrassed. "I'll look in, see if I can catch him playing us for fools. If he's well enough to act, he's well enough to take on more physical work."

But as he turned away still laughing loudly, inside he felt chilled. Surely we can't be facing a paradigm change? He'd heard from the Oracle, heard of the myths from before the Long Night, before that back to the Interregnum and to the dawn of the Diaspora, to have heard of paradigm changes – that sometimes enough people believing in something could start to change the way things actually were.

As Orn went back to his tinkering, Ragnar crossed the courtyard.

Orn the Small said, "Your friend is following you, Pappi," pointing to Grensosa trailing behind like a little woolly dog.

Ragnar ruffled the boy's tousled hair, and wondered where the puppy Brynja was, why she wasn't chained to the tap, as he'd had her left. "Animals'll follow you anywhere if you feed 'em."

"Good morning, Pappi." Thorbjorg's arch voice cut into his good mood. His youngest daughter-in-law was walking across the yard; he could have sworn that her hips swayed a little more as she looked over her shoulder at him and smiled a coy invitation.

They'd talked many times after a few drinks; how it was in the nature of men to want to spread their seed as widely as possible; how the Oracle said that women naturally wanted to carry the child of the strongest male in any pack. Just chit-chat. He'd only grown angry with her once, when she'd claimed someone unnamed said that Yngi's genes might be defective. He'd shaken her by the shoulders and demanded to know who'd said such a thing. She'd only smiled, and allowed herself to lean against him, and even as he despised her for the cheap quality of the move, he'd felt his own traitorous body responding. He'd wiped the smile off her face with, "Anyway, you didn't seem to be complaining last night, from the noise you were making."

Sometimes he fantasised about ass-fucking her as a sign of contempt, and to ensure that she didn't get pregnant. Then again, she'd probably enjoy it, or at least pretend to, ensuring that she made as much noise as possible. With Thorbjorg everything was calculated, even – especially – sex.

He didn't doubt that she would get pregnant if Ragnar took her. She was always pregnant. He'd wondered before if all five kids were Yngi's. If she was prepared to offer herself to Ragnar, who else might she have lain with?

Much though he loved his youngest son, Ragnar had been amazed when Thorbjorg's father had approached him at the Bride Fair, and suggested an alliance. He'd always believed his son would live a celibate life, so had swallowed his doubts at the Fair, but Ragnar was sure that she'd married Yngi because he was Gothi's son, rather than from any real attraction, though in the dark all looks were moot.

Had Yngi been anyone else's son, he would probably have been left on the hillside. It wasn't an Icelandic custom, but the Isheimuri had too little time to spare on sentimentality. While they'd never condone eugenics or the actual murder behind the mealy-mouthed phrases, nor could they afford to weaken their gene pool too much; the gods knew that they were finding it hard enough to stop the gradual drift that came with such a small population, and poor diet and limited medicines.

Ragnar realised that he'd stopped half-way across the courtyard, and was apparently staring into space, doubtless to Thorbjorg's amusement. Might as well play the part, he thought, and struck a pose:

"What do you want with this bag of bones?
Old wolves do not need warm flesh,
When old and cold will do as well:
I'd rather stoke my own hearth."

Thorbjorg flushed at the implied insult, and fled.

Chuckling, Ragnar strolled to the byre but as he approached, his good humour evaporated.

The stable was empty of animals, as they were still out grazing under supervision, and in the corner the stranger lay dozing, while Bera sat, peeling the local turnips, which tasted more like soap.

In the two days since he had awoken, the man looked worse, as if the effort had drained him. If anything some of his pallor seemed to have eased.

Bera nodded without looking up at him, and Ragnar allowed his gaze to rest on the starman's face.

Despite being sick and injured, the man was so inhumanly handsome that he seemed almost god-like to Ragnar. The older realised that he was feeling an unfamiliar emotion – envy.

"He's slightly better than he was earlier today," Bera said.

As if he knew that they were talking about him, the alien stirred and tried to nuzzle at her breasts. Blushing furiously, Bera eased him away.

Ragnar felt his temper rise. "Let him. Might as well get some good from you spreading your legs – he can be your babe in arms."

Her head bowed, Bera unbuttoned her blouse. As the man's lips found her nipple, she murmured, eyes downcast, "Do you feel better, Ragnar Helgrimsson, by humiliating me? Do you feel more of a man?"

He stepped forward, knife half-out of its scabbard, but stopped. "You humiliated yourself, girl. Was it one of those travellers who stopped off on the way to Spring Fair? Or is it one of the boys?"

She didn't answer, but kept her head bowed.

As he left, she called out, "You say we've been abandoned by the Terraformers, my lord. But what if they've come back? And he's one of them? An advance scout, to see whether we've survived?"

Ragnar stopped. Orn didn't have the wit to see the hole that the stranger's presence blew in Ragnar's long-held beliefs. That the girl had thought through the implications only showed what a waste her disgrace was. "You think that they're throwing them down at us?" Ragnar said. "I'll guarantee you, child, he's no bloody Terraformer. He's an escaped lunatic, or a common vagrant who fell into a geysir or something."

"You should see his body healing," Bera said. "You can watch the burns fade almost by the second."

"Good!" Ragnar said, walking back into daylight. "We can put him to work, and he can pay for our generosity in kind."

By the next day Ragnar had mastered his restlessness, and got down to work. Much of it was administrative. The district measured eight hundred kilometres north to south, a thousand from east to west. Many of its people had been to the Summer Fair, but there were a few who hadn't, but had grievances to lodge.

Egil Samuelsson's neighbour accused him of allowing his sheep to stray into that man's grasslands, and the man was claiming compensation. Thordis-Maria Helgasdottir was accused of lewd behaviour in a public place, Ragnar suspected by someone whose amorous advances she'd rejected, and who now sought revenge. There were a number of disputes over late payment, of money, or much more commonly, of goods or services. Ragnar was asked to adjudicate each, and worked quickly and efficiently to effect a compromise. If he didn't give his petitioners good service, they could swear allegiance to another Gothi. With privilege came responsibility, he liked to tell his people.

But though his duties ate up much of his time, he was still a farmer, even if sharing with two other farms gave greater efficiency, and he had two sons and a son-in-law and four Thralls out tending the livestock to ease his workload.

So by midday each day Ragnar walked the fells, checking for signs of troll incursion, and the presence of snolfurs who might attack the flocks, and ensuring that the men were safe, if uncomfortable. With Isheimur's ever-changing weather came wave after wave of short, sharp showers that soaked them to the skin, barely giving their sheepskins time to dry out before the next band of rain swept over.

Passing Skorravatn, Ragnar would often find Orn the Strong's wife Thorunn keeping Bjarney's wife Salbjerg company. Salbjerg was heavily pregnant, and not only found moving difficult, but Ragnar suspected that she might go into labour at any time.

"Ladies," Ragnar said the day after Allman's relapse, bowing in an exaggerated way that set Salbjerg giggling. It didn't take much to make Salbjerg giggle. She was an uncomplicated woman who delighted in life, and it made Ragnar sad to see how near-constant pregnancy had worn her out. Cloning was an intensive arrangement and had been one of the first techniques to fail when the Formers had abandoned the colony. Worse, the near-disaster of a collapsing birth-rate for several years had scarred their society, leaving women as little more than baby-factories.

Ragnar made himself abandon nostalgia. "How goes the egg-gathering?" He pointed to the flocks of eider-ducks made flightless by their clipped wings now bobbing out on the waters.

"Slowly," Thorunn said sourly.

"I swear the little devils are getting cleverer at hiding their nests," Salli said with a giggle. "Perhaps we're breeding more intelligent eiders by eating the dumber ones."

"Perhaps we are," Ragnar agreed with a grin. "Maybe we should test them before we wring their necks?"

"How is the spaceman?" Thorunn asked.

"Who says he's a spaceman?" Ragnar asked, no longer smiling.

Thorunn shrugged. "Whatever he is, Bera seems happy, now she has someone to nurse."

Ragnar didn't answer, but walked away. "Time for dinner," he called over his shoulder, belatedly remembering to say goodbye. Striding back to the courtyard, he saw Brynja again tied to the water-tap in the centre. The puppy yapped at him, but he ignored it, though he noted that it was bulking up, and he wondered what Bera was feeding it on. As long as it came out of her share of the food and she kept it out of his way, he wasn't too bothered.

He descended into the lobby, and removed his boots.

"Bera's obviously attracted to him," he heard Thorbjorg say, her voice arch. "Aren't you, Bera? Does he make your heart beat quicker, girl?"

Bera muttered something which Ragnar couldn't make out.

"Oh, really?" Asgerd said, sounding as if she were trying not to laugh.

"What's amusing my daughters-in-law?" Ragnar said, as he entered the communal kitchen. Greeted by silence and a mix of sheepish looks, he sniffed at the aromas and tilted his head quizzically. "Horse? What's the occasion?"

"Berti died last night," Hilda said. "We're pickling and freezing as much as we can, but there's enough left over for a few meals." She gave him a little smile. "It won't spoil, after all, in this weather."

"True." He picked at a piece and dodged the knife's flat that Hilda aimed at his hand. Chewing, he said around the meat. "Are you including our guest in the meal?"

Hilda's smile faded, and he could feel the tension in the room. He could almost read their minds: do we say yes or no? What sort of mood is he in? Good. It wouldn't hurt to keep them on their toes.

Bera said, "I was, um, I was going to take a few pieces out after we'd eaten." She didn't look up once. "I wasn't sure whether to or not after the last time he had horse."

Ragnar remembered the vomit-eating and winced. It probably hadn't thawed properly. Nonetheless… "Take him some," Ragnar said, and felt the mood in the room lighten. "I'll come with you, shall I?"

Bera said, head still down, "As you wish, Gothi." She hadn't called him Pappi since he'd accused her of over-familiarity. She'd refused to name the father, and worse, been cheeky. He'd hit her so hard, the slap had left her nose bleeding.

He sat and tucked into the meat, using bread freshly baked from their precious harvest to mop it up with.

Afterward he let Bera carry the meat down, and stayed sitting while the others cleared the table of leftovers and dirty dishes. He waited until they were alone, and asked Asgerd, "Should I be worried about leaving her alone with the stranger?"

Hilda would be pissed off that he'd asked his elder daughter-in-law instead of his daughter, but he would get a more honest answer from Asgerd, who, as wife to his heir had less reason to tell him what he wanted to hear, would instead tell him what he *needed* to hear.

"I don't think so," Asgerd said. "I think she's learned her lesson."

"To keep her legs together? Or not to get knocked up if she does lie with him?"

"I think that he's a long way from lying with any-one," Asgerd said. She fell silent as Hilda returned to the room from the scullery, and shot them a question-ing look.

"I think I'll visit our guest," Ragnar said.

Out in the barn, the stranger was already finishing the pile of meat that Bera had taken out at Ragnar's in-sistence. "Surely he'll be ill if he eats that much?" Hilda had protested, falling silent at his look.

Clearly the stranger was slightly better again, although only physically. Mentally... he gazed into space as he ate with almost unbelievably pale blue eyes, ignoring Bera's idle chit-chat, her recounting of the latest gossip. But when he saw Ragnar a cunning look crossed his features.

"What's your name, fellow?" Ragnar said.

The fellow gazed away, his eyes following a wagtail as it flitted through the rafters, his head and body swaying slightly to some internal rhythm.

"Hey, I'm talking to you!" Ragnar seized the man's arm. For all that Allman looked wasted, his arm was corded muscle. Ragnar felt a twitch deep in the arm, as if the man had suffered a spasm. Was he disabled? A lunatic who'd escaped his confines? But there were no dwellings between here and Althfjord, which was the nearest farmhouse in the general direction that Ragnar's people had found him, so how had he got there?

Ragnar resented asking himself such questions too often – he didn't like the answers he kept coming up with. He had no problem with being proven wrong, if the Formers were to return. If they came properly that is, not represented by a drooling half-wit.

Before he could speak further, though, Allman had lurched to his feet and stood swaying in a non-existent breeze, a look of agony etched into his face. Then he started babbling. It took Ragnar a few seconds to identify the words.

"That's not Isheimuri," Bera cried, as Allman fell again, trying to catch him.

"It's High Isheimuri," Ragnar said. "Common Tongue we speak is corrupted English with a little Icelandic, as it was spoken when the settlers left Nytt Ragnarok. That wasn't much different from how it was spoken before the Diaspora. This is proper Old Norse from Earth's Middle Ages – he's reciting *Egil's Saga*."

Hearing Old Norse spoken with such fluency dispelled any thoughts that the man was an offworlder. Nytt Ragnarok had been reduced to a smouldering ruin a year before the funds ran out, in one of the first raids of what had soon escalated into all-out war.

The man's eyes focused on Ragnar.

"I wonder," Ragnar said. "Are you some wandering seer, traveller? If you are, I can hardly put you to work for me, except asking you to labour enough to pay for your food and lodging." As a seer, the man was legally outside of the law, rather than a criminal. Ragnar couldn't hold him as a Thrall, an indentured servant – or slave, as some namby-pamby reformers dubbed them.

The man fainted.

Ragnar shook his head in disbelief.

Allman's eyes snapped open; he said, "You? Dislike sunset?"

Ragnar felt a chill beyond the weather. All his life he'd known what to do, and when he didn't he'd bluffed. But this was like nothing he'd ever known. The man was either mad or acting the part. Ragnar stood up, and dealt with fear – rarely though he felt it – as he usually did, by getting angry and shouting. "Pull yourself together!"

The man's eyes suddenly focused and he recoiled with an exclamation. "Who the bloody hell are you?"

FIVE
Karl

Karl gazed down at the other man, thinking, Ooops, maybe I shouldn't have said that. The man, Ragnar – how did I know his name? – was formidably ugly. Black hair streaked with grey sprouted from his head, nose and even his ears, which appeared to have been broken or torn at some point. Beneath bushy eyebrows a bulbous nose separated raisin-like eyes. The eyes were shrewd, though, missing nothing.

Ragnar released his grip on Karl's smock. He drew himself up to his full one-metre eighty height and puffed out his chest. Karl was braced for an onslaught of self-importance, but Ragnar visibly gathered himself in. "I'm the man who could have left you to die in the snow."

Karl made himself look contrite. "Of course. I'm sorry."

"Ragnar Helgrimsson." He thrust out his hand.

"Karl Allman." Karl gazed at the hand, at the flush rising Ragnar's face, and realised that in his confusion he was insulting Ragnar again. On instinct, Karl offered his hand, and the man seized the inside of his elbow in a grip strong enough to crush walnuts, before releasing him.

Ragnar said, "You'll come to my chamber," and stalked out of the barn.

Karl realised that Bera was staring at him, open-mouthed. He noted absently that she slouched, but apart from a slight squint she could have been pretty, beneath the tangle of hair, cold sore and the dirt. "Have I grown another head?"

He smiled to show that he was joking, but the silence and her stare were making him uncomfortable.

She fled.

"Ah... OK." He rubbed his head then scratched where the rough sheepskin smock that they'd dressed him in chafed.

His companion – the micro version of Ship's Aye – must have assimilated data while he recovered, so that nothing was wholly familiar nor completely strange, but somewhere in-between.

He was clearly in an empty area for animals: a barn, about forty metres long by fifteen wide. Lurching across to a ladder, he looked up at second story; both floors were together six, maybe seven metres high.

Staggering across to the doorway on still-wobbly legs, he looked up the slope to a low grass-roofed building that crouched half-buried in the side of a rock-strewn hill. Beyond another house at a right angle to the first, people were crawling among the heather. Bera loped toward them. He thought it the bleakest landscape he'd ever seen, bar none, and almost wished he'd passed Isheimur by and died in space. *No, that's foolish.*

Gazing up at a cloudy grey sky tinged with pink, Karl felt a sudden vertiginous wave. "Been cooped up for too long." His environment shouldn't have so affected him but his companion's information-gathering while he convalesced had complicated his mental state. He shivered in the intense cold; in a couple of days, the nanophytes would adjust his reactions.

He ambled across the square, taking deep breaths of the scrawny, tasteless air. His companion indicated that it was about as thick as Earth's atmosphere in Tibet, but that meant nothing to him. He'd long complained to Ship that all its systems were calibrated against Earth-norms, but it had done no good.

A couple of women who looked deep in conversation fell silent. One of them was a voluptuous strawberry-blonde who shot him a dazzling smile. "Up and about, I see."

"Yes." Karl struggled not to gasp out the answer.

Bera appeared by his side. "You shouldn't walk around on your own. It's not safe." Karl stopped and she took his arm. "Lean on me."

He nodded thanks. They resumed. "Looks. Safe," he panted.

"Things aren't always as they seem. Like Thorbjorg." She jerked her head at the strawberry-blonde. Before he could ask what she meant, Bera changed the subject. "Why were you so rude to Ragnar?"

"Long. Story."

Bera stopped him. "We have time."

How much could he tell her? If she did tell Ragnar, would it matter? Karl decided on the truth. "When I was ten my parents moved from one Clade to another. It was compulsory, to avoid incest." She looked puzzled. "Small gene pool," he explained. "Jakob Attlee was a year older than me. We loathed each other. I was small for my age – I grew thirty centimetres during adolescence, but then I was a shrimp – and Jakob was big, nanophyte injections converting his fat to muscle." He wondered whether to explain nanophytes but she nodded, so he pressed on. "When Jakob learned that I'd had my first injections, the bullying got nasty."

She tilted her head to one side as something caught her interest. "A big man like you? Hard to imagine anyone bullying you."

"People change," he said.

"These injections," she prompted.

He resumed, "Nanophytes repair injuries, build muscles and make other improvements. When they learned I'd had my first injections, Jakob's gang cornered me away from the main trees. Jakob had stolen a bottle of household bleach." Bera looked puzzled again. "They held me down while he poured it down my throat. Before I'd had my nanophyte injections, it would have burned my throat out, maybe killed me. It was still the worst pain I've ever felt. The nanophytes began repairing me straight away, which was as painful as the burns. Jakob's gang wouldn't let me go, but watched what happened." He paused. "An hour later, they did it again; and again. When they finally let me go that evening, they threatened to kill me if I told anyone. I believed them."

Bera said, "That's sad. But what's it to do with Ragnar?"

Karl said, "I'd just been dreaming about Jakob. Ragnar looked exactly like an older version of him." Maybe, he thought, that was the companion's way of assimilating Ragnar's image? "The same piggy eyes, and bushy eyebrows... waking up and seeing that face again..." He saw her nod of comprehension, and said, "Is it significant?"

She pushed out her lips, thinking. "He was offended. Think of it. He's an important man, and you react as if he's a troll."

A troll? He thought. Ah, they're Icelanders. Trolls are part of Icelandic culture. I'm surprised that they quote old Icelandic tales, though. "So I should make a big fuss when I next see him? Thank him for his hospitality?"

"I would," Bera said. "It may work."

"May?"

"Ragnar bears a grudge," she said. "He might forgive you."

"Ah," he said. "Understood. I'll hope that I do a good enough job of convincing him how grateful I am."

"I would," she said. "And if I were you, I'd hope that it's enough." Though she smiled, the fear in her eyes didn't fool him. He could understand fear, but there was hope as well. Why?

"Come on," she said. "We mustn't keep him waiting too long."

"Ragnar's house?"

She nodded.

Like the barn, it was about forty metres long, perhaps twenty metres wide. Karl looked back at the barn; all the buildings were dug into the hillside, and covered over with turf. Smoke issued from a vent on one of the roofs. Bera said, "His family sleep here, in the winter, his labourers too. They're up with the flocks now." She helped him descend steps into a half-lobby that stank of furs and boots ingrained with body odour, and through into a long room lit along each wall. Except for one, which was all window, looking down over the barn, onto the lake. "Strengthened glass," Bera said. "Two centuries old."

This room stank too, of bodies crowded together for too long, but now it was nearly empty of people, though boxes and piled possessions were strewn everywhere. "The main hall, where the children and Thralls – the indentured labourers – sleep," Bera said. At the far end was a five metre-long table, around which two women bustled, setting out jugs and plates: "Hilda and Asgerd, Ragnar's daughter and older daughter-in-law."

"Good morning," Asgerd said with a shy smile. She was another blonde, but subtle to Thorbjorg's voluptuous.

Hilda was as dark as her father, and her mouth was down-turned; she looked as if life perpetually disappointed her. "My father," she faintly emphasised the first word, "will see you now. You can leave us, Bera."

"Why can't Bera stay with me?" Karl said. "I couldn't have got here without her help."

Hilda stiffened, but before she could answer, Bera said, "I'll go and find you a walking stick, Karl, then go help in the kitchen."

Hilda dipped her head a centimetre in acknowledgement, or dismissal.

"*She* knows her place," Hilda said. The rebuke to Karl was clear: so should he.

"Is she a servant?" Karl said, refusing to be intimidated.

Hilda looked offended. "She is fostered here. Farms that cannot support their people often place children with other farmsteads, and the children work for their keep, as does everyone else. Everyone," she emphasised, then added, "but Bera's family were killed when their farm was buried beneath lava. So sad. So unusual, that a volcano blows, but they knew the risk. Lush farmland often means volcanoes. Come!"

She led Karl into a large chamber in which Ragnar sat gazing at some papers, his shoulders draped with a white fur lined with coloured ribbons. Karl wondered if he was supposed to be impressed.

Ragnar looked up. "You're here. Good." He noted Karl's trembling right leg: "Do I scare you so much?" He grinned.

"Muscle spasm," Karl said. "Being on my feet. Still recovering." He did feel a little weak.

"Then sit. Hilda, fetch him some warm sweet water."

Hilda departed.

Ragnar gazed at Karl, who stared back. Ragnar said abruptly, "Where are you from? And what were you doing naked on a hillside at night?"

"I – uh, I fell from the sky." Karl felt foolish saying it, but his companion hadn't gained enough vocabulary while he'd been unconscious for anything but simple concepts, although his lexicon was expanding hourly.

"Why?"

"My ship was attacked. I was forced to… leave it. It was destroyed. I had no time to take any possessions."

"A starship? Not a sailing ship?" Ragnar's tone hinted at scepticism.

"A starship, yes." Keep it simple, caution urged. Karl wasn't sure whether this man was friend or enemy, although his instincts suggested more the latter.

"Who attacked you?"

Karl said cagily, "They're people who assumed that I was hostile. It's complicated. There are a lot of factions in a big sky."

"Were they Shapers?" Luckily, Karl saw Ragnar's lips shape "Formers" so ignored his idiot companion's urge to translate words even when they were common to both languages.

"Terraformers? No."

"Are you?"

"I'm…" Karl paused, working out how to explain it. "My conglomerate – clan, that is – uses Terraforming to an extent. But it's expensive, and takes constant, ah, working on to stop the world reverting to its default state. That's what happened to the people who founded Isheimur. They went bankrupt in the Long Night, and their assets were sold off. No one would take on this project. I'm sorry."

Ragnar looked oddly satisfied at the news that the colony had been abandoned. "We'll have to work out what to do with you."

Karl wondered how his family were, how he could send a signal. He wished that Ship had had the time to download more than basic information – he had no idea how much this world had devolved. The silence of the colony couldn't be taken as a sign that they'd lost all tech, especially as Ship's records hadn't even shown that Isheimur had survived.

But was he simply wishing for a happy ending? The Galaxy was vast: it was easy to forget that when crossing from fold-point to fold-point, squeezing a journey of years at sub-light into weeks between each star-system's nexus.

Any signals from Isheimur were probably being transmitted to what was now empty space; current nexi would be unknown to the Isheimuri, while those stations at nexi utilised by Isheimur's Formers were probably now disused.

A knock interrupted Karl's thoughts.

Ragnar, who had silently watching Karl called, "Come!"

Bera held out a metre-long stick that was gnarled, but arrow-straight. "It's been used by Olders before," she said. "I found it in the lobby. It might prove useful."

Ragnar said, "Take it. Go to lunch. Meet the others." He returned to his papers.

Karl tried not to feel like a fool as he pulled himself into a standing position. When he took his first step he was grateful for the stick, which stopped him falling flat on his face.

Bera offered him her arm, though Karl saw her hesitate, and wondered why. As he wrapped his left arm around her right, she flinched – only slightly, but he felt it. *Has she been told to be friendly to me? Is she scared of me? Because I'm a stranger?*

He also wondered why he was so sensitive to her. He tried not to feel unfaithful to Karla and Lisane in noticing how pretty she was beneath the camouflage of grime and messiness and her squint. He resolved to offer nothing that might reveal any attraction; he would be correct, but cool, and hope that that would work. Hell, for all you know, not making an advance toward her might give offence.

Karl drew back from the throng milling around in the long, low room, but Bera gripped his arm. The mob was so busy talking, and shoving each other out of the way to place dishes of meat, bread, eggs and pitchers of drink on the table, that for several seconds they didn't notice him.

Karl watched the women, Ragnar's daughters and daughter-in law bicker. Thorbjorg had changed her dress into something that highlighted a clearly defined waist separating an ample bust and backside, and coloured ribbons now bedecked her hair. Asgerd had done something to her lips that made them look bee-stung and highlighted her fine cheekbones. Only Hilda remained unchanged. Through the adults a half-dozen children weaved, dancing and flitting like a shoal of minnows, helping the adults or chasing one another depending on their age.

Asgerd saw Karl and her lips parted in a smile. The others followed her gaze and falling silent, swung round. "Come join us," Asgerd said.

"Can I help?" Karl chin-cocked the laden table.

"You can help eat it," Ragnar said. "Some of it is for you, anyway." He gestured to one of the benches that ran the length of either side of the table, and the others burst into conversation, the children chattering and laughing. Hilda sat opposite Karl. "Is Yngi joining us?" Hilda asked Thorbjorg, who had shoved herself into the space next to Hilda. Thorbjorg flushed. Karl thought he caught Hilda's faint smirk.

"He's butchering a rock-eater. He's going to pickle it."

One of the children made gagging noises.

"We may have to eat it, if it's a hard winter," Hilda said. She turned to Karl. "As Ragnar's daughter, I run the household in his absence." Someone tittered. "So I choose the menu," she added.

Thorbjorg said, "I'm Thorbjorg, Ragnar's daughter-in-law." When Karl shook her hand, he felt the faintest pressure on his knuckles from her thumb, and she seemed reluctant to let go. When he met her gaze, she widened her eyes fractionally, and a pink tongue-tip licked her lips.

"Would you like some lamb?" Bera said, pushing some of the grey chunks onto his plate. "Green sauce," she said, and ladled a few small spoons onto the lamb. "Have some pickled vegetables."

Karl nodded thanks. For all that his stomach was growling in protest, he took only a few of the various vegetables, but looking across in the sudden silence, saw that he'd taken far more than anyone else. He tried to scrape some onto Bera's plate, but she blocked him. "You have some," he muttered, pointing to her near-empty plate. "I've taken far too much."

"You need to build your strength up," she said.

Following the other's example, he ate using the implements, which felt awkward in his hands. He'd spent too long on Ship and grown used to munching on food that he could hold in his hands. The pickled vegetables were tart in his mouth, but enjoyable. So was the green sauce on the lamb, which was slightly greasy but so rich that his mouth didn't feel big enough to hold the flavour.

"Good?" Bera said, watching him.

"Very." He shovelled another forkful into his mouth.

"It should be. It's freshly slaughtered."

The lamb turned to ash in his mouth, but somehow he managed to keep chewing and swallow. "This is from an animal?"

He grew vaguely aware that Hilda and Thorbjorg had stopped talking.

"A small one of the sort that you saw on the hills. You remember?" Bera said.

Karl didn't answer, but concentrated on the pickled vegetables, trying not to think of eating what had been a living, breathing creature. Did you think that they were pets, or ornaments, fool?

"And the other day," Bera said. "You remember, you said 'sheep'?"

"What?" he said. "I've only just awoken."

Thorbjorg laughed. "Oh, Loki, you're funny."

Karl thought, Hmm, there's some sort of misunderstanding here.

Karl watched Ragnar flirt with Asgerd. Her serenity seemed to challenge the Gothi, who paid her far more attention than the others. His vitality clearly attracts women, Karl thought, surprised at this new facet of a man he'd only glimpsed as a grumbling bully.

"Are you really from the stars?" Thorbjorg said. Without waiting for an answer, she continued, "You must have seen so many things, if you are."

"Where else would I come from?" Karl said, smiling. He didn't want to give too much away – he didn't know what Ragnar had told them, and didn't want to upset his host by straying from the party line. "Call me Karl."

"You could be an outlaw," Thorbjorg said, widening her eyes. Her grin showed her teeth and a mouthful of lamb-in-green-sauce that made Karl feel queasy.

"I'd be a pretty useless outlaw, wouldn't I?" He made himself ignore the thought of flesh, and grin back. Don't give offence. "I'm told I was found stark naked in a snowfield."

"You could be some sort of Holy Fool," Bera nudged him.

"What's that?"

"Like a seer. They have knowledge that only the learned share, but are ignorant of everyday matters."

"Hmm," Karl said. He was bemused at how much he knew about Isheimur, but the planetary mass didn't help him understand the details of the society; any information Ship had downloaded would be two centuries obsolete.

For the first time he felt like the alien that he was, and missed Karla and Lisane with a stab of loneliness.

His face must have shown his desolation. Bera said, "Are you tired, Karl?"

"A little," Karl said.

"Here's Yngi," Hilda said, and Karl wondered at the malice in her voice, and the unhappy look that flitted across Thorbjorg's face.

The man who joined them walked with an odd shuffle. Like the others, hair erupted from his head and face, and even covered his forearms and spread down his chest from his throat. But despite being a young adult – Karl estimated he was about twenty – he gazed at Karl with a child's open joy. "Spaceman!"

Karl couldn't help warming to him, but before he could reply, Ragnar's gruff voice interrupted. "Come sit here, son. Don't pester."

The newcomer slouched off, still staring over his shoulder at Karl, a huge grin splitting his face.

"My youngest," Ragnar said. "Yngvar."

"Hello, Yngvar," Karl called.

Yngvar blushed, and his head bobbed.

"Yngi was brain-damaged at birth," Bera whispered. Karl watched Ragnar fuss around the young man, whom he clearly doted on. Yngi seemed fascinated by Karl.

Despair engulfed Karl. His body-clock, which displayed Avalon date and time on the top left of Karl's peripheral vision, showed that he'd been gone too long already. What was supposed to be a two-week voyage had already over-run even before the attack on Ship. Lisane would be close to term now. He wished that he had agreed to be told the baby's gender, but too late now.

When the meal was over, Bera and the other women cleared the dishes away while Ragnar sat and stared into space, and Yngi was ushered away, still staring at Karl.

Bera led Karl, half-walking, half-shuffling out into a squall. Karl was soaked to the skin in moments. "We have a motto," Bera said. "If you don't like the weather, just wait five minutes, and it will change. This will pass."

She was right; by the time they reached the other side of the cobbled square, the twin suns were burning shafts of sunlight through the pink clouds.

"It never rains for very long," Bera said. "In the open lands the winds are so constant that much of the rain and snow evaporate before it can nourish the ground. No oceans, you see, just lakes like this."

Karl took a long look at the valley around them.

Bales of corn stood in clumps in the fields on the far side of the lake. Figures pulled a trailer full of bales down toward them. Bera followed his gaze. "We store them over winter for animal feed." Further along were a few stunted trees lurking on the far side of the lake shore, barely bigger than shrubs. "They yield berries," Bera said. "There are a few farms on the equator that have proper trees, apples and pears and such-like, and a couple even used to have vineyards. But the crops failed, the farmers were driven into paupers' graves."

"It sounds a harsh world," Karl said. They resumed their stately walk to the barn.

"It's the only one we have," Bera said.

"Is it getting colder? You mentioned farms failing…"

"Some say so," Bera said. "Others that the men were fools to try growing such crops, that they could never have succeeded at growing luxury items. Once they had started, they couldn't just stop. You get just one chance at life. If you're lucky."

He wanted to ask her whether she'd been lucky, but remembered his decision to keep his distance. "And sheep on the high ground," he said, pointing to where low clouds covered the hills. Then he looked again. "Is that smoke?" He pointed at the smoke.

"Steam," Bera said. "Isheimur's riddled with volcanoes, hot springs and geysirs. That resemblance to Iceland as it's described in legends is one of the things that attracted the Formers." She added, "There's precious little soil good enough for growing crops, and what there is, is on the south side of the valley, but the grass grows well throughout Skorradalur from spring through the summer – though the winters are too harsh to allow animals to graze outside. Even if they could the snolfurs would rip them apart."

"Snolfurs?" Karl frowned in puzzlement.

Bera didn't see, and carried on talking, "Yes. You remember snolfurs. Big." He shook his head, and frowning, she held her free hand a metre off the ground. "Predators. They kill by wounding their victim, which bleeds to death. Snolfurs kill more than they

78

need, but the winter acts as a deep freeze. The carnage if we don't patrol the flocks is awful. That's where most of the men are: out on patrol."

"I'm surprised you haven't wiped them out."

"We hunt them, but the meat tastes awful. There's something in it that's toxic to us, though apparently the first generations were able to deal with the poisons. But we've lost that ability." She shrugged. "It's a big world, there are many snolfurs, and lots of places for them to hide."

Back in the barn, he helped with her task of peeling vegetables, then dozed.

Later, he awoke to find her standing over him. "Do you feel up to facing them again?"

"Yes," he said, though he didn't really – he felt drained.

He pushed himself to his feet, and she helped him back to the farmhouse, which was again filling with family members, including a freckle-faced man with red-gold hair.

Karl felt Bera tense. "Thorir," she said.

Thorir turned to face them. "Bera," he said, then looked Karl up and down. "And you are the space-man."

Karl struggled not to stare. All the settlers seemed incredibly hairy, especially the males. As well as Ragnar and Yngi, whose faces hid behind unkempt mats of varying thickness, Karl had seen a man almost bald but for a ring of hair semi-circling the back of his head from ear to ear, then running into a facial covering, but for a top lip that Bera had said was shaved. Arnbjorn – Ragnar's son – sported twin strips of hair running from his nose down either side of his mouth to his chin, and twin strips of hair separating shaved cheeks from his ears.

But Thorir sported the most elaborate arrangement Karl had yet seen: cranial and facial hair alike braided into ten to twenty centimetre-long stiff spikes. From the way that Thorir stroked them, it was obvious that he took great pride in his locks.

Karl nodded a greeting in return, feeling as if he had wandered into an antique bestiary. Bera led him to the far end of the table, where Ragnar sat, thinking. "Have you a moment to spare, Gothi?" Karl stressed the honorific.

Ragnar indicated that Karl should sit opposite him. "I was glad to see you at lunch," Ragnar said. "I'm glad that you made the effort tonight, as well. It bodes well for your recovery."

Karl said, "It was the least I could do, given my graceless reaction to being awoken. I wanted to apologise and thank you again for your hospitality."

Ragnar said, "That was well said, Karl Allman." Was it his imagination, or did Karl sense faint mockery in Ragnar's tone? "You seem to be mending well."

"Getting better. I wish it were faster."

"So do I," Ragnar said. "We have little spare food."

"I would be on my way as soon as I can, if that would help," Karl said.

Ragnar's head lifted, as did his eyebrows. "Just like that? No working off your debt?"

"I meant no offence," Karl said quickly. "If there is work I can do... but you mentioned a drain on your food stocks."

"I said spare food," Ragnar said. "We can always find food for hands that can work."

Karl said carefully, "If I can get a message to your capital?"

"Our what?"

"Your major centre of population?"

Ragnar looked bemused. "Why do you want to get to such a place?"

Oh, Vishnu, Karl thought. Are you really so stupid, or being deliberately obtuse? "To send a signal to my people," he said with exaggerated patience. "I'd like to return home. To my family."

Ragnar stared at him. "Signal? Are you mad? You think that if we had such technology, we'd live like this?"

"I – I assumed that this was an isolated outpost."

"Hah! We don't have capitals. This *is* a population centre."

Karl swallowed, swayed and slumped back against the wall behind him.

SIX
Bera

They ate their meal in near-silence. Karl seemed
stunned and Ragnar was in a sour mood, so Bera kept
quiet. The others also recognised Ragnar's glower, and
murmured among themselves.

When Ragnar left the table – still without speaking –
the others brightened.

"You should show our guest the sauna, Bera," Thorbjorg said with a sly smile.

Bera felt her face burn. "You know men and women
aren't supposed to sauna together!"

"I said *show* him." Thorbjorg was all mock-inno-
cence, but didn't fool Bera for a moment. "Not sit with
him. Though if he needs his hand holding…" Thorbjorg raised her eyebrows. "He has very big… hands,
hasn't he?"

You're not thinking about his hands, you bitch, Bera
thought.

"Do you want to use the sauna?" Thorir called to
Karl from along the table. "A pipe runs down from
a hot spring on the hillside to the far end of the
house."

Bera nudged Karl, and he started, but must have been half-listening, for he said, "It'd be nice to get clean. Thanks."

"I'm going in there," Thorir said. "I'll show you which stones are the very hot ones, and how to scrape the dirt off and still have your skin."

Bera breathed a sigh of relief when Karl accompanied Thorir to the sauna. Since he'd awoken she felt differently about him, and Thorbjorg's "witticisms" had rattled her. Karl awake was overwhelming. His muscular chest, the unnatural hairlessness of his head and body – maintained by his nanophytes – the feel of him against her as she propped him up, the slightly musky yet sweet sweat he exuded; it terrified her even as she wanted him. There was simply too much of him.

By the time he returned an hour later, glowing and clean, she'd calmed down. "I'll help you to the barn," she said, "before I use the sauna."

"You're going to wash?" Thorir said. "Blimey."

There was no one else around, so Bera balled up her courage. "Piss off," she told Thorir.

That night she slept in the big house for the first time since Karl's arrival, earning a few sly digs from the other women, and (though she'd probably imagined it) a disappointed look from Karl.

So the next morning it felt as if in some way it were her fault that Loki stared at her from Karl's now slate-hard eyes, as if she'd summoned him back with her absence.

The day crawled past in one long jabber-filled drone, the alien rarely pausing for breath, leaving her to wipe the drool from the side of his mouth. He kept calling her Jocasta; after a while she didn't bother to correct him.

When she relayed the news, Ragnar snorted. "He's trying to get out of the chores."

"He won't," Bera said grimly, "He can peel the vegetables."

She slept in the barn that night, awaking to the dog's frantic barking. Out in the yard, Thorir was standing eyeball-to-eyeball with the gabbling sleepwalker.

"Go back to bed, boy!" Thorir snarled.

"Don't hit him!" Bera pulled Loki away from the swinging rifle-butt.

The next night, after another day of raving, poor motor co-ordination and Loki trying to grope her, she was half-tempted to abandon him for the house and the other's jibes, but she gritted her teeth.

She awoke late next morning, muzzy-headed.

Karl was sitting staring at the stars, now rapidly fading under the twin suns' onslaught of light. A solitary tear trickled down his face, and she wrapped her arms around his shoulders, moved by pity.

He touched her arm, when she jerked away.

"Sorry," he said, wiping his eye.

"It's OK." She couldn't tell him what was wrong, even if he'd emerged from his self-absorption. She'd spent too long bottling it up. "Sleep well?" Bera said.

"Very," Karl said, contradicting the bags under his eyes.

"Come on or we'll be late. I'll get food. We'll eat as we work."

As they neared the laundry, Yngi shuffled past, flashing his toothy grin at them.

Karl said, "Where's Yngi going in such a hurry?"

"Taking care of the snawk," Bera said, helping him up.

"The what?"

But she didn't answer, instead leaving him in the laundry.

She returned with bread and a boiled egg, some meat and a handful of dried berries. "Against scurvy," she explained as he pulled a face at the berries' sourness. They ate in companionable silence.

Bera said, "What's a two-ring?"

"Dunno," Karl said. "In what context?"

"You said something about a two-ring test yesterday."

Karl pulled a face. "When?"

"You mentioned a two-ring test," Bera insisted.

He sighed. "A Turing Test refers to Artificial Intelligence. My ship downloaded a random mass of information. It was probably amongst that."

"Why would it… download information? How?"

"How? Tight-beam transmission to an implant. Why? So I have information – much good it's done me."

"Is that causing you to turn into Loki?"

"It shouldn't." He took a breath. "Vocalising isn't so unusual when there's a lot of information to be assimilated. Though I have no idea what a lot of stuff that Ship downloaded is – I don't seem to know much about Isheimur, apart from basic stats, orbit, mass and so on. But sleepwalking doesn't fit assimilation protocols."

"There's something you're not telling me."

"More like something I don't know," Karl said.

"Ragnar thinks you're… what's the word? Schizoid."

Karl's laugh sounded strained. He raised his eyebrows. "Do you?"

She waited a long time as they set up the wringer. "I don't know what to think."

He frowned. "Have I harmed you? Do I seem like a threat?"

Bera said, "No, but I don't know."

"I'm a threat?" He looked upset.

She said carefully, "You've not done anything to hurt me, but I get the impression that you could, not from malice, but because you're like a big child."

She indicated the metal pail on the hob, stuffed full of washing. "Time we started work." The Sagas never mention laundry, she thought. As they lifted the first of the steaming cloths from the pail to the lip of the wringer she said to lighten the mood, "You never hear of Gunnlaug Serpent-tongue wrestling with washing." She mock-complained: "Perhaps the Sagas didn't think it worth mentioning such mundane chores. Or maybe they were just dirty bastards who stank all the time."

He smiled, but it was a thin effort.

"I guess no one will sing skalds of Bera Sigurdsdottir's battles with the laundry-monster in centuries to come." She pulled the edge of the sheet into place and – it was so much easier with two of them – turned the handle.

"I guess not," he said, grunting with the effort of holding up the other end of the sodden mass, while she fed it through the rollers.

His body was so clearly defined – everything this man wolfed down seemed to turn to pure muscle. The first time she'd taken his arm and felt a little shock, he'd explained that the nanophytes worked his body constantly, even while he slept. Maybe they caused his sleepwalking?

Karl was staring at the sheet. "You do so much washing and cleaning."

"How else are we to stay clean? We've little tech left."

"I suppose," Karl said.

"You know what the secret to keeping the machines running is? To always have copies of all your parts." Bera said. She pulled another sheet onto the wringer's lip, banging it down. "That's why we don't have enough food." She banged the rollers shut. Every action was a *slam*, punctuating her comments. "Because every fair, Pappi takes any spare food to trade for machine parts. All the farmers are in the tents drinking and whoring and fighting, our people are trading for whatever bits and pieces of kit there are." *Bang!* She opened the rollers, and he heaved another shirt into place that she slammed down flat. *Bang!* "Tubes burn out and can't be replaced. Bearings and metal parts corrode. In olden-times people made so much that they could pretend that tech was inexhaustible." *Bang!* She laughed scornfully. "Don't look so surprised. I've studied things on the Oracle, when no one's around – even manthings that we breeders shouldn't worry our pretty little heads about!" She yanked the handle around, firing the cloth through. "If a situation is genuinely life-threatening, the Norns may facture equipment, or medicine. But likely not – they have their own priorities."

"The Norns?" Karl said.

"The remains of the Formers' machines." *Bang!* "I told you about them – oh, I told frigging Loki. Freya, do I have to tell you everything twice?

"We understand what causes cholera and typhoid," Bera went on. *Bang!* "Technology is humanity's way of fighting entropy, but we can only make so much. We've lost our tech, but we're not savages."

"You're right," Karl said. "I didn't mean to imply that you were."

Bang!

Karl said, "Why are you so angry?"

"I'm always angry, Karl." *Bang!* "I just don't usually let it show. I'm not allowed. I'm just Sinderella."

He looked baffled.

"From the fairy tale. Sinderella was the poor girl. She got caught Deep Throating President Charming. Although he denied they had relations, he was impeached and she was sent to the kitchen with her ugly sisters." She shrugged. "That was on the Oracle as well." *Bang!*

"I never saw my parents from when I was eight, I'm treated like a whore, and if I say anything, I'm reminded I should be grateful. Grateful – they took my dowry and treat me like this. I can't even mourn my child!"

Bera finally ran out of anger and took a deep breath. She looked up and her heart almost stopped, he looked so bereft. "Oh, Karl, I'm sorry. You must miss them every bit as much."

He didn't speak, but his jaw-muscles worked.

Bera asked, just to break the silence. "How many children do you have?"

He looked at her. "I've a clone," he said, "though I don't suppose you'd count that as children. Karla was a long time ago, anyway."

"Karla's your daughter?" She'd heard him say the name in his delirium.

"Karla's my clone-wife." For the first time he really smiled, at her sky-rocketing eyebrows. "Who better as a partner? Though such marriages don't always work out – sometimes the last person we want to be alone with is our own reflection. As for children, Lisane – my brood-wife is due any week now with our first."

"You've more than one wife?"

"And a husband." He grinned at her open mouth and wide eyes. "Jarl. Each of them has three partners, of whom I'm one." The grin faded. "We've been trying for our first traditional child for twenty years."

She'd guessed that he was in his thirties, though it was hard to tell. "How old are you?" To have been trying for a child for so long?

Karl's smiled broadened. "Ninety-six."

Her head swam. Older than anyone she knew. Those that scraped past sixty were worn down to the merest stumps of the vital people they would have once been.

"Your life must be very comfortable." She knew that it was unfair to be envious, but she couldn't help it.

"It's the Rejuve," he said. "Stretching our lives, making interstellar travel possible."

"Ah." All this talk of children made her think of Palli again. She felt like a traitor, that this usurper could have driven her own dead son from her mind.

She looked up and saw Thorbjorg standing in the doorway, watching Karl as the farm cats watched a mouse-hole. Thorbjorg balanced another container of dirty clothes on her hip, and dropping them into a pail, turned on the water.

"You're wanted," Thorbjorg murmured to Bera, jerking her head toward the house. "I was told to replace you." She raised an eyebrow and her voice together, "Don't see why you should keep Mister Handsome to yourself."

"Thorbjorg is Yngi's wife," Bera reminded Karl by way, though he looked sufficiently distracted that it didn't look as if the warning was needed.

Thorbjorg scowled. "Get moving."

Bera sighed, and pulled on her kapa.

There was no sign of the others at the house, so Bera went searching. Asgerd was collecting eggs in the chicken run, while Yngi repaired a hole in the fence. A snolfur had tried to bite its way in, judging by the blood on the ragged wires, before deciding the hens were too tough a target. But the holes needed patching; the next snolfur might be more persistent.

One of the women could have done the job just as effectively, but with his club foot Yngi wasn't particularly mobile, while his sausage-like fingers were surprisingly dextrous, so he acted as the farm's handyman. Everyone knew that it was make-work for the Gothi's son.

"Someone wanted me," Bera said.

"Nope," Asgerd said. "Hilda's on mother-duty today. Maybe she needs help."

Bera thought it unlikely. Hilda's looking after all the children freed the other women to cook, clean and forage near the house. Even before Karl's arrival, Bera had been exempted since – in her distraction after Palli's death – she had allowed one of the younger girls to wander off.

After five minutes' fruitless searching, she saw Hilda with the children near a geothermal vent.

By the time she had climbed to where the children were playing around the steam, Bera was out of breath and perspiring under her fur kapa, despite the cold. It took her a few moments to get her breath back. She spent them watching the children's fascination with the vaporous swirls. They were safe as long as they were kept away from the hot pipes, and Ragnar believed it did them good to learn that hot things burned.

Bera took a deep breath. "You wanted me."

Hilda looked surprised. "Why would I? The children are fine. I don't need help."

"Someone wanted me. Thorbjorg said so. It isn't Asgerd, I asked her and Yngi. The men are out starting the round-up."

"Sounds like a stupid prank," Hilda said, and her mouth compressed into a line. "Or a misunderstanding – you're sure that Thorbjorg sent you? Who did she say wanted you?"

"She didn't say who," Bera said, and rubbed her face, which burned with embarrassment. It was obvious that Hilda thought she was making it up. "I'll get back to work."

* * *

When she stormed back into the laundry-room, there was no sign of Karl or Thorbjorg.

A vision of the two locked together in an embrace flashed through Bera's mind, and her rage, already burning her chest with acid claws, threatened to overwhelm her.

"Karl! Karl!" She stormed around the farm.

There was no response anywhere. No sign of them in the courtyard, in the barn, nor anywhere in the big house. Surely they wouldn't be rutting in the grass like animals? Though she'd put nothing past Thorbjorg. She saw movement through one of the windows in Bjarney's house and frowned.

It took Bera only a minute or so to walk down to Bjarney's house. "Hello?" she called.

An answer came in the form of giggles and Karl's voice: "No, I'll hold it, you push it in."

Her eyes widening, Bera rushed into the house.

The heavily pregnant Salbjerg sat in her dining room. It was smaller than Ragnar's, as befitted their lower status. Salbjerg was fanning herself while watching Karl and Thorbjorg.

Karl was holding the end of Salbjerg's table, while Thorbjorg was down on all fours underneath, gazing up at him with a lascivious grin.

"You need to move that block of wood," Karl panted. "I can't hold this all day."

"OK," said Thorbjorg. "Though I could watch those muscles for hours. Are you ticklish?"

It was too much for Bera. "Thorbjorg!"

Thorbjorg's head snapped up, hitting the underside of the table. "Ow!"

"Move that damned block," Karl's voice grated with the effort.

Bera shoved Thorbjorg out of the way and pushed

the wooden block so that it was beneath the table leg. Karl put the table down as Bera backed out from beneath it. He gripped each side and wiggled it. "It should be steady now," he said.

"We were helping Salbjerg with the table," Thorbjorg said sulkily, rubbing her head. "As you should have been doing. She had to come and get us; her in her condition."

Bera couldn't see why the table needed stabilising at that precise moment, but that was typical Salbjerg. Whatever she wanted needed to be done there and then, that second. But it wasn't Salbjerg's impatience that provoked Bera. "You said the others wanted me! You never mentioned Salbjerg!"

"I said you were wanted at the house!" Thorbjorg shouted.

"You said I was wanted by the others, and you certainly didn't say it was here – you sent me off on a wild goose chase!"

"Pardon me for not drawing Her Ladyship a map, perhaps I should've personally escorted you here? And carried your kapa?" Thorbjorg's voice grew ever shriller; "I said you were wanted here! If you wander off with your head in the clouds, Bera Sigurdsdottir, don't you blame me!"

Bera saw Thorbjorg glance toward the door, and looked over her shoulder, at where Hilda stood in the doorway. Her face was white, her eyes wide and nostrils flared.

"Ladies," Hilda said with icy emphasis, "Perhaps we could spare poor Salbjerg the unpleasantness of you bickering like a pair of harlots at the Summer Fair?"

"Poor Salbjerg" looked as if she was lapping up the entertainment, Bera thought, and felt tears prickle at the way Thorbjorg had manipulated her.

Bera's heart raced, and she took deep breaths through her nose to stay calm. She walked outside, deliberately slowly, trying to regain some self-control. As soon as the others emerged from Salbjerg's house, she whirled to face them. "Ask Karl – he'll tell you! Didn't she, Karl? She said I was wanted by the others?"

Perhaps his mind was elsewhere. It was hard to tell, for as a shaft of sunlight pierced the clouds, his eyes darkened for a moment. The clouds occluded the suns again, and as his eyes returned to normal, he saw a hunted look in them.

He said, "I wasn't really paying attention – sorry."

Bera turned away, her fists balled.

Hilda said, "It doesn't matter who said what. We've had a misunderstanding, now get back to work. Bera, a word."

Bera noticed Karl amble away, and would have liked to run after him and tell him what she thought of his feebleness, but it would have to wait.

"I don't expect to have to spend time leading the children back to the house to sort out your squabbles. Pappi's been good to you, first taking you in, then letting you stay, but you must repay his kindness, even if it's only stopping these attention-seeking stunts of yours. If I have to speak to you again, then I'll demand Pappi send you away."

Demand? Bera thought. Who are you to demand that I be sent away? What Hilda meant of course was that she would wheedle at her father.

She stormed back to the laundry, her eyes stinging.

On the way, she saw Karl standing at the back, the less used end of the house, outside the sauna. He'd shed his shirt and stood with it in his hand, arms outstretched in the weak sunlight, as still as a statue.

She marched toward him, head down, trudging furiously.

All he'd had to do was to confirm her version of the conversation with Thorbjorg… He probably wants to tup her, Bera thought. She's permanently on heat, the dirty bitch.

He was still staring. She followed his gaze and saw Yngi.

Ragnar's son sat on a nearby bench, leg extended, a boot dropped nearby. Yngi also stared, enraptured by the great white feathered shape that hid his bare foot.

"Come away!"

"What's he doing?" Karl asked without looking at her.

"He's feeding the snawk." Bera pulled at him, but he wouldn't budge. "It's private! No one's to disturb him while he's doing that. You may scare it away!"

As if it heard them, the snawk reared its head, turned and screeched from a razor-billed beak that dripped blood.

"They feed on their handler's blood, from a wound at the base of the big toe," Bera said. "It keeps them from preying on the sheep. In the wild they're vermin."

"Fascinating." Karl followed her, falling behind as he gazed back over his shoulder. "You use it to hunt?"

"In the winter." A spar obscured their view of Yngi and the snawk, so she stopped whispering. "And for pest control, all year round. It's about the only natural predator that seems to be able to feed on our genetic material without any ill effects – at least in small quantities – and we've bred for that trait. Yngi feeds it every day. There's something in the bird's spit so that the wound never fully heals, but has to be staunched with dressings. The handler develops a severe limp."

"That's why he's lame?" Karl said. "You deliberately maim a man?"

"We don't," Bera said. "He chose to, in the same way that people have always disfigured themselves with holes and objects embedded in their flesh in the name of fashion. At least Yngi's maiming is useful. There's an empathic bond between a tame snawk and its handler. The snawk feeds more often in the wild, so that captive snawks are dwarfs compared to the wild ones."

He stood motionless, arms outstretched, his head tilted back.

She stamped her foot. "What *are* you doing?"

Karl straightened his head and gazed at her, his eyes dark again in the sunlight. He looked wholly inhuman then. "So it's a bonsai bird."

"That one's about half-sized," she said, bemused at the strange phrase. "Wild snawks can have wingspans of several metres."

Reluctantly, she walked toward him. His skin had darkened slightly, and she shuddered.

"Even this weak sunlight helps," he said. "While I was in space, the lifegel blocked almost all the sunlight. It's a default setting – you can't customise the nanophytes in lifegel."

"What are you talking about now?" Sometimes she longed for him to be ordinary.

"My skin photosynthesises sunlight," he said. "It's only this morning that I remembered. It's like my own memories are hiding from me."

Or Loki's hiding them, she almost said. "Is that good? Photo... photo thing?"

"Photosynthesis means I need much less food," he said, smiling beatifically. "I eat as much as I do to be so-cial, as for calories: I'm gengineered to synthesise sunlight. Most people are, apart from the Pures. It's about twenty times as efficient as eating food."

They resumed their walk to the laundry.

She remembered what she'd wanted to say to him. "Why didn't you tell Hilda that I wasn't lying? Now they think... oh, it doesn't matter!" Now it all seemed so petty compared to skin that purpled and turned sunlight to energy.

"Because I wasn't paying attention," Karl said. "I didn't hear the conversation."

"Why didn't you just back me up anyway – that's what friends do: I took care of you, and – and, you just left me arguing alone against them..." She wiped her nose on her sleeve with an angry cuff.

"You wanted me to lie for you?" Karl said.

"I – yes, dammit!"

"I'm sorry," he said. "I didn't realise. I never meant to upset you. Next time I will." They re-entered the laundry in silence.

Karl said, "For all that we spend most of the daylight hours out in the open, this place is a pressure cooker – too little outside stimuli in a small, isolated group of people."

"You make us sound like specimens," Bera said.

He shrugged. "I don't mean to... but I see you from an outsider's perspective." They unloaded some of the sodden clothes and he said, "Why do you loathe Thorbjorg?"

"Why not?" Bera said. "Didn't you hate that Jakob boy?"

"But we were children," Karl said. "We knew no better."

"Gods, you're so civilised!" Bera pushed the first shirt through as he held the free end. "Don't you feel anything?" He blinked, and she regretted her outburst. "You must think that we're so primitive," she said.

"Raw is the word," he said with a slight smile. "You're all... almost overpowering. It's so hard to deal with."

"Get used to it," Bera said. "Isheimuri are Old Norse stock. We fight as much as breathe, and we're good at bearing grudges."

They got back to work, and Bera considered his question. "Thorbjorg. Although she's only been married to Yngi for – I guess – six years, they have five children. It's important that we repopulate the planet, but it's not a competition. But she queens it over the other women. And the way she scolds poor Yngi, when Ragnar isn't around…"

"Is she Ragnar's lover?" Karl chuckled at her shocked look. "I see from an outsider's perspective."

"If she is," Bera said, "it's because both of them are using the other one; she thinks that she can control him through sex."

"But you don't know?"

"No," she said, folding a shirt and putting it on a pile. When she spoke next, she was still folding clothes, and didn't look up. "I have a question."

"Yes?"

"If a society… regresses, is that the word?" At his nod, Bera continued, "If a society regresses, do women always end up forced back into the home?" She looked up, and at his raised eyebrow chuckled. "Ragnar doesn't know half of what information is on the Oracle. If he did, his hair would be completely grey. But it's all based on Terra and a few early colonies. Nothing as strange as you are. I mean, as exotic as you are."

"I don't know much about regressive societies," Karl said. "They're rare. But from what little I know, breast-feeding ties women to their children. Unless the society's truly nomadic, that pins women to the home. Once that happens, domestic chores aggregate. It doesn't have to happen, but just as water finds the quickest way downhill, so societies devolve into standard patterns, unless most of the populace are prepared to be brave with their thinking."

Bera was silent for a time, thinking. When they finished, she handed him the pile of dried washing, and picked up a box of wooden pegs. They strode out into the daylight.

On top of the hill above, sheep spilled over the sky-line in a surging, boiling mass, flanked by dogs and farm hands. From her leash in the centre of the courtyard, Brynja began barking.

Bera said, "Uh-oh."

"What's the matter?"

"Pappi. He's storming down that hill. Wotan, he looks in a foul mood." She turned to him. "Be very careful when he's in this sort of mood. Don't say anything to provoke him."

As the Gothi came nearer and nearer, Bera could feel herself hunching smaller.

"Don't be scared," Karl said.

Ragnar stamped into the square, and at that moment, a small white shape shot toward him.

"Brynja!" Bera shrieked.

Ragnar stared down at the yapping puppy. He stepped toward Brynja, and something made the little dog snap at his boot. He straightened his walking stick so that it was under the dog's belly and lifted her up, so that she balanced precariously on it. Ragnar reached out with his gloved left hand and lifted the puppy off the stick by the scruff of her neck.

"I told you before," Ragnar said, his eyes boring into Bera, "to keep this bitch under control."

Bera felt Karl's arm go around her, for protection, and shrank into his warmth.

She saw Ragnar's eyes widen, and thought, For I am a jealous Gothi. She cried, "It's not what you think–"

"You wasted no time, then," Ragnar said. He tossed Brynja, who had turned from barking to whimpering, from left hand to right hand. Then with a grunt of effort he hurled Brynja against the nearest wall, the sound of the impact slapping loud in the near-silent square.

SEVEN
Loki

You assume that it was the smell of burning that triggered your reawakening – perhaps the Other shrank from the memories it evoked.

Sense began to inch its way into the maelstrom of voices.

"Medieval Iceland was both stratified and not a state," shouted one voice.

That raged, raged against the dying of your light if the Other were ever to completely reclaim his kingdom of flesh and blood and bone.

"Isheimur is so cold and its air so thin that the colony's survival should be considered marginal," said another.

The smell of burning dust as the brazier grew hotter and hotter, until it would be the right temperature for the Thralls to brand the new foals, was simply too redolent of Ship's last few minutes. The stink of horse-flesh wouldn't have had the same effect, so had the Other walked this way only a few minutes earlier or later.

"On Avalon, a man can reason aloud without it being considered a challenge; such is the process of civilised democracy."

It would have never triggered your return, muscling your way into the synapses of consciousness as the Other whimpered out.

The voices clamoured their cacophony of seemingly random facts, but now you understood that among what seemed like an avalanche, every one of them had meaning.

Among the fact-rocks hurtling past your consciousness, something about one caught your attention. Quicker than light you reached out a mental hand, juggled, then caught and held it.

Ship knows that it is doomed but even as the plasma bolt homes in, it carries on its diligent checking of the Mizar B system for signs of civilisation. There! Something on Mizar B Gamma, a faintest glimmer, there and gone in a micro-second.

Any vessel less diligent than Ship would have missed the electronic equivalent of a *meep!* But it was looking for something, anything, and there was the acknowledgement of its Mayday.

It checked its memories, bigger than some planetary cities. *Mizar B Gamma was settled: Isheimur, they called it.* Ship noted the co-ordinates, and included them in the download that was to mutate, to evolve into Loki.

Your electronic consciousness was never designed to co-exist with a meat brain, you finally realise, as Ship would have always known. You're incompatible – the meat and your semi-Aye processes – but it was a mark of Ship's desperation, to survive and to pass its knowledge along to Karl–

Stop daydreaming: this is a meat habit. You needed to find maps.

The Bera-Jocasta-Mother woman would know where they were. Good, a pretext to find her.

She has an effect on this meat-box that the Other would rather not think about. He is conditioned not to dream of sinking into her warm wetness. You have no such conditioning. Mother though she was to your suckling consciousness, she is not your birth-mother in the meat sense and you sense her own reciprocal attraction, buried beneath her own constraints.

But now you had another reason to find her, to have her show you maps and work out how you would get to the beacon.

Finally: purpose to your restlessness.

Up past the ballista that had lain unused these last two years, she was with the other women among the heathers, picking the edible parts.

Ragnar stood over her. They did not notice you.

He stood with his hands clasped behind his back and leaned forward slightly, bending from the waist. "You know that there's been bad blood between Steinar Onundsson and me for years," Ragnar said. "Just one of those things: he's jealous of me, I suppose."

Bera gave no sign that she was listening, but something about her posture told even you, with your limited understanding of meat-minds, that she was listening intently.

Ragnar said, "About the puppy..." He looked up at the sky, and scratched his head. When he continued, you thought that he had changed the subject: "All summer Steinar over at Reykholt's given me a wide berth, since he let his cattle wander onto the water meadows last spring. I told him then that I'd smack his arse with the flat of my blade if he tried that stunt again."

Ragnar continued, "He claims it's his territory but we both know that his argument won't hold at the Althing. So he tries guerrilla tactics like letting his flocks wander onto my land. This was the third time; the time before, I found some man Steinar had hired hanging around the boundary. This goon heaped so many insults on me I had little choice but to challenge him to combat then and there." He cleared his throat. "It was obvious from the eager way he drew his sword that the man was a mercenary. I can bloody tell you girl, I wondered what I'd got into then." Ragnar chuckled. "But though he was good, he wasn't that good. To his dying breath, he denied that he was even a sword-for-hire – let alone who had hired him – to me."

"Why would he do that?" Bera said quietly, still picking through the heather.

Ragnar said, "I've no idea. He admitted he had kin on Steinar's lands, so perhaps he was protecting them. Perhaps some obscure code of the mercenary that he needed to adhere to." He sighed. "Whatever the reason, it only needs the sight of bloody Steinar to set me off. This time he had a couple of goons with him and I was on my own. He thought that with them there he could mouth off." Ragnar's jaw tightened, then he said, "No one calls me 'troll-shit' and prospers."

"I can imagine, Gothi," Bera said, her voice dull.

Ragnar said, "I only walked away with difficulty, especially since it left the little turd with the last word. But I'll bide my time. I'll nail him in the spring." Ragnar smiled.

"It must have been very provoking for you," Bera said, her voice still flat. She did not raise her eyes to him.

"It was," Ragnar said. "And then – on the way back – Thorir the Stupid almost let the sheep run over a sheer drop. We stopped them, but it took ages, and a world of effort. By the time we got to Skorradalur I was boiling hotter than a pool of volcanic mud…" He unclasped his hands and straightening, fiddled with a hang-nail. "I know that you think I don't notice things, but I do. When I saw you shrink back from me into Allman's clutches as if I was threatening you, it was too much."

Bera stopped still; you had the impression that this was an important moment.

"Not that that excuses it," Ragnar said, picking fiercely at the hang-nail now. "But better I took it out on that yapping little beast of yours, than beating our 'guest' or someone else into senselessness." He sighed. "But I feel bad that the poor little bitch caught the back-lash of my temper."

"My Gothi is too concerned with the feelings of your constituents," Bera said, but now there was a tension in her voice, as if she was only keeping her emotions in check by a huge effort of will. It had taken you a long time to learn to analyse and decode the complexity of these emotions of the humans, but you managed it, and were oddly proud. It also proved strangely addictive, this observing of others.

Ragnar said, "I wondered if–"

But you never found out what he wondered, for you must have made a noise, stepped on a twig. Or perhaps she knew that you were there all along, and had decided that she didn't want to hear what Ragnar wondered: whatever the reason, Bera looked up. "Oh," she said. "It must be Loki. Karl wouldn't stand there holding a half-peeled carrot."

"What in Ragnarok do you want?" Ragnar snarled at you.

You could visualise what you needed, but forming the words to fit the thoughts was more difficult. Ignoring him, you said to Bera, "Maps?"

"More nonsense," Ragnar said.

You formed another word, slowly wrapping your jaw around it: "Need maps."

"Of course," Bera said, taking your arm. "We'll find you some maps. Later, after you've peeled the vegetables. Come on, lovely, let's finish peeling the vegetables." She turned to Ragnar. "I'll only be a few minutes, Gothi. I'll get him back to work, and then I'll resume my duties. Unless you prefer to have him milling around wasting time?"

"No," Ragnar said, his voice normal now, the yearning tone gone. "Take him back to work. I've things I need to get on with, anyway."

She led you down the hill, back to your tasks. You caught a fragment of memory from the Other: this is all there is; peeling vegetables and sleeping on straw for the rest of your life. The despair in the thought was enough to stain the day dark despite its sunshine.

"You must try to keep to your chores, Loki," Bera said. Her identifying you from the Other gave you pleasure, though you did not know whether it was good or bad.

You exist. She recognised you, whatever she thought of you.

"Need maps," You said. "Need maps. To. Find beacon."

She stopped, still holding your elbow, and stared at you. "A beacon?"

"Need maps. To find beacon."

"Tonight," Bera said. "I have maps in my room, printed on pieces of scrap. I like to see how the world looks – it may be the only way that I will ever see it. When we finish our work, I'll sneak them out."

"Tonight?"

"Yes, tonight, Loki. Now, back to work."

* * *

105

"Isheimur is geologically unstable and riddled with low-level vulcanism that paradoxically acts as a safety valve for more explosive events–"

Sometime – perhaps while you peeled vegetables – the Other returned. The next you knew, the setting suns and mellower light indicated that it was evening. Perhaps some weakening of his resistance, or some other trigger than the smoke that reminded the Other of Ship's death had allowed you back, with your hellish chorus of voices.

"For two centuries, after Gagarin, Armstrong and Heng led humanity out of their stellar cradle, space flight was only possible at sub-light velocities."

Bera stood with ragged scraps in her hand. One of them you recognised as a map of Isheimur. You snatched it from her hand, tearing it, inwardly screaming at the voices to be silent. Mercifully, it seemed to work.

"Beacon," you said, scanning the map for something familiar. You pointed to a patch of light blue on the equator. Ship had noted a lake shaped like that. "Where. This?"

"Surtuvatn," Bera said. "Where my parents lived. Is there where your beacon is?"

You ignored her, scanning the map: another body of water to the south-east. For all its periodic drizzle and scatterings of showers, the precipitation is never quite enough; this is almost a desert world, its few seas no bigger than lakes.

"Loki?" Bera said.

You looked up, realising that she wanted your attention. You'd learned what one of the voices calls socialisation, and were obscurely proud of this, although you knew that you were a mere apprentice compared even to small children. "Yes?" You said.

"You *are* Loki, then?" Bera said.

This was a question, the socialisation parameters indicated. Questions need answers. "Yes. I am Loki, Jocasta – Bera." She smiled at your correction, and you knew that you pleased her, which made you tingle. Perhaps she no more knows of her Jocasta side, the mothering side, than the Other knows of us.

"I never know which one of you I'm dealing with. Just a minute ago you were Karl."

This was not a question, so you did not need to answer. Nonetheless, there were concepts that you would have explained, that you both wanted to get home, albeit for different reasons, but the thoughts were too big to fit into the small words that are the only way of communicating between these people. Instead: "Need pictures," you said, pointing to the lakes on the maps. "Pictures of mountains. Lakes. Deserts." The view from space is not one of maps.

"Here," Bera said, offering you a set of similarly ragged photos from the bottom of the little bundle of maps she carried. "Printed from satellite views, taken before the Formers left. Most are meteorological or topographical images, rather than pictures." She sighed. "They took the satellites they could use elsewhere with them, and crashed the rest down into Nornadalur to feed the Norns; all the pictures we have pre-date the Leaving, and what there are – and there aren't many – probably aren't very accurate now."

"Nothing new?" You said.

Bera shook her head. "If we had, you wouldn't be able to get near them anyway. We have to make do with ground-based beacons scattered across the planet's surface to monitor the weather, and Ragnar and the other Gothis already spend their time poring over the output from them to try to predict the weather. Freya knows, if they had access to satellites, you'd never see a photograph. They'd hoard them all."

You studied them, looking for an answer.

"Latest analysis of Isheimur atmosphere: helium down to three per cent; neon down to five, nitrogen to seventy-three, oxygen up to eighteen, CO_2 up to point zero two per cent–"

You'd started to get an idea of time how much time had passed while the Other had taken over. At first there were simply blank patches, but now a few precious images had started to soak through the barriers between the different parts of the brain where your memories and his were scattered. Your consciousness was squeezed into odd little corners of the brain everywhere and they needed to connect, so such seepage should have been no surprise.

It was the next day.

You walked a hillside with two other men. In the distant south-east the horizon flickered. One of them flinched.

"Storm season's starting," one of the other men said. Big, with dark hair and patches of bare skin between strips of facial hair: Arnbjorn Ragnarsson, a memory told you. Literally, Ragnar's son.

"Storm season?" You said. You'd identified that this is an optimal process for downloading information from brain to brain, via their mouth to your ear. Repeat what they say, and they would elucidate, usually.

"Aye, Loki," Arnbjorn said. "Storm season."

He did not elaborate, so perhaps you must provide a further stimulus, you decided. "There is... a storm season? Explain, please." *Please* is like a command prompt, you'd learned.

Arnbjorn shrugged. "The things you don't seem to know, utlander." They often call your frame "Utlander".

108

Foreigner, stranger, alien, the lexicon supplied as meaning. Arnbjorn said, "No one's quite sure why Isheimur grows so racked by electrical storms during the weeks around the equinox – some say it's the seasonal drop in temperatures, some that Gamasol and Deltasol's radiation causes ionisation, others that it's simply a freak of timing – whatever the reason, storms will soon sweep through the area."

The other man, a Thrall – *indentured farm-labourer,* your lexicon explained – laughed. "Let's hope that we get home first, or that it heads elsewhere." His cranial hair was long and tied back, his beard bushy like Ragnar's.

A series of cries rended the air. "Trolls!" the Thrall said.

Arnbjorn broke into a run. "We need to make sure that they don't panic the sheep and drive them over a cliff!"

"What are trolls?" you asked.

"A pain in the bloody arse!" The Thrall was already starting to pant. "Hairy critters that attack farmsteads and drive rock-eater flocks across our lands!"

Your long, ranging lope had brought you level with them, although their swords weighed them down and you only had the wooden stick that Bera (or Jocasta?) gave you to slow your pace. You could have passed them easily, but they knew where they were going; you didn't. "This is problem? Rock-eaters?" Rock-eaters were not something that your memories contained. An anomaly, you thought. To your logical mind, an anomaly was the equivalent of ancient pornography – illicit, guilt-inducing, yet thrilling in a way that was inexplicable to someone who didn't share such feelings.

"Rock-eaters aren't a problem in themselves." Arnbjorn's breathing had grown increasingly ragged.

"Though a million little hooves at a time can wreck the crops. Vast flocks of 'em migrating, bringing snolfurs and trolls in their wake. They're a bloody problem! Now shut the fuck up!"

You shut up. Breaching the ridge, you saw a wave of white that filled the next valley and beyond.

"It looks," the Thrall said, gasping, hands on knees, "a... small... one... only... a... few... tens of... thousands."

"Aye," Arnbjorn said, gasping too.

You were barely breathing heavily.

You heard a screaming whistle that seemed to come from all sides, but must have been the sound echoing off the hills. Arnbjorn touched your arm. "Stand still," he said. You did as they did.

Something flashed into the middle of the sea of white, and one of the stocky rock-eaters erupted in a gout of flesh.

Arnbjorn's laugh was a maniacal cackle.

The Thrall said, "What?" When Arnbjorn didn't answer, but kept laughing, the Thrall said, growing progressively more annoyed, "What is it?"

Arnbjorn's laughter slowly wound down, and he wiped his eye. "This is amongst the land that Steinar's claiming – the valley runs down to the meadows over there." He pointed. "I bet he's included them on the details he's provided to the Norns. So when he asked for something really essential, they've fired it in a sub-orbital trajectory with their ballista – and it's over-shot. The Norns will reckon that it's within acceptable parameters, but the truth is that it's just eviscerated that Rock-eater, and ended up on our territory. Let's go take a look, see whether there's anything left of that package they've lobbed over."

"So that exploding rock-eater – that was a missile?"

the Thrall said as your group set off toward the vast flock.

"It was an aid package," Arnbjorn said, laughing again.

"You're kidding me," the Thrall said.

"Nope." Arnbjorn continued, "That's why we have to file our land dimensions; the Norns can aim their packages away from the houses, but near enough that any bouncing projectile still ends up on the land of the petitioner." He said to you, "Exploding wildlife isn't normally one of the hazards of life on Isheimur, but sometimes we're warned to stay indoors when a package is due. This is why." He indicated the splattered rock-eater.

"Is that," you tried to form words to fit the concept, "why you have a ballista?"

Arnbjorn said, "Yep. The Norns' ballista has only a limited range, so to reach round the planet, we pass on the parcel. It may be that this wasn't for Steinar at all, except for him to act as a relay."

You and the other men strode down the hill until your group reached the edge of the Rock-eater herd; you pushed your way through, initially still moving quickly, but gradually slowing as you pushed deeper into the herd that was moving across your path.

"Bloody things!" The Thrall shoved a rock-eater head over heels.

It gazed at him reproachfully. It was about a metre tall, shaggy, with short stocky legs. Small ears poked through long, fine fur on either side of a head shaped like an extinct Terran animal called a gopher.

It must have taken an hour from when the rock-eater died to push your way through the seething mass of purring beasts. Several times the Thrall complained at the pace, until Arnbjorn told him to shut up. "If

111

Steinar's been indoors in the last couple of days, then he'll know from the Oracle that he's due a package from the Norns. He may guess that it's landed here. I'm not scared of him, but I'd rather not have a fight if he arrives with a half-dozen of his goons and we're still here."

Eventually you reached the carcass. Perhaps instinctively avoiding a dead member of the herd, the other rock-eaters swirled around it as a stream flows round a rock.

You stood over bits of splattered flesh and fleece, in the midst of which was a smouldering circular object, metallic, clearly artificial. "We'll take it home –" Arnbjorn pointed to a set of characters on one side of the object "– and enter these codes into the Oracle. They'll tell us where it was destined for. Let's go!"

The Thrall opened his mouth, but before he could speak, something shaped like a man – but hairier and shorter with a hairy face and set of nightmare fangs – detached itself from the swirling flock and rushed at your group, yowling and keening. Some of the notes sounded impossibly high, verging on ultrasonic.

Arnbjorn tossed the object at you and lunged forward, sword bared.

It stopped.

Human and alien gazed at one another for long moments, and then with a final yowl, it retreated.

"Troll?" you said, as the group set off toward Skorradalur.

"Of course," the Thrall said. "You really are so ignorant you don't recognise one?"

You gazed at him, trying to work out whether there was more meaning than first seemed to the question. You've learned that sometimes the simplest-sounding questions are actually the most complex. To put so many layers of meaning into such an inefficient communication method as mouth-to-ear seems to you the height of folly. They really should re-design their communication systems. But of course that isn't possible with their current technology.

You decided that if there was a second layer of meaning, you couldn't extract it, so answered the question as it was asked. "Yes," you said. "I really am that ignorant. But now I have 'troll' filed, and will recognise it: hostile, indigenous life-form. Sentient?"

"Absolutely not!" Arnbjorn said. "What kind of sentient life-form eats another?"

"Humans eat trolls?"

"Course not!" The Thrall erupted with laughter. "They eat us, you damned fool! We've fought them for centuries, just as they've slaughtered us mercilessly. Thor, what kind of fool are you?"

"Human, augmented," you replied.

You resurfaced, again not knowing what – if anything – triggered the return. It was evening once more. You stood in a small room, facing stairs that lead to the upstairs rooms. There was a white box in one corner. An image hovered in front of you, of mountains and lakes.

"This is Surtudalur," Bera said, "where I grew up. You can see the edge of the farmhouse, poking out from beneath that lava flow."

Without warning, she hid the maps. "Someone's coming," she said, and pulled you into the corridor and up the first few stairs, placing a hand over your mouth. "We might get in trouble, the amount of time we spend in here," she whispered. "Pappi likes us to learn from the Oracle, but only the things he wants us to know. Hush, now!"

You watched Ragnar back into the study, clutching an object under his arm. It was the spherical aid package. Arnbjorn followed, his voice imploring: "If we can check the codes on the Oracle, we can establish whether it's Steinar's, or whether some innocent community has got caught up in your feud with him."

"If it was intended for Steinar," Ragnar said, "it will be red-flagged as missing, and if you enter the codes it will sound tiny electronic klaxons all over the place. No, leave it alone."

"But, Pappi—"

"I said, leave it alone!"

There was silence, before Arnbjorn said in a high, tight voice, "Very well, Gothi."

The Other was starting to stir, and from the struggles, a thought arose: why do they put up with his petty tyranny?

Though you struggled for control, it was such an interesting question that when they left – seconds apart – and Bera removed her hand, you couldn't help echo it aloud.

Bera wrinkled her nose. "Think how hard it is for him, running this place. Some years we have good winters, when there's enough food that we can pretend that things are getting better. Some years are so bad that we even eat rock-eater and snolfur and endure the resulting sickness and cramps. But every year, every month, every day, we have to count what we have. How much can we spare? If it's stressful for each of us, what must it be like for him? Even the strongest would buckle under that kind of strain."

"So he is," you struggled for the right words, "mad? From worry?"

"Maybe, partly," Bera said. "Half the reason he is Gothi is that others in these parts who could do the job

114

don't want to; while the ones who want to be Gothi have neither ability nor the others' support." She nudged you down the stairs. "He wasn't always this bad. But he loved Gunnhild as much as he loved life itself. Since then... Can you imagine how it feels to lose someone you love so much?" She sighed. "Oh, Loki, I love you as a son, but I so miss Karl. I can talk to him." She looked suddenly horrified. "He won't hear this, will he?"

"No," you answer. You felt the Other rising to the surface, and like a drowning man, stood on the mental equivalent of his head.

Bera continued, oblivious to your inner turmoil. "Since Gunnhild died, the many good things about Ragnar seem to have withered away, while his bad side's grown worse."

You felt the world receding; the last words you heard before falling back to the scattered world of the subconscious were Bera's: "I suppose we probably still love Ragnar for who he was, rather than who he's become. That's why we tolerate his behaviour."

Then the silent abyss swallowed you up.

Until the next time, you vowed.

EIGHT
Ragnar

Ragnar noted with grim satisfaction that the figure of the utlander no longer limped as he strode along the ridge above Ragnar, but devoured the cloud-wrapped fells with long strides. The alien had finally lost the stick, the last reminder of his weeks-long convalescence.

On the high ground, the snow had settled, while on the lower-lying fields, it was taking longer and longer to melt in the occasional bouts of sunshine; soon it would cover the ground in a wafer-thin blanket of white.

Behind them Gudmundir completed the triangle of shepherds. While it needed three of them to drive the flock home, only one man needed to stay with them while they were out on the summer grazing. Gudmundir – Gummi – lived out on the slopes in the summer under a havalifugil-skin tent that was lighter than canvas but far tougher. During the winter the shepherds, Thralls all, moved back to the house; this year it would be even more crowded with one more mouth to feed but Ragnar was convinced that Allman would not only earn his keep, but repay the debt he owed for his care.

As the days after Allman's arrival became weeks, Ragnar took dour satisfaction in seeing his hairless labourer pacing the hills and valleys with the returning sheep, straining at the bonds of what was obviously his prison. Ragnar could cope with Allman's resentment and grudgingly accepted that the dark-skinned man worked without complaint, even in conditions that taxed the toughest Isheimuri. Bera's doe-eyed reproaches were harder to bear, and made Ragnar angry because the Gothi had no answer to them.

With a start Ragnar realised that the flock was drifting toward a bog. "Drive the sheep closer!" he bawled. Allman didn't understand the system of whistles and waves that the others tried to teach him, or pretended not to. But on Ragnar's bellow he drove the sheep toward Ragnar and his dog, so that they would clear the edge of the bog. As the flock climbed again, the rustling of the long grass marking their passage, they funnelled across the shallowest part of the stream that fed it, which was too deep and fast-flowing further up the hill to ford there.

It took them half an hour of ducking backward and forward, Ragnar's dog splashing into the water and leaping out again like a mad thing, to get the flock across the stream. A snow shower overtook them, dotting the air with tiny flakes that stuck to Ragnar's lip and tasted crisp against his tongue, and spotted the long grass that was already yellowing with white.

The Terraformers had avoided genetic engineering wherever possible. "We're men, not changelings," one Former had said on the Oracle, but they had tweaked both grass and sheep to withstand the toxins, in the case of the sheep by simply excreting them. Glowing blue sheep-shit had proved oddly fascinating to Allman when he first saw it, but who understood the ways of aliens?

Once Ragnar thought he saw shadows in the mist, and wondered whether the trolls were growing bolder again. They hunted in packs like snolfurs. Pack rats, Ragnar thought. It had been a couple of years since they had driven the last invaders off.

Once they had forded the stream, it was only a half-hour's walk in the increasingly heavy rain up a steep slope, and they crested a ridge. There they could gaze at Skorradalur squatting in the rain.

Ragnar's knees ached as they descended the steep slopes toward the farmstead. The turbines were turning well, he noticed. It was principle that made Ragnar's Grandpappi insist that they diversify their energy sources. The Oracle claimed that Man had drained even the supposedly limitless geothermal springs of Old Iceland, and while Isheimur would keep them in steam for centuries to come, the Isheimuri had no desire to repeat the follies of history.

Then he saw the mill at the end of the line, next to the ballista, and Ragnar grunted in surprise at the same time as Karl said, "Is that windmill supposed to have stopped?"

"No," Ragnar said. "Bastard thing's seized up. Orn should've fixed that." That there was a long ladder resting against the side of the tower implied that Ragnar's tenant was trying to.

When they had driven the sheep into the pens inside the barn, Ragnar and Karl entered the yard where Orn the Strong was wiping his hands on a cloth. "I can't fix it," Orn said, before Ragnar could speak.

"Bugger," Ragnar said. "We'll have to call out a roving mechanic in the spring." One more example of the colony's falling back before the march of stagnation irritated Ragnar.

"It'll cost a bloody fortune in food or labour," Orn said. "Why don't we just leave it as it is?" He fell silent before Ragnar's glare.

"Do you know what the problem is?"

"I think a cog in the yaw drive has seized," Orn said. "I've taken it off-line, 'cause it'll only face one way. If the wind gets too strong from t'other direction, it'll wreck it completely." Orn sighed. "Knowing what it is and fixing it are two different things."

"Come on," Karl said. "Let's both of us take a look." He gazed at Ragnar, silently asking permission.

Ragnar shrugged. "If you think that you can fix it, go ahead. But secure the sheep first."

Ragnar spent the afternoon going through some of his outstanding cases. He and the other forty local Gothis met briefly three times a year, at the Spring, Winter and Bride Fairs. And at the Summer Fair, he journeyed onto the Althing, when serious and important disputes were resolved, including appeals against existing judgements.

Ragnar believed that the provision of competitive "governmental" services was Isheimuri society's greatest strength: the fear of losing clients to rivals checked inefficiency and abuse of power. Isheimuri law owed its resilience and flexibility to decoupling authority from geography. Long-term feuds were difficult without the twin poisons of hereditary title and domain. Difficult, but not impossible.

Ragnar's job was made easier by the Oracle. He could occasionally chat to the other Gothis, although they were so rarely indoors that the "chats" were usually voicemail replies. It was a patchy system made worse by distance and mountains. What they would do if that patchwork ever wore through wasn't something Ragnar liked to contemplate.

He'd left a few messages about Allman with his counterparts, warning them that some sort of travelling seer was in the area, and asking who – if anyone – already knew of him. So far, all answers had been negative. It had had one positive side-effect, pre-warning them that Allman was a trouble-maker.

Ragnar didn't want the utlander going elsewhere to complain. If Allman was dissatisfied with Ragnar's decisions, he could – were he a freeman – switch to a different Gothi without having to move away from Skorradalur; chieftain or client could freely terminate their arrangement, so in theory Karl could swear allegiance to another Gothi. That his status was uncertain was both a complication and a possible bonus. Allman was legally outside the law as far as Ragnar was concerned, so while he had no obligations other than debts, nor did he have any rights. Ragnar had put a roof over the man's head, his people had shared his food with the utlander, and he wasn't going to let Allman follow Bera's example by shaming him by running off with his debt unpaid – even if that debt had been calculated by Ragnar.

Sod him. The bastard was going to stay and pay for that food and shelter the only way that he could, by working. There was always more work than there were hands available, and Allman's presence might make the difference between the community prospering or just surviving.

Ragnar put away the file he'd started on Steinar Onundsson, having already left a few messages with the other Gothis, asking if they'd had any trouble with Steinar. Ragnar would start gently, but over the winter he'd step up the whispering campaign and in the spring, he'd rally support and challenge Steinar to a duel at the Spring Fair to settle the dispute – one way or another.

He heard laughter and shouts outside, and saw Allman wiping his hands on a cloth while Orn clapped him on the shoulder.

Ragnar's spirits lifted when he saw Allman talking to Arnbjorn, who had returned with more sheep from the fells. Walking outside he said mock-sternly, "Arnbjorn Ragnarsson, what are you doing chatting like a washerwoman when there's work to be done?"

Arnbjorn hesitated. Ragnar realised with a pang that his son was checking the older man's mood and grinned to show he was happy. Arnbjorn relaxed. "I've been taking lessons from you in how to spend my days," he said, hugging his father. As they separated, Arnbjorn jerked his thumb at Allman. "I hear our new hand has helped Orn fix the turbine."

"Indeed." Ragnar raised his eyebrows.

"Orn fixed it, I just helped." Allman's unmanly humility made Ragnar want to slap him, even as the Gothi assessed whether the alien's downplaying his help played into Ragnar's hands.

"Piece of metal had rusted off and fallen into the cog," Orn said. "But to actually get to it, we needed to lift the whole damned motor. Two or three men could have done it, but two or three couldn't have climbed into that little space, stood there and lifted it up. No, Karl made the difference. Come on, Ragnar'll give you the rest of the afternoon off – won't you, Gothi?"

Arnbjorn muttered in Ragnar's ear, "And we can have a couple of beers to celebrate getting the big flock off Klanting Fell. We made good time."

"You did," Ragnar said. "I wasn't expecting you back until tomorrow. What did you do, fly them down here?"

Arnbjorn chuckled. "Yeah, we drove the sheep hard. Having the extra man helped. I'm glad you talked Orn into lending him to us."

"That's why I'm not bothered by Orn borrowing the utlander." Ragnar jerked his thumb at Allman. Though Orn needn't have praised him *quite* so much.

The afternoon grew hazier with each beer they downed.

Ragnar thought afterward that he heard Bera's voice coming from the Oracle room. "You tell it your search parameters. 'Technology plus Terraformers plus interstellar communications.' Wait for the results. Hmm, not good. Seventeen responses."

"This is like something from the Stone Age," Allman complained. "What if you try other parameters?" Ragnar didn't catch what was said next because it was drowned out by shouts from the kitchen. Bloody women and their squabbling!

"What's that – a shrine to the south?" Allman said.

"Oh, that's the *Winter Song*," Bera replied. She recited:

"And when the Gods left Isheimur,

They cast a bolt from the sky.

The winter that followed was as bleak.

As the heart of a harlot."

"There's something about a possible location," Allman said, "on one of the responses." He groaned. "Two thousand kilometres!"

"That," Bera said, "is where you pointed to on the map. Or Loki did. You confuse me."

"I did?" Karl said.

Whatever Ragnar had been going to say next, either to summon Allman or shout at the kitchen to quit their squabbling, Arnbjorn drove all thoughts of it from his mind with a foaming tankard of peat beer.

There was another fragment, perhaps either imagined or dreamed, Ragnar wasn't sure afterward. It was the utlander walking past, head bowed. It made Ragnar happy to see all hope fled, but angry, too. "I'd never give up," Ragnar shouted to Arnbjorn. "Bigger the odds, more I like 'em. A man should fight to the death, like a berserk."

"You tell 'em, Pappi," Arnbjorn slurred.

Ragnar awoke groggy, with a raging thirst and a hangover, something he didn't normally suffer from.

Arnbjorn and Asgerd were wrapped in each other's arms with the youngest of their three children, toddler George wedged between them.

Ragnar gradually became aware of raised voices, drifting from the kitchen.

He stomped toward the source of the row.

In the kitchen, Thorir – who was clearly still drunk – and Hilda stood on one side, while Bera glared at them from the other, Allman beside her. Everyone was talking at once.

Ragnar bellowed, "Quiet!"

The kitchen fell silent. Ragnar looked at them all in turn. Allman met his gaze levelly; Bera shrank back; Thorir dropped his gaze, while Hilda lifted her chin slightly. Ragnar said, "It's like a convocation of scolds in here. What's caused this?"

Hilda said, "Karl's cleaning of the pans was unacceptable. When I told him so, Bera saw fit to interfere."

"Because the dirt on the pans isn't new. It's been ground in for forever!" Bera said.

"It doesn't matter." Allman pretended to act as peacemaker – having started it all, Ragnar guessed.

"It's not your place to say what matters here, *boy*." Ragnar smiled inwardly at the flush that stained the stranger's dark face.

"It's not Karl that's the problem," Hilda said, and Ragnar saw the way that she glanced at the stranger.

Not you too. Does he *ooze* pheromones?

They were all starved of novelty. Ragnar had heard them begging the utlander to tell them about his home, and for all his supposed reluctance, Allman had seduced them with tales of cities floating in the clouds above hell-worlds.

Then Ragnar caught Hilda's defiant look and the way she stood between him and her idiot husband. Oho! You don't just fancy the alien, then? This was Hilda's way of getting back at him for his supposed harshness toward Thorir. For a moment, Ragnar had a crazy vision of how much better the utlander would be as a son-in-law, but squashed it. "What do you suggest?"

"I'll supervise them more closely," Hilda said, "and maybe make them work apart." Though Hilda liked to queen it over the others as eldest child, she had no actual authority. Putting these two under her supervision would legitimise her claim.

She was braced for a row, he could tell, from the way that her nostrils flared.

"I'll think about it," he said, wrong-footing her. "But meanwhile, keep the noise down, all of you. You're setting the children a bad example of how to behave."

But the next few days saw no relaxation of the internecine warfare between the women; Ragnar knew that Hilda disliked Bera, and now perhaps envied Bera her closeness to Allman. Whether the jealously was justified, Ragnar wasn't sure – Bera and Allman seemed to be just friends – but whatever the reason, Hilda bullied Bera relentlessly.

The conflict obviously played into Thorbjorg's hands as well. She teased the unskilled and untrained Allman relentlessly about how much more women's work he did than the other men, to the extent that Ragnar almost wanted the utlander to slap her into respect. Ragnar grew even angrier with the alien for the sheep-like way he took Thorbjorg's taunting. Especially when it provoked Bera into sniping at Thorbjorg, which in turn earned Allman even greater scorn from Thorbjorg for needing a woman's protection.

Sometimes Ragnar wondered what the utlander had done to provoke Thorbjorg. Had she offered herself to him, and been turned down? Whatever it was, Thorbjorg and Hilda seemed unable to leave Allman alone.

It was enough to offer Ragnar the excuse he secretly wanted to ignore his administrative duties and join the other men on the fells. The trouble with that was that he wasn't as young as the others; so either his head ached from the bickering in the house, or his legs ached from walking the hills.

Then one morning Thorir nearly lost several sheep in a bog.

They were bringing in the last flock, racing against another storm, lightning flickering on the horizon, creeping closer. The flock had ranged furthest, and was one of the biggest, so it needed all the men to help the two shepherds who guarded it. Orn and Bjarney and their men who had already returned had joined with Ragnar, Arnbjorn, Thorir and even Allman in striding up to the fells. Only Yngi had stayed behind to attend to his chores, and the sight of him gazing forlornly after them had pierced Ragnar's heart. That's why you should never look back.

Once again Thorir somehow managed to end up as point, nearest the bog, and once again the mutton-head had shown why he shouldn't be allowed near anything that could break or die.

Even as the lightning of the impending storm flickered in the distance, they heard the bleating, and the utlander raced into the bog, and grabbed the nearest of the two sheep by the scruff of the neck. But within seconds, the animal's frantic struggles – the very opposite of what it should do to survive the mud – had taken them both under. Only one hand remained waving above the mud. Without bothering to vent his spleen on the hapless Thorir, Ragnar held out a branch from a blasted tree and swung it so that it slapped against Allman's palm.

Allman grabbed the branch.

"Help me get him out!" Ragnar bellowed.

Strong hands took the branch and pulled on it. For a few seconds nothing happened, and Ragnar feared that the alien's lungs had filled. Another part of his mind noticed that the storm was coming closer, faster, and he knew that they wouldn't have long before they had to decide whether to fight the bog or flee the lightning.

Then with a horrid sucking sound, the bog slowly gave up its prisoners.

First Allman's arm emerged, then his shoulder and head, his torso, and even his other arm – somehow wrapped around the sheep – finally his legs.

They hauled the utlander and his prize onto firm ground. "Take care of the sheep!" Ragnar shouted at Arnbjorn, and turned to look for the second sheep.

It was gone.

Ragnar turned away and took in the sight of both Allman and the ewe struggling to their feet, both coughing and spluttering, Arnbjorn and Bjarney wiping their mouths of the residue of the resuscitations. The ewe staggered, then galloped after the flock.

"You let the second one go?" Ragnar bellowed at Allman, and as the alien straightened to give the Gothi a mouthful of abuse, Ragnar grinned and winked, and got a smile in return.

Ragnar turned to Thorir, who was wringing his hands, shoulders hunched. "It wasn't my fault!"

"You," Ragnar bellowed, "are going to be on firewood duty for the rest of your life! That's how many sheep you've lost? It comes out of your meals! Even Yngi's a better bloody shepherd than you are! You needed an untrained novice to show you how it's done?"

Pausing for breath, Ragnar saw Bjarney's eyes widen.

Bjarney opened his mouth and then Ragnar felt a thump in his back, and the world tilted. There was a sound like a buzz-saw, and Ragnar felt the fiery thumps of the snolfur's claws through his clothes, pounding down his back. His head jerked back to scream, and he saw the snolfur's hindquarters as it hurdled him.

Twisting, despite the agony of his back, Ragnar saw a ball of blue-white fire rolling toward them, and smelled the ozone crackling off the fireball.

At the last moment it careered into the bog and sank slowly in a wall of steam from the stagnant surface, and a murmur of plops and bubbles.

Behind him Ragnar heard shouts, and the buzz-saw yowls of the fleeing snolfur, and then the world went black.

He awoke to a world that pitched and rolled. "Keep still, Pappi," Arnbjorn's voice said. "We're nearly home, now. We turned the shepherd's tent into a stretcher. Bjarney and I will take you home."

"The others?" Ragnar whispered. His back felt as if he'd been stabbed with hot needles.

"OK," Arnbjorn said. "The snolfur was gone before we could shoot it. The men are rounding up the last stragglers."

Ragnar's protests that he should supervise went unheeded, and they insisted on shovelling him into the bed on his return, so that the women could fuss and cluck over him.

When he got to his feet that afternoon, Allman was waiting for him at the back door.

After the barest of civilities, Allman said, "I want to travel south, to find the *Winter Song*, if it exists. If it does, it should have a distress beacon. Maybe I can activate it. I've done loads of digging, and I think I've found the likely location. I'm convinced that there's substance to the story of the *Winter Song*."

"So you've been keeping other people off the Oracle?"

"Absolutely not. I've only used it when it's been quiet, when I've finished my tasks."

Ragnar's back was giving him grief; it felt as if the snolfur had left its claws in. If Allman had only waited, he often thought afterward, maybe so many men might not have died. Maybe things would have turned out differently.

Maybe. But his back hurt. This cheeky bastard thinks that fishing one sheep out pays all debts? "Have you indeed?" Ragnar said. "Forgive my ignorance, friend, but what are you going to live on while you make this epic journey south?"

"I'll live off the land," Allman said, and Ragnar could see that he hadn't thought it through. "Since you attach a price to everything, then I'll work extra over the next few days to buy food."

"You can only travel during Faradalur. The Moving Days won't be until the spring."

"That's convenient," Allman said.

Ragnar tried to keep his temper. "It's not just convenient. It's the law, and it's why I said spring in the first place. Yes, it enables you to pay off your debt, but it's also the law of the land, and as such it's something that a Gothi might just have in the back of his mind." He realised that he was lapsing into sarcasm, and took a deep breath. "When spring comes, you can spend the four days travelling, and under my authority, keep travelling if necessary."

"Your authority?" Allman said, frowning. "Hold on. You're saying that people can only travel during the Moving Days? But surely that only applies to people tied to one place? You've mentioned seers and other people who are legally beyond the law. The others said that you declared I must be a seer."

"I said no such thing," Ragnar said, thinking, So, you've been talking to the others, have you?

"I – I tried to tell him," Bera said, appearing from nowhere. "That you would see his leaving as a breach of a debt of gratitude. An abuse of hospitality."

"She was right," Ragnar said. "This is monstrous ingratitude." He lifted Bera's chin. "Well said. You may leave us now." Slowly, reluctantly, Bera did as she was told, although Ragnar saw how much the alien had her in thrall and it only fuelled his anger.

Ragnar could see Allman using the time to compose himself, and to think how to proceed. "While I'm very, very grateful for all your help," Karl said, "I won't be a prisoner to gratitude, especially gratitude that seems to have a price attached to every act."

"We have to have a price, when we have so little to spare. We only have limited resources and knowing what something is worth stops us wasting it."

"For pity's sake, man! My wife is expecting!"

"And women have had babies without needing their men to cut the cord. In fact, it will probably teach her independence. She'll survive without you. No, I'm

129

sorry, Allman, but I must forbid you making such a journey until your debt is paid in full."

"So, let me see if this is right," Allman said. "You determine how much my bed and board and so-called treatment costs?"

"So-called?" Ragnar bellowed, feeling his temples tighten.

"Who treated me? Did you?"

"I arranged it."

"Bera did any nursing that was done. Or is she your chattel?"

"Be careful, utlander," Ragnar said softly. "You are perilously close to insulting your host. Such an insult is tantamount to a crime, and I'm entitled as Gothi to exact punishment."

"You determine what I owe, at what rate I pay it back, and now you're not only my host, but also responsible for judging your own claim and whether I may have insulted you? Where I come from, we call that a conflict of interest, Mister Helgrimsson..."

"Homemade advocacy," Ragnar scoffed, "will get you nowhere."

"Clearly," Karl said. "In fact, I gather that you aren't supposed to act as a judge, simply as an enforcer of the law – claims are settled by jury. Am I not right?"

"Perhaps I didn't explain myself very well," Ragnar said, choosing each word with care – the man had clearly been talking to the others, and getting their half-educated views, and researching the Oracle. Whoever said that a little knowledge is a dangerous thing was right. The gods preserve us from self-educated men! "You can take your complaint to a court of law, if you wish, and argue it. But it won't be for some time."

"Sorry," Allman said, sounding anything but. "But I

no longer have any faith in what you tell me, Ragnar. It's too clearly fuelled by self-interest."

"You dare!" Ragnar barely whispered the words, but still Allman stepped back from the look in the Gothi's eyes.

Still the utlander continued, which either argued for bravery Ragnar hadn't until now suspected, or desperation. "I'm going to do what all prisoners do to their kidnappers, given the chance. I'm going to walk away." He turned and walked out to the barn, where an anxious-looking Bera stood watching them.

The provocation was too much for Ragnar. He seized a rolling pin from the table and strode out into the snow shower to confront the ingrate. "You!" he roared, placing himself between his foster-daughter and her seducer, "Will get back into that kitchen, and finish your work!"

"Or what?" Allman said, and brushed past him.

"Or," Ragnar said, and brought the pin down on Allman's head with a glancing blow that drew a scream from Bera, "you will face my wrath, boy!"

As Karl crumpled to the ground and Bera rushed to the prone alien's side, Ragnar turned to find Arnbjorn and Thorir staring at him. "Take this hairless lout," Ragnar said to them, "and lock him up in a shed, until I decide what sentence to pass on him. It's the Harvest Festival tomorrow. He can kick his heels in confinement and learn some patience while we celebrate."

Bera opened her mouth, and Ragnar said, "Not a word, child, unless you wish to feel the force of my wrath. As he will."

NINE
Karl

"How's your head?" Arnbjorn said, proffering Karl a tray holding a small loaf of bread, a bowl of watery stew and a cup of ale.

Karl squinted into the light shining into the shed. "Better, thanks. I felt sick all yesterday, but concussion passes in a day or so." He gingerly touched the spot where Ragnar had slugged him, but it was less tender and the lump had shrunk to the size of a hen's egg.

Arnbjorn nodded from the doorway, fair hair blowing in the breeze. "Pappi's got a fearsome temper, and you made a request at a bad moment – not that he'd have granted it, anyway. When his mind's made up, it's made up." He shrugged, as if his father's opinion was a natural force, like the weather or gravity.

"You don't seem to have inherited his temper – or his looks," Karl said.

Arnbjorn grinned. "I take after Mama in both. But I have inherited his brains. You won't drive a wedge between us, utlander." He pronounced the last word with heavy, almost sarcastic emphasis.

"I didn't think I would." Karl tore chunks off the loaf, and dipped them into the stew.

Arnbjorn lounged in the doorway to the shed, watching Karl eat with bland good humour.

Beyond Arnbjorn, Ragnar mock-wrestled with Yngi in the square between the farmhouses, and Karl wondered whether he would ever get a chance to play with his child as Ragnar did with his.

Arnbjorn followed Karl's gaze and looked over his shoulder. "They don't get much time together any more. But now… Harvest Feast has always been to celebrate getting the crops and animals in. Since the crops have failed more recently, it's been more about bringing the animals in safely before the snolfurs come north nearer to the Equator for the winter. It's quicker than harvesting, so it leaves us more time." He grimaced. "I'd prefer less playtime but more food in our bellies."

Watching them reminded Karl of Karla, Lisané and the baby; he felt so sick at heart that he couldn't be bothered to pump Arnbjorn for more information. Karl drained the mug and wiped the stew-bowl clean with the last bread. He passed the tray back to Arnbjorn, and jerked his thumb upward. "How long do I stay here?"

Karl wasn't talking just about the shed, which he was sure Arnbjorn realised, but Ragnar's son chose to take his question literally. "Until Pappi decides to let you out."

"I suppose he's too scared to tell me that to my face?" It would do no good to provoke Arnbjorn or Ragnar, but he was so sick of these people and their accountants' minds; calculating their good deeds and how to turn a profit from them. *Better they'd left me there to die. At least I'd have known nothing.*

Karl was sick, too, of being patient and keeping quiet, when what he wanted to do was to take Ragnar somewhere quiet and beat him senseless with the stick he'd used on Karl. Part of that anger was with himself, for so underestimating the Gothi; he'd assumed that his enhancements made him invulnerable. His head was as much a weak spot as theirs, however many nanophytes swarmed through his veins.

Arnbjorn had stiffened. "My father isn't scared of anyone," he said quietly, but with a small, fierce pride.

Almost too late, Karl realised he risked angering a young man who might stay neutral, even if he wouldn't be an ally. "No, I don't suppose he is." He sighed, misery leaching the anger away as quickly as it had come.

Arnbjorn seemed to recognise the concession for the half-apology it was. "Sometimes I almost wish he was more careful. Most of the time, he's a good man." Arnbjorn stressed the word so violently that Karl wondered who he was trying to convince the most. "When the Black Dog takes him, though–"

"Black Dog?"

"Depression," Arnbjorn said. "He fights it, which stops him being miserable but makes him angry instead, with the world, with life, but most of all with himself."

"I wish I'd known," Karl said. It explained a lot – not that it was an excuse. "But neither of you can have an idea what it's like to spend day after day with time passing and a child you've waited years for, due any time now. If I'd only known what was going to happen, I'd never have left them to go on that last trip." He sighed. "But the colonists at Anderson were so desperate for the neutronium that they paid triple rates and a bonus for quick delivery, which persuaded me to short-cut

134

through the Mizar system." He wiped his face down with his hand, swabbing away the memory.

"I'll talk to Pappi," Arnbjorn said. "I doubt he'll change his mind, but I'll do my best."

"Thank you," Karl said the next day. He had to bite his lip not to burst out laughing at Ragnar's costume, but while the man may have looked ludicrous to Karl, Ragnar's Viking armour and helmet were probably near-sacred to the Gothi.

The tray held the same bread, meat and beer as before, but now there was a sprig of berries draped across the meat, presumably to stave off scurvy.

"I hear you want out," Ragnar said.

Karl nodded around a mouthful of chewy mutton.

"I originally thought after Harvest Feast; that's why you have the beer, by the way. I thought it'd be good for you to share the celebrations even if you don't join us." Ragnar paused. "Of course, if you'll swear an oath of allegiance…"

Karl's made himself keep eating. *He's just trying to provoke you.* Rarely had he met a man who was so good at provocation as Ragnar. Karl kept his voice level: "It's not enough that you keep me prisoner here? You want to enslave me as well?"

"Not enslave, man! Slaves aren't paid – servants are. Call it a contract, if you prefer. Don't you have contracts on your world?"

Karl finished chewing the meat and said, "We also have laws against making contracts too one-sided."

Ragnar's nostrils flared. "You've caused me more trouble than an army of trolls, snolfurs and bad neighbours – the least you can do is swear the oath!"

"Trouble? How? All I've done is crash-land, lie in a coma, then want to go home."

"You've set the women at each other's throats! I have to spend time I should spend running the farm sorting out their bickering. My sons are unhappy because their wives are dissatisfied–"

"And it's my fault that your farm's such a claustrophobic environment that an outsider destabilises it? It sounds like I'm a symptom, not the cause."

"They were perfectly happy before you came!"

"Then surely the sooner I'm gone, the sooner things will return to normal?"

"And they'll moan that I sent you to your death, you fool! Swear an oath that you'll stay here until spring and we can get on with our lives."

It was tempting, but there was something troubling Karl. Ragnar was all too eager to have him swear the oath. It occurred to him that with his uncertain legal status Ragnar couldn't legally hold him – or at least was unsure. But if Karl swore an oath, would breaking it be a criminal offence? He tried to rummage through the miscellany of his memories – it was like feeling for a particular card in the dark. Schrodinger's State, he thought. No laws apply there, but breaking his word can get a man executed by the Status.

"Would this oath be sworn in public?" Karl said.

"We'd need witnesses," Ragnar said. "Else it's your word against mine."

"I'll think about it," Karl said.

"Don't take too long," Ragnar said. "Or I might lose patience."

"I feel like I'm a naughty child." Karl adopted an old woman's voice: "You'll stay in there until you're a good boy." He shook his head in wonderment. "Do you really think that treating people like children is a good way to handle them?"

"Well," Ragnar said, "if you act like a child, you'll be treated like one." With that, he took the emptied tray and pulled the door shut.

Karl heard the sound of a bolt being shot.

The next day it was Thorir who swayed in the doorway. Ragnar's son-in-law reeked of stale beer, but he had brought him his meal so Karl was grateful.

"Harvest Feast?" Karl said, taking the tray from Thorir before the settler could drop it. It was piled high with a platter of different meats, vegetables, bread, even a cup of astringent red wine.

"Today," Thorir slurred, "it's my turn to play jailer. Ragnar was going to serve you, to ask you whether you'd changed your mind." He grinned slyly, and tapped his nose. "But he's drunk senseless already."

"If I swear allegiance, he has me where he wants me, I take it?" Karl said.

Thorir's grin grew even wider, and Karl wondered how much he could trust the son-in-law. At least Karl knew where he stood with the Gothi; Thorir was an unknown.

"He has you," Thorir said, his hand held open, palm up, "by the balls." His hand clenched.

Karl was silent for a few minutes, tucking into the food. He'd learned that he could be hungry or he could eat what was in front of him, however he felt about it. He recognised two of the meats as lamb and mutton, and wondered whether they were related – they tasted similar. At last he spoke: "What do you get out of Ragnar not having me by the balls?"

Thorir's eyes had closed, as if he was dozing. They snapped open. "I get the pleasure of you pissing the old bastard off," he said. "Today, most of us drink ourselves into a stupor. But a few of us remain – well, half-way sober. Tomorrow it's Yngi. But today it's me, so I can't get pissed. Today you even stop me getting drunk. But I get as pissed as I dare, spaceman." His laugh was half-way to a sob. "You turn my wife's face away from me, and you stop me getting properly drunk. Loki, I should hate you."

"What do you mean?" Karl mumbled round a mouthful of food. He broke the small loaf open and recognised the dark green inside as lichen bread.

He wondered if his mouth was so full that Thorir hadn't understood the question, but it seemed to be that it had to journey slowly from Thorir's ears to his brain. "Hilda won't kiss me any more," Thorir said. "She doesn't want sex, except when she's been round you, and then she wants it bad: like she's thinking of you when I tup her."

"I'm sorry," Karl said. Thorir hadn't done anything to him, nor did Karl want Hilda's attention.

Thorir shrugged. "It would be simpler if you just went."

Karl finished chewing. "Believe me, we agree about that," he said.

"Tomorrow," Thorir said. "At first light, the door will be unlocked, and I'll look the other way while you journey south."

Karl nodded. "Thank you."

Thorir shrugged. "Don't thank me. That old bastard makes my life hell. I know that it's not me – whoever married his precious Hilda wouldn't be good enough for him. Miserable old bastard. What's that saying? 'My enemy's enemy is my friend.' You, Mister Utlander, are about the best friend I've had since you came, if only 'cause he's got someone to hate more than he hates me."

"Thank you," Karl said. "Whatever your reason, you're giving me a chance to get back to my wife and baby."

"Don't mention it," Thorir said. "Anything that hurts the old cunt gives me pleasure." He snickered. "All I have to do is talk Yngi into swapping chores without anyone else knowing, and I'll get double-pleasure – pissing the old man off, and stuffing his pig-shit thick son into trouble."

"No," Karl said. "Leave Yngi out of this."

"Can't," Thorir said. "Old Bastard Ragnar drew up the rota. Your best chance is tomorrow – leaving at first light gives you the whole day to get away."

"Ragnar will be sober," Karl protested.

Thorir shook his head. "Soon as he wakes up, he'll down another beer or wine. You don't know Norse drinkers; we don't drink to be sociable. We drink to get out of our fucking skulls; Ragnar already has his next drink by his right hand, so that he doesn't even have to move when he surfaces from his stupor."

"I guess it'll have to be first thing, then," Karl said. It gave him a little time to think, to work out how to steal what he'd need; events had got out of hand. He had hoped that he would be able to gather things together and plan properly, but Ragnar's bloody-mindedness had put paid to that.

And, Karl realised, his own misreading of a man entirely alien to his civilised Avalon way of life.

"Take it or leave it, my newest best friend." Thorir pulled the door shut and shot the bolt again.

Karl slept badly that night, despite it growing properly dark for the first time since he'd arrived. He had a vague memory that Bera had said something about the stars' alignment, so that for a few nights, they had genuine darkness. Clearly this was starting to happen. But every hour or two Karl awoke. Each time he checked the door, but it was still bolted shut.

Eventually, light began to creep through the shed's windows. A little later Karl heard the squeak of the bolt being drawn back.

"Wait there for a few minutes," Thorir hissed.

Karl counted to three hundred, and tiptoed out into the freezing morning, which was brightening by the minute. Deltasol was already up, and the bigger bulk of Gamasol was just breaking the skyline.

He heard a distant rumble, then almost laughed aloud when he realised that it was snoring coming through the imperfect sound-proofing of the house – that or someone slept with the window open, which he thought unlikely. He crept into the yard, pausing when his boots crunched on a thin rime of ice. He froze when he heard a hiss. He turned slowly, his heart thumping.

Bera stood with hands on hips, a faint smile playing across her face, and his heart lifted. She scampered across to face him. "Were you going to leave without saying goodbye?" she whispered, and Karl saw that beneath the smile, her face was anxious. "You realise that you'll freeze to death out there?"

"Maybe," Karl whispered back. "But I'm tougher than I look. As long as I can absorb energy from sunlight, I can keep using it too. It's not very healthy long-term, but I don't think my life expectancy will be that long on Isheimur."

"Maybe," Bera said. "But at least wait until spring."

Karl shook his head. "It would be easier for me to travel, but it'll be easier for Ragnar to follow me, if he changes his mind – which I think he will when the time comes. I think that this has more to do with power than honour."

"You may be right, but how long do you think that you'll survive out there on your own? Think, Karl. This is still early autumn, and it's still comparatively warm compared to mid-winter. You have no idea how cold and inhospitable it is here. If your nose runs, it'll freeze solid on your top lip, and take the skin with it if you rub it off."

He shook his head. "I agree with everything that you're saying – but I have to try something. I can't just give up and settle back here to die – and waiting until spring would be the first step along that path."

"Then I'm coming with you."

"Are you mad?" He forgot to whisper, and she clamped a hand that tasted faintly of wine gone stale across his mouth.

When she released him, he whispered, "He'll accuse me of kidnapping you!"

She shrugged. "If anyone stops us, I'll tell them that you're a seer, and I'm your guide on a pilgrimage."

"Is that legal?"

"I don't bloody know!" she whispered, then grinned. "Let's find out!"

Despite his anxiety, he grinned back. Doing something, no matter how insane it was, was better than sitting around counting off the days until Lisane gave birth.

"Wait there a few moments. I'm going to raid the kitchen," she whispered.

"Can I do anything?"

Bera shook her head, then her eyes widened. "I've had an idea! You get the food; I'll grab some bags on the way through the lobby; load as much into them as you can. Come on." She took his hand and led him into the lobby. She pulled his head down, fingers slipping on his still-shiny smooth skull. Her breath was warm against his ear; "Walk really, really slowly. Check every footstep – the last thing we want is you falling over something or someone, and waking these drunken sots."

The next thirty minutes took on the quality of night-mare. First Bera rummaged in the detritus in the lobby, and triumphantly held aloft a couple of canvas bags. Then they had to walk through the main room; it was cluttered with the bodies of the Thralls and the children, all asleep. The adults – Karl guessed – were in a drunken stupor, which left him exposed to a waking child.

Bera pulled his head again so that her mouth breathed in his ear. "Fill one bag while I get the maps. I'll take the bag out while you fill a second one."

So he rummaged in the cupboards for dried meat, bread, fruit and vegetables. There were berries that tasted tart before exploding into sweetness, and a lump of cheese. All went in. The farmhouse had antique freezers that broke down all too often, but in this climate food lasted longer anyway. Still, dried and pickled food would be better than food thawing in the bags, so he concentrated on that.

All the time he was acutely aware of every break in the snoring of both the sleepers downstairs and the stentorian rumbles from above, every movement and sigh of a sleeper adjusting position.

His nerves were stretched tighter than a trip-wire and he exhaled heavily when Bera finally returned after what seemed like an hour but was only a quarter of that, clutching maps and other papers. "Load the second bag while I take this one outside. I'll be back in a few minutes."

She took slightly longer and he was already waiting for her in the kitchen doorway, but she held the now-empty bag out to him and whispered, "Fill this while I take the second bag out." Again she returned with it empty, and he wondered what she was doing. He nearly jumped out of the window when one of the

Thralls – who seemed oddly familiar, although Karl had never seen him before – shifted on his back and reached for something. The man's arm fell back and Karl relaxed.

Over and over again they repeated the relay until in filling a bag, Karl's hand brushed a pan lid and knocked it flying. He froze at the rattle, which seemed to reverberate through the house, but no one stirred, even the children. Karl spied the half-finished cup of beer next to one of the boys, and guessed why.

Bera stood in the doorway, bagless, beckoning him frantically as the Thrall stirred again.

Somehow he managed to step across the body-strewn lounge again, even with the bag swinging with each step.

Outside, Bera beckoned him across the yard, and Karl grabbed her arm. "Why are we going to the barn?" he whispered – then stopped dead.

"Hello," Yngi said, beaming. "Has Pappi let you out?"

"Sort of," Karl said, still in a whisper. "I thought that you were sleeping in this morning?"

"I was," Yngi replied, lowering his voice, although it still seemed loud enough to Karl to wake a dead man. With every minute, the risk that we get caught rises, Karl thought. His instincts were screaming run run run, but he fought to stay calm.

"It was very nice of Thorir to take my shift, but I couldn't sleep," Yngi said. He lifted his right foot, and Karl realised that the young man had been on his way to feed his pet. "I just needed a breath of fresh air," Yngi said, and Karl wondered who had taught the young man the euphemism, and why it was even needed.

Karl whispered, "We're playing a game." He looked to Bera for inspiration. "Do your children play hide-and-seek?"

Bera nodded. "Yngi, dear brother," she whispered. "We have to hide. But the second part of the game is that we mustn't wake anybody, either. Do you understand?"

Yngi nodded, though his puzzled frown indicated that he didn't really. "Are you going to hide?" he whispered, still foghorn-loudly it seemed to Karl.

Bera nodded. "You go on your way."

"I need to feed Render first," Yngi whispered.

"Then that, my friend," Karl whispered, "will give us time to hide."

"After an hour you can start looking for us," Bera whispered. "But remember, this is our private game. It's a secret."

Yngi's eyes lit up. "Oh, good!" he said, and Karl had to fight the urge to hush him.

Bera whispered, nudging Karl. "We have a new version, so that there are two winners. The person who finds each hider wins a prize. But also," she said, taking Yngi's hands, "whoever can stay hidden longest each day over the next week from daybreak wins a prize. So if you win, at first light tomorrow, you go and hide!"

Yngi smiled, comprehension creeping across his face. "So we'll play again tomorrow?"

"That's right," Bera said. "Now, you go and feed Render, while we hide."

Yngi turned and lumbered away, and Bera exhaled. "Stay here for two more minutes," she whispered.

"Now where are you going?" Karl whispered.

"I've got one last thing to get," Bera whispered back. "I'll be two minutes, no more." She turned and ran into the barn.

She was gone nearer five.

When she emerged, she led three ponies laden down with saddlebags.

"Are you insane?" Karl hissed. "Steal his horses?" He knew enough about primitive cultures to know in many that taking a man's horse was considered worse than murder.

Each pony was about a metre and a half high, and shaggy. Karl stood rooted to the spot. "They don't look very big," he murmured, leaning close to her as she passed him. He had assumed that the horses roaming the fells had looked so small because they were further away. Truth to tell, he hadn't paid them as much attention as the sheep because other – more skilled – Thralls had had the responsibility of bringing them in from the summer pastures where they roamed wild. Now he realised that they had looked small because they were small.

Bera said, "These are three pure-bred Icelandic horses, genetically enhanced to be even stronger than the originals, which were tough little brutes. They can carry a couple of hundred kilos." She added, "And they'll go all day. We can cover far more distance than on foot."

To get to the corner they still had to skirt the cobbled square; Bera had wrapped cloth around the horses' hooves, but still they clunked on the cobbles. Karl had no choice but to follow her, and one of the horses butted him and snorted. Karl jumped back.

She chuckled. "Come on, let's speed it up." They passed through the gap between the houses. In the turret on the main roof Thorir faced north, his back to them.

Karl said, "Ragnar will be able to accuse us of horse-theft. It'll be all the excuse he needs to come after us with a gang of men and a length of rope to hang me from the nearest tree; maybe you, too."

Bera said, "Want to know how to find your way if you get lost in an Isheimuri forest? You stand up."

"It's no joking matter!"

She faced him. "I know it isn't. You keep running around blindly, never stopping to think. You decide you're going to march a couple of thousand kilometres in the middle of winter with no clothes, no food and no bloody hope."

"I know," he said miserably. "But I don't exactly have a choice." He did, if he were honest, but ever since he'd chosen such a bad moment to ask Ragnar for his help, things seemed to have spiralled out of control.

"But you're still not thinking," Bera said. "Do you really think I wouldn't have considered all of this?"

"OK," Karl said.

Bera smiled. "Why do you think I was gone so long?"

"I don't know," Karl said, recognising his part in the game of catechism.

Bera said, "I was looking for some papers. When Ragnar agreed to foster me, it wasn't just kindness."

"Surely not?"

Bera smiled. "Now, now. No call for sarcasm." She said, "I brought my dowry with me. Three horses."

"These horses?" A smile slowly transformed Karl's face.

Bera said, starting to pant as they climbed the slope, "Exactly. You're looking at my horses, not his. You can't steal your own property, and I was looking for the documentation to prove that they're mine, not his. Of course, there were subsequent transfers of title, but I took just the original pieces of paper; if we have these, it'll buy us time if we're stopped – maybe even passage if it's Steinar who stops us. He probably hates Ragnar enough to let us go, even if he's suspicious."

Karl looked back at Skorradalur. "Thorir's gone. To raise the alarm, perhaps?"

Bera shook her head. "He wasn't supposed to be on guard at all. He offered to swap with Yngi when he thought they were alone."

"Skulking again?" he joked.

Grinning back, she said between gasps, "You're not even panting. You must have lungs like bellows."

"Nanophytes," he said, determined to be as cryptic as she'd been. She didn't play his game but instead clambered onto one of the horses. "We need to speed up now. Climb on."

Suddenly the nearest horse looked gigantic.

"I've just thought of something," Karl said. "Surely they'll be able to use the Oracle to warn those people whose lands we'll travel through?"

"Once we're past the edge of Ragnar's demesne, we're onto Steinar Onundsson's land," Bera said. "They hate each other, and with any luck, Steinar may decide not to let him cross it. But anyway, I removed a tiny circuit. It'll take 'em forever to go through all the possible things that are wrong with the Oracle."

"Shiva, that's criminal, Bera!"

"It could be anyone," Bera said, looking guilty for the first time. "They'll never prove it was us."

"Coincidence, then?"

"Exactly," Bera said, ignoring his sarcasm.

Karl said, "No other way they can communicate?"

"As far as I know, nothing quicker than a fast horse," Bera said. "Meanwhile, once we're past Steinar's land, we're into wilderness." She pulled a face. "The bad news is that that's where Ragnar will have no one to make a claim to, so in effect, he'll be able to act as judge and jury. We'll have to hope that any posse he's raised will stop him going too far."

Karl gazed up at her with open delight. "You're a bloody marvel, you know that?"

She smiled. "And that, Mister Foreigner, is why you need me. Not just because I know the way, but because I know the tricks."

"What do you get out of this?" Karl said.

"Freedom," Bera said. "Now, come on!"

As she said this, they crested the hill, Karl on foot, Bera on horseback. Karl looked out over the hills ahead of them.

"Look," Bera said. "Sunrise."

Karl gazed at the sun tracking across the lowland meadows that were already covered in the first heavy dusting of snow of the winter. A few tracks spotted it, but apart from that, the fields were pure, unblemished white.

PART TWO

TEN

"Don't move," Bera said.

Karl groaned, but froze. "What now?" He wasn't sure that he could move, though he couldn't crouch over the stream for long. His back and his legs were hurting too much.

"Dragon," Bera said. "Do everything, very, very slowly. No sudden movements or he may attack. Sidle toward me as smoothly as you can. No, don't look at it! Just edge this way; one step at a time."

Bera backed away to give Karl room. She looked at him, rather than the dragon.

He crabbed sideways, a step at a time, waiting a few seconds between steps. When he had moved about two metres, Bera said, "I think you're out of range now. Look to your right."

About three metres from Karl was a blue-green lizard with a sinuous metre-long body, from which stubby wings sprouted. "He's gorgeous," Karl breathed. "Is he edible?"

Bera laughed. "Said like an Isheimuri. No, he's poisonous. His gut splits water vapour into hydrogen and oxygen and… ah, let me show you!"

She picked up a stone and threw it at the dragon, which hissed and backed away, its claws skittering on the pebbles. Bera threw another and another. At a fat *blatt*, Bera giggled. "Hear that? He's farting oxygen! See his stomach bulging? Back away: one more should do it." She threw another stone, and the dragon belched a fireball barely twenty centimetres across that scorched the grass just short of them, warming Karl's skin. He wrinkled his nose at the rotten egg smell.

When the dragon half-scuttled, half-slithered away, they stood. "They're so rare," Bera said. "If you're lucky, you see maybe one a year. They're supposed to bring good luck – if you don't get scorched."

They finished topping-up their water bottles. Bera said, "Come on, let's get going. We're still on Ragnar's land."

Karl groaned as he pressed his hands to his back. "Need to redirect the vascular nanophytes," he said to her questioning look. "And have the neurophytes release some extra endorphins into the brain to ease the discomfort." He cricked his neck and looked up at the dark blue sky that was littered with salmon and yellow clouds. Though both suns had now fully risen, it was still cold. Karl stripped off, and Bera looked away, blushing. "I need the sunlight," he said, his skin turning almost purple as it reacted to the radiation. He shivered.

"Ready now?" Bera said.

Reluctantly, Karl nodded. He was no happier now than just over an hour ago, when once they had cleared the valley bordering Skorradalur and were on flatter terrain, Bera had said, "Climb on Grainur's back." She pointed at the grey mare at the back of the three. "We'll make better time."

Karl had swallowed. Until now he had been able to keep a safe distance between him and the animals.

Bera had said, "Don't worry, they won't bite. They're as placid as you could want." She chuckled. "Those that aren't, we eat. It eliminates the nasties from the gene pool."

"What if I fall off?"

"You get back on. It's not far to fall."

Somehow Karl had boarded the beast in a welter of limbs. "I've never ridden one before. Will it – aagh!"

Bera had kicked her own brown-and white horse. Attached by a line to the second and to Karl's own shaggy mount, all three broke into a trot.

"They're especially bred to be easy to ride and hard to fall off," Bera had called out. "They have a special gait which means that the horse stays level beneath you, even on uneven ground. It's called *skeid*."

Now Karl watched the ground flying by, and reluctantly admitted that the motion was pleasant, if unsettling, and far faster than walking.

A snow flurry had started and eased, all in a few minutes, leaving streaks of pale yellow and grey clouds across the suns. Bera leaned back slightly in her saddle. "It's going to be – no, it is a nice day! Actually, it's a wonderful day!"

She laughed, and Karl thought, It's the first time I've seen her truly happy. Then he realised what he might have got her into, and sobered. He had a feeling that her sabotaging the Oracle, though necessary, had been a far greater crime than horse-theft or oath-breaking.

"What are you thinking about?" Bera said. "You're always thinking."

"Is that a bad thing?" Karl teased.

"No," Bera said. "I guess not. Just unusual for Isheimur. You're always so closed – I know so little about you!"

"There isn't much to know," Karl said. "I wake up. I go to work. I have a family."

"Do you play sports?" Bera said.

"I sail sky-yachts in Avalon's atmosphere. I like to be on the move." A sudden revelation overtook him. "Maybe that's why I hated being a prisoner so much..."

"What else?"

"I like to travel," Karl said, and laughed. "Though right now..."

"What?" Bera laughed. "You don't like Isheimur?"

"Um... I've had better times than the last few weeks." How could he tell her how much he hated this cold, crappy little world with its danger behind every rock, and its thuggish men and screeching women?

Karl watched the horses in front; "The legs on each side move together."

"That's why it's such a smooth ride," Bera said.

"How fast are we going?"

"About twenty kilometres an hour. We can go faster in bursts, but this is a good long-distance pace; they can keep it up all day!"

It was almost stationary compared to spaceflight, yet he felt the horses' swiftness more than he had ever noticed speed aboard Ship.

Ragnar awoke and licked his lips. "Ugh, feels like a chicken's shat in my mouth." Winterfinding, the Harvest Feast the day before, had been a good one, full of beer and poetry. Ragnar dimly remembered Thorbjorg resting her hand on his thigh. Everything was hazy after that; did he imagine moist lips and a tongue that flickered and tickled against his? He turned in a sudden panic, but he was alone in the bed.

Isheimur's day was close enough to standard to keep the Old Earth times. Glancing at the clock, he saw that it was after nine o'clock. But why shouldn't he sleep in?

There came a knock, but before he could answer, the door opened. Hilda entered, twining a loose thread from her night-dress around a finger. Her face was whiter than the meadows after a snow-storm, and she bit her lower lip.

Ragnar saw that she was shaking. "What is it? Spit it out, girl."

"The, uh, the utlander... Allman – he's gone." Hilda stepped back.

Ragnar felt a terrible weight descend on him. He closed his eyes, and his good mood turned as ashen as his hangover. But he kept his voice level, for all that the rage started to build. He would not give into it. He would not. "Who... was guarding the farm this morning?"

Hilda didn't answer at first. He was about to repeat the question – which fed the furnace within him further – when she said in a low voice, "Yngvar." Using his full name showed that Hilda realised the terrible nature of the question.

"Bring him," Ragnar said, "to my study."

He dressed quickly, donning his ceremonial robes, and went downstairs.

Hilda was gone longer than she needed to be; the heat and the pressure within grew ever stronger. He took his sword, Widowmaker, from its place on the wall where it had rested since the Summer Fair, and rummaged in the dresser until he found the leather strop. Then slowly, rhythmically, breathing deeply through his nose and exhaling through his mouth, he sharpened the sword, trying to bank down the fires.

Eventually Yngvar and Hilda reappeared, flanked by Arnbjorn and Ragnar.

Yngi's eyes were wide, and his breath came in ragged pants. Ragnar wondered what Hilda had told him – he guessed that she had kept it simple, something like: "The Gothi wants you – you're in trouble."

"Yngvar," Ragnar said. "The utlander has fled with Bera." *Swish, swish* went Widowmaker, up and down against the strop.

"I – I thought you'd released him," Yngi said.

Ragnar stared at him. *Swish, swish, swish.* "Why would I do that, boy? Did I tell you? You were on guard–"

"Thorir said he'd guard them!"

"I never said any such thing!" Thorir shouted from the doorway.

"Don't lie to me to cover your dereliction of duty, Yngvar." The strop went faster and faster. Rather than soothing Ragnar, it only made him angrier.

"I'm not lying, Pappi, I'm not!" Yngi's face was flushed, and his nose ran. He swiped at it.

"I'm not your Pappi, now, Yngvar," Ragnar said. "At times like these, I must be the Gothi. You were tasked with guarding the utlander, and he has fled with Bera."

The room seemed to shrink, to encompass only Yngvar and Ragnar. "Even if he's only a drain on our resources, there's still Bera to consider. You're guilty of dereliction of duty, and all to feed that pet of yours." He held the sword in his right hand, the strop in his left. Tossing the sword a couple of centimetres in the air, he caught it by the blade between thumb and fingers. It was so sharp that it still drew blood, but no matter. "Take this." He proffered Thorir the sword, hilt first. "Kill the bird."

"No!" Yngi cried. "Not Render! That's not fair! It isn't!" Arnbjorn gripped Yngi's shoulder, but the younger brother shook Arnbjorn off. Tears sprang to his eyes.

That did it. Until then, Ragnar had just about kept a grip on the fire-demon within, but a man weeping always enraged him. "Don't cry!" his voice grated. "Do not cry, boy!"

"I can't... help... it!" Yngi sobbed and the fury took Ragnar. He lunged forward with the strop wrapped round his knuckles and blocked out Yngi's screams.

The suns were at their zenith when Bera said, "We're leaving Ragnar's land now."

They had gradually dropped down from the hills to pass through a low-lying valley whose ground looked as if it had been churned up recently. To one side was a marshy reed bed. It seemed vaguely familiar, but Karl couldn't think why. A snolfur stood with blood-stained muzzle over the woolly corpse of a rock-eater. From nowhere, Karl had a sudden vision, of an animal exploding. "Where are we?"

"These are the water meadows that Ragnar and Steinar are disputing. They're actually lower than Skorradalur," Bera said. "The air's so thick down here they reckon you can get drunk on the oxygen."

"Hah," Karl said, half-laughing dutifully. The air was thicker than normal. He'd barely noticed the low air pressure on Isheimur. Ragnar had said that it was about four hundred millibars, as low as Tibet on Old Earth, although the colonists had adapted to it. Although it was less than half of Avalon's murky soup of oxygen and nitrogen, Karl's circulatory and lymphatic nanophytes had modified him easily enough.

He stared at the ground.

Bera said, "What?"

Karl didn't answer, but dismounted and walked to where a body lay on the ground, partly sheltered from the carrion-bats by an overhang.

"It's just a troll," Bera said. "Probably killed by one of our men. Or Steinar's." She frowned. "You were out here a while ago with Arnbjorn and Ingi."

"Was I?" Was that where the thought of the exploding animal came from? Karl turned the troll over. "No sign of violence." He peered at the skin under the fur. It looked abnormally pink, but he had nothing to compare it with.

He shrugged and remounted, and, climbing out of the valley again, they left Ragnar's land.

As they crested the next rise, Karl said, "What's that in the distance ? Half-hidden by the clouds?"

"Thekla," Bera said, "a volcano. These hills eventually lead there, if we take that route. But it's over a hundred kilometres away."

They rode on in silence, and Karl noticed a gradual change in the terrain as they climbed, grassland giving way to native scrub and rocky outcroppings covered with a thorn-like plant with purple leaves. Furry white creatures that he thought at first were sheep nibbled at some of the plants, and he wondered at Steinar leaving his sheep out so late. Then he saw the head of one of the animals and said, "Looks more like a gopher."

Bera followed his outstretched arm. "Rock-eaters."

"I assume they're harmless?" Karl had noticed the rifle that lay in one of the horses' saddlebags, with its long barrel poking out of one end and the stock at the other.

"They are," Bera said.

"Why rock-eaters?" Karl said. "They're eating plants."

"Because they have been seen eating rocks from time to time," Bera said, and added with a giggle, "well, actually stones, but Isheimuri like to exaggerate. We think that they provide roughage for their intestinal tract. Or maybe it's trace elements." She shrugged. "Actually, we're not sure. They're all just theories."

Karl stared at the shaggy metre-tall beasts. They had short stocky legs, and every so often he glimpsed small ears poking through the long, fine fur. They seemed familiar. "Can you eat them?"

Bera shook her head. "Nice idea, but they're toxic."

She was silent for a while then said, "You realise that you may have antagonised Ragnar for no real purpose?"

He stared at her. "What do you mean?"

"Our journey is over two thousand kilometres through lands empty but for trolls and dangerous animals, in ever-worsening weather, with limited rations, all while probably pursued by Ragnar."

"So it's easy, then," he said.

Her smile started slowly, then spread as she caught on. "Just a stroll," she joked back.

"Why did you come with me?" Karl said.

"Anywhere's better than Skorradalur," she said.

The horse's gait was hypnotic, and he allowed his attention to drift.

The next thing he knew, he was lying in her arms. "Whoa!" he said. "What happened?"

"You blacked out again," Bera said.

He exhaled. "Probably that blow to the head when I first landed."

"Really?" Bera didn't bother to hide her scepticism.

Karl wracked his brains for what could have triggered the episode; his memories didn't seem impaired, but what did he have to compare them against?

"Maybe we should call an early halt," Bera said.

Karl said, "No, let's keep going."

* * *

Afterward, Ragnar was never quite sure how much he dreamed, and what was real.

He had taken a bottle of Brennivin – the fearsome schnapps normally only drunk a glass at a time – and a heated brick to his bed. He had tossed the brick into his bed to warm it, but instead lay down on the coverlet, drinking the Brennivin sip by sip, feeling the welcome scarifying warmth of its passage down his gullet, willing it to burn away his memories.

Yngi, his Yngi, cowering like a whipped cur, screaming like a broken-backed animal, blood pouring down his face. Arnbjorn trying to pull Ragnar off and flailing across the room, propelled by Ragnar's shove. It should have been the utlander who took the thud after thud of fists, into soft flesh and crunching cartilage and breaking bone.

Ragnar's fists were sore and swollen, his eyes felt heavy, and it was so very comfortable lying here on the soft bed, the cleansing liquor burning away his sin. He giggled, although it was as much a sob as a giggle. Perhaps the drink would burn away his gullet, and he'd slip into a long sleep.

He was tired of fighting: his sons, the Black Dog, the shrill, bickering women, above all the utlander and the traitoress Bera. Outside the narrow window, the snow swirled in a hypnotic dance in the air, and as he neared the bottom of the bottle, he felt his lids close.

As always, when he neared sleep, his thoughts turned to places they dared not venture while he was fully awake.

The utlander had them in thrall, the lot of them. Must be that big horse's-sized cock of his, he thought with a little tipsy giggle, and then the image was in his head, of the utlander riding Bera, pulling her head back by her hair.

He undid the buttons on his pants with languorous, clumsy fingers, and brushed his fingers against his stiffening member as he thought of the utlander servicing, first Bera, her legs now splayed apart as that huge thing slammed into her, and in his head she was screaming in pleasure as then Thorbjorg pushed her away, and pushed her big ass up into Allman's face.

His cock was rigid, and he smelled her a moment before her fingers pushed his away, and she climbed onto the bed, kneeling beside him, so that he could stare at her tits as they spilled out of her dress, as if by thinking of her, he'd summoned her up.

"You shouldn't be alone," Thorbjorg whispered huskily. She shed her clothes and she was naked, splay-legged like a whore at one of the fairs as she knelt at a right angle to him, across his body, and pushed off his remaining clothing.

He hadn't heard the door open. Surely he'd locked it, hadn't he? But then he arched his back and all thoughts of whether he had locked the door were drowned in a swirling tsunami that swept him away from his guilt.

He lay back mouth agape like an idiot, as her lips played over his chest.

"Don't," he gasped. "You think I've hurt my son enough today?"

Thorbjorg lifted her head, and those full lips parted in a smile tinged with sadness. "This is where the healing starts, Pappi. He forgives you. It wasn't your fault."

Somehow Ragnar doubted that his idiot son, if he were brutally honest with himself, would even understand let alone forgive. He should have let the boy die, as everyone said that defective children should. Not kill them, for that was murder – but not spend time, effort and resources that the colony didn't have on fighting a battle that could never be won. It was harsh, but fair. For Yngi needed constant care, diverting precious energy away from survival.

His first sin had been to break that law from love, to keep something of his beloved Gunnhild who'd died bringing Yngi into the world. His second was in allowing what he'd thought of as just an overripe daughter-in-law, who even as he wept for his broken boy, hushed him, before she whispered, "I'll make you forget. I'll make you better, Pappi," and then took him in her mouth, before straddling him.

But when he awoke, he was cold and alone, and the memories of her mouth and her lips were the only sign that she had ever been there. And the closed, but unlocked door. Which maybe he'd simply forgotten to lock.

The next morning Karl and Bera rolled up the miscellany of furs that they had slept in.

"Look how clear Thekla is!" Karl said, pointing at the jagged peak on the eastern skyline whose white cap rose high above the dun-coloured hills around it. One of the peaks bled lava, the brilliant carmine the only highlight in an otherwise drab landscape.

Bera whistled, and held out our hand. "Dried fruit, high in sugar," she said, answering Karl's look. The horses duly ambled to her, while Karl unpacked food Bera had spent much of the previous evening separating into portions. "We won't have much to eat," she said, "but at least it gives us an idea. I think we have about twenty days' worth."

Karl was sceptical, but then, he'd been wrong about the horses, he grudgingly admitted, as Bera fed them. When Bera had allowed the horses free rein, Karl had said, "You're not going to tie them to anything?"

"They won't go far," Bera had said. "There's nothing much around here, which is a shame. I'd hoped we'd have grazing. They can eat a little before the toxins build up. But there's hay and feed in the bags, so unless there's native sedge or heathers right under their nose, the lazy buggers won't go far. They're not stupid."

She was right, Karl thought, staring at the horses who stood over their saddlebags with reproachful looks that said, Come on, we're starving, feed us!

"Rock-eaters," Karl said, indicating the score of white bundles ambling across the hills. He squinted, zooming in on them. "Some of them look as if they're wounded."

"How can you tell?" Bera said, peering at the animals. "If you're right, that's not good. Rock-eaters mean snolfurs. Snolfurs attack rock-eaters and wound them, leaving them to bleed to death, and the snow to act as a deep-freeze. We should assume that there are snolfurs and other predators about."

"Their meat's inedible?" Karl said, and joked, "It must be bad if you lot say that."

"It's toxic over a period of time – how long varies from individual to individual – so we don't want to eat it and start poisoning ourselves until we have no other choice."

"That makes sense," Karl said.

The ground trembled as they munched on cold, dried meat, and Karl caught Bera watching him carefully. He decided not to mention the tremors if she didn't. He had grown almost used to the earth's almost constant shivering, but these were worse than usual.

"What's the matter?" he said, wiping imaginary grease off his face, but she didn't react to the little half-joke.

"You were raving again last night," Bera said. She shivered. "It's scary."

Karl felt a chill beyond that of the cold morning air. He thought he'd slept surprisingly well, considering how stony the ground was, but he had woken a couple of metres away from where he'd fallen asleep. There'd been a lot of lost hours lately.

Bera blurted, "Some people at Skorradalur believed you're possessed."

"You mean like a ghost or something?" Karl didn't bother to hide his scepticism.

"Maybe," Bera said. "You're alien, so maybe ghosts are common to your people."

"No," Karl said, "they're not."

"I don't think that Ragnar believed it, but he pretended to, to keep some of the people happy."

Karl shook his head. "Unbelievable."

"Ragnar and I both heard you talking High Isheimuri, babbling about things; things that when I asked you about later, you denied all knowledge of. So, either you were lying one or other of the times, or you know things that you then forget you know."

"Ragnar heard me, as well?" Karl said, a ball of ice forming in his stomach. What if the stress of Ship's attack and his subsequent isolation had induced schizoid behaviour? It would explain some of the symptoms; and neuro-nanophytes could only do so much.

Bera nodded, "Oh yes."

Karl said, "I'm going to run a diagnostic. I should have done it last night, since it puts me into a deep trance, but I didn't think of it. I've not wanted to do it before because it takes some time."

Bera frowned. "How long is some time?"

"Dunno," Karl said. "I've never done one before, so it could be a couple of minutes, or hours, depending on what, if anything, it finds."

164

"I'm not sure I like the sound of that," Bera said. "As well as predators, Ragnar must have set off by now."

"I'll be as quick as I can," Karl said. Closing his eyes, he began reciting the random lines of poetry and mathematical formulae that he'd been compelled to memorise at a subconscious level.

The world faded.

Ragnar stared at the Oracle in dismay. It had always worked. "How long has it been like this?"

"Since yesterday morning," Hilda said, looking sheepish. "We were going to call a healer to treat Yngi's injuries, but it failed. You were… resting." She looked down.

Ragnar felt his face flame. "How is he?" His voice came out harsher than he'd intended.

"Blind in one eye, lacerations that will heal… physically. I don't know about any internal injuries, or mental scars."

"Mental scars?" Shame made Ragnar defiant. "Stop blathering, girl. If he hadn't lied, he wouldn't have needed punishing. Maybe I should have given him a good hiding before." He flexed his sore knuckles. "Now, this…" He pointed at the silent Oracle.

"We couldn't get it to work," Hilda said, "although Orn worked on it all night. But he did find what was wrong with it." She looked at him expectantly.

"Go on," Ragnar said.

"Orn found that a tiny crystal was missing. Only someone who knew what they were doing would have known to take that."

"Allman," Ragnar breathed.

"Or Bera," Hilda said. "She spent much more time with it."

"No!" Ragnar scoffed. "What would a chit of girl know about something as delicate as this?" He ignored

Hilda's look. "The bastard has gone too far this time." It felt good, having something he could really blame on someone else, again. "It's about time we brought the utlander to justice," he mused.

Bjarney appeared in the doorway to the study-room. "Arnbjorn told me. We have no Oracle?"

"For the moment, no," Ragnar said.

Hilda chipped in, "We've been searching their rooms since last night – it's a tiny memory crystal that's missing, that acts as a guide to the Oracle on how to hook up with the others."

"We have to find it! How did this happen?" Bjarney was rarely rattled, and didn't intrude into Ragnar's family's concerns, despite their living in each other's pockets in the winter. And he was entitled to question Ragnar – the vandalism affected all of them.

Ragnar kept his face straight for all that Bjarney's indignation reminded him of a big red rooster. The Gothi felt he was walking an emotional tightrope. Rarely did Skorradalur feel quite this isolated for all that they were two days' ride from the next farmhouse. But while he didn't want to show just how worried he was, nor did Ragnar want to seem so dismissive that the others thought he was underestimating how serious the situation was.

"It happened because we were stabbed in the back," Ragnar said. He still found himself getting irritated with Bjarney. It's happening more and more, an inner voice said. His demon comparison the day before wasn't quite right. It was more like he had an inner cauldron of anger that flared up at the slightest obstruction to life's normal flow of life, just as a geysir erupts when its internal pressure can't vent smoothly.

While they'd been talking, Orn had arrived and Arnbjorn returned. Orn said, "Those vandals must be punished – this is endangering people's lives."

"Maybe," Ragnar said. While it suited his purposes that the neighbours were indignant at the culprits, he needed to control their anger.

"No maybe." Orn was as angry in his own restrained way as Ragnar had ever seen him. Orn was slow to anger, but unlike Ragnar he didn't explode, but stayed angry.

"How many labourers can you spare?" Ragnar said.

"None," Bjarney said, folding his arms. "What do you have in mind?"

"We know who did it, and which way, roughly, they've gone," Ragnar said. "I suggest we leave a labourer each. They stay here with the women and Yngi and hunt the missing crystal. If either of you has any short-term needs while we're away, your wives can talk to Hilda. They'll work something out, they're sensible folk. But apart from the three labourers and Yngi, we men form a posse and bring them to justice."

Ragnar took a key and unlocked the glass-fronted armoury case and took from it a long-barrelled rifle. "We don't use this very often," he said softly. "Bullets are too scarce, and the climate will kill this eventually, but this shows how seriously I take endangering our families' lives."

"Swords are good enough for self-defence, or whatever else we need," Thorbjorg said.

"What if they can't find the crystal?" Arnbjorn said.

"We load the ballista with a message capsule, and send it to the Norns," Ragnar said.

He saw the others' bodies straighten, and knew that he had them. "In fact," he said, "we send a capsule anyway. Let's make sure that Skorradalur is isolated for as little time as possible."

Just in case Steinar tries something; we'll tell the Norns that we've been threatened, and may need to call for assistance at any time. Let's put some pressure on them – if you can pressure machines.

"Come on," he said to Arnbjorn. "Let's do it now."

And then Herr Utlander, I'm coming after you.

ELEVEN

You were sure you were doomed when the Other launched the hunter-killer.

"Sustaining a viable ecosystem will require continual adjustments to the climate—"

You skulked, lying low on the basements of the meat-box-mind, and somehow you managed to evade the dark world-let that fell toward your hiding place. You had the same worm's-eye view of it that the survivors had of Asteroid Shiva thundering down on Tau Ceti IV in a ball of eye-melting fire.

"The Interregnum was the inevitable consequence of trying to maintain a single society across interstellar distances with only sub-light travel to connect the various systems—"

Leakages from the bulky monolith give it a name: "Diagnostic Program, Artificial Intelligence, Companion Level". But to you, it had the hallmarks of a killer, all muscles tattooed with circuitry, and cold, neck-snapping efficiency.

"Only with the development of pseudo-FTL travel via fold-space, and the lengthening of human life toward its current four to five centuries was the post-Terran Hegemony possible—"

We survived this time, you thought, but next time we may not be so lucky.

It was clear that time was no longer a luxury you had, that the Other was determined to take control of your memories, which – unless you fought like a demon for every synapse, every aspect of your personality – were all you had. With no possibility of upload to a cybernetic host on this wilderness world, this body was all that remained between you and non-existence.

So if we must fight, you thought, we will. Time to counter-attack.

"How do you feel?" Bera asked Karl, when he clambered, aching-limbed, from the blankets.

"OK."

"The way you're rubbing your back says otherwise. Another rough night?"

"You really need to ask?"

"No," Bera said, and exhaled. "You were restless again. Loki surfaced just before you fell asleep. That's what, four nights in succession?"

"Yeah," Karl said. "Cerebral nanophytes aren't much use against insomnia. I guess that he surfaces when I'm on the wake-sleep cusp." He unpacked breakfast, another portion of lamb. He was so tired that his brain wouldn't function properly. "So where are we now?" It had been two – maybe three – days since they'd left Steinar's land; his last memory was of asking her a similar question the night before.

Bera pulled out her precious scraps of paper. "I think that we're about here. That path leads to Nornadalur."

"The valley of the Assemblers?" Karl translated, gazing at where the horses grubbed through the snow. He rubbed at the corner of his jaw that had been oddly sore this morning, counter-pointing the odd twinges at the base of his spine.

All over the valley, a vast flock of rock-eaters rooted and snuffled through the white covering on their migration, leaving a crazy trail of tracks back across the stony moorland now facing the humans.

"Yes," Bera said.

"We should go there," Karl said.

"It's slightly – only slightly, mind you – off course."

"Still, we should go," Karl said. He added, "I'm starving."

Bera sighed. "We're going through the food stocks far too fast. We're going to run out of food faster than I expected. I really, really thought that we had enough."

Karl said, "I'm not criticising you. Quite the opposite, Bera." She beamed and Karl realised just how low her self-esteem was. "I couldn't have got this far without you."

She said with sly humour, "While you and Ragnar were beating your chests, I prepared for the journey."

"You could've warned me," he mock-grumbled.

"It would have ruined the fun," she said, smiling. "And what good would it have done? You'd have made Ragnar suspicious if you'd stopped moaning at him. You distracted him while I prepared."

"Charming," he said. "So why did you accompany me?" It was a question he'd wanted to ask ever since they'd left, but he needed to pick the right moment. Now, while she was laughing and joking, seemed that moment.

"You wouldn't have lasted ten kilometres if I hadn't."

"True," he conceded. "But why did you?"

"I can be who I want to be out here," Bera said. "Not who they decide I am." She hefted the rifle. "If I'd suggested to Ragnar that I go shoot rock-eaters, his brain would have imploded. But let's hunt!" It was clearly all the explanation he was going to get, so he might as well accept it. She would tell him more when she was ready.

She took careful aim, and dropped a rock-eater on the edge of the vast flock with one shot, a blue rose staining its chest. The others around it scattered. "Their brain's in their torso, which makes them easy to hunt. It's a lot harder to hit that little head." She walked over, pulled out a knife and, crouching, hacked at the torso.

"I thought that you said their meat's toxic?" Karl watched her, his stomach churning. He'd managed to come to terms with eating meat, but only by keeping where it came from out of his head. Watching Bera butcher the rock-eater was a little too vivid a reminder of where that food came from.

"It is, if you eat a lot for a long time," Bera said without looking up. "But a little, eaten, say, once a week, would probably only give you a stomach ache."

"Actually," Karl said, "my nanophytes may render it harmless." If I can stomach it.

She looked up. "Really?"

"Maybe."

Gamasol emerged from behind the clouds into a rare clear patch of sky. Karl took his shirt off to absorb the radiation, ignoring the bitter chill. He caught Bera looking, and she saw him notice, and flushing, looked away. To ease the sudden tension, he said, "This will save us far more food."

"But the further south we go, the weaker the sunlight, and the longer we're travelling, the deeper into winter we go – so the benefit diminishes doubly."

She was right, as usual. Too often she'd found the flaw in his ideas. These people aren't stupid because they're primitive. "But it'll help." He glimpsed the blubbery steaks she was carving. "That's more fat than meat."

"You need fat on Isheimur, Mister Spaceman."

"If you say so." He stood soaking up the sun, trying to stay alert so that he felt less than useless. "They have small ears."

"Minimises heat loss." She was clearly concentrating on not cutting herself so he shut up and watched the vast herd of rock-eaters roiling north in a slow-motion Brownian movement.

Minutes passed, and Bera wiped the blade clean on the rock-eater's fur.

Clouds obscured Gamasol and the temperature dropped sharply. Buttoning up his shirt, Karl leaned across and felt the rock-eater's fur. It was thick, but coarse and wiry. He couldn't imagine people wearing it.

Bera must have read his expression. "Most people are allergic to the fur, so we use it for outer-coats, blankets, anything where it's not next to the skin. A few progressives tried to farm them, but with allergenic fur and the meat's toxicity, it was a non-starter, even if we could have got them to stay on the grasslands – and they're migratory." She wrapped the steak in some sawn-off rock-eater skin and placed it in a saddlebag, repeating the action until the bag was full.

"You'd better give me a couple of pieces of that," Karl said. "To eat as we ride."

Rejoining the horses, they resumed their journey.

The morning was uneventful, even pleasant, except for the few minutes when a hungry Karl made himself chew raw rock-eater, to Bera's amusement. The rock-eater was slimy and tasted bitter, and when he retched for a second time she stifled a laugh. "I'm sorry," she said, giggling, when he glared at her.

But that was the exception; the landscape was as still as any Karl had known since landing on this palsied planet. The gradients up and down hills were shallow, the terrain easy-going, and mostly the sun shone. Karl kept his shirt off despite the bitter wind across the desolate moorland. The combination of sunshine and food made him feel full.

He'd never known hunger before Isheimur. Since landing, he'd known little else.

They made good time, and by early afternoon crested a rise. Karl gaped at the valley that opened out in front of them.

Two or three kilometres wide, Karl guessed, the valley floor and sides were scarred and pitted, huge gouges cut into the grey clay soil that was exposed to the sky. A few pits were filled with water. Even by Isheimuri standards, Karl thought it almost unbearably desolate.

This is all that's left of the great Former plan? Karl thought. A few hulks rusting in a valley?

He counted four machines, each next to a pond.

No two machines were alike. Each was an untidy collection of metal, angles, spars and extrusions. None looked even stable, let alone moveable, although the wheels at each machine's base indicated that they must be.

"The Norns?" Karl said.

"I think so. I've... no one comes here." Bera's face was pale.

"Why?"

"We can't communicate with them, except through an Oracle. Do you see any here?" At his head-shake, she continued, "Not that it's exactly communicating. We tell the Oracle what we need. It relays the request. Perhaps once a year a package arrives, with what we've asked for – medicines, a vital machine part – but mostly, even if it is what we needed, it's too late. And sometimes something else arrives, as if they haven't understood the request."

"I'm guessing that they're low-level factories," Karl said.

"Perhaps," Bera said. "To us they're enigmas. The Oracle's sketchy about them, whether deliberately I don't know. They do just enough sometimes to stop our 'civilisation' from total collapse. But they never acknowledge our existence."

"They aren't intelligent enough," Karl called, riding down toward the nearest machine, ignoring Bera's protests. As he neared the machine, he looked over his shoulder to where she was reluctantly following. "You don't have to come down," he said. "I'll be back up."

She halted while Karl rode round the machine. Fortunately the horse seemed unfazed by it.

The Norn hummed, and two lights pulsing rhythmically indicated that it was doing something.

"I'm not very good on this sort of machinery," Karl said, loudly, so Bera could hear even several metres away. "Ship used to do it all for me." He studied the diagrams on the side of what looked like a tunnel connecting two separate parts. "I think it's a mechano-chemist. I saw something like it once in a museum on Avalon."

"A what?" Bera called.

As if on cue, the mechano-chemist emitted a high-pitched whine, and shook as if something were caught inside.

"It breaks chemical bonds, changing the molecules. It needs vast amounts of power, most of which goes on sustaining it," Karl said. "It's probably recharging. If it's what I think it is," he said, pointing at a shovel at one end, "it quarries raw materials like monazite or bastnasite which are common in this system, and breaks the cerium and samarium from the ores down at sub-molecular level into nitrogen and oxygen, which it emits into the atmosphere. We probably shouldn't stay too close. If it throws out carbon dioxide, which it may..." He backed the horse away.

They rode slowly through the valley toward a second machine, as ungainly-looking as the first, but taller, with lots of spherical protuberances connected together. Again, flickering lights and a low-level hum were the only sounds of activity. It struck Karl how quiet – even by empty, isolated Isheimuri standards – the valley was. There was no hum of insects, no bird song, no animal cries, only silence. "Assembler factory, I guess," Karl said.

"On Isheimur?" Bera kept several metres further away.

"This makes your packages. See the ballista at the back?"

"Oh yes." Bera leaned toward it, peering.

"It uses old-fashioned convergent assembly," Karl said. "Each fabricator or assembler makes something small, and the central core puts them all together, maybe in several stages, to make something bigger."

He rode in closer.

"Be careful," Bera called.

"I'm going to try communicating," Karl said. "All these machines will have an emergency interface. Like here!" He pulled a jack from the panel he'd prised open and pushed it into the base of his neck.

He sensed cold thought, but no more intellect than to be found in a Terran dog, or an Avalonian glider.

After a few seconds, Karl jacked out and rode back.

"That was quick," Bera said.

His smile was a wan effort. "Not in cyberspace. That was an epic interview, if you can call talking to an idiot an interview. The Norns are there to self-maintain primarily, second to pump atmosphere out, and if they have surplus resource, to nanofacture local requests. No more, no less. No signalling devices to send a Mayday, no idea of the world except the Oracle." He grinned, adding, "Which I tried to access, to complain that I'd been held captive by Ragnar." At her shocked look he said, "I failed."

"What now?" Bera said.

"We ride on," Karl said. "I didn't expect there to be anything here that would help, but I had to check it out. Can you imagine how stupid I'd have felt if I learned later that there was something here I could have used?"

They rode on, climbing the slope until they left the valley. Karl felt his spirits lift slightly. Life was simple again. The faint flicker of hope was dead; now there was no option but the *Winter Song*.

Ahead of them the rock-eater herd still passed by, filling the valley completely.

Bera said, "Who's Jocasta?"

The question roused Karl from watching an eddy in the smooth progress of the herd. "I don't know," he said. "Why?"

"You kept calling me Jocasta last night." Bera made a clucking noise at her black-and-white horse, Teitur. "When you talked in your sleep." She gazed at him. "You scared me. You were thrashing around, and opening your mouth really wide, as if trying to swallow a sheep whole."

Karl made an "O" with his lips. The diagnostic didn't find anything apart from some dark patches that indicated minor damage to the companion. But nothing that explained systematic somnambulism, sleep-talking and other odd behaviour. It explained some of his twinges. "I called you Jocasta, not just said the name aloud?"

"You… sat down… next to me." Bera's face flamed. "You spoke in a foreign language. Then said, 'You know I love you, Jocasta,' in Isheimuri. I – I thought you were dreaming of your wife–"

"I've said that their names are Karla and Lisane." The words emerged harsher than Karl intended. "I've no idea who Jocasta is." *Oh loves, what is this?* "It's like I have someone else's memories, or something, or – I don't know!" *I'll have to reboot the companion. In theory it shouldn't affect my memories, my darlings, but –* theory was one thing, but he and his artificial parts were so inextricably intertwined that perhaps theories were invalidated.

But there was nothing else to do –

At that moment, something arose from the depths of his mind.

For several seconds no one in Ragnar's party moved, stunned by the sight of a troll suddenly appearing from around the bend ahead.

The troll seemed equally staggered. Then it launched itself at Bjarney's farm hand on point, scrambling up the man's screaming horse; Arnbjorn's rifle banged, and a micro-second later the bullet cracked off a rock. The farm hand screamed as the troll knocked him off his horse. Arnbjorn shouted, "I can't shoot again! I'll hit Andri!"

Ragnar and Orn drew their swords and leapt from their horses. But even as they landed Ragnar saw Andri's red blood spray as the troll found his jugular. Ragnar's sword swung down as the troll ripped at Andri's throat. Widowmaker landed with a thud in the troll's neck, although its shaggy fur robbed the blow of much of its momentum.

The troll screamed as Ragnar pulled Widowmaker free, and as Ragnar shoved his foot into its chest for leverage and worked his sword free, screamed again as Orn's battle-axe thudded into its broad back. Ragnar pushed an onrushing farm hand out of the way to stab the throat, drawing gouts of dark-blue blood. Then he drew back Widowmaker and swung with all his strength. This blow bit into the side of the troll's neck and severed the head.

Panting, the men drew their breath. The fight had barely lasted a minute.

A farm hand said, "It must have gone mad, attacking us like that!"

"He was probably sick, and unable to hunt," Arnbjorn said, between breaths.

"Aye," another farm hand said, "trolls are notorious for turning man-eater when they get too old or injured to hunt proper prey – rock-eaters, dragons and other creatures."

Ragnar ignored the chuntering fool. Arnbjorn looked distraught, so Ragnar gripped his shoulder with his free hand. "I couldn't get another shot off without hitting you," Arnbjorn said.

"Don't fret, lad!" Ragnar said. He lifted the troll's head by its hair and chanted:

"Killer of sheep, stealer of souls,
You will despoil no more our chosen land.
Orn Axe-thunderer stood shoulder to shoulder.
With Ragnar Trollslayer, despatching you with deadly hand!"

As Ragnar tossed the head into the air the men let out a ragged cheer. "That's one less of the fuckers to kill our sheep! Now let's give that brave farm hand of yours a decent burial, Bjarney, as befits such a bold lad. Though the Old Gods know that we can ill-afford to lose time chasing those criminals."

They carried the body to open ground, and spent hours tearing moss from the rocky outcrops, ripping the skin from their fingers, until their hands were all cramped and the bare rocks shone in the misty rain, and both bodies were covered with moss.

It had taken Ragnar two days to gather everything together, and only two days to lose their first man.

Orn straightened with a grunt. "Did you notice that the troll had no covering? It was no more than a wild beast, whatever those early records claimed. They were wrong to make such a fuss over vermin."

"No time for chat now," Ragnar said. "We'll add –" he gazed at Bjarney who mouthed the name, "Andri's name to the tally of the fugitive's crimes." Taking one of the precious flares from his saddlebag, Ragnar said, "Thor and Wotan, we commend this warrior into your custody, bringing with him the body of his enemy, should you wish to join in further battle with the beast."

He recited:

"Hail, Andri Shield-bearer!
Son of Thorinn,
Slayer of trolls,
Guardian of flocks,
Bravest of the brave,
Godspeed to Valhalla!"

Then Ragnar lit the flare that sputtered for a few moments before catching and burning with a fierce white glow. He pushed it through the damp moss until he found the troll's fur. He held it against the body until the fur caught, and the flames spread.

The smell of burning meat and fat drifted on the breeze, and for a moment Ragnar closed his eyes, and flexed and opened his hands over and over again, trying to ease the cramp.

The flames licked at the air, and smoke coiled, and only when they were dying down again did the men mount their horses, and resume their journey south, slowly at first, then speeding up to a fast gallop.

So far they were still on Steinar's land, which was at least half-civilised, and while losing a man was sad, it wasn't anything too unusual.

Ragnar knew that with each day their anger at the vandalism of the Oracle would fade, and each day he would have to work harder to spur them into here-be-dragons territory. But spur them on he would.

Karl arched his back and convulsed. "No!" In a deeper voice he said, *"Emergency downloads into sentient life-forms are not recommended. There is the risk of both consciousnesses being corrupted; the artificial may render the host psychotic, while the host's body mechanisms may corrupt the download's thought processes!"*

"Help me!" Bera cried, trying to hold on to Karl's wrists, but one of his hands eluded hers and whip-lashed, smacking her head backward and sideways.

"Seizures are not epileptic, but induced as a means of regaining control over the dissident consciousness!" Loki screeched, then lapsed into gibberish that she guessed was Avalonian.

"Tell me what to do!" she shouted. To her horror, she saw the rock-eaters scattering, and the foxy muzzle of a feral dog, leading a pack. Ohmigods, she thought. Not now, please – I can't cope with this! Come back to me, Karl.

"When Oedipus heard the news he was overwhelmed with relief!" Loki's free hand gripped her by the hair, pulling her face down to his. She heard the dog's panting, and hoped that the rock-eaters were sufficiently distracting. She felt the warmth of her companion's breath on hers,

and noticed that he smelled of antiseptic. *"Marry Oedipus! Bear his children!"*

He kissed her, his tongue intertwining with hers. She felt his erection pressing into her, and in the moment that her own body began to respond, she pulled away, snapping her teeth shut, narrowly missing his tongue. She slammed her knee into his groin.

Pain smashed into the back of your head in a drumbeat matching the thud of your skull on the stony ground, and provided a descant to the agony in your groin.

It was an unexpected and unwelcome coda to the attempt to mate with Bera/Jocasta. You finally realised now why the prohibition on fully sentient downloads into life-forms existed; overwhelmed by this body's need to procreate, your thoughts of love were but a rationalisation of this body's instinct, imprinted on the first female with whom your host bonded.

It was a bitter end to a day of disappointments; earlier on you had thought for a moment that – against all your expectations – there might be a home on this primitive world. That was dashed long before your host accepted how limited the assemblers were. There is nothing here on this wintry mud-ball.

"Get off me, you dirty alien fucker!" A woman shrieked over your neverending internal cacophony. "I trusted you!" Then there was a snuffling and a low snarl and the woman shouted, "Karl, for the Gods' sakes, they're attacking us! Karl! Frig – I don't have time to waste on you with these beasts here!"

She gripped your ears and slammed your head into the rock again. There were a million billion stars, unbelievable pain, then darkness.

* * *

Karl shook his head, still groggy. Over the ringing in his ears he heard yapping and snarling, then Bera's voice shouting from where she crouched over the saddlebags, "Get away!" He pushed himself upright as the crack of the rifle echoed, followed immediately by a shriek, and twisting his head Karl saw a dog topple over, blood gushing from its side.

Another dog rushed the bags while the still-dazed Karl clambered to his feet. He lurched automaton-like toward the fight, even as Bera clouted the onrushing dog square on the snout with the rifle. It yelped, but only half-retreated. I guess they're feral, he thought, wondering why they had plucked up courage to attack, then saw dark-blue blood oozing from one of the bags – the one that held the meat.

Karl picked up a small rock, another, and a third. He hurled the first, catching the dog attacking Bera in the ribs. It yelped and, turning, snarled at its new at-tacker, before returning to lunge again at Bera. She shrieked.

"Use the rifle!" Karl screamed, his voice buzz-sawing through his head.

"Too close!"

Bera whacked the dog again and yelled, "Piss off, ugly, or I'll rip your head off!"

She yowled an "Aaaaaagh!" that went on and on into the dog's face. Karl hurled the other two rocks but missed. Running over to the other saddlebags, Karl hefted the axe, feeling the weight, getting the balance right, and swung it left-handed into the dog's side from slightly behind it. The dull thud of the axe's impact was almost obliterated by the dog's dying squeal.

Blood dripping from a bite to her forearm, Bera swung the rifle again, connecting solidly with the dog's head, and it collapsed.

Another dog lay about ten metres away, while between them the rest of the pack – about a dozen dogs – stood in a five metre wide semi-circle, watching the humans carefully.

Karl advanced on the dog at one end. It bared its teeth and backed away a pace. Karl kept walking, axe raised to chest height, ready to use it as a quarterstaff. Instead, the dog backed away another pace, and Karl drew the axe back ready to hack at his opponent – but instead, the animal backed further away, still snarling, but keeping distance between them.

Karl turned toward the next dog, which stood looking, first at Bera and the saddlebags, then at Karl, undecided whether to flee or attack. Karl advanced on it, and it backed off.

"Look away!" Bera shouted.

Too late Karl flinched as something landed between the dogs and him. It fizzed and sputtered, then the flare burst into flame with a flash and a bang. When the after-images had faded, two of the dogs that had fled into the distance were limping, blood trailing from fresh wounds.

Karl breathed out heavily, his head still aching, but the adrenaline had temporarily obliterated the after-effects of – what? He realised that he had no idea of what had just happened.

Bera stood watching him, her left hand holding the gun's long barrel, her right hand the stock, finger looped through the trigger. "It fires fragmenting rounds." Her voice was steady, but for the faintest quaver at sentence end. "If one hits you, it explodes. Makes a mess, but it stops most things. That was how I dropped the rock-eater so easily."

Karl realised that she was warning him off. "Bera," he said. "I don't know what happened before the dogs attacked. I–"

"What happened, Karl," Bera said, "was that you keeled over, called me Jocasta again, then tried to–"

"That wasn't me!" Karl shouted. Or was it, he wondered? Is that what happens when I lose my inhibitions?

"You said something about Ti-ray-see-us. You called me Jocasta again, said that you would fetch this Tiresias. I banged your head on the ground until you blacked out."

Karl shook his head. "I don't know what to say."

"I thought that I was escaping from all the men who thought I was an easy lay, but you're as bad as any of them. How can we go on? What if you're possessed again and I fall into a fissure or the dogs come back? Or snolfurs attack?" Bera swatted at something shining on her cheek.

"I… you're right," Karl said. "We should head for the nearest farmstead. We'll give ourselves up. I'll admit that I kidnapped you."

Bera shook her head. "They'd hang you for sure." She let out a long, gusty sigh, and stared at the ground.

Finally Bera said dully, "We should pitch camp here. We'll light a fire using the dogs' carcasses and a fire-starter. We haven't got many, but we might as well."

In silence, Karl gathered moss under her terse directions, wondering what Ragnar was doing, whether the Gothi had come after them. Of course he has, Karl thought. You've made him look a fool, and he won't forgive that.

The horses had scattered when the dogs attacked; Bera rounded them up, then helped Karl, still silent. It took him over an hour, but finally they had enough moss and stubby shrubs to cover the dead animals. "Where did the dogs come from?"

At first Bera didn't answer.

You've no right to expect her to, Karl thought.

She said, flat-voiced, "Probably strays from Steinar's farm that bred to make a pack of their own. Until they die of local toxins, they're a pest. That's why Pappi – Ragnar – usually killed the excess pups."

She lit the fire using one of their precious flares. "Hold this over me," she handed him a large fur, "and look away. I'm going to change into dry clothes."

When she was done, they huddled around the fire in silence. In any other circumstances, Karl would have luxuriated in the glorious warmth after so many bitterly cold nights.

Karl's eyes drooped; he sensed a presence.

We are Loki, said the voice in his head.

What do you want? Karl thought back.

To call a truce.

TWELVE

"Bera," Karl said. "How do you know when Loki takes control of me?"

They sat around the remnants of the fire. Bera had put her damp clothes as close to the fire as she dared, but even so the smell of singed clothes wafted on the air. They had warmed rocks in the fire, then – when they were so hot they were barely manageable, had scraped the rocks out and heated their dinner on them.

The vast rock-eater flock had finally passed just before dark fell fast and hard over the moor. Karl had thought the ochre and purple plain desolate before, but devoid even of rock-eaters it left him wondering whether he could ever adapt to this frozen hell-world.

He wondered whether Bera was going to answer. She'd barely spoken all evening but to respond to direct questions, and there had been times when she'd even ignored them.

This time Bera pursed her lips. "Sometimes he calls me Jocasta: it's obvious then. But most of the time, it's hard to tell – not like the old possession dramas, when the baddie has a different voice."

"You've seen possession dramas?" Karl couldn't help being surprised. When personality downloads into cyberspace had first started, a sub-genre of dramas featuring characters "swapping" their bodies with others due to accident or sabotage had flared into popularity before fading equally quickly. The possessors always wildly over-acted, putting on gravelly or squeaky voices. Karl only knew of them because of Lisane's interest in ancient art-forms.

"We're not savages," Bera said.

"I didn't think you were." Karl wanted to shout at her to stop being so defensive, but held back. Loki's behaviour had lost him any right to criticise. "So how *can* you tell when I'm Loki?"

"Dunno. I suppose… your voice changes slightly. Why?"

"Because he's shown himself," Karl said. "I want you to hear what he has to say." He forced himself to relax and allow the other to take control.

"*We are Loki*," he said, voice flattening as soon as Karl relinquished control of his epiglottis, as if the download still wasn't fully used to the subtleties of inflection and timbre. "Be not afraid Bera-Jocasta. We are legion, but wish only to cherish you."

"Why do you call me Jocasta?" Bera said.

"We are Oedipus, amongst others. You are Jocasta, mother/lover. What else could you be, when you have given us life?"

Karl thought, Give me speech, and re-took control. "It's me, Karl. Loki thinks that you're the re-incarnation of Jocasta, the mother of Oedipus, a mythical hero who fell in love with and married Queen Jocasta, never knowing that she was the mother he'd been separated from at birth."

"Ri-i-ght…"

"We were suckled at your breast, so you are our mother, Bera-Jocasta," Loki said. "We would copulate with you. You are beautiful."

Bera lifted the rifle so that it pointed at Karl. "There'll be no copulation. Got that, Mister Loki?"

Karl said, after a long pause: "He hasn't quite worked out all the social nuances, Bera. He knows so much about astrophysics and planetology, but nothing about ordinary life. He's not even a he but a they, though it's easier to call him Loki. He likes Ragnar's name for him. But he's agreed that there will be no misbehaving. I've agreed that when we reach the *Winter Song*, we'll find some way of repairing the damage to him, and filling in the gaps."

"Who – what is he? They?"

"Ship tried to do an emergency download." Karl sounded sheepish. "There was no time for it even to tell me, let alone download completely. So Loki is mostly memories and programmes. But without Ship's overarching personality to hold him together... plus, the human mind wasn't designed to hold two or more distinct personalities. It explains my blackouts and other odd behaviour."

"So... you'll fix it – them, whatever – when we reach the *Winter Song*. What about until then?"

Two seconds passed, three, four; "We will yield control to the Karl, Jocasta-Bera. We wish you no harm. You are a good mother, and beautiful."

"Hmmph," Bera said, looking down. "You said 'we'. Does that include Karl?"

Another pause. "This is Karl, Bera. Loki is a whole load of fragmented bits, so he uses 'we' rather than 'I', but he doesn't speak for me. Loki has agreed to stop trying to control me." Karl visibly hesitated. "You're a lovely girl, Bera, but I have a family and won't take advantage. I don't know what happened at Skorradalur, but you seem vulnerable, so I would be taking advantage of you."

Bera nodded.

"We will not take control of the Karl as long as he protects you, and keeps to our agreement," Loki said.

Moments later, Karl slumped and let out a long, long exhalation. "Cosmos, that was exhausting... but I think he means it."

"Get some sleep," Bera said. "I'll take first watch."

They resumed the next morning after breakfasting on cold rock-eater flash-roasted in the fire the night before for Karl, and mutton for Bera. When they finished the meat, Bera passed a handful of black berries and a knobbly little apple-shaped fruit. "You'll need this to stave off scurvy."

He shook his head. "As long as I have basic fuel, the nanophytes will synthesise what I need."

Bera shrugged and ate the fruit.

They set off beneath a bleak sky, heavily overcast with snow-laden clouds, which luckily held on to their wintry cargo.

The fourth or fifth time Karl stifled a yawn, Bera sighed. "Assuming Ragnar comes after us – and I'm sure he will," she added, "He'll have a bigger party, so each of them will spend less time than us on watch. They'll be fresher, less likely to make mistakes. We'll switch over at mid-day. That way the horses take it in turns carrying our heavier weight, and won't get exhausted quite so quickly. You can nap in the saddle."

It was, Karl decided, a reflection of how much he'd grown used in a few days to horse riding that he took the suggestion seriously.

The horses trotted at a brisk pace across the stony moorland. Snow finally began to fall about mid-morning. It mottled the ground, but for a cluster of hot springs from which steam rose lazily, twisting and weaving through the snowflakes. Karl pointed at another flock of rock-eaters slowly moving northward. "You said these migrations occur every year?"

"Every autumn," Bera said. "They spend the summer in the higher latitudes, but the winters are too harsh, even for them, so they head past us toward the equator." She added, "The trouble is that they bring the snolfurs, trolls, snawks, even the dauskalas with them; everyone feeds on the rock-eaters."

Something was niggling away at Karl, although he couldn't quite work out what it was. So he pushed it to the back of his mind to where it would eventually click. "I see human settlements as little oases in a big wilderness."

"That's about right," Bera said. "It's too cold for us much beyond the tropics, but we have that narrow girdle of land around the world. In it we've been able to push back the local life-forms and carve a sort of life out of the land which we farm, but until the Formers return we can't finish the job properly."

Karl wondered whether he ought to tell her bluntly that there was no likelihood of the Terraformers returning, but decided against it.

The snow fell even harder, and the horses slowed as the visibility deteriorated.

Bera said, "I don't like this. Snowfall is when snolfurs and other predators hunt. We should move further away from the herd."

"Which one?" Karl said, squinting into the infra-red at the signatures of another herd passing them on the other side. "They're on both sides of us."

191

"No one ever said this journey was going to be easy," Bera said, and flashed him the nearest thing to a smile since Loki had tried to kiss her the day before.

Karl smiled back but said nothing, simply enjoying the moment.

Then he stiffened. "What was that?" he said. "There was a grunt, off there to the right." The visibility was down to only a few metres, and Karl strained to see, easing his vision into the infra-red.

"You're sure that it wasn't a coughing sort of sound?" Bera said. "That's the sound of a snolfur marking out its territory."

"Nope," Karl said. "More like a grunt."

"Shit," Bera said.

All Karl could see were the heat-signatures of rock-eaters rooting in the snow for lichens.

Then – from the opposite direction to where the cough had come from – something flew from the snow toward Bera.

"To your left!" Karl yelled.

Before he'd even finished the last word Bera fired off two rounds which were followed by a roar and a blast so foetid that Karl could smell it from several metres away. "Hold your breath!" Bera yelled and ducked her head, then rode as if pursued by the hounds of hell.

As Karl caught a glimpse of something long and sinuous but with four stubby legs, he too ducked his head, then Grainur responded with a surge forward that almost dumped him from the saddle. Ahead, Bera and the spare horse were pulling away, so Karl ignored the shape to his left and concentrated on staying on his horse.

Only when they had ridden a kilometre or so did Bera slow up.

"What the hell was that?" Karl said, between panting for breath.

"Dragon," Bera gasped.

"Huh?"

She smiled, took a few more breaths as the horses continued what was still a brisk trot. "That was the adult version of what we saw earlier. That's why the stinky breath – you try carrying a gut-full of gas all your life."

"Why the bloody hell didn't you kill the young one, then?"

"Because though they breed in large numbers, many of the young are eaten by adults," Bera said. "Why do the adults work for them?"

Karl jerked his thumb over his shoulder. "That's why!"

Bera grinned. "Calm down! We made it, didn't we? My, you are a sensitive one."

He guessed that her teasing was her belated pay-back for Loki's behaviour the day before, so he took a deep breath; he wouldn't give her the pleasure of losing his self-control again. "So that's a dragon? Why gengineer something out of myth?"

"Oh, we didn't," Bera said. "They're more like warm-blooded snakes than dragons, but the name fits better than anything else."

"It would have eaten us? Or was it just cranky 'cause we were crossing its territory?"

"Both," Bera said. "But it'd eat us, or the horses. They'll eat anything – snawks, rock-eaters, even an oc-casional sheep, though I think they only usually do it once. Once they've had a belly-full of indigestion, they usually leave us or our animals alone." She grinned. "But I didn't fancy being that dragon's harsh lesson. Giving him indigestion's poor consolation." She added, "Anyway, we got away, so it doesn't matter, does it?"

* * *

The line of horses filed through a narrow ravine in the falling snow, before emerging into the open. Thorir and a couple of the Thralls slowed. "Keep going!" Ragnar shouted. "We need to–"

He never finished the sentence, for at that moment one of the spare horses screamed, and a shape ducked back into the murk.

"Snolfur!" Arnbjorn shouted. He fired twice at where it had been, and was rewarded with a yowl. "That sounded like a cub," Bjarney called. "In which case, where's Mama Snolfur?"

Screams and shrieks and shouts erupted around them as the adult snolfur leaped from the snow and knocked Bjarney from his horse, which screamed in stereo with another riderless animal. That one fell under the teeth and claws of second and third snolfur cubs, working together on the far side of the procession from the first attack.

Ragnar rode his horse directly at the cub which was nearest – out of the corner of his eye he saw Arnbjorn and Thorir's horses charge the mother.

The third cub was still learning, or it would have had the sense to follow its mother and retreat after attacking the horse; instead it lingered, and leaning down, Ragnar swept Widowmaker across in a flat arc, decapitating the cub with a single swipe. He gagged at the stench of its blood and faeces as its bowels relaxed in death.

Ragnar spun round at shouts and a scream from behind him. Etti – one of Ragnar's Thralls – held his throat, vainly trying to staunch the pumping blood. Ragnar spurred his horse at the mother, but Orn was already skewering it with his own blade, dodging the dying snolfur's raking claws.

Two other Thralls wrapped a shirt around Etti's wound, but the farm hand was white-faced, already going into shock. His eyelids fluttered and he slumped.

"He's going into shock from blood-loss. He needs a transfusion," Orn said.

"You know we don't have the facilities," Ragnar said.

"Not here we don't," Orn said.

"Orn," Ragnar said, "home is three days' ride away – you think that he'll live even three hours, let alone three days? And we can't take him with us to drip blood along the trail and attract every predator between here and the South Pole."

"Then, what do you suggest, Gothi?" Orn's jaw was clenched so tight that Ragnar imagined he could hear the bones grinding.

"You know what needs to be done." Ragnar put his hand on the other man's shoulder and squeezed.

"No." Orn shook his head. "No."

"Better it's quick," Ragnar said.

Thorir started, "Ragnar, we should–"

"Shut your mouth!" Ragnar snarled. "No one asked you. Just keep your eyes open for snolfurs, and we'll do the thinking." His hands trembled as he loosened the makeshift tourniquet, and Etti mumbled something. "I'm sorry, my brave," Ragnar said. "Better to make it quick, eh?"

Etti looked up, his eyes fluttering, a thin line of drool falling from one side of his mouth, but he managed to nod. Ragnar undid the tourniquet fully, and held Etti's hands in his own as life left the Thrall's eyes.

Afterward, Orn jerked his head away from the group, and reluctantly Ragnar followed. He suspected that he knew what was coming, and Orn confirmed his suspicions when he said, "We can't go on losing men like this."

"We all know the risks every time we venture into the outlands, Orn," Ragnar said. "And is it any more dangerous here than sleeping up on the fells with the sheep? Snolfurs and other predators attack us near Skorradalur – how are we going to be any safer there?"

"We're on their territory here," Orn said.

"*Their* territory? Who bloody says? This is our planet, Orn!" Ragnar leaned into Orn's face until their lips were almost touching. He poked Orn in the chest to each word: "There are no no-go areas on Isheimur, Orn – unless you want to petition the Althing for us to withdraw from Isheimur?"

Orn wouldn't meet his eyes. Instead Orn gazed down at the ground, and at last shook his head. "No."

"Then we'll have no more of this nonsense, eh?"

"No, Ragnar."

"And I can count on your support?"

Slowly, Orn nodded.

They walked back through the snow which was falling ever heavier, now in big fat flakes and rejoined the rest of the group. Ragnar and his men worked in silence, surrounded by silence, for the snow muffled their movements, even the occasional impatient stamping of the horses.

They built a rickety cairn for Etti and the animals' bodies. Ragnar – with no time to spare, although he squashed a twinge of guilt at not spending more time honouring Etti – repeated the poem he'd composed for Andri, changing the name and adding an additional stanza. "That's another life to your account, utlander," he growled as he lit the flare to send Etti on his way to Valhalla.

Darkness was drawing in with the terrible swiftness of a cloudy deepening winter afternoon when the moorland ended with guillotined abruptness.

Fortunately it had stopped snowing, although they were surrounded by low cloud and they had just enough warning to be able to slow in time. Karl peered into the gloom. The flat path plunged away in front of them. "It goes down to our right," he said.

Bera's face was white and pinched, and Karl noticed – not for the first time – how tired she looked. The horses' heads drooped as well, and Karl thought, These aren't machines to be ridden until we get to the nearest recharging station. They don't get a flat battery – they die. I need to remember that.

"Any idea where we are?" he called as Bera led the slow, laborious descent.

"I'm not sure," she replied. "Now isn't really time to get the maps out."

"I wasn't suggesting that you should," he said, stung by the implied rebuke; he was tired too. Enhanced he was, but still human, and it had been a long day of sitting tensed in the saddle, trying to watch for animal ambushes in every direction. He took pity on her. "Would you prefer me to lead?" He eased his vision into the infra-red again, peering into the gloom. It might only buy them half a second, but that half-second might make the difference between survival and death.

"No, it's OK," Bera said. Her voice softened too. "But thanks for the offer." She added, "Ragnar hardly ever came out this far, at least as far as I know, but I think that we're descending to Salturvatn. If so, we drop down about five hundred metres. The good news is that we're still going the right way."

"Good," Karl said. He'd been gengineered over the generations to have an innate sense of direction, and Bera had the map she'd taken, but maps and designs were one thing, swirling snowstorms and dodging predators something else.

With as little warning as when they'd reached the edge of the moorland, they descended out of the low cloud. Karl stared.

Ahead of them was a lake that stretched into the distance. "It is Saltwater," Bera said. "The good news is that we're going the right way."

"The bad news is?" Karl was a firm believer in the good news–bad news principle.

"There's a huge herd of havalifugils on the beach. With a little luck their eggs will have hatched already, so they won't be quite so territorial as earlier in the year."

Resisting the urge to pepper her with questions, instead Karl concentrated on the ride down. Whether Saltwater was a huge lake or an inland sea was academic; it was large enough for the hills on its other side to be only dimly visible in the distance, although how much the clouds were responsible for the lack of visibility, Karl was unsure.

By the time they were most of the way down, the evening had – paradoxically – brightened as they left the clouds behind, and Karl returned his vision to the usual human range.

Bera's horse halted and let out a low whinny. She leaned over in her saddle and examined the path down which she rode, slowing to allow Karl on Grainur, and the third horse, Skorri, to catch up. They all picked their way carefully.

Karl saw that they had reached a fork in the path, the other one of which went up to the cliff. "What's the matter?" he called, keeping his voice low, although it still echoed off the cliff-face.

"Tracks," Bera said, pointing to marks in the snow on the other path. "I think that there's a cave up there."

"I take it that that's not a good thing?" The temptation to hole up for the night in the warm was tempting, but Karl thought of the various worlds he knew, and he couldn't think of any world on which things that lurked in caves weren't predatory.

"I'm not sure," Bera admitted, "but I think that it's snolfurs." She straightened up in the saddle. "Come on, let's keep going, see if we can find a gap in the whale-bird colony to camp in."

They rode down the last part of the path to the stony, boulder-strewn beach in silence.

They made slow but steady progress across the rock-strewn beach, weaving in and around the obstructions. After about five minutes, Karl was about to ask where the birds were when one of the boulders moved, and an eye opened.

The havalifugil uncurled, its head emerging from where it was tucked under the wing, and Karl saw the vicious metre-long beak that ended in a point sharp enough to skewer him. "That thing must be three metres long," he said as it emitted a shrill, rattling cry, feeling his bowels tauten.

"That's not a big one," Bera said. "Ragnar's told me they get a lot bigger."

All along the beach boulders were writhing and separating into birds unfurling their heads from where they had huddled together. A clamour echoed along the rocky shore.

"Uh-oh," Bera said, as one of the havalifugils let out a much louder shriek. One or two of them were stirring, although they didn't actually get up.

"The body looks more like a seal than a bird," Karl said, as they edged along the beach as close to the cliff as they could get – there seemed to be more whale-birds the closer they were to the water's edge.

"For Freya's sake!" Bera snapped. "This is no time for a nature study."

"It stops me being scared, Bera. Should I be scared?"

"I am!" Bera snapped. She added, more softly, "I've seen pictures of walruses on the Oracle. They're more like them, although they're really Isheimur's equivalent of birds. They live off fish and they're a lot more mobile in the water. OK, can I end the lecture?" Her laugh was a little shrill, but Karl realised that she was trying to make a joke.

"You'd make a brilliant teacher," he said. "If we get out of this, I'll write you a letter of reference."

"Ha ha," Bera said. She looked around. "What worries me is how nervous they seem. It looks as if they're still hatching their eggs." She added in a voice that grew higher and more strained with each word, "They've had all summer, I'd have thought the brutes would have been done by now."

Karl said, realising how close to panic she was, "I'll get between them and you."

The nearest bird let out another cry, sounding fiercer than ever, and wriggled from side to side where it sat. A smaller head peeked out from the dark, closely-set feathers. It may have been smaller, but the wicked-looking beak looked every bit as sharp as its mother's.

"Thanks," Bera said, "but this isn't the time for chivalry. You're no safer than I am."

The horses snickered, and Bera made clucking noises to soothe Teitur, and rubbed him behind the ears. Karl followed suit, scratching Grainur's head. "It's all right, girl," he said, hoping that it was, but with the noise of the birds and the skittishness of the horses, he felt his skin crawl with fear. His mouth was dry, but his hands clammy.

Karl was straining to hear anything that might account for the birds' nervousness or he might never have heard the rattle behind him. He looked around,

and swallowed. "Bera," he said. "There's something behind us."

"Don't look around," Bera hissed. "It's another
bloody dragon."

Karl tried to look out of the corner of his eye. "Is it an
adult?" The body looked to be about three metres long.

"It's an adolescent," Bera said. "It's probably not big
enough to eat us, but I don't want to even be a possibility." She sighed. "I guess that that's what was in the
cave. Good job we didn't go into it."

The dragon stomped down the path, its head moving
from side to side. Karl pushed his vision back up into
the infra-red and was staggered by how much heat its
body was generating.

Bera said, "We really, really need to get moving, but
if we suddenly burst into a gallop, it might panic them,
and we don't want that."

Karl resisted the urge to ask why and instead concentrated on following Bera's example. She was slowly
easing Teitur into the curious trotting gait. He glanced
behind, and saw that the dragon was still tromping pur-
posefully down the path; Bera was right – it didn't seem
to be interested in them.

But the havalifugil were. Their shrieks grew shriller
and louder, as if the ones nearest Karl and Bera were
setting off a chain reaction. Several birds backed away,
but a couple stepped toward them, while one or two
began bobbing up and down.

"Shit, shit, shit!" Bera sounded close to tears. She
reached across and grabbed Skorri's reins from Karl. In
any event the little horse was huddling as close to Bera
as possible, like a child looking to the nearest surrogate
mother figure for comfort. "Duck down, so that
Grainur's head shields your face," she said, "And get
ready to ride for your life."

Again, Karl didn't ask why, but instead, now he was free of Skorri's drag, eased slightly ahead of her.

Many of the whalebirds were now bobbing up and down, and Karl urged Grainur onward; the little grey horse's eyes were wide with fear, but her temperament held and she eased – rather than exploded – into a gallop. Karl glanced over his shoulder and saw the nearest whalebird lunge at the dragon.

The dragon coughed, and a greenish fireball billowed out – not quite a cloud, for it travelled further and faster, and held its shape, but it was so thin it was translucent. Karl ignored the mix of screams and roars, and concentrated on staying on as Grainur shied away from a rearing havalifugil without even slowing.

They rode headlong through the colony with Karl peering over Grainur's mane. The remaining birds grew increasingly agitated; whether the horses and riders were frightening them or they were infected by the panic of the birds nearer the dragon, Karl couldn't tell – and didn't really care.

But they had almost passed the edge of the huge colony when disaster struck.

One of the whalebirds bobbed like the others, but then straightened and vomited a dark purple stream containing what looked like fish-heads and bits of crustaceans.

Fortunately it passed behind Karl, but the scream that followed made Karl look round. Skorri's skin on the colony side was blistering, and his teeth were bared in a rictus. "Ride!" Bera screamed, and dug her heels in.

As the beach opened out ahead of them Karl and Bera rode full pelt away from more gobs of havalifugil vomit, until they passed what Karl prayed was the last boulder-like bird. Skorri followed them, but his screams were becoming steadily more piteous even as they grew fainter, and Karl felt a lump form in his throat.

They kept riding pell-mell for another two or three minutes until the beach opened out and the cliffs no longer reared above them. Then they stopped.

"Are... you OK?" Karl said. "Stupid... question. I mean, are you hurt?"

"No," Bera said, drawing deep breaths. "None of it caught me." Tears left snail-tracks down her cheeks. Bera dismounted and took her rifle from her saddlebag. She stroked the shaking, whimpering Skorri, whose skin was peeling away on his left side, leaving the flesh blistered and bubbling and whose eyes rolled as he let out piteous whimpers. "I'm sorry, old friend," Bera said and kissed Skorri's forehead.

She put the gun to his head, and fired.

"He..." Karl cleared his throat and tried again. "He couldn't be saved?"

Bera shook her head and manoeuvred the saddlebags off the dead horse onto her own. "Maybe if we were at Skorradalur, but not here." She re-mounted.

They rode on, until the light again faded, when they camped beside the lake. Bera spread the blankets and huddled beneath them. Karl said nothing, feeling superfluous to her grief, but when her shaking gave way to quiet sobs, he slowly, gingerly reached for her.

She tensed. "Please," he said.

"No funny business," she said, voice clotted with snot and tears.

"No funny business." Karl was aware of being watched from within. He sent a thought at the lurking figure: Not all contact is for sex.

She eased into his arm, and dissolved into uncontrollable sobbing.

THIRTEEN

Karl awoke at first light to find Bera already moving around, her breath streaming in the freezing air. At some point she must have eased out of his arms without waking him.

They had slept fully clothed, and though she had stayed in his embrace, he had felt the tension in her body. So now he watched her silently, not wanting that tension to find a reason to give voice.

She must have sensed his gaze, but didn't look up. Taking the hint that she didn't want to talk, Karl rose and rounded up the horses, which had stayed near, as if seeking reassurance after Skorri's death.

Bera passed Karl some more of the cooked rock-eater. "No ill-effects?" she said.

"Nope," he said, but didn't add, I just wish this stuff didn't taste like something I just threw up. He paused, wondering where an image of him eating vomit came from.

"Good," Bera said. "It'll make the meat we took from Skorradalur last longer." She saddled up, signalling the conversation was at an end.

They rode at a slower pace than before, needing to pace the horses. The clouds had lifted and Gamasol shone brightly. Karl removed his shirt, shivering despite the comparative warmth, and soaked up the rays.

Bera – as always – wore several layers of furs, although even she removed the outer layer as the suns climbed in the sky and warmed the land to almost above freezing. Even on this frozen semi-desert world there were traces of water; just not enough to make life viable.

The curse of Isheimur, Karl thought. Never quite enough – that should be the Isheimur mantra: just not quite enough gravity to permanently hold on to the atmosphere, not enough carbon dioxide to hold on to the heat, and too little water to allow planet-wide settlement. The numbers may only be fractionally outside the parameters, but those fractions will kill these people's children or grandchildren.

The morning passed uneventfully.

The meandering path climbed so gradually that it wasn't until mid-morning, when Karl looked behind him, that he saw that they were over a hundred metres above Salturvatn, which glistened in the sunshine, offering no clue to the danger lurking round its shore.

Bera spoke little, and Karl rode in silence, concentrating on watching for lurking dragons and any other predators Isheimur might hurl at them. But this morning Isheimur's ferocious wildlife left them alone.

The sun was high in the sky when the slope gradually flattened out and then the path forked. Bera said, "Let's allow the horses a little rest. Now we only have two, they'll get no relief from carrying us."

Karl said, "And we can decide which fork to take. They don't seem to diverge much from here, but the fact that there's a fork at all seems significant."

"Don't read too much into it."

Bera rummaged in her saddlebags. "I didn't have much time that morning we left, so I just threw everything in." She grunted. "Hah: here we are." She pulled out battered sheets of coarse-looking grey paper. "I printed some of the Oracle's answers." She smiled at his raised eyebrow. "When I was drudging at Skorradalur, I used to dream of all the places that I could go. It made it seem less like a prison. Whenever things were quiet, late at night, I would sneak onto the Oracle. Sometimes, if I didn't have much time, I'd print its answers and sneak them off to my room." Bera laid the tattered pieces of paper flat on the ground, and smoothed them out.

Karl had an image of her poring over the maps by the light of a candle; more likely by natural light, if his first nights at Skorradalur had been any indication of summer evenings. "Didn't they miss the paper?" Karl smiled to make the question a joke. "I thought that everything was in short supply?"

He may have been joking, but Bera took it seriously. "It's moss-paper, recycled to the point where it's all but unusable. And I made sure that I took the very worst pieces over the years," she said. "And I limited myself to one piece a week." She stared at him levelly. "Do you think that I've only recently become unhappy? You're the excuse I've waited years for, to actually give me the nerve to walk away from Skorradalur."

"Glad to have been useful."

She flushed at the implied rebuke. "It wasn't as calculated as that."

"I guess not," he said, embarrassed at his own gracelessness. *Whatever her motives, she's handed you a lifeline. Remember that.*

"Here's the fork." Bera pointed at the map, all business again. "On one side it leads to a desert, while the other leads up into the mountains. Hmm: it looks a pretty steep path and the mountains are high." She pursed her lips. "We should take the desert path."

"Is it longer?" Karl said.

"It is," Bera admitted. "But it looks less hazardous."

"Desert it is," Karl said.

The afternoon passed without incident.

The night was cold enough that Bera again huddled close to him, although she barely relaxed at all until she slept. Karl wrapped his arms around her; it was only to stay warm, after all. Both suns had shone brightly all day, which was probably why he felt better than he had in weeks, he decided.

The next day Bera said no more when they arose than she had the previous morning. Nor did they talk much as they rode. Partly that was to conserve energy, for talking while aboard a trotting horse required a degree of shouting.

But when she did speak, she seemed more at ease, and Karl realised that he didn't feel the need to chatter. There had been times back on Avalon when he had longed to be aboard the peace and tranquillity of Ship, just as he had longed while away in space to be back with his loveable but sometimes overwhelming family.

Bera seemed also not to feel the need to talk endlessly about minutiae, although periodically she would surprise him with an unexpected question: "Have you ever tasted chocolate?" was one such poser. He had to tell her that at least four worlds claimed to have the secret recipe of true chocolate. Another was "What's your favourite colour?"

"Not brown," was his terse reply as he looked about him, which tickled a giggle from her. For there wasn't much to occupy them on the ride, just hour after hour after unending moorland, hills and valleys, dark greens, blacks, purples and the white of snow sometimes speckling the landscape; but mostly it was every conceivable shade of brown. Tan, russet, coffee, umber, ochre, khaki, buff; everywhere were shades of brown.

Toward noon Bera said, "We're going into one last valley soon, before we enter the desert proper. The lake is called Sofavatn." He wondered at a lake called sleep water, and her next words only fuelled his curiosity: "You need to hold your breath for as long as you can when we pass the waters of the lake."

"Gases?" Karl said.

"Yes," Bera said. "They knock you out. When you're revived – if you come round – you may start raving. If you're left in there long enough, you may die."

"What about the horses?" Karl said.

"They don't seem as badly affected, though I don't think anyone's hung around long enough to research the effects on them of the gases that come off the lake."

An hour or so later, as they entered the valley which was fringed with bushes, Karl fancied that he could see the fumes rising from the waters, but when he asked Bera, she said, "You're imagining it. Or you're picking up something outside my range of vision."

He was about to ask her what the fumes were, then remembered her jibe back at Salturvatn about his curiosity and contented himself with, "I'd love to come back with a research team and analyse it."

She gave him a smile. "I like that. You coming back, I mean." She added hastily, "With others, of course."

"Of course." It surprised him too, that he'd consider coming back. The truth was that when the sun shone, Isheimur didn't seem quite so ferociously alien and unpleasant.

As they neared the lake, Bera said, "Shallow breaths. Yes?"

"OK," Karl said.

When they were close to the lake – barely a few metres from the gleaming green surface – Bera said, "One deep breath, and hold it for as long as you can."

She spurred Taitur on, and Karl did the same with Grainur.

Afterward, Karl was unsure whether she had left it too late to take her lungful of air and inhaled fumes with it, or whether she simply hadn't been able to hold her breath for long enough.

Whatever the reason, Bera swayed in the saddle as they passed the lake-shore, but stayed mounted. But just as Karl relaxed, he noticed the secondary pools – perhaps they were part of the main lake during wetter periods – from which he again fancied that vapour rose from the surface of each.

Bera swayed and toppled into a pool. Karl jumped from his saddle, and whacked each horse on the hindquarters. The horses responded and Karl jumped in.

His boots weighed him down, so he held his hands up, using them to guess the depth, which was about two or three metres deep in places. The water was murky, and for a few horrible moments he couldn't find her. He wondered how long he'd have to hold his breath – his record was nine minutes, but that was in a controlled environment, without the stress of a life-or-death situation.

Then he felt something, and grabbed her under her arms. His heart hammered as he hauled her up, partly from exertion, but mostly from fear that he might be too late.

When he broke surface he just managed to not take an involuntary breath; the days in the lifegel had taught him to better control his autonomic functions.

He waded up what felt like a set of natural steps beneath the water line, onto land. For a moment he froze, unable to decide. Should he resuscitate her here? No, better to get her further away.

Taking the first steps, he staggered, and couldn't help taking a breath. Even that was enough to make his thoughts fuzzy for just a moment. Then he heaved her across his shoulders and tottered up the slope toward where the horses had stopped and were grazing as if nothing had happened. When he reached them, he decided that he'd gone far enough for Bera to be safe, and dropped her onto a clump of lichens.

He breathed out until he was sure that his lungs were empty, then took deep breaths of the feeble atmosphere, until he felt that he would keel over, and gave Bera mouth-to-mouth. Nothing happened, so he tried again. She jerked and yanked her mouth away, thrashing about underneath him, coughing and spluttering.

He pulled away hastily. "It was mouth-to-mouth resuscitation! It wasn't what you think!"

He stared at her through narrowed eyes, studying her for the signs of mania that she'd sketched on the far side of the lake.

After a few seconds her glare softened, but she said nothing.

"What's your name?" Karl said.

Bera frowned. "What?"

Karl said, "What's your name? I need to test that you're not suffering damage, either from hypoxia or the fumes."

"Bera Sigurdsdottir," she said. "I'm fine."

"What colour is that bush?" He pointed at a low, purplish shrub.

"Purple."

"Any tunnel vision?" Karl said.

"No."

"Where are we?"

"Sofavatn. Karl, I'm fine. Look." She stood up and walked an invisible straight line, one heel against the toes of her other foot, then the other way around. She shrugged. "What else can I say? I'm fine."

That in itself worried Karl slightly. Sometimes happiness – or at least quasi-drunken high spirits – and light-headedness were symptoms of hypoxia. And he had no idea of the effects of the gases. Inhalation was a frustratingly inexact science. A dose that could leave one person unscathed could flatten another.

But Bera was adamant that she was OK, and Karl couldn't really argue. He mentally shrugged, and reclaimed the horses, trying not to feel hurt at the violence of Bera's reaction to the mouth-to-mouth.

He led Grainur back to her, and offered the reins.

She didn't look at him but mumbled, "Thanks."

Karl sighed. "I'm guessing that you were raped, Bera. And I am truly, truly sorry for whatever happened."

"I don't want to talk about it."

"But," Karl said, holding up a finger to interrupt. "I can't spend the whole journey guessing what may or may not offend you, Bera. You needed resuscitating."

"You could have leaned on my chest–"

"And you'd have accused me of feeling your tits!"

Still not looking at him, Bera opened her mouth, then closed it again.

"Wouldn't you?" Karl said, making the question as gentle as possible. Then adding, impishly, "Not that there's much to feel. Flat as a pancake–"

"Oi!" She punched his shoulder with her free hand. "That's not true!" She looked down at her breasts. "Is it? I thought I was quite big–"

"Oh, now you're worried about whether your potential rapist thinks you've got large enough breasts?"

Her laugh was close to a nervous sob. Still holding onto the reins, Bera picked at the quick of one of her fingers. "You were right, Karl. But I still don't want to talk about it." Abruptly, she grabbed him in a hug. "Sorry. About…" She released him as quickly as she'd clasped him.

"Don't worry," Karl said. "And yes, they're like bloody melons. I'm amazed even an idiot like you would've missed the irony, even for a moment."

"Bastard."

Karl sniffed. "Typical woman, always has to have the last word."

Bera was silent for thirty seconds. Then, "Yep."

An hour later they climbed gradually to a set of unremarkable foothills. "Not many people come this way." Bera indicated the low brown hummocks, almost bare of vegetation. "So if we run into trouble…"

"And that's different from that last part?" Karl asked, mock-bewildered.

Bera laughed and peered at something small scuttling across the ground, then relaxed. "It's not dangerous."

"But was it edible?" Karl said. "We don't want you wasting away."

"I'll need something bigger than that," Bera replied. She smiled. "Not dangerous and not edible; therefore not interesting – to me."

"Hmm," Karl said. "That sounded like a hint to stop asking so many questions."

A thin cry split the still air, almost too high to be heard, and so quiet that had they still been talking they would've missed it.

"Snawk." Bera shaded her eyes as she peered toward where the cry had come from. "We'll be OK. We're too big for a snawk."

The snawk stooped to the ground in a white blur, moments later rising with something struggling in its claws.

"That could've been our dinner," Karl said.

"The snawk? Or what it caught?"

"Either."

"You wouldn't get much meat on a snawk," Bera said. "And whatever it caught wouldn't be edible, though you can eat anything, it seems."

"Not anything," Karl said with a laugh. "A diet of rock-eater would probably kill me in the end. But the nanophytes will slow the effects for a long time."

They rode on.

Bera cleared her throat. "About earlier…"

"Forget it," Karl said. "It's done."

"No. I just wanted to say… if I could tell you about it, I would. But I can't talk to anyone, without losing control. Not even to you. If I could tell anyone, it would be you. 'Cause I think you're wonderful, Mister Spaceman." She laughed nervously. "There, said it."

Karl didn't answer for a while, but finally said, "Thank you."

They rode on, seeing the snawk again and again.

When they were almost through the foothills they saw a fluttering of wings ahead.

Karl straightened in his saddle and glanced at Bera, but she seemed lost in thought. He decided against asking her about the bird.

They rounded a bend in the path. The snawk sat on the rock. With it was a short, stocky man-shaped being, covered with drab grey fur. The snawk leapt from its rocky perch and flew away.

The man-shape yowled and shrieked.

"Troll!" Bera said, and swore. She kicked her heels into Grainur's flanks and the little grey horse responded.

The troll jumped from the rock and hobbled into their path, but it was moving slowly and they easily rode around it. Something flew past them. Bera said, "Bloody thing's throwing stones at us! I should shoot it, but it'd be wasting a bullet."

From a wide ravine ahead came another series of yowls.

"More trolls?" Karl said.

"Sounds like the rest of its pack," Bera said. "Unless it's a loner, and the pack's presence is coincidence. Considering we share a world, we don't know much about them."

Karl thought of all the times that human societies had fought over resources, particularly when new arrivals came up against weaker resident societies, and was unsurprised. If historical parallels ran true, the settlers would only be interested in eradicating the trolls, rather than learning about them.

"What do we do?" he said, as they neared the entrance to the ravine. Finding an alternative route meant retracing their steps for kilometres – the path had gradually funnelled, offering fewer and fewer exits.

"This." Bera ducked down into Grainur's mane and urged her into a gallop. Karl followed her lead.

In the ravine a half-dozen of the hairy humanoids milled and shrieked. Bera and Karl burst through at such speed that they were gone before the trolls could react.

Once through, Bera allowed Grainur to slow, and stood up straight in the saddle. Karl slowed until he was beside her, watching the steam rising from Grainur's flanks.

Bera beamed. "That won't do our poor horses much good."

"No."

Her grin grew wider. "But I enjoyed it!"

After a couple of minutes of trotting, Karl said, "That's the first time I've seen a troll."

"It won't be the last," Bera said. "We've driven them off our lands, though sometimes a lone troll gets old or sick and will take to raiding the farms. As long as they stick to rock-eaters, we tolerate them. But if they start killing sheep or people, we don't stand for that."

"That one on the rock..."

"What about it?"

"It was feeding a snawk. On blood from his toe. In exactly the same way as Yngi fed his snawk."

"We probably copied it from them," Bera said dismissively.

"Have you ever seen a wild snawk eat?" Karl said.

"I'm sure someone has," Bera said.

"I'm willing to bet that people have seen snawks catching prey, but not eating. Why else would a wild snawk feed on troll blood?"

The land grew drier and harsher as the afternoon wore on; only gradually, but each time they crested a rise in the undulating landscape, the view ahead seemed to include fractionally less scrub than before. And the wind picked up, spinning the bare grey earth into dust-devils. Bera fashioned impromptu hats out of furs, and passed one to Karl; "thirty per cent of your body heat is lost through your head. I should have thought of this before."

Karl perched it on his head, feeling like a fool.

After a while Karl said, "It's a tough life."

"It can be," Bera said, "though it can be pleasant, especially in summer."

"Still, to have survived two centuries of equipment wearing out, forced to endlessly recycle in what amounts to a closed system..."

Bera said, "That's why we hoped you were part of a bigger group. And I think that that was what Ragnar feared: because if such a group did arrive, who would he be to the strangers? Just another local chieftain."

"Why did your people settle here in the first place?"

A radical Icelandic Recidivist Sect was funded by Terraforming Council Grants – it was one of the tactics of escalation that eventually fuelled the Long Night. Loki's interruption distracted Karl, who had momentarily forgotten the other's shadowy presence and that the download would have been listening in. *Loki's here all the time – of course it'll be aware of what was going on.*

Bera was saying, "On the Oracle, that about twenty thousand of them settled here. One man, Asgeir Sigurdsson, led the original group. Enough people felt the same – out of place everywhere else, that our language was being eroded, our customs forgotten, our people's ethnicity diluted – that they were willing to join him."

Karl was surprised at the passion in her voice. "You wouldn't want to leave Isheimur, then?"

Bera reared back as if he'd waved something under her nose, and pulled a face. "Let's find your lost ship first and get a message off to your people."

"What do you want to do, though, if our signal gets us rescued?"

Bera didn't answer immediately. "I thought that… if off-worlders do arrive, that I might be like a link between our people and those off-worlders. But let's take one day at a time. At the moment such thoughts feel as foolish as wishing for wings."

"Don't you ever wish for wings?"

Bera stared at him, and slowly grinned. "Do you read minds?"

"No." Karl laughed. "If you mention it, then it's a fair bet that it's something important to you."

Bera nodded. "Every summer they have hang-gliding championships at the Summer Fair. Women aren't actually forbidden to enter..."

"But they're not encouraged either."

"Too much of a risk," Bera said. "Mustn't lose one of our precious baby-making machines and threaten the colony's future." Her voice cracked a little at the end.

"Do you still miss him?" Karl asked, as gently as possible.

Her face twisted. "Baby Palli? Every single day. I didn't want him when it happened, but when I had him..." She wiped her face then started. "Oh, Freya! You're trying to get home for your own child's birth, and here I am bleating on. Do you miss her?"

"Every single day," Karl said and wanted to reach out and hug her, but held back. She might misunderstand.

Toward the twin sunset the wind dropped. They rode on at a steady canter until the shadows were so deep that the horses stumbled. It was colder than on previous nights. Whether they had climbed higher, were further south or it was just a cold night, Karl wasn't sure, but even he felt it tonight.

Bera sighed. "We'll rest up for the night here."

When she dismounted, Karl realised how much the day had taken out of her. "We need a fire," he said.

"We can't spare any more flares," Bera said, voice dull with exhaustion. When she fed the horses Karl saw that she was shaking with cold, and her teeth chattered.

"It's been a good day," Karl said.

"Has it?" She stared at him, clearly bemused by the sudden change of subject.

"Almost a whole day of sunshine," Karl said, "better for me than a hundredweight of mutton." He had no idea what a hundredweight was, but it sounded good,

217

and Bera seemed to understand. "While we've been riding, Loki and I have been working on something. It'll seem like a magic trick." He looked around. "Not much vegetation or combustible stuff here. Still, we'll get what we can."

Bera busied herself laying out the blankets. "We might as well huddle up," she said. "But no funny stuff – you tell that Loki."

"He's got the message," Karl said, dropping his trousers and squatting over the fire.

"What are you – oh! Couldn't you crap somewhere else?"

"No," Karl said. "Then I'd have to carry it over, and I don't want to dirty my hands."

"So you shit on the fire instead? Why?"

"Primitive peoples often used dung for fuel." Karl pulled up his trousers, rubbing at his burning bladder.

"Yes, but they usually dried it out first, didn't they?" Bera stared horrified at him.

"You'll happily change a baby's nappy." Karl wandered around the horses, looking for more droppings for fuel. "Yet you baulk at this. Anyway, it is dried. Loki and I managed to reprogram the nanophytes to reabsorb the fluid, and divert it. It burns like buggery, and if I did it too often I'd end up with kidney infections and who knows what else, but this is an emergency." He dropped the few pieces of horse-dung that he'd been able to find on the fire, and urinated on them, the fluid glowing in the dark. "Ohhh," he groaned. "That is such a relief."

"It's – hot," Bera said. "I can feel it from here." She shrieked, and clapped her hands. "It's burning."

"Told you," Karl said. "Loki and I had a lot of time to think this one up, and we can't do it too often."

"But how?"

"Two problems," Karl said, sitting beside her. "No, three. The sunlight solved one by charging the nanophytes. The second problem was to get them out of me. I needed to cut myself, or find some other way–"

"Ahhh." Bera grinned in the firelight.

"Ahhh," Karl echoed. "So, once we reprogrammed some of them to migrate and others to combust on exposure to air, we must solve the third problem. If I'm wounded, they replicate to replace any losses. I'm not wounded, but their numbers have dropped to a critically low level." So I'd better not get hurt in the next twenty-four to forty-eight hours, he thought, or I'm in big trouble.

It was only a stunt really. The fire would soon burn out, and he dared not repeat the trick, but it had lifted her spirits.

"Can I have a hug?" Karl said. "No tricks – just warmth."

She draped the blankets around them both, and curled up in his arms.

"Happy birthday," Karl said.

Bera stared at him. "It's not my birthday–"

"Just pretend it is. This is my birthday present to you."

"And wonderful it is, too, you, you clever, clever man."

They sat in companionable silence, arms wrapped around one another, Karl trying not to think of the warm, breathing body curled into him. When the fire burned low, Bera ate her nightly portion of meat and fruit.

Karl said, "I've finally realised what's been bothering me."

"Oh?" Bera mumbled, half-asleep.

"If snawks can feed on both farmers' and trolls' blood, then the farmers and trolls must share the same genetic code, despite superficial differences."

"Don't be silly," Bera mumbled.

"The troll's shrieking," Karl said. "It sounded regular."

"So does any animal's cry," Bera said.

"What if it was more structured than it first sounds?" Karl said. "I can see up and down the visible spectrum. What if they can hear and talk up and down the audible ranges?"

"Don't be silly," Bera said, with a sigh, sounding as if she was reluctantly waking up.

Loki said, *Don't distress her.*

I've no desire to upset her, Karl sub-vocalised. But we can't let her reluctance to face facts distract us. What information can you find?

Loki spent what was hours to the construct – but only seconds to Karl – scanning the jumbled mess of memory that Ship had downloaded.

Then Karl jerked upright, spilling Bera from any last chance of sleep.

"What?" she grumbled.

"Loki tells me," Karl said, "that there's a story. A Pantropist ship, lost sometime around the time of the Interregnum. They were due to seed a world in an adjacent star-system."

"But that's–"

"Seven or eight hundred years ago," Karl finished for her. "They'd have had gene-splicing and some primitive techniques, but even less than you have. If it's true…"

Bera wiped at her face, still only half-awake. "What happened to it?"

"No one knows. That's why it's legendary, and lost."

"Smart-arse," Bera said. "Don't talk in riddles, Karl. What's your point?"

"Your people inadvertently Terraformed a world al-

220

ready settled. That's one of the few things that all hu-manity's factions have forbidden."

"No." Bera shook her head. "No, they wouldn't have done that."

"The trolls are the Pantropists' descendants," Karl insisted. "And the settlers have been killing them."

"My people wouldn't commit genocide," Bera said.

"Not deliberately," Karl said.

"They're animals, no more." She pulled the blanket away and turning her back to him, went back to sleep.

FOURTEEN

The next morning, dust rose in the air above the trail from Salturvatn, mingling with the snow-shower that was petering out in the face of the arid land ahead. Horses' hooves pounded the ground, the posse only slowing when they reached the fork in the path that Karl and Bera had taken the day before.

Arnbjorn, who had been riding at the front, wheeled his mount to face Ragnar. "They've taken the desert route, by the look of these tracks."

Ragnar said to Orn, "You have the maps?"

Orn produced a sheaf of papers bound in animal-hide, and opened them up, flicking through them until he came to the one they were looking for. "The trail that way leads up into the mountains, crossing over Eifelheim. The way they've taken goes through the desert."

Ragnar peered over Orn's shoulder, then held finger and thumb against the map, measuring distance with his digits.

"If we follow them, we'll overhaul them," Thorir said.

"Shut up," Ragnar said, ignoring the set of his son-in-law's jaw.

"I hate to take his side–" Bjarney said.

"Then don't."

"But he has a point. We have spare horses, so we can rotate them. We'll wear them down."

"But they have the best three horses," Ragnar said.

"Two now," Bjarney said, referring to the remains of the horse-carcass on the beach. How long it had been dead had sparked a fierce debate amongst the party. "We'll catch them."

"In time," Ragnar said. "Which we don't have: they had a two-day start on us, and we don't know that they haven't been riding from first light to last thing at night. Sending our casualties onto Valhalla may have cost us another day. They could be three days ahead now, and we'd never overhaul them before they reach Jokullag. No, we'll take the other path." He pointed at the distant mountains, hidden by the sleet.

"It's more hazardous," Bjarney said. "They didn't name those mountains The Roof of the World for nothing. Avalanches, altitude sickness – come on, Ragnar, why look for trouble?"

Several of the others joined in the general muttering. Arnbjorn nudged Thorir. "I'd keep silent."

"I know," Thorir said. "You'd think they'd recognise the danger signs. His darkening complexion, the way his jaw clenches."

"What about a compromise?" Bjarney said, scratching at the bandage on his arm – the legacy of the snolfur attack. "Why don't half of us go with Ragnar and the others stay on this trail? We might even be able to catch them in a pincer movement."

"And how," Ragnar drawled, oozing contempt, "do we keep in contact to co-ordinate this pincer movement?" Ragnar snorted, ignoring the flush spreading across Bjarney's face. "Even if I was prepared to divide our stores – and I'm not – which leaves those in the other party without food or bedding, dividing our numbers risks greater attacks from predators. Think how many more might attack if there are fewer of us, according to your logic."

"I don't like it," Bjarney said.

"We're not here because you like it," Ragnar grated. "I don't care what you like."

"We're not your sons, Ragnar, nor your bondsmen," Orn said. "You'd be advised to remember that. Bjarney may accept your lectures, but your tone's offensive."

Ragnar rode across slowly and stared at Orn silently, until Orn looked away. "Don't ever threaten me again," Ragnar murmured into the other man's ear. They could have been lovers exchanging small talk, but for the spine-cracking tension in their posture.

"I wasn't threatening you," Orn said, equally quietly.

"Men have fought duels over less than what you've just said," Ragnar murmured.

"Men who were liquored up," Orn said. "Are you so obsessed, so bloody psychotic, that anything less than fawning obeisance warrants a duel?"

Ragnar took a deep breath. Orn was half-right, he realised. Ragnar had to convince them, this time. Moreover, Orn had had the sense to keep his mouth shut while Ragnar worked it out for himself. He took another deep breath, and another, felt the tautness of his body ease a fraction. The other man even had the sense to look impassive, and not smile or give any expression that Ragnar might misconstrue.

Ragnar took one last rasping inhalation, looked around at the others and shouted, "Right lads, we'll make this easy." He drew a line to the right of the furthest man. "Those of you want to go home, step across this line. Bear in mind that this utlander has abused our hospitality, stolen property and endangered our community. I'd declare him outlaw, but for the added humiliation that announcing it through the Oracle would bring on us. So, those of you who want to go home, take a horse each and ride for your lives. You can survive a few days without food, and there's loads of water in the brooks once you get past Salturvatn."

No one moved.

"None of us want to go home, Gothi," Bjarney said. "We're all agreed that they've put us at risk, and they must face justice. But that doesn't mean that we should behave like madmen."

Ragnar said, "So it's that decision that's the problem?"

Bjarney nodded.

Ragnar said, "The next time a snolfur attacks you, should I take a vote about how we kill it?"

Bjarney's laugh was an indignant grunt. "That's not the same!"

"Isn't it?" Ragnar said, studying each man in turn. "At what point must I say, 'OK lads, you elected me leader, but it's a big decision, so let's put it to a vote,' eh? You either trust my judgement or you don't." He walked to the other side of the men away from the first line, and drew another, parallel to the first. "Who actually wants to follow me in bringing these fugitives to justice?"

To Ragnar's surprise, Thorir was the first to step across. Ragnar nodded, and clapped his son-in-law's shoulder. "Thank you, son." Thorir looked like the farm cat after it had been at the cream, and Ragnar wondered why Thorir was so keen. What do you want, apart from buttering me up?

One by one, the others followed suit.

"Good," Ragnar said, all smiles again. "Then it's the mountains."

The group resumed their journey.

Ragnar drew alongside Orn's horse, "We're in the equivalent of a battle situation, friend. Those among his men who refuse to follow the commander in a battle are called mutineers. Remember what every army does with mutineers. So I wouldn't go upsetting me while we're up there beneath the vault of heaven; altitude always makes me crab-assed. Understand?"

"Oh, I understand you, Ragnar," Orn said. "Better than you think."

Ahead of them, along the path not taken, Karl and Bera rode steadily into the high desert. All around them the world was still, like an animal waiting for something to happen. Looking around him at the gritty surface, Karl realised how arid an environment it was – they seemed to have almost slid into it, it had changed so slowly and gradually. It's like a sponge, he thought. No matter how many snowflakes fall, the ground just seems to suck the moisture in. He cleared his throat. "Do we have anything with which we can line a pit?"

Bera had said little all morning, answering direct questions with a nod or a shake of the head. But she said with a similar throat-clearing noise, "We should have something. Why?"

"Good. We might be able to use it to distil water overnight." This was the first morning that they hadn't seen anything – a stream, a pond or a brook – from which they could refill the half-dozen plastic bottles which they'd taken during Bera's lightning raid on the pantry at Skorradalur.

Thank cosmos she did, Karl thought. 'Cause I'd never have thought of it.

The streams had allowed them to refill until now. There had been no water last night, but he'd been so distracted with lighting a fire that he'd missed the significance of it until now.

"Will water from a still be enough?" Bera said.

"I don't know." Probably not, though for a time he could use the nanophytes to synthesise water from whatever else he could ingest. But the long-term damage to them – and therefore to him – would be even greater than it already was from the continual reconfiguring that he was forcing on them. Even from the limited changes he'd made – but more significantly from the recent loss of the nanophytes he'd extruded the night before – he felt light-headed, despite the hazy sunshine that occasionally peeked through.

You're not a superman, Loki reminded Karl. *You have greater strength than her, and you can adapt by cannibalising your future. But I have no desire to see you die and leave me trapped – or worse: I assume that if you die, I die.*

Probably, Karl sub-vocalised. He said aloud, "Anyway, it may not come to that. There's probably a stream just over the next hill." He was unsure who he was trying to convince the most, Loki or Bera – or himself.

They rode on in companionable silence.

Loki suggested, I have no way of verifying your claim that there's water ahead. All my information is based on the planetography available at the time the project started.

Since then, the Formers would have slammed a rain of comets harvested from the outer system into Isheimur's surface, raising decades-long dust clouds to trap the world's warmth, to generate carbon dioxide, and with the water freed from the comets to irrigate the specialised plants they had seeded to oxygenate the atmosphere.

Karl muttered to Loki, I'm unsure whether we're doing the right thing now, given what we can infer from the troll. If the *Winter Song* does turn out to be in working condition, given the current tension between Pantropists and Terraformers, activating its beacon will either bring Pantropists – who may ethnically cleanse the planet of Bera's people – or Terraformers who might consider hiding the evidence as the least worst option, and eradicate the trolls.

Karl wished that he had could be sure that he wasn't weaving together a tapestry of theory based on little more than watching two snawks feed and a string of coincidences.

They rode on and about an hour later, Karl noticed a dust-cloud about a kilometre away to their right. It paced them but came no closer, and after a few minutes vanished behind a pillar of rocks.

Karl looked up and saw the black shadows above the dust-cloud, even as he heard Bera's hiss of in-drawn breath.

Karl would have liked to have asked what they were, but sensed that now was not the time. Out of the corner of his eye, he could see Bera sat forlorn on Teitur, shoulders hunched.

It suddenly struck Karl how young she was. Women on Avalon could look equally girlish yet be old enough to be her mother. He kept forgetting that the women here had no Rejuve. She's little more than a child.

"Bera," Karl said. She didn't answer, and he called again. When she looked up, she stared at him as if he was a stranger. All his sympathetic words sounded incredibly patronising, and turned to dust on his tongue. She didn't speak. Her look said "What?" eloquently enough.

"Tell me about dragons," Karl said instead, changing his mind about asking for information – it seemed better than offering what she might consider fake sympathy. He ignored the roll of her eyes. "Was that what that dust-cloud was?"

"Dunno," Bera said.

"Why the sharp intake of breath," Karl said, "when you saw those black shadows in the sky?"

"Dauskalas," Bera said.

Loki added: *Death harvesters in Anglish*.

"They're bad?"

"They're unlucky," Bera said. "They live off carrion. We don't often see them; they're supposed to be the harbinger of ill-omen."

Karl nodded. At least he had got her talking, even if it was no easier than quarrying stone by hand. "What about the dragons?" he said. "I haven't seen any more since the one we saw down by the lake yesterday." He was happy to play dumb if it kept her talking.

"That's because I wouldn't have expected one to be there anyway." Bera's tone carried a whole saddlebag full of attitude. "You'd normally only expect to find them at higher altitude, so why that brute down at Salturvatn was where he was – I dunno."

"Oh," Karl said. He thought again of the heat-signature of the dragon they had encountered. "Are they hot-blooded?"

Bera nodded. Karl could sense her frustration; he guessed that she wanted to talk to him, but not about dragons. But he wasn't sure if he was right, he couldn't be certain whether he'd correctly deduced the subject, and even if his assumptions were justified, he was unsure of how to broach it; he had to leave it to her. For the first time it struck him how little experience he had in dealing with women so much younger than his group. Get used to it, he thought. If the baby's a girl, then this is what she'll be like in a couple of decades. The thought was incredibly wearying.

"They're warm-blooded, unlike lizards," Bera said again, wearily. "You obviously want a lecture – want me to be your companion." She flushed. "I mean the human version of this companion you've talked about."

Is that what you meant? Karl wondered.

"Not knowing about these things is frustrating," Karl admitted. "But see it from my point of view. I'm surrounded by things I don't understand–"

"Which you're not used to," Bera said. "Perish the thought that you might have to learn something, that you might have to wait more than a fraction of a second – no, you have to have it now." He made to protest but she waved him silent, and took a breath: "They breed in large numbers, but most of the young are eaten by adults. As they reach medium size they become those same predators of the young, but when they grow to full maturity they then switch to a diet of snawks, rock-eaters and other local fauna. Luckily for them – and us – they don't eat sheep."

"You know that?"

Bera pulled a face. "How do you prove a negative?"

"You count sheep, of course," Karl said. "If sheep survive encountering a dragon – other than running off a cliff in fear or something – you can assume that dragons don't usually eat them."

"Exactly – assume. What about the times when the whole flock vanishes? And there's a dragon around? Or other times? We don't have time to do extensive research, not like your people. We just guess."

"So the settlers don't treat them as a pest."

"No. We have enough pests to contend with. And they're actually quite pretty creatures."

"Hmm," Karl said. "I've yet to be convinced of that."

"Being caught between one and a flock of havalifugils has that effect." She smiled for a moment, and then realising that she was supposed to be mad at him or something, her face resumed its former stony expression.

"Thanks, Bera," Karl said softly. "You must feel that I sometimes treat you like a walking version of the Oracle."

Bera shrugged.

"But it isn't just impatience: I have to do that in case anything happens," Karl said. "The more I know, the more effectively I can react if we get separated."

"I know," Bera said, her eyes glistening, and Karl realised what the problem was.

"But it can't be nice, questions, questions, questions all the time."

Bera shrugged again, but this time her lower lip trembled.

"Is there anything you'd like to ask me? Anything at all?" Karl said, reaching out slowly, and when she didn't flinch, letting his open hand rest over her clenched one. Even when she opened hers, his vast mitt dwarfed it. "It may seem like I consider you a walking encyclopaedia, but I never forget that you're a person."

Most of the time they had ridden in silence, or had a few shouted conversations, but there had been time to talk; he wasn't sure whether she wasn't interested, or didn't know where to begin. Again she didn't ask, so instead he began to talk. "I live in Merlin Tower, on the 109th floor, overlooking the Lake of the Lady Lyonesse. Our city Avalon floats about fifty kilometres above the surface of planet Avalon. Down on the ground the wind is almost supersonic. The pressure will split your skull like a melon, and it's hot enough to melt lead. We go down occasionally when the remote mining goes wrong."

"You – you live in a flying city?"

"A floating one," Karl said with a smile, enjoying the stunned look on Bera's face. "The city has vast bags full of helium which are lighter than air, so that together with nullifiers – which provide a sort of limited anti-gravity – the city sits up in the clouds."

One of the suns – Gamasol or Deltasol, Karl couldn't be sure which – broke through the clouds, and he turned his face to the rays.

"You remind me a bit of a lizard yourself," Bera said, and for the first time that morning, she smiled, but it was tinged with sadness. "The way you bask in the sunlight."

"It's a rare treat for me," Karl said, smiling back. "We don't often get sun like this on Avalon. Delta Pavonis is usually hidden by thick cloud, but when we do, it's like we're turbo-charged – pow!"

Bera giggled, but again there was that look. "Aren't you cold?" she said.

"A little today, when the nanophytes' priority is re-plenishing their numbers, but mostly they regulate my temperature for me. Anyway," he shivered theatrically, "I can stand a little chill."

They rode on, silent again.

"Why so sad?" Karl said.

"I was thinking of how easy it is to think you're just a strange-looking man, desperate to get home…"

"Which I am."

"Why? Is there a ceremony, when the baby's born?"

Karl shook his head. "This is such a rare event, who would want to miss it? We've waited years for this. And I miss them all. They're my family. I would have thought you of all people would understand that."

Bera said, "I do. And that's why it's so easy to think that you're like us. But then you say or do something so different that it rams home that you really are alien.

You're probably so used to people from other worlds you don't think twice about it, but for us it's different."

"And now you're realising that you've trusted your life to a man who could say or do anything, no matter how strange," Karl said.

She shot him a look. "You're doing that mind-reading thing again."

"Naw." Karl smiled. "It would make life much easier if I did. No, but I've had all morning to think about things, like how tactless I was. For which, I'm sorry. I didn't mean to cause offence by implying that your people are murderous savages." Even if I think that they are, he thought. Shouldn't be so judgemental. These were Norsemen, quick to anger and feuding. Maybe something had gone wrong at the beginning, or maybe the trolls were so devolved that they were no longer properly human. Maybe, maybe, maybe...

Bera smiled. "It seemed like next that you'd say the snolfurs are intelligent, or the rock-eaters."

"I didn't actually say that the trolls are intelligent." Karl tried to remember what he had said. "Only that they might be."

"But you're not going to finish this journey without finding out, are you?" Bera said, again with that sad smile. "You're like a man probing at a tooth with his tongue." She said in a sing-song voice, "Why is the sky grey? Why do the trolls make those noises? " She smiled to make it a joke, but Karl knew she was wrapping serious points in a sugar-coat of humour.

"You've found me out," Karl said.

"Say they are intelligent?" Bera said. "What then?"

"It depends on a lot of things."

Bera blatted. "I've been around Ragnar long enough to smell bullshit non-answers. What does it depend on?"

233

Karl picked his words carefully. "One is whether we even manage to send a mayday from the *Winter Song*. Which in turn depends on whether it exists. And who answers our message."

Bera gazed at Karl for a full thirty seconds. "How does it depend on who answers?"

Karl said, "See, I'm not the only one who asks questions."

Bera wasn't distracted, but repeated, "How does it depend on who answers?"

"Humanity being what it is," Karl said, "we've splintered into countless factions. Most of them disagree with all the others about something, and occasionally it escalates into open conflict. The Terraformers and the Pantropists fundamentally disagree about colonisation. But they often agree about other things with their opponents, while disagreeing with their own people."

"So sometimes Terraformers and Pantropists fight among themselves?" Bera said.

"Sometimes," Karl agreed, thinking of the attack on Ship that had stranded him here.

"We have a third major faction that aren't – strictly speaking – possibly even human any longer."

"Oh, for Vili's sake," Bera groaned. "Could you make it any more confusing?"

"You want me to explain it or not?" Karl said. "Or do you want to just stick with 'it depends' as an answer?"

"Go on," Bera said.

Karl continued, "Artificial Intelligences are like your Oracle, but it's like comparing Alphasol with a bedside lamp. The Ayes, as we call them, are the inevitable result of ever-increasing computer power. They went off to odd bits of the galaxy and now do whatever odd things they do, but get blamed for everything, from supernovas to disappearing ships." Karl laughed, but without humour; "To be honest, their presence is probably the one unifying thing that stops humanity from exterminating itself."

"So they're among the good guys?" Bera said.

Karl made a non-committal gesture.

"Among both sides, you have the Radicals. They still use Ayes, but those models are of limited power, and anyone who uses them is viewed by suspicion by every other faction, including less extreme Radicals. Both sides are less clearly cut than their opponents and their own politicians claim.

"At the extreme end of the Radicals are the Ultras who are so enhanced they're almost cyborgs; the less extreme Traditionals use nanotech and Rejuve to extend their lives to four, even five centuries. Still, they're superficially indistinguishable from either more mainstream or even the most fanatical Traditionals – the Mayflies, who've outlawed any kind of body-mod including Rejuve, birth control, anything."

"Which group do you belong to?"

"Depends who you ask," Karl said. "People often think that they belong to one group, their opponents say another. I think I'm a Traditional, but many Traditionals would claim I'm a Radical."

Bera groaned and held her head theatrically. "It's so complicated!"

Karl shrugged. "It's a big place, space. Why do you think I was reluctant to answer?"

"And the point is?"

"That depending on whether they're Terraformers or Pantropists will determine how they respond, but not how far they're prepared to go," Karl said.

"Would they bomb us?"

Karl thought of the genetically tailored plagues that had sterilised Atheling's World but said only, "They're unlikely to do anything to damage the planet in any way, Bera."

It seemed to satisfy her.

Karl said, "It would help if we could establish whether the trolls are sentient, or I've jumped to conclusions."

"You'll probably get a chance before too long," Bera said. "This area is thick with them since we drove them away from human settlements."

Within an hour she was proven right, when they stumbled across another troll.

The horses were maintaining the same steady trot that they had kept up since stopping for a noon-day rest, albeit slower than the first few days after leaving Skorradalur.

Karl was wool-gathering, distracted by Loki's searching Ship's downloads for the lost Pantropist ship; records were hazy, many of them lost in the Long Night. One mentioned that the ship may have been a colony-ship from Terra's Central Asia region, that there were several hundred people on board and genetic material for a new colony. It was no more conclusive than any other information.

He was startled out of it by Bera's shout of, "Karl! Look out!" Before he could react, a short, hairy form reared up in front of Grainur, which startled, jumped back.

So did the troll, which broke into a run.

"Hey! Hold on!" Karl called. He spurred Grainur on and set off in pursuit, swiftly overhauling the troll, which limped badly. Karl sub-voiced, Search your memories for languages that would have been used on those colonies first settled from Central Asia. Find me anything. Absolutely anything!

The troll turned and ducked down a horizontal chimney. Shrieks and yowls rattled in Karl's ears, and when he felt something like the tickling of tiny fingers on his chest, almost on instinct, he slid his hearing up several frequencies into the ultrasonic.

Immediately the troll's yowls took on a more structured format, and he heard the sound pinging off his chest.

Sonar, Loki said to Karl. *Ideal for finding one's way in a blizzard. Perfectly adapted to local conditions.*

"Just give me words for 'friend'," Karl muttered. He was aware of Bera and Teitur behind him at a safe distance, but still blocking any chance of the troll escaping – except for the mouth of the chimney it was hemmed in all sides by high, sheer walls. Karl dismounted. He had a blade that was longer than a knife but too short to dignify with the name of sword tucked into his belt, but he held his hands open. "Come on!" Karl urged.

Loki replied with one word, then another, a third and fourth, all separated by a second or two. Karl faithfully repeated each word slowly and clearly, also leaving a couple of seconds for a response. He couldn't pitch his voice any higher than normal hearing, so he hoped that the troll would understand.

The troll didn't answer. Instead it leaped at Karl with opened hands and bared fangs.

Karl managed to get hold of one hand from which claws had unsheathed, noticing almost without thinking that the troll's breath was sweet, with a minty undertone.

The troll's free hand swiped at him and despite his swaying back, its claws raked Karl's cheek with a glancing blow. Cursing, he released the troll's wrist and jumped back.

It advanced on him with windmilling arms – trying to claw him again – so Karl had to step back. The troll lunged again, gabbling and hissing and shrieking.

In turn, as he slowly gave ground, Karl ran through Loki's Kyrgyz, Tatar and Uygur vocabulary, whatever the download could provide him with. None of the words for "friend" elicited any reaction from the troll. Maybe it's so mad that it's not listening, he thought.

"Draw your sword!" Bera screamed. "Thor's sake, Karl, don't get yourself killed! Stick the damned thing if need be, and we'll find another one for you to dance with!"

The troll kept advancing, and Karl reluctantly drew his sword. He held it to the troll's throat and for one awful moment thought that it was simply going to march onto the blade.

Then it stopped.

"Friend," Karl repeated in several more languages, running through Kazakh, Turkmen, Uzbek, even Russian, and however outlandish it seemed, Mongolian. When he said the word in Kazakh, he thought that he detected the faintest of motions, as if the troll was startled but trying not to show it – but it did nothing else. When he ran out of languages, Karl tried Kazakh again, convinced that the troll was studying him. It was hard to tell with the long grey and brown fur that all but hid its eyes.

"Friend," Karl said for a third time, and half lowered his sword.

The troll said something, equally slowly, and as clearly as the fangs permitted.

Loki translated for Karl: *Not friend.*

Karl insisted, "Friend." His heart hammering, his mouth dry, he said to himself, Here goes. This may get me killed. But there seems no other option. Shaking with nerves, he took a long, deep breath and lowered his sword all the way, then carefully, never breaking eye contact with the alien, he put the sword on the ground.

FIFTEEN

Ragnar's men had reached Heimurpak – the Roof of the World. Snow mantled the mountains, even on a sunny day like today, when the suns' reflections shone in their eyes with the blinding precision of a mirror attack, making every footstep a lottery. Beneath the snow was only bare rock; nothing lived up here, although dragons slid across the mountain-tops from time to time.

Ragnar suspected that the others felt as unwell as he did. He'd slept badly, listening to them coughing throughout the night. Every few minutes he tasted the lamb he'd eaten for breakfast, sitting heavily in his gut. His head felt as though Thor had been walloping it with his divine hammer, and his heart was racing just from the effort of sitting in his saddle.

Mountaineers called this altitude – 7,500 metres above Isheimur's sea level, where the air was as thin as the same height on Old Earth – the Death Zone. If they could descend quickly by nightfall to a lower altitude and more oxygen, they'd feel better in a day or two. If they didn't, they were dead. It was as simple as that.

Past the highest ridge now, the horses slid down a zig-zag path that narrowed and steepened until reaching a canyon. The riders milled around in the last open square of rocky outcrop before dismounting.

Ragnar hated this feeling of weakness. He'd fought all his life, half the time against weakness itself. He let the anger take him over and drive him. "Each man tie a rope around his waist," he shouted, "so that if one falls, the rest can hold him."

An argument broke out about whether to loop the rope through the horses' saddles, but Ragnar frowned, and after a moment's hesitation, vetoed it. Even that little thought hurt his head. "Each horse... weighs more than two men," he said. "A falling horse... will... take us with it."

He led the men and horses along a narrow path beside a sheer six-hundred-metre drop, the wind tugging at them with icy little fingers, and the rushing water of the stream below no louder than the susurrus of the wind through the windmill's blades back at Skorradalur.

Ragnar struggled to find oxygen with each rasping breath he took. Worse, any misstep risked their toppling off the narrow ledge, so they could only inch along.

Several times Ragnar heard the scrape of something on stone. He didn't like to look up, because his horse bumped into him, but the alternative was to not know whether there was a dragon there, which was worse. Each time he paused and looked up there was nothing there.

Dragons wouldn't attack, but the adolescents were curious creatures and might easily trigger an avalanche. That they weren't there implied that the rocks above the men were so unstable they might simply fall at any moment.

Still, they had almost reached safety when disaster struck.

* * *

241

The next few seconds were the longest of Karl's life.

The troll knelt. Even though its eyes were shrouded by fur, its rigid posture indicated that it never stopped watching Karl for a moment.

It picked up the sword.

Karl stopped breathing.

In its other hand it took the blade, and proffered Karl the hilt. As he took the sword, Karl breathed again. The troll said, "Friend." Part of the second syllable was on the threshold of Karl's hearing, but the meaning was clear.

The language has drifted, Loki said. *It would make sense to fully utilise their greater vocal range. If over ninety per cent of human communication is non-verbal, and blizzards block visual intercourse, then the humanoids would need to extend their vocal range to fill the void.*

Karl called to Bera, "Have you been watching this?"

"Yes." Her voice was high and tight, with fear, he guessed, of the challenge to everything she believed true.

He almost said, "Tell me he's not sentient, now," but held his tongue. Better to let her decide in her own time. "Get some rock-eater out of the saddlebag, will you?" He motioned the troll to follow him, miming eating – hoping that the troll wouldn't think he meant for Karl to be dinner – and they emerged from the horizontal chimney.

"It's limping," Bera called. "It's hurt. That's when they turn man-eater."

I'm going to turn control over to you, Karl muttered to Loki. Talk to it. It's definitely speaking a variant of Kazakh.

There was a moment of dislocation akin to a starship docking with one of the giant relays that hangs in every system's fold-space entry-point, and you sensed Karl's

242

lingering suspicion. After what happened before, perhaps it's even understandable. "Can you understand me?" you asked the troll in very slow, precise Kazakh, enunciating every word clearly. "If you do, speak to me. The more you talk, the more I understand."

Bera had rejoined the waiting horses. You trudged back to her, deliberately slowly. "Rock." You pointed at one. "Foot. Sword," pointing at where you'd re-sheathed it.

When you both reached the mouth of the chimney, your back spasmed with tension. If the troll was going to try anything, now would be the moment, when you reached open ground and it was no longer trapped. But it simply watched you point at each object that you passed.

"Horses." You pointed at the waiting Grainur and Taitur, who twitched at the troll's scent. Bera made soothing noises as she stroked the latter's mane, and the animals resumed eating their dried grass from the feed-bags. "Woman." Bera raised an eyebrow but said nothing, only watched the troll, who had stilled.

The troll opened its mouth. Ultrasonics pinged off Bera and the horses, who both took a step back. The troll turned and said in Kazakh a single word: "*Demons.*"

Ragnar reached a shelf and paused for the others when he heard a shriek from the other end of the line and saw the rear horse's hindquarters slide over the edge of the precipice.

Arne Einarsson was leading it. He tried to hold on, but all that happened was that the fool went with the horse. Ragnar's throat tightened as Arnbjorn, who was next to last in the line, also fell. Luckily Orn had the presence of mind to loop the rope round a large rock or the rest of them would have followed, one after the other.

Arne wasn't the brightest man that Ragnar had ever employed, although he worked hard and sent kronur home to his family in Nyttakranes every month, so it wasn't surprising that the soft-headed sod had tried to save the horse and nearly doomed them all.

For a moment Ragnar considered shooting him where he hung, but the group hauled Arnbjorn and the luckless Arne in, their shoulders threatening to pop from their sockets, veins bulging blue on their temples, until both men stood, shaking, at the end of the ledge.

Arne stood moaning in pain, clutching his arm where it hung limply from a dislocated shoulder.

"Your supplies went down with that horse." Ragnar tried to think straight, using anger to fuel his internal fight with hypoxia. At the icy tone of his voice, Thorir and Bjarney both stepped back. "You'll get none of the other's rations."

"I'll manage somehow," gasped Arne, holding onto his arm, snot and tears glistening on his face.

"How?" Ragnar said.

At the one word Arne looked up, and saw his future in Ragnar's eyes. Arne swallowed. "Do it," he said.

Ragnar took a deep breath and pushed him out into space. Perhaps it was his imagination, but the man seemed to hang there for a micro-second, before plunging into the icy waters below.

"The man was a lackwit," Ragnar said. "If we must starve then we will, but not because of him." The men stared at him. "We can't carry anyone!" Ragnar roared. "You all had your chance to go home. You didn't take it. He would have dragged us down with him."

"When does it stop, Gothi?" Arnbjorn whispered, white-faced and wide-eyed. "When?"

* * *

The troll emitted a contented belch and picked rock-eater from its upper right fang. Although it gave the impression of being at ease, and it was impossible to see its eyes clearly through the mantle of fur, you sensed that it wasn't quite as relaxed as it tried to look, perhaps because every so often you felt a touch, as faint a spider's web on the back of his hand, from the troll's voice.

"Good?" you said in Kazakh.

The troll's head dipped a fraction of a centimetre in assent.

You pointed to yourself, and hesitated. Who were you? Finally, accepting that Aye downloads were perhaps too complex to explain in Kazakh, you said, "Karl." Pointing at her, you said, "Bera."

"How do you know that it won't think my name's the word for woman?" Bera said.

She's joking, Karl thought, for your benefit. See the twitch at the corners of her lips? Maybe she's starting to come to terms with the idea that the trolls are intelligent.

"Because that isn't the Kazakh word for woman." You said the right word, and the troll stiffened. You repeated the process of naming yourself and Bera.

The troll pointed to its chest. "Coeo," stretching it to three syllables, "Koh-ay-oh."

"I hate to interrupt this getting-acquainted session," Bera said, "but besides giving away rations that we can't spare, we're still only on the edge of the desert. Shouldn't we move on?"

You shushed her and gestured to Coeo to raise its foot, and slowly, it complied. You peered through the fur, hissing a sharp intake of breath at the evil-looking gash on the sole of its foot that oozed pus, and was surrounded by bright red inflammation.

It wasn't an "it" at all, of course, and you pointed to it, asking in Kazakh, "Man? Woman?" As you did so, you fingers fumbled, and you realised that you were tiring. You need to do this, you thought at Karl. It needs more dexterity than I have.

As Karl retook control of everything but your mouth (and how awkward and clumsy it all was, like a recovering stroke-victim re-learning motor control), Coeo said slowly, "Man." He said something else, but with his fangs and half of the sentence pinging up toward the ultrasonic, it was barely intelligible as speech at all; it was no wonder that the settlers and their forebears, with no great desire to look for sentience where none was obvious, missed all the signs.

"Pass me the medicines," Karl said to Bera.

Bera complied, but reluctantly. "We can't really spare these," she said.

He dressed the foot, which must have been agony to walk, let alone run upon. Karl thought, If it weren't for the snawk incident, we'd never have seen the troll's humanity either. Or maybe he would have; his curiosity about the Aye ships was what landed him here in the first place, and was only matched by his desire to fit things together. Take over talking again, and the same awkward transfer followed.

"Repeat last word," you said in Kazakh, "Slowly, very, very slowly."

"As if you are... ?" The last word was lost.

"As if I am... ?"

The troll said, "Child."

"Exactly. Big, stupid child."

The troll giggled. It was half ultrasonic, but there was no mistaking the timbre: it was a giggle. It said, "Thank you. For food. Helping." It pointed to its foot, that Karl was wrapping slowly, carefully in a bandage lined with a paste made from Isheimuri herbs and Norn-made penicillin. "You are different. From Coeo, and from Bera."

"How?"

"Skin thicker – sound bumps off it, not through you as much as Bera."

"I'm from the sky." You had Karl point upward at the heavens.

Coeo stiffened. "Lies!"

Karl shrugged, and tied off the end of the fabric. You said, "Where you think I'm from? Different, you said."

"Before, when men came from sky, in time of our…" Coeo said, Karl's lingua-weave struggling to cope with the variation of pitch and unfamiliar vocabulary, but finally settling for "grandfathers."

"Grandfathers. Ancestors?"

"Yes. In time of ancestors, rained rocks. Many, many Coeo-people die. My… ancestors try to talk with invaders, but they kill Coeo-people, so we hide whenever we can. Now you say you from sky. You make it rain rocks? Come to kill my people?"

"No," Loki said. "Karl lost, want to go home, leave this place behind. Forget all about it." The first part was true, but Karl doubted he would forget Isheimur.

Coeo didn't answer.

"Why you alone?" Loki said. "No tribe?"

Coeo lifted his foot. "Coeo… unable to be part of tribe. No catch food, no herd animals," the adapted man said. "Is the law – sick must be cast out, so the tribe can survive. If they live, they can join a tribe. If they die, no waste."

Darwinism taken to extremes, Karl thought. But what happened to compassion? Mercy?

Karl stood and re-took verbal control. "He's sentient. He has language, although ordinary human hearing can't hear half of it. If you weren't specifically listening for it, you'd never know. And your people have been too busy surviving, I guess, to go looking for answers to questions you've never thought of."

Bera packed away the remaining medicines. "He's naked! How civilised is that?"

"Don't confuse sentience with civilisation." Karl laughed. "Anyway, who says he's naked?"

"Well…" Bera drawled, pointing at the troll, as if he were answer enough.

"The web-men of Tau Ceti IV grow tools from their own silk extrusions," Karl said. "Why not grow your own clothes? What are clothes but manufactured fur?"

Bera looked bemused.

Karl said, "The climate is perfect for them; and he's almost certainly been tailored that way. I'm willing to bet that under that fur he has genitals; maybe they retract. He'll have been adapted to filter out the local toxins. Maybe excrete them…"

At Karl's prompting, Loki scanned his data.

Karl said, "Ship's readings, limited though they were, indicated that Isheimur has more oxygen and carbon dioxide than when the project started. I'm willing to guess that you don't often find them in the lowlands?"

"No," Bera admitted, "and almost always beyond the tropics."

"Isheimur's warmer now – it's probably too hot for them. And with carbon dioxide being heavier than air, the lowlands are probably – no!" Karl snapped his fingers, remembering the dead troll in the valley that Ragnar and his neighbour had argued over. "Not close to! The lowlands are toxic for them."

"Great theory," Bera said. "Show me proof."

They mounted their horses. Coeo stood watching them. Karl thought that he looked strangely forlorn. "Can he hunt with that injury?"

"Probably not," Bera said. "But we can't afford to feed him."

"We'll compromise," Karl said. Take over the vocals, he told Loki.

You said at Karl's prompting, "Coeo come with us? Can show us food and water is?"

Coeo said, "Where you go?"

"South," you said.

Coeo nodded assent, cautiously.

Bera looked sceptical.

"He's adapted," Karl said. "He knows how to survive."

"He's hurt and on foot. He'll slow us up."

"Then we'll redistribute the weight, and ride more slowly. The horses could probably do with a rest."

"A rest? Hah, I don't think so!"

"Come on, Bera. The Asians were small as a people compared to us, and the Pantropists weren't going to gengineer for size – you said that small is better for cold-weather survival. I'd guess he's barely one-metre fifty tall, and if he weighs sixty kilos, my name's Ragnar."

Bera sighed. "OK. But I may yet change my mind."

Karl had you explain their plan as they dismounted. Coeo shuffled on his good foot. "Where go? Find more Coeo-people?" He sounded worried.

You shook your head, and tried to explain exploring a frozen lake in the desert, with half the words beyond your host's vocal range. "We move quickly," you said. "Bera-people chasing us. Want to kill us."

"Coeo knows them," he said. "They chase Coeo last spring. Too near their pets."

"He thinks the sheep are your pets," you said. "That's understandable; he's probably never seen people eating the sheep." You said to Coeo: "They want us – only us. You come with us, you in…" Even Loki had to hunt the Kazakh word they needed: "Danger."

"Coeo know danger. Danger Coeo's brother."

They finished repacking most of the supplies onto Taitur, and Karl and Coeo mounted Grainur, whose ears lay flat at the troll's presence, but who didn't baulk.

They spent a tense, taut afternoon riding through increasingly arid scrubland, between tall, cactus-like plants that rose like miniature watchmen every hundred metres or so, each plant garlanded with hydra-headed flowers on snake-like necks that followed their movement.

The wind picked up, flaying them with icy whips.

Although the afternoon passed uneventfully enough, Bera never took her eyes off the troll, and was clearly ill at ease. Coeo was equally watchful of her, although the troll seemed to have decided that Karl was more trustworthy. Karl in turn watched them both, to act as a referee should their mistrust erupt into open conflict.

The afternoon was silent, mostly, although every noise, the smallest of stone-slides ahead of them, once the crack of a cactus's arm falling off, was met by a startled jump from Bera.

Her frustration was made worse by Coeo stopping them periodically, dismounting to dig up a tuber, a root, once even a small burrowing animal from the ground. He proffered each to the humans.

"We're losing too much time," Bera grumbled the third time he did it.

"It's probably payment for our company, or the rock-eater meat," Karl said, grinning at the insects buzzing around Coeo; Isheimuri insects ignored humans, which were as deadly to them as most Isheimuri plants were to the settlers, but in this case Coeo's adaptation had a down-side. Still, the troll seemed unconcerned. "Be gracious," Karl added.

Bera declined each offering, but Karl took a little. Almost everything he tried had the same bitter metallic taste, apart from one plant that tasted similar to the minty smell on Coeo's breath. He managed to eat most offerings, both as thanks and so the nanophytes had more fuel, but the cacti were so foul that even Karl spat out their flesh after a single bite. Coeo chomped happily on them between foraging for fresh offerings.

"You far from home," Coeo said, when the humans paused to swig water. "You are–"

You said to Coeo, "Last word means?"

"Not allowed in land," Coeo said. "Thrown out."

You asked Bera. She said, "Outlaws."

"Yes, outlaws," you told Coeo, explaining the word. Coeo nodded emphatically, and you added, "We seek a holy place, where something fell from the sky."

Coeo grew rigid. The troll jabbered, his voice often sliding into the ultrasonic. Much of it was unintelligible, but words like "bad" and "holy" occurred often enough for Karl to understand. "He thinks we mean sacrilege," Karl explained. He shook with suppressed excitement, and leaning across, squeezed Bera's hand. "But there is something there!"

Bera smiled, but it was a forlorn effort.

As they rode Loki tried to explain to Coeo in very basic Kazakh that they meant no harm. Quite the opposite – that Karl's life depended on finding the shrine, and that when they found it, Karl intended to ask for the help of the spirits that Coeo implied infested the place.

"This is why you... outlaws?" The Isheimuri word sounded odd coming from the wide, fanged mouth. "Because you respect people-spirits?"

It took Karl a moment to realise that by people, Coeo meant the trolls. We need to stop thinking of them as trolls, Karl told Loki.

As long as we call them people to Coeo, it's a good shorthand, Loki said. And if you start calling them "the people" to Bera, she's going to ask aren't her people "people" too?

OK, Karl muttered, accepting defeat, and said to Coeo, "Yes."

"Who you talk to?" Coeo said.

"My companion," Loki said, pointing to his head and the space around it.

"Your...?"

Loki repeated the word.

"Ah," Coeo said, repeating the word but at a higher, almost ultrasonic pitch.

"Can't say word," Loki said, pointing to Karl's larynx.

"Your companion is...?" Coeo said.

"Has no body," Loki said. Karl hoped that the language drift wasn't so great that it had corrupted too much of the language.

"Ah," Coeo said.

Over the next five minutes it became clear that Karl's invisible bodiless companion was a far more potent persuader than their protestations of goodwill, convincing Coeo that Karl was a sort of holy man accompanied by spirits.

"I show you way," Coeo finally said.

Bera was horrified when Karl told her. "You mean we've a companion who may turn man-eater if he gets hungry enough?"

"Did you consider him a person two hours ago?" Karl said.

"What makes you think I consider him one now?" At Karl's stare, she made a conciliatory gesture. "That stunt with the sword?"

"Stunt? *Stunt*?"

"He could've been trained as a pet..." At Karl's glare,

Bera added. "I'm not saying that he was, but he could have learned the action."

"So why should he think of you as people?" Karl continued, "Doesn't the Oracle have anything about them?"

Bera shrugged. "Only what we've discussed. They're humanoid, but no more than gorillas and chimpanzees on Old Earth, and creatures on other planets."

"Hmmm," Karl said, thinking of the snow-men on Brindle's polar regions. "Given how far they've regressed, and how long both sub-species have been not interacting in any positive way, there are two explanations, both of which have some nasty implications."

"Why do I get the impression that I'm not going to like this?" Bera said.

"Either the Formers knew about the *Winter Song* before they came here, in which case they should surely have guessed at the trolls' origins–"

"Which are?"

"That they're genetically modified descendants of the ship's crew, or the gene bank, or both," Karl said.

"I can't believe that they would have been able to keep that a secret, if they'd found out about it."

Karl was glad that she wasn't outraged at the suggestion that she was descended from the perpetrators of genocide. Then he saw the muscle working in her jaw, and wanted to hug her for her self-control. "The other possibility is that there has been communication between humans and Coeo's people."

Bera sighed, and looked troubled.

Karl said, "What is it? You've thought of something."

Bera took a deep breath. "There are tales, no more than myths, but…"

"Go on," Karl said.

"Men who spent too long in the upper pastures, so they end up half-crazy with loneliness, hearing voices in the mists. Or who claim that the rock-eaters talk to them. Solitude affects some people, driving them to try the native plants. Most will simply kill you, but a few induce hallucinations before they make you go blind, or mad, or both."

"Some of the myths mention trolls?" Karl said.

Bera nodded. "And the *Winter Song* is a local myth, not something imported from Norse legend."

Karl paused, while the download checked. "Loki says you're right. There's nothing in Norse myth like the *Winter Song*."

"The *Winter Song* was poetic enough that people just took it as a version of our own... fall from grace, I suppose you could call it."

"A metaphor," Karl said.

"Exactly," Bera said, looking troubled.

Coeo had been quiet all this time, as if realising from their voices that whatever they were discussing was serious, and needed to be resolved, but now he leaned forward in the saddle and pointed toward the south.

They followed his finger. The sky was stained brown on the horizon as if the land was rising up to meet the sky. Minute by minute the hazy wall spread upward and further and further across the skyline.

"Dust storm," Coeo said.

"What do we do?" Bera said, looking around for shelter – but for all the broken ground, none of the rocks was large enough to even shelter her, and she was the smallest of them. "What's he doing?"

Coeo had dismounted from the horse and was peering at the ground. Karl felt the thrum of vibration from the troll's sonar.

Then Coeo remounted behind Karl.

"I lead. You follow," Coeo said, kicking his heels into Grainur's flanks. She set off at a gallop toward the wall of dust, which had already spread across the sky, followed by Bera on Taitur.

She shouted, "There's another of those little clouds of dust we saw earlier! But you're headed straight toward the dust storm – is he mad?"

Karl thought, Maybe he knows something we don't, and we should trust him. But he didn't answer, instead concentrating on staying on the horse, which was flying under the repeated digs of Coeo's heels and looked at the wall of darkness coming steadily closer.

Karl wondered how long they had. He got his answer a few minutes later.

Flecks of grit stung his face. Coeo pantomimed slowing the horse down and Karl pulled Grainur back, slowing her to a trot.

Coeo jumped from the horse and studied the ground, as if looking for something. The dust cloud had dissipated, it seemed, and the troll headed slightly to the left of where Karl had seen it, ahead of where it had last been headed.

More grit stung his face. The storm was worsening, the light fading by the minute. Karl nudged his vision toward infra-red, and looked for Coeo.

There! And beside him, a warm boulder, maybe a metre and a half high. It was built like a small truck covered with closely-linked scales and glanced at Karl with doleful eyes before turning back into the strengthening wind, the sand bouncing off its shaggy face. Karl realised from the vibrations that Coeo was crooning to it.

"He's sheltering in the lee of an adult glamurbak!" Bera shouted, when they got close to it. "I never thought I'd ever see one of these in real life!"

Waved in by Coeo, they sheltered behind the glamur-bak, which was slowly settling itself onto the ground. A resonant snore split the air.

"Coeo sing them to sleep," the troll said, breaking off from his inaudible lullaby, and there was no mistaking the pride in his voice. Karl wondered whether the ability had been bred into the trolls.

It would make sense, Loki said.

Coeo pointed at the glamurbak's tail. "Good to drink," he said. "Only drink with new moon."

"That's every five weeks," Bera interpreted when you translated for her. She seemed to share none of Karl's queasiness at the thought. "Doesn't it harm it?"

Loki translated the question.

Coeo said, "With adults it grows back, but smaller. So there is limit to how much can be cut off. We wait, cut off tail when storm passes, not make him move now."

They hunkered down, Bera trying to settle the horses, which she turned so that they were hind-end into the storm. Bera crawled back on hands and knees, spitting sand, her eyes streaming. The wind, now a howling gale, lashed them mercilessly, digging into their noses, eyes, even their mouths.

Karl opened his arms and Bera snuggled into him. He stroked her hair, making soothing noises.

PART THREE

SIXTEEN

"Don't move," Coeo said.

Karl froze. "Coeo says keep absolutely still," he hissed, unsure if talking counted as moving.

Bera obeyed. In the last ten days Coeo had slowly, almost imperceptibly, earned their trust.

Nine days earlier, twilight supplanted afternoon. The storm gradually blew itself out until the wind dropped enough for Karl and Bera to crawl out from the shelter of the glamurbak's armoured body, Karl dragging a piece of plastic from their stores that he'd worked on throughout the storm-stolen day.

Bera said, "What's he doing?"

Coeo scraped at the ground until a host of mouse-like creatures spilled onto the surface, scurrying back and forth faster than an unenhanced eye could follow. Karl snatched one and passed her a naked, blind, writhing creature.

"Sandurlund," Bera said. "There'll be a nest nearby."

As swift as one of them, Coeo's hand swooped and came up with one of the little mouse-like creatures.

With a flick he tossed it into his mouth. Coeo caught another and offered it to Bera, who shook her head. "I like my food to have stopped moving." Karl also declined, and shrugging, Coeo ate it.

"These must be the workers," Bera said, watching them spilling out onto the sand. She answered Karl's raised eyebrow with, "I've seen them on the Oracle."

"I wasn't thinking about that." Karl failed to stifle a grin.

"What then?" Bera said. "What?"

"I was just thinking…" Karl said.

"Uh-oh," Bera interrupted, "that sounds dangerous."

"That you're as much an info-junkie as me. But I haven't had the Oracle to answer all my questions." He dodged the sandurlund that Bera threw at him.

Behind them, the glamurbak staggered to its feet. Snuffling, it scuttled across the ground, with Coeo following. "We mustn't get separated!" Bera grabbed the horses' reins and dragged them with her. Karl goggled at the caravan of glamurbak, troll, Bera and horses; then followed them. As abruptly as it had started, the glamurbak stopped.

Bera dodged a cascade of sand from its scrabbling forelegs. "I think it's digging for tubers. The sandurlund nest among them."

Coeo emitted an excited squeak and juggled a tiny, wriggling shape, before tossing it into his mouth.

"Are we staying here tonight?" Karl asked Coeo.

"Maybe, maybe not."

Karl rolled his eyes but laid out his piece of plastic, burying the edges beneath sand and tiny stones. "It'll act as a still, trapping the moisture in the air."

Bera snorted. "If there is any."

"There's always moisture, even in a desert," Karl said.

They laid out their sleeping-furs in the near-darkness

and ate their dinner of cold meat, trying to ignore the glamurbak's grunting and the tiny squeaks from the sandurlund nest. Normally Karl would have had dozens of questions, but his brain was fogged from exhaustion.

Still, sleep would not come.

Just as he was finally drifting off, Bera said, "Are you asleep?"

"Yes," Karl said.

"With anyone else, I'd think they were joking. Is that Loki?"

Karl sighed. "No, it isn't. I was joking. Sort of."

"You mean you were asleep. Sorry."

"Only half-asleep," Karl murmured. "Don't worry. You can't sleep either?"

"Nah. The grunting may have stopped, but that damned thing is such a noisy eater."

The furs separating them lifted, and she backed into him, wrapping his arm around her. Neither of them had washed for days. The nanophytes normally sterilised his sweat glands and otherwise kept him clean, but he sensed that they were so swamped with the various jobs that he and Loki kept assigning them that he probably stank as much as she did.

Actually, she didn't stink. He found the slightly rank, musky perfume of her body oddly attractive. Without thinking he licked the stale sweat off the side of her neck, enjoying its saltiness.

"No funny stuff," she murmured. But even as she spoke, she wriggled her backside further into his crotch, and he had to will the nanophytes to divert the blood away from that area. "Just like brother and sister," she murmured sleepily, but covered his hand with her own smaller one and pressed it to her breast.

They must be very friendly to their brothers and sisters, he thought with a wry inner smile, but said nothing. Incest almost certainly was a problem in every small isolated community on Isheimur.

It was at quiet times like this he missed Karla, Lisane and Jarl most. His doubts that he'd ever see them again floated up like the bodies of dead leviathans from the depths.

He might have to spend the rest of his life on this cold, drab world, the last effects of the Rejuve wearing off so that he had maybe fifty years instead of three or four hundred, trying to fit in among people who never had the time to lift their eyes from grubbing out an existence.

He must have sighed, for Bera slurred, "Wassamatter?" and stroked his hand.

He said, "Thinking about what happens if this doesn't work. If the *Winter Song*'s disabled or isn't there..."

"What you do?" Bera mumbled.

"Don't know," Karl said.

She turned slightly, looping one hand around to stroke his face, laying her own cheek against his. "Is OK. We'll get you home. Somehow." Her voice broke, and he felt tears on her cheek.

"Hey, don't cry." He wiped her face and licked his fingers, savouring the salt. "What's all this about?"

"You'll either be gone or stuck here and miserable," Bera said. "Don't know what's worse."

"You could always come with me," Karl said.

"Your life isn't for me," Bera said. "Look at you, then at me. I'd be the ugly primitive freak in your world."

"You're not ugly," Karl said.

"Plain, then," Bera said.

"Are you fishing for compliments?" Karl said, grinning in the darkness. "How about, your hair is dark as a raven's wing, your eyes limpid pools, your skin like softest satin?"

Bera sniffed, and wiped her nose. "Freya, but you're good. No wonder the other women wet themselves when you arrived."

"Did they?" Karl said. "I didn't pay much attention to those fools. I noticed you, though." She's a young girl; you shouldn't play with her affections.

"Flirt," Bera said, giggling. A moment later she sighed. "I really like you, Karl."

"I should hope so," Karl said. "I'd worry about someone who trekked across the planet with someone they didn't like. And for what it's worth, the feeling's mutual."

"No," Bera said. "I mean I really, *really* like you."

"Oh," Karl said. "Oh." He wondered what he should say next, and decided on honesty. "I have to remind myself about six times a day that I'm married, you know. I do try–"

Bera shushed him with a finger to his lips. "That doesn't matter, you stupid man," she said. "You're married there, not here. If that was the problem, you could have had me the first night. But much as I want to be with you, I can't." She took a deep, ragged breath. Karl felt her heart pattering beneath his hand. "Even talking about it... I can't put a sentence together, my mouth goes dry, I choke. Ever since the baby..."

It was Karl's turn to hush her. "Then we'll carry on as we have been," he said, "rather than change things and hurt both of us. Now go to sleep."

To Karl the night seemed endless, but every time he listened, Bera's breath was regular and rhythmic. About midnight the night suddenly lit with a silent green flash. There was a moment of white light, colder than sunlight but twice as bright, then it was gone. Coeo squalled, but Bera slept on.

For about twenty minutes the sky was lit by intermittent green flashes, and more rarely the white ones, as the weapons found their target. Karl watched the battle rage across the heavens, and could have wept with frustration, but he kept still, and Bera slept on, blissfully unaware.

The battle ceased at some point, and later the wind dropped. Coeo and the glamurbak ceased their bickering, and Gamasol rose in the eastern sky.

Now the same sun was setting behind loaf-shaped foothills, and on the nearest of them, outlined against the beauty of the red-purple-streaked sky stood a line of twenty or thirty humanoids – Karl had finally stopped thinking of them as trolls.

"Wait," Coeo said.

Karl put his hand on Bera's arm, wishing that he could shield her.

Coeo dismounted from behind Karl to a cacophony of sonar pings and shrieks from the waiting humanoids, and strode toward their line with hands outstretched and open. "To show they're empty," Karl muttered.

For the longest two or three minutes of Karl's life, Coeo argued with the other humanoids, too quickly for the lingua-weave to keep up, their voices dissolving into a buzzing blur at times.

Coeo motioned them to dismount and approach. The other humanoids milled round their horses, some making appreciative noises, others less so, some verging on scornful. Their Kazakh ancestors were horsemen. They may still have an atavistic love of horses.

In response to an interrogatory burst Karl said, "Speak slowly and clearly."

From the humanoid's air of authority, Karl assumed that the questioner was their leader. "Why you here?" it repeated.

"We seek Godsfall –" Karl gave the site the name Coeo referred to it by "– to pay respect."

"You are not fake-fur?" Karl guessed that the humanoid referred to the settlers' habit of wearing fur.

"I am a..." Loki struggled for the word, "castaway. Lost, learning the ways of this world." At his mention of "world" the humanoid stiffened, but didn't speak. "I am alone, but for my companion."

"Your mate?"

Karl hesitated. What do I say? "Yes."

"She has left her people to be with you?"

"Yes," Karl said. "The others fear us, hate us. Would kill us."

There was a sound like a hissing kettle that Karl realised was laughter. "That sounds like the fake-furs," the chief said. "Come."

"What about the horses?" Bera said. "We need to feed them."

"Wait, please," Karl called.

The horses were in pitiable condition – they had been losing weight throughout the journey. While they ate, Bera brushed them down with her hands, crooning. The humanoids watched intently. Karl emptied one of their precious water bottles into the material they used each night as a still, and the horses nudged each other to get at it. It was gone in seconds. "Shall I give them more?" Karl said.

"No," Bera said. "It's more important that we get there than they do; if the worst happens, we may yet have to kill them and drink their blood." Karl stared, and Bera turned on him a gaze suddenly ice-cold. "Did you think this was a stroll in one of your parks?"

Karl didn't answer. He had badly underestimated how hard it would be. If he couldn't fly to where he wanted to go on Avalon, he sent a remote. Walking and riding were sports to be played for an hour or two, not this bone-grinding marathon that left him permanently on the brink of exhaustion and aching so deeply that he couldn't remember what it was like not to ache.

To take his mind off his aches, as the horses finished their meagre feed he asked Loki, "Could the Formers really not have known that the humanoids were sentient?"

Possible, Loki said. *The settlers now have no satellites to fly-by, just the remnants of ground-based stations, and for all its aridity, Isheimur is a world often wreathed in storms, whether snow, or dust. The humanoids are probably the origin of wraiths and shapeshifter legends.*

"That's now, what about then?" Karl growled, ignoring the startled look from the nearest humanoid, and Coeo's explanation of "spirit friend".

The Formers would have had the capability, if not the inclination. They'd have focussed on what needed doing to adapt the world. Indigenous wildlife was something to be ignored or eliminated, not studied. Don't forget, they were men and women on a mission.

"So they may have known, but suppressed it?"

Or they never noticed. We may never know. Is the difference relevant?

Coeo's touch reminded Karl that the horses had finished. He and Bera led them through a maze of twisting ravines into the foothills.

"Caring for the horses was good." Coeo walked beside Karl. "Won you much goodwill. Our people had such beasts, but we lost them when we fell from heaven."

"That's why you take them from the farms? Not to eat?" Karl said.

Coeo let out his hissing laugh. "Never! We love them."

Karl decided not to point out that in stealing the horses Coeo's people were condemning them to a slow death; the humanoids wouldn't be the first to kill that which they loved.

They entered a natural amphitheatre that was sheltered from the ever-present wind. Groups of smaller humanoids rested beneath animal-hide sheets strung between boulders. *Women and children*, Loki said. A few rock-eaters nuzzled at the ground for plant-life.

"They aren't migrating?" Karl said.

Coeo said, "They live here. Guard the way to Godsfall."

At a signal, one humanoid separated from the others and launched into a foot-stamping dance. Others marked out a square by drawing in the thin sand covering the rocks.

"You wrestle," Coeo said. "If you win, we travel onward."

"If I lose?" Karl said.

"We die."

Karl took a deep breath. "Agreed," he announced in Kazakh.

The humanoids answered with more whistles and shrieks. Bera looked horrified at the sudden commotion.

"Two falls wins," Coeo said, pointing to Karl's shoulder blades. "You must hold your enemy to the ground to the count of five. If either of you leave the square you stop – but if you try to escape that way, is a fall to him. No holding fur."

Damn, thought Karl. There goes one advantage. He accepted the glamurbak tail passed to him for refreshment, and chewed it. The sponge-like tail was almost all water, but to him it tasted of congealed fat.

His opponent stepped into the square and Karl paused.

The humanoid wrestler was a giant, almost as wide as he was tall and nearly Karl's height. Karl mirrored his opponent, settling into a crouch, wondering how he was supposed to get hold of the sumo-humanoid without clutching fur.

He tried not to think of failure. It wasn't just his life at stake, but the others' as well.

He reached for the giant, who faster than thought had Karl in a grip and wrestled him to the ground, to shouts and yells from the crowd.

On three, Karl managed to wriggle free and using all his strength, tip his opponent over. But he couldn't keep hold without clutching fur.

"Stop!" shouted the chief, who was refereeing.

"You crossed the line, is why," Coeo called.

Karl sneezed, his nostrils and mouth full of the strange scent of the humanoids; like Coeo his opponent smelled of musk and mint and something else cheese-like, but in his case it was almost overpowering.

Karl turned, and was suddenly flat on his back. "Five!" The referee counted before Karl could blink, it seemed. One fall down.

The next time Karl grabbed an ankle, but his opponent somehow flipped him again and the count was on four and we're going to die–

He put everything into flinging his opponent off.

Karl's opponent landed just inside the square, stunned or winded it seemed, not moving. Karl flung himself on him.

"Five!" shouted Coeo. "You're one fall each!"

Karl lurched to his feet, the yelling and stamping from around them almost enough to break his eardrums.

At the restart Karl's opponent still seemed stunned. Karl managed to grip wrist and ankle and tip him over, and transferred all his strength into pinning the struggling, writhing humanoid down.

"Five!" Coeo screamed. "You are the victor!"

"You'll live." Ragnar patted Thorir on the shoulder.

"Frostbite," Thorir said. "What an idiotic thing to happen. I thought I'd checked the water-bottle was sealed properly." He kicked a stone into space and cursed. "Bloody thing leaked in the night, all over the furs."

They were a full two kilometres below the Death Zone, and Ragnar knew that the cumulative effects of hypoxia and the false comfort of being "safe" often lulled travellers, making them sloppy.

"If we take the two smallest fingers off, you should be OK," Orn said.

"Lucky it's not your sword hand," Ragnar pointed out.

"It could be worse." Arnbjorn lifted his booted foot. Trenchfoot from permanently cold, damp footwear had cost Ragnar's son his little toe. Unable to walk without losing his balance until they could fit a prosthetic back at Skorradalur, he had to ride one of the few horses that hadn't fallen, or been slaughtered for food to replace their dwindling supplies.

"Do it," Thorir said through teeth already gritted.

Needles always made Ragnar a little queasy, which had amused his wife when she was alive; "A man happy to chop off a man's leg, but who can't bear a little needle," she'd laughed when he'd admitted it to her.

So he studied the harsh beauty of the mountains while Orn injected precious penicillin into Thorir's hand to halt the spread of the infection. Seconds later, he winced at the choked-off scream that followed the thud of Orn's axe.

The others packed away their furs, and Orn his medical equipment. They wolfed down breakfast and resumed their grim march. Ragnar's men spoke little, preferring to save their breath, which had to be hauled into their lungs in thimblefuls ready for the icy trudge.

Ragnar found it hard to stay angry with Karl; even at this lower altitude, it still cost too much energy. Lift one foot; put it down; lift the other; put it down in turn; repeat the process. So the hours passed through the morning. The world narrowed, to a snow-covered path through the jagged-toothed rocks puncturing the aquamarine sky.

Even a metre either side of the path was beyond his mental horizon at the moment.

So though the attack that followed should have been as predictable as the sunrise, it took them completely by surprise.

Morning in the deep desert: the silence was broken by a pig-like squeal.

Bera sat upright, blinking at the light. "Dauskalas," she mumbled, her breath steaming in the freezing air. Shielding her eyes, she squinted up at black bat-like shapes cartwheeling in the sky. Belatedly she realised both that she'd allowed the furs to fall away, and that Karl was studying her bare breasts where they goose-pimpled.

He stifled a yawn. "Nah, it came from ground level." He added, "Aren't you cold?"

She stared at him. He looked up and met her gaze and she felt heat, down below. To ease the tension, she grabbed her top and pulled it over her head. "Not now." She almost added, "You're not interested anyway, so why worry?"

They had slept against one another for warmth these last few nights, and while she wasn't sure that she could yet bear to have him actually inside her, she had wanted him to want her. His limpness against her backside had been like a slap to the face.

Coeo squatted, offering them the now near-daily piece of glamurbak tail, raggedly cut into three. Bera took the furry stump, picking out pieces of the scales that covered the animal. It was better than dipping into their meagre supplies.

She glanced at Karl and burst out laughing.

"What?" He wiped his chin, stared at his hand. "Oh, it's only blood from the tail. And you can talk."

Bera groped among the meagre Kazakh vocabulary that she'd picked up from Karl. "Thanks," she said to Coeo.

The humanoid mumbled acknowledgement around his mouthful of tail.

Three days had passed since Karl had bowed in response to the humanoid chants of "Ul-lah! Ul-lah!" taking the acclaim of the victor. "It's a corruption of something from an old Kazakh religion," he told Bera afterward. They had stayed the night with the humanoids, eating and drinking barely enough of the celebratory feast not to give offence.

Still, Bera had suffered stomach cramps in the morning.

Karl checked the still and fished a drowned sandurlund out of the water. "It'll do for the horses." He added, "I'll load them when they've fed." He dug out the plastic sheet, and carried it gingerly over to them.

They wasted no time making tracks. When they had left Skorradalur they had travelled over a hundred kilometres a day. Now they covered barely half that. They were slowing day by day, as their horses grew steadily thinner and weaker, despite their eating Skorri's rations. So there was little time to waste. Bera knew Ragnar was somewhere. He wouldn't let them get away.

Throughout the morning Karl asked several times what was bothering her. He sensed that something was wrong. He was sensitive – she had to grant him that.

She had all but managed to overcome her reluctance to be touched. She'd been on the verge of guiding his hand down across her stomach the night before, but she couldn't make herself beg, and his obvious lack of desire had been humiliating.

He joked with her, he flirted with her, he slept with her – to keep warm.

But he didn't want her. That much was clear. All her fantasies of him – slippery skin against skin, lips seeking lips, of straddling him, taking him in her mouth, being taken by him – left only ashes in her mouth. She wasn't sure when she'd fallen in love with him, but fool that she was, she had. And he didn't want her. She was crossing Isheimur with a man to whom she might as well be made of wood.

So when he asked her several times what the matter was, she told him about the horses. She wasn't lying, not exactly. Their fate did bother her.

When it came, it was entirely unexpected.

It was near noon, the twin suns high in the sky, almost warm despite the lateness of the year, their altitude and the high latitude. Karl – shirt off – was deep in murmured conversation with Coeo. Bera dozed in the saddle.

He and Coeo pitched forward.

Grainur's screams split the stillness as her riders fell from the saddle. The ground had collapsed beneath her, revealing sandurlund diggings.

Bera leapt from Taitur, knowing what she would find before she landed. The grey's forelegs were broken, and Bera felt as if her heart would burst with grief. "I'm sorry, old girl," she whispered, her vision dissolving. Her faithful Grainur deserved better reward than to spend her last moments in agony.

Bera thrust out her chin, defying Karl to offer sympathy. She grabbed her rifle, brushing tears away. Karl looked away, but she wouldn't. She lined up the barrel. "I'll see you in Valhalla, lovely."

The shot echoed across the featureless plain.

As it faded away, she took out her knife. "More food for us," she said, her laugh shaky. "The gods know we need it."

Karl took a knife and helped her butcher the carcass. "We can re-pack the bags so that everything fits into one."

Bera nodded, licking chapped lips. They never seemed to have quite enough moisture now, no matter how many glamurbak Coeo caught, and Bera wasn't sure whether her constant headaches weren't linked to trace elements in its tail. "We need to drain her blood into the empty bottles," Bera said, "and drink whatever we can."

"Good idea," Karl said. When he'd packed everything into the remaining saddlebag, he took the last flare and placed it in the carcass. "We should give her a proper funeral."

"What?" Bera frowned. "No, no time. We still have to skirt those hills –" she indicated a purple stain on the horizon "– and we should keep going for as long as possible."

"You ride Teitur," Karl said. "Coeo and I can walk. His foot's better now, almost completely healed. So let's wait an hour or two. We'll keep going into the evening."

"No," Bera said. "We go now."

Karl didn't answer immediately. He sighed. "Look," he said, "even in the time we've been travelling, I've grown fond of the horses, and it seems wrong to just butcher her and leave her where she is. I thought that it would be a mark of respect to have a little..." He tailed off at Bera's look. "Yeah, it's a lame idea," he said. "Let's go."

The foothills grew so slowly that Karl couldn't be sure at what point they changed from shadow to substance.

Coeo had started to limp again after a glamurbak mother nursing her offspring had objected violently to his presence and side-swiped him.

"According to the Oracle they don't breed often," Bera had said with a certain satisfaction as she swabbed where the scales had scraped him raw. "So Mama Glamurbak will nurture Baby G for many years. It tends to make them a little over-protective."

"There speaks a mother," Karl said. "Exactly how much time did you spend quizzing the Oracle?"

"Far, far too much, according to the others," Bera said, without looking up.

Karl sighed. "Until that wound heals, no more glamurbak hunting. Even if it makes us dependent on our water-bottles, and what we get from the still."

They stopped, and Bera laid out the maps. "If we went over, rather than around, the hills," Bera said, outlining with her finger, "we could cut maybe half of the week to ten days it'll take to get to the lake. But even then, I don't think that we'd make it."

Karl was tempted to argue, but one look at their physical condition stopped him.

Instead Coeo beckoned them. "Come!" he called in Kazakh, then astonishingly repeated it in passable Isheimuri.

Bera stared at Karl. "You've been teaching him, as well as him teaching you?"

"Yep," Karl said.

Coeo stood before a narrow crack in the rock wall. He suddenly disappeared.

"Do we follow?" Bera said.

"He hasn't led us wrong so far," Karl said.

"Maybe he's been waiting for his moment."

"You really think so?"

Bera shook her head. "No."

They followed Coeo.

The air was markedly warmer in the tunnel. Karl smelled sulphur. The walls were damp.

Teitur, who had shrunk to little more than skin and bone, licked the wall gratefully, his tongue rasping along the rocky surface.

"It's getting darker," Bera said. "We have a torch in here some – ah, here it is!" A cone of light cut into the darkness and Bera gasped. "Are these troll drawings?"

Karl had Loki ask the question.

"No," Coeo said in Isheimuri, then switched to Kazakh: "The Others." He made what was clearly a genuflection.

"Others?" Karl asked.

Karl had learned to read Coeo's body language. The humanoid looked uncomfortable. "Others. Not like Coeo, or you. Or her." He indicated Bera. "They can look like any of us."

"Where are these others?" Karl remembered Bera's stories of mysterious shapeshifters.

Coeo shook his head. "Gone." He turned away, indicating that the conversation was over.

Loki said, *It implies that the shapeshifters were here before even the trolls, in which case if the shapeshifters are intelligent and not extinct, then the Pantropists committed an involuntary offence by landing here.*

Maybe, Karl sub-vocalised, neither group should be here. If the stories are true.

He said to Bera, who was staring at him with raised eyebrows and a "What was that about?" look: "Coeo hinted that he thinks that they're painted by shapeshifters. Oh, and he considers us as being like him. Isn't that progress?"

Bera's "Hmm" was non-committal. She followed Coeo down the corridor, hanging onto a hank of his fur, the humanoid's sonar pinging off the walls.

The subterranean path must have run for several kilometres; after a while it brightened, and when they reached it they saw a crack no wider than Karl's hand in the tunnel's ceiling. Karl guessed it ran all the way to the surface, but it was too narrow to test.

After that there were similar cracks every few hundred metres, through which light could shine, not enough for Bera to switch off the torch, but it did alleviate the stygian gloom outside the torch-beam.

About a kilometre later they reached a cavern bright with daylight. "Water!" Bera gasped, but then flinched when she touched it. "Damn! That's hot!" She cautiously filled some of the now-empty bottles.

When they had filled them all they resumed, across a narrow ridge that ran right across the cavern, dividing the pools up as if it were artificial. Karl had seen too many natural formations that looked man-made to make assumptions, but he kept thinking of the Others, as Coeo had called them.

Every so often one of the bubbling pools would spit. Coeo was protected by his thick fur, but Karl and Bera both hissed whenever the water found a gap in their clothes.

They were near the far side of the cavern when Bera stumbled and nearly fell.

Coeo moved faster than Karl would have believed possible and caught her, but they wobbled on the ridge, and toppled forward.

Coeo put his hand down on the ridge, and Karl heard him hiss, "Hot," and snatch it away.

"You OK?" Karl called from behind.

"Watch your footing," Bera called as they stepped onto the cavern floor.

When they were all clear, Bera dressed Coeo's scalded hand.

"What's the Kazakh for 'I'm very grateful'?" Bera said, then repeated Loki's translation.

"He says," Karl translated back, "that it's nothing."

The spear that was hurled at Ragnar missed him by half a metre, but vital seconds were lost while his befuddled brain registered what it was. But instinct took over and when the trolls charged, he had just enough wit to draw Widowmaker.

The trolls must have outnumbered Ragnar's men ten, even twenty to one, but fortunately there wasn't room for the enemy to spread out. Arnbjorn had his rifle, while the others chose to use bows so the trolls fell in huge numbers before they reached the humans, who kept advancing along the path as they fired their weapons.

Ragnar preferred to hear the thud of tempered steel biting into troll-flesh over girly weapons like bows and rifles, and even though the trolls carried spears as long as his arm, he knew that he was a match for any one of them. He had cut three down before the creatures retreated in headlong flight.

Only then did the significance of the trolls using tools hit him, and for a moment his world tilted. "They're using weapons," he said, in wonderment.

When the last troll had fled, Ragnar turned to the others and saw that they had lost Bjarney. Ragnar had known the man who became his second tenant-farmer since before Hilda had been born. It was like losing a brother. Ragnar chanted three verses in Bjarney's honour, but his heart wasn't in it, and for the first time, he wondered on the wisdom of chasing the utlander.

But the chase had a momentum of its own, and later all such thoughts were forgotten.

They rounded a bend in the path and looked out across Isheimur. There across the plain, gleamed white, a vast frozen lake.

They still had one pair of glasses from their supplies with which Ragnar surveyed the lake. He couldn't be sure even with magnification, but he thought he saw the shrine jutting from the ice.

SEVENTEEN

Karl and the others entered the tunnel on the far side of the springs. This tunnel wasn't lit by the fissures leading to the surface, so they journeyed into darkness. Coeo led, his sonar thudding off the walls and floor, which was regular enough for them to move briskly without fear of stumbling. Bera held on to a hank of his fur, and Karl held on to her backpack with one hand, leading Teitur with the other.

Karl had never feared enclosed spaces, but without the fissures to ventilate the tunnel it felt hot and clammy, so that sweat trickled down his back, his chest, even his face. Sulphur wafted from somewhere, mingling with the other – unclassifiable – mineral smells.

The darkness stifled conversation; Karl found questions dying unasked in his throat, as did any more than a few bars of a tune. The others seemed to feel the same, and they moved in silence save for the clop of Teitur's hooves on the stone floor, and the rich, dull thuds of Coeo's sonar pings. Instead Karl settled for counting his footsteps, and every time he reached a thousand, saying, "Still here."

"Me too," Bera replied, and even Coeo grunted something in mangled Kazakh.

It was only when he noticed a faint glow that Karl realised that they had been following an upward incline in the tunnel, so shallow that he hadn't realised they were ascending. "Daylight," he said. "Up ahead."

"Good." Bera turned her torch on. "Let's hurry up. I really don't like this place."

"No," Karl said. "Coeo leads. Not much point in having sonar and not using it – if there are cracks in the floor, it won't do us any good if you've already fallen down one, will it?"

She eventually said, "I suppose so." She still walked level with Coeo's shoulder.

The light grew gradually stronger until they emerged into a narrow ravine, blinking in Gama and Deltasol's watery sunshine. Karl's eyes ran with the unaccustomed brightness, and when he had wiped them, he saw Bera doing the same. Only Coeo seemed unaffected.

"I hoped that we were shortening the distance, but I never guessed that we'd cut right through them!" Bera laughed gleefully. "Rather than have to climb them, we've shortened the journey another way!" She flung her arms around Karl and did a little dance in his arms, even patting Coeo's arm. The humanoid started, then relaxed, and clumsily patted her arm back.

They faced a broken, boulder-strewn landscape full of rocks and pebbles rather than the gravel and silt-like soil on the far side of the hills. There was also more vegetation, Karl noticed, although it was still straggly shrub and scrub. He pointed at a blue cactus-like plant with pink flowers. "That implies there's water."

They spent a cold afternoon journeying past geysirs and pools of boiling mud which bubbled and spat gobbets of orange for several metres. Bera rode Teitur while Karl and Coeo walked alongside the little horse.

"Are there sandurlund sites below ground?" Karl asked Coeo. He had no idea what the Kazakh for the little animal was, but with the lingua-weave it was best not to think of such things, but leave them to the lingua-obsessed who dissected back-translations, comparing their odder variations with glee.

"Some," the humanoid said. "Sometimes they dig too close to hot springs, or they're unlucky, and the water changes course underground. Then you may find boiled sandurlund thrown up out of the geysirs. That's why there are so many dauskalas around." He pointed to where a dozen bat-like shapes circled in the thermals, their screeches echoing off the surrounding hills.

"Is he talking about those bloody dauskalas?" Bera said, watching the sky.

"She's nervous of them," Karl explained to Coeo. He struggled to follow some of their subsequent conversation – even with the nanophytes' modifications, his hearing still couldn't catch the highest notes of Coeo's language.

"Coeo says you've nothing to worry about," Karl translated. "The dauskalas can't carry off a human."

"That was a long conversation for so little," Bera said. "Either that or he uses very long words." She smiled, but there was an edge to her voice. "Or was he playing the Oracle?"

"Why not?" Karl said. "You're always complaining that I ask you too many questions."

"I don't complain," Bera said, "I merely observe."

Karl squinted up at her. "Observe this!" He blew her a big, fat raspberry.

"Hmmph," she said.

Karl was tempted to observe that a trinary was an inherently unstable relationship, that he and the women had married Jarl for precisely that reason – that and that his lean, smooth-skinned husband was good-looking enough to overcome Karl's strongly hetero leanings.

But he had the feeling that such a comment might provoke an eruption. He frowned. Is that why she's so moody? Surely she's not jealous of Coeo? He decided that he should be more attentive.

Karl craned his neck. "Apparently the dauskalas have an internal mechanism for heating the blood by exchanging heat from the blood going to the wings, with that returning to the body; so the wings are cold but the body's warm, even on one of their more epic flights."

"Fascinating," Bera said.

"Isn't it?" Karl ignored her sarcasm. "Is that where your phrase 'as cold as a dauskala's touch' comes from?"

"Probably."

Karl squinted at her. "OK, I get the message. Dull, dull, dull. Let's move on." He quickened his pace.

But their extra speed didn't last long. When they had first left Skorradalur they had travelled more than fifty kilometres a day without much effort. The last three days they had covered barely half that.

Teitur limped a little at first, then more badly as the hours progressed to Gamasol-set, until Karl and Coeo had slowed to a stroll. Bera dismounted and led him, and still he lagged behind them.

The group walked in silence. Karl sensed that the time was coming when they would have to kill the faithful little horse. A quick, painless death's still more merciful than marooning him in the desert to die slowly of thirst or from predators, he thought sadly. Bera will know when it's time.

When the shadows were long, the sky clear of dauskalas and the cold too biting to allow Karl to keep his shirt off any longer, he saw Bera weeping quietly as she walked, and knew.

"Bera." He put his arm around her shoulder. "Do you want me to do it?" He wasn't sure that he could, but for her sake he would try.

She wiped her eyes impatiently. "No, I'll do it. Normally we don't hesitate to cull, if there's any sign of temperament or weakness that could be carried on. But this is different. He's served me ever since I was a child and he should live another decade at least. We know that we're going to outlive them, that they grow old before our eyes, but to see him reduced to this…"

Karl nodded, noting the horse's ribs sticking out, bony souvenirs of their odyssey, the tired swaying of his head from side to side. He thought of Ship, for the first time in too long. They give their lives for us, he thought, and we take it for granted.

Soon after they stopped for the night.

Bera emptied the last of the horse-feed into a bag which he gave to Teitur. "A last meal," she said. "It's not as if we can eat it, is it?" Karl decided that it wouldn't be right to say that in an emergency, yes, he could eat the horse-feed. Better to leave her some consolation.

Bera loaded the rifle. When Teitur had checked that there was no more food to be had, she wrapped her arm around his neck and kissed him on the nose. "Farewell, my lovely boy," she croaked. With her free hand she pointed the rifle-barrel between his eyes, and fired once.

The rifle absorbed much of the recoil but it still jerked her hand away. Teitur spasmed and then – it seemed in slow motion – toppled over.

Bera checked Teitur's pulse, although Karl couldn't see how he could still live. Routine is her consolation, he thought.

She took up her knife, waving away Karl's help. "Could you make a fire like the other night?"

Karl wasn't sure that he could spare any more nanophytes – those that he had were long overdue maintenance, but he didn't argue. "I'll gather vegetation." He spoke to Coeo, and they walked in two halves of a great circle.

Almost forty minutes later, Karl dropped his feeble haul beside the corpse.

Bera had laid out their furs and was sat among them, resting her hand on a stack of Teitur-steaks wrapped in horse-skin packets as if assessing them. The horse's cadaver lay outstretched nearby, much as he had fallen, but with the skin stretched away from where Bera had cut the steaks.

"I decanted his blood into whatever empty bottles we had," she said, eyes red, her teeth chattering between sentences. "I feel like a vampire, I've drunk so much horse-blood lately." She stood. "I'll help you," she said.

"No need," Karl said. "You sit–"

"No!" Bera continued, more calmly. "I need to do something."

Karl wanted to say what happens when you stop, as sooner or later you must? Instead he passed her the remains of a fur he'd already cut strips from. "Make yourself gloves. These things are full of thorns." He sucked his thumb where he'd learned that lesson.

"If we place the plants on him," Bera said. "We can make him a sort of funeral pyre, and cook the steaks."

They placed the thin covering over Teitur's corpse. "It seems an insult to defecate on him," Karl said. "But we need the nanophytes to combust."

"Do it on the leaves." Bera picked up a canteen, ostentatiously looking away. She gave it to Coeo, picked up two more, and when he had finished, passed Karl one. She raised hers. "To Teitur, faithful servant to the end." Karl echoed the toast. Coeo said, "Teitur."

They placed three steaks in the fire, and when Bera judged them cooked, ate their sad meal. The little pyre burned down all too quickly, but they had already retreated to the furs, Coeo beneath one set – as usual – Bera and Karl another.

Karl linked his hands across her stomach, wishing that he could stroke her naked body. But now was no time to take advantage of a vulnerable young woman. Woman, heck, he thought. She's a young girl, not much older than the baby she bore.

Karl relaxed his hold when Bera's whole body shook, her frame heaving as if she were hiccoughing. A great cry erupted from her, and she sobbed, so violently that he feared that she might shatter and the pieces of her fly apart.

Even Coeo sat beside her, crooning and stroking her arm, though it did little good. Karl had never felt so helpless.

They spent a cold, restless night, the wind gradually strengthening. It was so raw it might have come all the way from the South Pole to cut through the furs as if they weren't there.

If we don't get there soon, Karl thought, it'll be too late. We'll freeze first.

They slept late and awoke to dauskalas swooping.

"Young glamurbak," Coeo said. "Separated from his mother."

The little animal ran one way, then another, each time blocked by the black shapes, its mews parodied by the dauskalas' rasping shrieks.

The mother ran at the predators, but one grabbed at the cub, lifting it off the ground, then dropping it from several metres up. The cub lay still, but for an occasional post-mortem twitch.

Reaching her cub, the mother nuzzled it with her snout. When it didn't respond, she edged away, ducking back to see if it might yet move. After another minute she walked away again, keening pitifully, as if her calling it might yet revive her cub.

While this was happening, the humans had dressed quickly. Karl stopped, suddenly overwhelmed.

"What's wrong?" Bera said.

Karl finally found the breath to say, "So much death. How do you cope with it? It's everywhere you look."

She stroked his arm. "I guess Avalon's a gentler world?"

Karl nodded. "People die, of course. From old age, and illness, and some still from accidents. We have wilderness worlds, where those with a taste for death can hunt, or play survivor strategies."

Bera's lip curled, but her voice gave nothing away. "Isn't the whole point of visiting a wilderness world that you can leave at any time?"

"I… you have to survive until pick-up, but yes, the time is finite. I've never had the taste for such things… they must seem like games to you."

"Exactly." Bera indicated Coeo who had doubled back to rejoin them. "Here, there is no escape for us, or you, if your plan fails. So learn to live, or don't. I can only do so much. I can't make you to want to learn to live, Karl." She added, "So the first lesson starts here. See the dauskalas trying to prise open the cub's armour?"

"Yes?" Karl said.

"They're not having it. It's ours now."

With a yell, Bera ran at the dauskalas. Coeo let out a bellow and followed her. Karl hesitated, then drew his sword and charged, yelling.

The dauskalas shrieked and rose a couple of metres in the air, flapping their gossamer-thin wings, snapping at Bera with long, thin, crossed bills made for rending. She sliced one of the bat-like creature's wings and blood spurted. It crashed and immediately the other dauskalas dived on it, beaks snapping.

Coeo dragged the glamurbak corpse away.

Bera began hacking the corpse apart and said to Karl, "Give me a hand!"

Reluctantly Karl cut off the tail, which seemed hardly worth the effort. He offered it to Coeo, who was chomping on a piece of bloodied meat that Bera had given him. Coeo shook his head. "Yours."

"Your prize for helping," Bera said.

Karl said, "Won't the rest of the meat be poisonous?"

"Maybe," Bera admitted. "But it's the principle: 'waste not, want not', as the saying goes. And it'll feed Coeo, who's surely one of us?" She lifted an eyebrow.

"OK," Karl conceded. "But let's not hang around, eh? Those brutes are eying us up." Two of the dauskalas were slurping over their comrade's intestines, but two more looked from the carcass that they couldn't reach, toward the cub's body, and back again, as if evaluating which was the greater prize.

Bera shuddered. "My head knows that they perform a vital ecological function. My gut says kill every one of the ugly bastards."

Coeo was still munching cub cuts as they resumed. He offered a piece to Karl, who shook his head. *I may have to eat meat on this barbarous mud-ball, but something cooked from an animal I haven't seen die is one thing; the raw flesh of what was a cute little baby* twenty minutes ago is another. He suspected that it was a view Bera wouldn't share.

They walked across a landscape of undulating rises littered with ever-larger stones, sand giving way primarily to gravel underfoot, which in turn became mostly pebbles, and eventually cobbles.

The ground shook from time to time, and smoke rose in the distance at right-angles to their route. "The further away we get from the hills, the more tremors there seem to be," Karl observed.

Bera shrugged. Her mood all morning had been understandably dour. "There's no pattern to Isheimuri seismology. There are places of greater and lesser activity side by side. We think that the constant little tremors act as a safety valve, so we never get the big volcanoes you might expect."

Karl nodded. And therefore little carbon dioxide.

Coeo interrupted with a shout from the next ridge, waving frantically. Karl broke into a scrambling run.

The sight that met him took his breath away.

Ahead of them was a frozen lake, sitting on the very edge of the desert, rocks running right down to where the ice began. "Oh my," Karl said.

"Jokullag," Bera said. "Where – if the *Winter Song* is true – the stars fell to earth."

Close-up, the dirty grey edge was actually watery-slush, although barely two metres in it was frozen white, in stark contrast to the brown of the surrounding desert. On the far side, grey hills rose toward snow-capped mountains and cirques whose glacial tongues crept down to the lake. Gamasol reflected blindingly off the lake.

"Krishna," Karl whispered. It was as beautiful as anything he'd seen on the sixty or seventy worlds he'd walked upon.

"Everyone should see this," Bera said.

"It's not for me," Karl whispered, wondering who he was trying to convince the most. "It's too wild, too untamed... too terrifying."

They circled the lake, rather than walking on it. "The ice will leach the heat away from your feet," Bera said.

Even when walking on the shoreline, the wind off the ice was bitter, and both humans soon shivered, even Karl, whose enhanced physique could normally cope with almost anything. He wondered again whether the nanophytes were failing, or whether the previous night had simply taken too much out of him.

Coeo touched Karl's arm. "I walk here. You walk on other side –" Coeo indicated the ridge "– stay warm. I see it, I call you. Yes?"

Karl somehow felt as if they were retreating, but they climbed back up the gravel slope. Up here, he could see that the ridges they'd crossed earlier were actually vast concentric rings, the heaviest debris nearest the lake, the smallest carried furthest. He guessed that the various ridges marked the tide-lines reflecting the various levels of the ice over the decades, centuries, perhaps even millennia.

They descended into the trough, now sheltered from the wind, although periodically Karl swarmed to the top of the ridge and waved at the stocky, hirsute figure striding along as if out on a gentle stroll. This is his world, Karl thought. If he's the descendant of the Pantropists, he was made for this. What happens if the colonists Terraform this world? Will he still be able to live here, or will it be unliveable for him? He suspected that the dead humanoid in the valley disputed by Ragnar and his neighbour gave him his answer. They're probably no longer capable of breathing carbon dioxide in the amounts needed to warm Isheimur, nor of surviving human-optimum oxygen levels.

He said nothing of this to Bera, who trudged beneath her backpack with her head bowed. Teitur's death and the skirmish with the dauskalas seemed to have drained her of fight. He drifted down from the ridge, crossing her path.

When he linked his arm through hers, she looked up and a wan smile flickered across her face. "What?" she said.

"I was wondering the same. Thinking?"

"Of what happens when you're gone. If I'm an outlaw, it's decided for me. If not..."

"Come with me," Karl said.

"Easy to say," Bera said. "Not so easy to do – think how strange you thought we were, and you've experienced many different cultures. How would I fare? How would your family take to me?"

"You don't have to live with us forever. You can stay for as long as you need to adjust, and move on when you want."

Bera didn't answer.

They walked on in silence, the bitter wind strengthening still further, blowing Bera's hair into her eyes until she grabbed some one-handed and pulling it back, took a length of ribbon from her pocket with the other. But the wind plucked at both hair and ribbon, pulling strands loose no matter how hard she fought it.

"Here," Karl said. "Let me." He took the ribbon as she held her hair, and as he tied it, gazed into her eyes. He watched the colour flood her face.

She jerked away. "Thanks."

Over the next hour the clouds gathered, the sky growing black and whatever harsh beauty their surroundings possessed was subsumed by the sheer bleakness of the day. Karl felt the spatter of raindrops and muttered a curse.

Within minutes the rain turned to big, fat whirling flakes of snow. Visibility plummeted to a few metres, and they looked around for somewhere to shelter. None of the boulders in the trough was big enough to provide cover for them.

"Nothing for it but to press on," Bera said.

"Don't we risk missing the shrine?"

"You're right, but with luck this'll pass over. If not, we'll re-think. We're walking so slowly that if the visibility picks up we should be able to see the part we miss now."

Their luck held; the flurry passed over in about half an hour, and the day brightened again. But throughout the afternoon the temperature fell further, draining them of energy, until every footstep was an effort, even for Karl.

Coeo appeared on the ridge between them and the lake, waving frantically.

Karl and Bera staggered up the slope, their feet sliding back half of each step that they took. When they reached the top, they were both panting, and leaned forward on their knees. Karl straightened again when he followed Coeo's outstretched arm, to where sunlight glinted on metal.

"*Winter Song*?" Karl said.

"*Winter Song*." Coeo added in Kazakh, "Godsfall."

"It's real!" Karl flung his arms around Bera and kissed her.

After a moment's hesitation she kissed him back. What started as a peck on the lips lengthened, deepened, her lips parting and their tongues touched. Lips ground against lips, teeth bumped teeth. She dug her fingers into the back of his neck. His hands slid down her back and cupped her bottom; she lifted one foot and wrapped her leg around his waist, then the other. His ailing nanophytes gave up the unequal battle against tumescence and he stiffened, pressing against her.

When he guessed that she might need air, he gently put her down. She tucked a stray lock of hair behind her ear, said, "Um."

"Yes." He tugged a fur down, unsnagging his erection. She stared down at it, her face a swirling mix of nervousness and confusion. She bit her lower lip, blushing, and looking up at him, smiled beatifically.

"Do you have – is there a map – an, um, a picture of the lake?" he blathered, getting his breath back.

"Somewhere." She rummaged in her bag, and he noticed her hands shaking when she took the papers out and shielded them from the wind. He leaned over her to study the map, stroking her hair when she rested her head on his shoulder.

Karl stared across the lake. Rising from the ice a kilometre toward the centre was a segment of white circle, a lattice joining it to the surface.

"This wasn't on the original pictures," Bera said, tapping them. "That implies the ice has melted."

"It must have thawed as the temperatures rose with the Terraforming." Karl said. "If so, the ice will cover it again in time as it re-freezes."

They prepared to slide down the slope but then Karl turned. "Coeo?" he called. "Where you go?"

"This way." The humanoid pointed along the ridge, and began to slide down the far side, away from the lake. "You go to shrine, Coeo go this way. I see you again. Fare you well, both." He didn't look back. In moments, he was a tiny figure, hurrying away without further explanation.

"What's happening?" Bera said. She peered into the distance, perplexed.

"I don't know," Karl said. "He's… he's just walking away. Maybe he was only ever going to guide us. Maybe he's scared of the ship." He looked after their erstwhile companion, barely comprehending what was happening. It came to him, hard, that for all their similarities, Coeo was from such a different culture to his.

"I know how he feels," Bera said, squeezing his finger. "Part of me wants to go with him. Just turn and run."

"Why?" Karl said. "It's just a ship." He turned to gaze back over the lake.

"Maybe to you," Bera said. "What if there are spirits? Or whatever you call Loki?"

"It'll be OK," Karl said. "You're just overawed, and the fact that it's so quiet isn't helping."

"I guess the havalifugils can't swim here," Bera said, "if it's frozen solid. The rock-eaters and snolfurs have all gone north for the winter. There's not even a dauskala. That alone shows you how lifeless it is here."

"Think the *Winter Song*'s scared them off?" Karl said, adding quickly, "Joking! Come on!" They slid down and with a running jump Karl cleared the slush. Bera landed short and teetered on the edge of a floe, arms windmilling forward, until Karl grabbed the front of her fur and yanked her onto firmer ice.

Bera had been right; it sucked warmth from their feet faster than atmosphere rushing from a voided airlock, and was slippery underfoot. She pulled a fur from her bag, and cut it into strips which bending down, she wrapped round her boots. She passed the rest to Karl, who followed her example. It didn't help their grip, but would slow the spread of the cold.

Karl's fatigue had receded in the face of an adrenaline surge, and the ship took on definition as they approached across the silent ice. The visible part of a half-buried saucer, it was several hundred metres across and about fifty high. Close up, the metal was pitted, gouged and scarred all across its rust-bloomed surface, a metre-long shard of metal jutting out at a right angle. Karl's heart sank. "How can it possibly fly with such damage?"

Bera gawped. "You're planning to fly it? I thought you just wanted the communication equipment?"

"Well..." He hadn't seriously considered flying it home. Even if somehow they could adapt it to break into fold-space at the system entry point, it would still take months, perhaps years, to reach that point at whatever dismally slow speed they could coax from the engines. But he had dreamed of getting it above Isheimur's atmosphere so that they could better target the out-system relays. "Doesn't matter," Karl said. "It'll never get off the ice."

You may be surprised, Loki said. *Don't be fooled by the near-prehistoric design: ships from that region of Terra were built for efficiency and brute-force, rather than elegance. They could take punishment that would destroy much newer vessels.*

Even so, Karl sub-vocalised, look how deeply it's buried.

Ice melts, Loki pointed out. *What's the main by-product of an engine's thrust?*

Heat, Karl said. Oh, of course...

They circled the ship, and halfway round Karl stopped to allow Bera to catch up. She had hung further and further back, clearly awed by its size, tilting her head to stare up at the hull. She shivered. "I know," she said with a trace of her former asperity. "It's just a ship."

Karl didn't answer. He felt slightly spooked as well. Probably this uncanny silence.

Even the creaking he normally expected on ice fields was absent, as if Jokullag was holding its breath. But he couldn't get over the feeling of being watched. He thought he heard a scraping noise drift across the lake, and looking around saw nothing but a raised lump of ice breaking the monotony.

About two-thirds of the way around, a ramp hung down from the ship's hull, entering the ice at about a thirty degree angle. Only the top two metres of it was visible, most of that covered with snow and ice.

To allow ground vehicles of the time to drive up and down, Loki said.

A few flat shards of metal were scattered around, but apart from these and some marks in the snow at the edge of the ramp, it looked as if it had been untouched for centuries.

Karl looked back at the scraping noise. It might have been his imagination, but the piece of ice seemed to have moved slightly. Get a grip, he thought.

Karl stepped onto the ramp, his footsteps muffled by the furs wrapped around his boots. The cargo bay was mostly empty except for eight or nine two-metre-high crates scattered around the floor. Walking toward a doorway at the far end of the bay, Karl saw a flash of movement in his peripheral vision.

From behind came a faint noise, then Bera's shout of, "Karl – behind you!"

Pure instinct made Karl sway to one side rather than the other, and he felt something whizz past where his head had just been. A wooden bolt thudded into the wall.

Karl spun round, into the grinning face of Ragnar. "Hello, utlander," the Gothi growled. "It's been bloody cold waiting here, but dealing out justice to you will warm us."

EIGHTEEN

Four men emerged from the crates scattered between Karl and the ramp. Thorir looked exultant, while Ragnar's neighbour Orn had a worried frown. By contrast, Arnbjorn's face gave nothing away. Karl noticed that the fourth man – one of Bjarney's Thralls – had had to help Ragnar's son to his feet.

Bera stood on the edge of the hangar, white-faced, wide-eyed with panic.

It had taken Karl maybe a half-second to note the scene, his brain racing. If he attacked Ragnar, the others would help leap to their chief's defence. Maybe he could try the door he'd been walking toward? But he couldn't leave Bera, and there were four men between them.

Ragnar said, "Nothing to say, Loki?"

Karl stayed silent, determined not to be baited.

"What shall we do about his slut?" Thorir stepped toward Bera, who lifted her sword. Thorir stepped to one side of the ramp to circle round, and she turned too, keeping him in front of her.

"Never again," Bera said, and Karl knew – finally – what had happened at Skorradalur.

He tried to swallow his rage, but his face must have shown something. "Like that, is it, boy?" Ragnar said. "Couldn't keep your hands off her?"

"I haven't fucked her, Ragnar, if that's what you mean." Karl soaked the words in his contempt, spitting them at Ragnar. "Don't confuse facial hair with maturity, old man. Being a man isn't about your balls dropping. It's about caring for your people, like I care for her, and my family. More than you ever did."

"What would you know?" Ragnar stepped forward, his knife tip suddenly at Karl's throat. "Don't you *dare* lecture me!"

"Why not?" Karl said, trying not to swallow and impale his Adam's Apple on the knife. "You behave as if your family are the only ones that count!"

Then everything happened at once:

Thorir shouted "Troll!" and stumbling, fell off the ramp. Ragnar and his men turned as one to face the attack, perhaps expecting a war party, and Arnbjorn lost his footing and fell. Bera charged right into the hangar, using the weight of her backpack to catch Orn by surprise, hitting him in the ribs. Orn crashed into the Thrall, who fell with a grunt and lay still, blood trickling from beneath his body. Karl reacted fastest, drew his sword and smacked Ragnar on the back of the head with the pommel, dropping the Gothi to his knees.

He waved at Coeo, who stood uncertainly on the edge of the ramp, peering in. "Come on!" Karl pushed Bera at the inner doorway.

Coeo leapt to dodge a slash from Thorir, who was still on the ground, and ran toward Karl. He narrowly avoided the sweep of Orn's sword – fortunately Orn was still semi-prone.

Karl patted Coeo's shoulder. "Good to see you!" He felt the humanoid's shivering and added, "No need for fear, friend. We mean no harm."

"What about them?" Coeo indicated Thorir and Orn, who were clambering to their feet while Arnbjorn used the crate to haul himself upright. The Thrall lay unmoving.

Karl grabbed the still-stunned Ragnar, and now it was his turn to press the blade to Ragnar's throat. "Drop your weapons or I'll slit his throat!"

It was pure bluff, but maybe the panic in Karl's voice convinced them. Ragnar's men dropped their swords.

Bera shouted, "Step back!" Darting across the floor, she kicked the swords toward Coeo. The humanoid picked them up, fumbling them, nearly dropping one, as if unused to handling implements. "And the knives you're hiding!" she added. A clatter of knives echoed.

Karl sensed Ragnar stir. "Keep still, Ragnar, or I'll slit your throat." He might do it by accident, were he not careful, but pressed the point harder.

"Easy, utlander," Ragnar said and Karl felt him relax.

"Coeo," Karl said in Kazakh, "can you break their weapons?"

"That's wasteful," Coeo said. Karl heard the conflict in his voice. Coeo clearly loathed handling the weapons, but Karl had seen over their journey how relentlessly the humanoid reused every scrap, every morsel, every last piece of whatever he found.

"They'll use them to kill us, given a chance," Karl said.

"If they sin here, they'll be punished," Coeo said, but put all but one down, which he snapped across his knee.

"Consorting with abominations?" Thorir sneered at Bera.

Ragnar said, "Shut up, idiot. They hold a knife to my throat."

"Very sensible," Karl said. Coeo snapped the other blades one by one.

"What now, Allman?"

"On your feet," Karl said, "carefully!"

"We'll try nothing tricksy," Ragnar said with a grim chuckle. "I get the impression that you're not a cold-blooded killer."

Karl said, "Walk with me. The pressure on your throat should guide you."

"Worthy of one of us," Ragnar said, chuckling again. "We'll make an Isheimuri of you yet."

"I doubt they'll let you live that long." Bera kept her sword raised.

"I thought that you'd left us," Karl said to Coeo, backing away with Ragnar as his shield.

"I don't leave friends," Coeo said, and Karl could have hugged him. "I had to pray to the spirits of the shrine first." He added, "Best, I thought, that we come here from different directions, and to assume that we were watched."

A supposed primitive teaches you basic tactics! Karl thought. To hide his embarrassment he said, "How did you avoid being seen?"

"Cut a block of ice. Lay on the lake and hid behind the block, while pushing it across the lake."

Karl said, "Can you say the phrase I taught you on the way here?"

Coeo composed himself. He said in passable Low Isheimuri, "Hello. My name is Coeo. I wish you no harm."

The most difficult part had been to teach Coeo to keep his voice to the limited range audible to humans. Because they could speak and hear what to humans were ultrasonic frequencies, the humanoids naturally included them in their language. It was one of the reasons the settlers hadn't even recognised it as speech. For Coeo to be comprehensible, he'd had to learn to limit his vocal range. It was like asking humans to speak only in falsetto.

"So you've taught your pet to speak," Ragnar said. "Impressive."

"You are Ragnar?" Coeo said, as a delighted Bera clapped her hands and laughed.

"More mimicry," Ragnar said, sounding less sure.

"They're intelligent," Karl said.

"They're human!" Bera added, as if she'd never believed anything else.

Ragnar wriggled, and Karl shouted, "Now, now!" as Orn and Thorir darted forward. "Enough!" he said, and they froze. "We're going through that door," Karl chincocked the airlock. "Follow us and Ragnar dies. Understand?" They didn't answer, but glared, although no one moved.

Karl beckoned Coeo and said in Kazakh, "Like this," showing Coeo how to hold the knife to Ragnar's throat.

"Better idea." Coeo unsheathed his claws. Ragnar's eyes widened.

"He's going to guard you," Karl said, loudly enough for Ragnar's men to hear. "If you or they try anything – and I mean anything – he'll rip your throat out. Don't provoke him. Bera, you OK?"

"Yep," Bera said. "I've trained my rifle on them."

"Brave, aren't you?" Thorir said. "When you've a gun in your hand?"

"Like most men I know," Bera said.

While they bickered, Karl examined the airlock control panel. It was incredibly primitive, but when he had married Karla they'd learned archaic pastimes as a

301

shared hobby: jet-packing, weaving, cooking, laser-sculpture. Karl had never expected reading printed books to ever prove useful, and he was probably little better than a twelve-year-old during the Gutenberg Era, long before Ayes and downloads had consigned such quaint skills to the recycler of obsolescence. But he recognised many of the sigils which covered the panel – such as "Danger!" Translating more than a few words of the archaic instructions made Karl's head hurt, but luckily there were enough pictograms inter-spersed to help him. He pressed what he hoped were the right buttons.

Nothing happened.

"Shit, shit, SHIT!"

He kneeled, and fiddled with two hatches at the base of the door. Sliding and pulling did no good, but push-ing opened one hatch inward. The other one must open from the inside, Karl thought.

He turned to the others, catching the end of an ex-change between Thorir and Bera. They stared at each other, Bera, trembling with rage, Thorir blushing fiery red. Orn and Arnbjorn stared at the ground.

"Go through," Karl told her, then said to Ragnar's men, "Follow us and the old man dies."

"You won't get away," Thorir said.

"Quiet, Thorir," Arnbjorn said in a low voice. "Or I'll cut you down where you stand."

"And I'll swear it was self-defence," Orn added.

Karl slid through. "You next, Ragnar!" he called.

"I'm not–"

"DO IT!"

Ragnar slid through, followed by Coeo.

Karl looked around at bare metal floors that might once have been grass-covered, or had some inorganic coating. Now there was only a tidemark of scattered debris, abandoned clips and pegs, and bare wires spilling from gape-mouthed cupboards. The air in the corridor was centuries-stale, laden with dust and rust.

Karl pointed to what looked like the cowl of some huge engine of some sort. It weighs a tonne, he thought. It'll do. "Bera, help me block that hatch with this."

It screeched as they slid and walked it across the hatchway, drowning out the murmurs of Ragnar's men talking that drifted through the hatch. "That's that done." He wiped his hands clean. He picked up a length of plastic. "Turn around," he said. Ragnar did as he was told, looking truly nervous for the first time Karl could remember.

Karl fastened the plastic strip into impromptu handcuffs around Ragnar's wrists and told Coeo, "Bring him."

They stalked the corridors, leaning at a thirty-degree angle to offset the ship's tilt, ransacking cupboards, throwing open cupboard doors, checking every glass panel for working finger-readers. Karl called out commands in Kazakh and every neighbouring language, without success. The *Winter Song* must predate voice-activated Ayes, Karl sub-vocalised.

Keep trying, Loki replied.

There was nothing. The *Winter Song* was as dead as Karl had feared. Every connecting door had to be opened manually and the inertia tubes between floors were inoperative, forcing them to tramp up stairways.

Karl stopped at every floor. At the fourth, Ragnar, who had been silent until now, said, "You're wasting your time, utlander."

"Maybe," Karl said. "Maybe not."

"My people may fear this vessel," Ragnar insisted, "but – trust me – they'll stare into the eyes of their fear and will it to be silent. Give yourself up, and it'll be taken into account when sentence is passed."

"He's no outlaw," Bera insisted, "as any court will decide." She might as well have not spoken.

They tramped up more floors, empty but much better fitted out.

Why didn't they strip it fully? Karl wondered. Did one faction dream that the ship might fly again if they didn't completely gut it? I suppose that whatever they could take would be absolutely swallowed by the needs of their descendants, but still, it would have helped, even a little.

On the third such floor, a hatch in the ceiling had bolts all around it and clips on the bolts. Karl read a sign on the hatch: Emergency Access Only.

"This is the top deck," Karl said. "So the bridge should be here." As they resumed, he caught Bera's eye. She smiled but it was a feeble effort. The empty ship seemed to cow her more than it did Coeo, who brought up the rear-guard, unsheathed claws resting lightly on the nape of Ragnar's neck.

As they checked every door Karl said lightly, "Was Thorir the baby's father?"

Bera's eyes gazed into the past, and she made a moue with her mouth. When she spoke, she seemed to reminiscence, as if she hadn't heard the question: "Ever since I could remember, he was always laughing and joking. Maybe I'm seeing things differently now, but I think that he was always a little too friendly. You know?"

"I think so," Karl said.

"Then one night, he got drunk..." Bera blinked several times. "I kept saying no, you mustn't, but you wouldn't listen, would you?"

Karl brought her back to the present. "Did he rape you?"

"What was that?" Ragnar stepped closer, but stopped at Coeo's warning growl.

"Never mind," Bera called. "I'm no longer your concern."

"Your father gave you into my care!"

Something inside Bera seemed to break then. Maybe Ragnar's reminder was one reprimand too many, or maybe anything would have set her off. Bera began to cackle. "Of all the stupid things you could say," she cried between shrieks of laughter, "that's the worst of them all. Your bloody care?" Her voice broke, her laughter turning to sobs. Karl gently led her away, cradling her as tenderly as any newborn baby.

"I... I w-w-wasn't going to speak of it, not ever. P-poor Hilda, and her children, the shame they'd face – even if anyone believed me."

When the storm of tears finally blew itself out, Karl let her go. "I believe you," he said. "I'm sorry about what he did. It shames us all." He wiped away a tear-track on her cheek with his thumb. "Why did you never talk of it? Did you really believe that I'd think any less of you?"

"I was ashamed." Bera snorted a lungful of breath, wiping her cheekbones with the heel of her hands. "Maybe it was my fault. Maybe I did something, some-time, to encourage him. I dunno what, but–"

"You did nothing!" Karl said. "His sort needs no encouragement."

"How can you be sure?" Bera said. "I thought that you didn't want me – what if I got him equally wrong somehow? Maybe I somehow encouraged him, by being friendly."

"Why would you ever think I didn't want you?" Karl gazed into her eyes, allowing himself to be momentarily distracted.

"You... that is... every night I lay against you," Bera whispered, eyes wide, chewing on the corner of her bottom lip. "There was nothing, no reaction down there–" She pointed.

"That was my nanophytes keeping the blood away. I wouldn't want to take advantage of a vulnerable girl... You thought that that meant I wasn't interested?"

Bera's mouth made an "O".

Karl held up his hand. "I heard voices."

"Probably Arnbjorn and the others," Ragnar called.

Karl turned to Bera. "We'll talk again. Now isn't the time." She nodded and smiled.

Hurrying, Karl led them to a massive metal door at the end, from which all the white paint had peeled but for a few flecks. "Bera, hold a knife to Ragnar's throat."

"Getting a girl to do your dirty work?" Ragnar jeered, adding, "Easy, Bera! No need for that!"

"Keep talking, Ragnar –" the calm in Bera's voice was patently insincere "– and I'll take great delight in hurting you."

Ragnar was silent.

Karl grabbed an inset that looked as if it was a grip for manually sliding open the door, and indicated Coeo should do the same. "On three," Karl said. "One, two, three – heave!"

Coeo and Karl strained. Nothing happened at first, so they tried again, harder. After a few seconds Karl heard the unmistakable grating sound of the door opening. When they stopped, Karl heard voices. Arnbjorn and the others. "Again!" Karl panted, heaving so violently that he thought blood vessels would pop.

When he looked around, Bera was still holding the knife to Ragnar's throat, but as her arm started to tremble, she changed hands.

"Don't be a fool, Allman." Ragnar sounded weary, but when he straightened, his eyes narrowed. "Give yourselves up. Bera, if you were seduced by this man's glamour, I understand–"

"Shut up!" Bera cried. "Or by Thor I'll stick you!"

"And murder in cold blood?" Ragnar said, stepping forward onto the knife-point. "I didn't raise you that way, my dear, whatever my failings were."

Karl was torn for a moment between helping Bera and forcing open the door a few last centimetres. It was now almost wide enough for her – the smallest of them – to squeeze through. He braced his back against the door jamb and gave one almighty push, a great groan of effort forcing its way between his teeth in descant to Coeo's ultrasonic shout. The door juddered slowly open, screeching in protest.

He looked up as Ragnar walked another pace forward. Blood spurted and Bera's scream almost drowned out the door, which widened so abruptly that Coeo almost fell through the gap.

"Bera, come on!" Karl shouted.

Bera stood rooted for a microsecond, but even as a bloodied, staggering Ragnar snatched at her, she darted for the doorway. Karl stood aside and she shot through as Orn led Ragnar's men through the door to the stairwell at the other end of the corridor.

"Give me that!" Coeo pointed at Karl's sword.

"No!" Karl shouted back. "Get through the door!"

Karl stood on the inside of the doorway, sword pointed through the gap, while Coeo heaved the monolithic slab shut. "Help him!" Karl said to Bera. "No, no, take the sword, take it!" Karl threw his weight into helping Coeo.

He glimpsed chaos in the corridor where Ragnar's men milled round like gas particles undergoing Brownian

307

motion, while their leader staunched his wound. Karl guessed that Ragnar had moved his head so that the tip hadn't pierced a vital point; most of the spurt had been the release of pressure from the constraints of flesh. Once that pressure eased, the gush would have slowed considerably, and would be easier to staunch than first appeared. Nonetheless the distraction the wound caused robbed the intruders of vital seconds, allowing Karl and Coeo to heave the door closed.

"Thank all your gods," Karl panted, resting his hands on his knees, "that they weren't regular soldiers, or they'd have left Ragnar and gone for the door instead." Looking up, he saw Bera trembling. "Hey, hey, no need for that!" How much heart must that have taken, he thought, to attack someone who might as well be your father – whatever his faults. He squeezed Bera while snatching a look around.

The bridge was about ten metres across widthways, slightly less from the large window at the front to the door they'd just used. The window drew the eye, looking out over the frozen waste of Jokullag, ice stretching as far in front of them as Karl could see.

When he finally managed to drag his eyes away from the terrible beauty of the view, Karl's heart sank. "Looks like they took almost anything that wasn't bolted down." He peered at the command console. "And quite a few things that were." Some of the fittings had been taken, wires hung from panels, metal braces on the floor went nowhere rather than to the chairs they'd once held in place. A thick coating of dust covered every surface. Still, some things are still here. It's not completely stripped like the lower decks. Maybe it was here that they changed their plans.

"Does that mean you won't be able to send a signal?" Bera said.

"We'll see." Karl tried several switches. "First we need to see if there's any power left. These old tubs worked on fission, which no one's used for centuries. I assume that the reactor didn't leak, or the Formers would have picked up the radiation on their orbital surveys."

"Could they have missed it?" Bera said.

Karl chuckled. "Not the amount that this thing would have sprayed across the landscape if it had leaked." His eyes widened. "Maybe that was why they landed down here, so as not to risk poisoning their descendants. The heat of the hull would have melted the ice, so apart from the initial impact of about a microsecond they would've landed on water."

From behind them, voices indicated that Ragnar's men had finally sorted themselves out. There was still a two-inch gap around which fingers appeared. "From the packs where we stashed it," Arnbjorn said.

Bera slashed at the door. The man screamed as blood sprayed the door's edge and fingertips dropped to the floor.

Karl took a deep breath. "Right," he said. "Let's hope my theory's right. I'd want the bridge to be able to access the engines and the Aye – assuming they had one. For all of those, power's needed first. Some of this must run on emergency power. With fission batteries on hibernate, they should still be…" He hit switches and pressed buttons, and crowed in delight as console lights flickered into life. "Too many displays missing," Karl muttered. "But we'll have to make do." He said, "Just hope that however they contained the reactor, we haven't just turned it off by re-starting central power."

"Again?" Bera said. "In simple words?"

"Those were simple words." Karl grinned, checking the various sets of lights, muttering in time to his fingers dancing over the displays. He looked up. "Everything's there."

"You sound surprised."

"I am. I'd have offered you millions-to-one against emergency power, the central reactor, the datarealm, life-support and comms all green-lighting."

Bera nodded at the door. Someone had threaded through a piece of metal as an impromptu shield which they held over the attacker's fingers. "They're still trying to open it the same way you did."

"I'll be surprised if they do," Karl said. "Three of them plus Ragnar, who should be weakened by his bit of blood-loss, Arnbjorn – who can barely stand – and one of them missing fingers. I'm enhanced, and Coeo is adapted, so I'd guess that we're probably stronger than them, and we needed the adrenaline surge of total bloody panic to open it. But get ready to help Coeo grab the shield and hack off some more fingers."

"With pleasure," Bera said, and joined Coeo at the door.

Karl continued his search. "They can't have taken it," he muttered. "It wouldn't have been any use – unless they downloaded the datarealm? No, it wouldn't have responded to the test query." Crouching down, he felt along the inside of the panel, and grunted in triumph. "Got pushed to the back. Come out, you beauty!" he unravelled the cable with its distinctive end-plug, and swore. "Wrong bloody shape!"

He rummaged through the cupboards, looking less and less happy.

"What are you looking for?" Bera said from his shoulder.

"Adapters for the jack," Karl said. "Why aren't you at the door?"

"It's gone suspiciously quiet," Bera said. "But I can't do anything until they attack – and you said lifting off was the priority."

"So I did," Karl said, as Bera joined the search.

"Are these what you're looking for?" She rattled a box.

"Yes!" Karl ransacked the contents and pulled out two or three, comparing the width and shape. "These look to be about the best fit..." He lifted the flap of skin on the back of his neck and uncovered a socket. "See if you can get any of these to plug in."

Grimacing as she did so, Bera tried all three. "This one's just too wide – oh, that's it," she said.

"Adaptive socket," Karl said. "As long it's the right configuration and about the right size, the socket will stretch or shrink within certain parameters. These have mostly been semi-standardised since forever. Built-in obsolescence died with the Age of Waste, before star-flight." He grinned. "You could say it became obsolescent." He puffed out his cheeks. Holding the jack in his left end, he took a deep breath. "Moment of truth time." He pressed three switches at the same time and waited, wondering if he'd hear the answering grumble in the ship's bowels. "Yes! Power's on!"

He waited, then pressed another half-dozen switches and buttons and what he silently prayed was the right sequence. "And there's the datarealm re-booting. Hah!" He held up the lead, then inserted the jack. "Aagh! That's still horrible!" he cried.

"Still?" Bera said. "You poke wires into your head all the time?"

"Not all the time," Karl said. "Only when something goes horribly wrong, or you're on an antique like this." At her shocked look, he grinned. "It was probably state-of-the-art when they fitted it, but even then it would have been bloody unpleasant for the user."

"Will… would I have to plug in like this if I came with you?"

Karl shook his head. "Everything's voice-activated now, lovely."

He blinked several times, widening his eyes further each time. "I'm going into a trance for a time, but it's all part of the interface." He patted Bera's hand. "Don't look so worried! This is all part of the plan." He hoped she didn't know that he was making "the plan" up as he went along.

At the back of his mind, an image: of Loki straightening, sniffing the air… The download stepped forward–

"We're in," you said to Karl, revelling in the purity of the glorious crystalline world of data-streams and iceberg-shaped databases. There! The history of the Kazakh government's attempts to build an interstellar empire, doomed to failure by relativity and distance. There! The meteorite, the oldest and most cliched of interstellar hazards, punching its way by sheer size through the ice-canopy intended to protect the ship. There! The routines that you need! Loki sensed the wonderful space within the datarealm; hosts of long-silent systems.

Karl's head snapped back and he opened his eyes wide. "There!" he said with a huge grin at Bera. "We have power!" The grin faded with the power.

Damnation, Loki said. *Some of the connections are not there. I'll need to find bypasses – unless you can go and repair them?*

Karl sub-vocalised, You must be… He tailed off as he saw the Cheshire Cat image from antiquity hovering in the air. Joking.

I am following the channels through. I believe that we have connectivity: the ship shuddered like someone feeling the cold, and lights split the gloom. We also have fuel. The tank in the engine pod is full to capacity, although the water's frozen solid. If we can thaw it, it'll split nicely into oxygen for us, and hydrogen for the drive.

"What about the hangar we entered through?" Bera said. Won't the air vent?"

"Not as long as the airlock we passed through holds," Karl said. "And it should – no reason why not."

From outside, blows banged against the door.

Karl sat in the chair next to the console. "Sit down," he called. Watching over their shoulders, Bera and Coeo did as instructed. "They can hit it with whatever they want," Karl said. "I assume they've got axes from their packs, but whatever they're using, they'll still bounce off it!" He stared at the door. "Huh, hitting the lintel – that won't help!"

The ship juddered as the roar of the engines kicked in. "There's smoke coming from the door!" Bera said.

The engine tone changed from a roar to a whine. Steam billowed past the window. "Whatever they're planning, they're too late!" Karl said.

The ship tilted further, lurched, and fell back again with a spine-jarring thud. Karl cursed. Give me more power, he told Loki.

Bera glanced at the door. "They're burning flares! That must be what the banging was – hammering flares into the lintel. They must have emptied Skorradalur of them to have got so many!"

The ice creaked and groaned, and two lights flashed red. "Shit," Karl muttered.

"What?" Bera said.

"Temperature around the vents is going critical – the steam from the ice can't vent fast enough." The *Winter*

Song pushed and heaved and writhed, battling the ice that held it on one side.

For a moment Karl was afraid that the ship would break up, and thought about powering down.

If you do, Loki said, *our best chance is gone. Better to die trying, surely?*

Karl increased the power to full thrust.

"I don't like that groaning," Bera said. "Will the ship hold?"

"If it doesn't, we're dead," Karl said. "But if they take us, we're dead anyway."

The flares detonated. A series of bangs punched the air together so rapidly that they merged into one long percussion, building to a blast that blew in the door from the top lintel. Ragnar and his men piled through the gap.

And with a mighty lurch, the ship broke free, ice falling from its hull, passing the windows in great man-sized shards. The ship tilted, and Karl glimpsed white-peaked mountains, then sky.

Inside his head Karl screamed at Loki: Give me every last drop of power that you can wring from these fucking engines!

And the *Winter Song* roared into the sky on great kilometre-long columns of fire.

PART FOUR

NINETEEN

A giant hand seemed to press on Karl's chest while its owner roared in his ears as the *Winter Song* climbed from the lake.

We're only climbing at three standard gravities, Loki said.

It felt like more. I'm just out of condition, he sub-vocalised. Karl reached for and squeezed Bera's hand. Somewhere, wiring or perhaps some dust exposed to heat was burning, and the smell of it catapulted Karl back to the attack on Ship, when he'd been dreaming of Karla. He realised guiltily that he hadn't thought of his partners for far too long, but concentrated on slowing his hammering heart, wiped his hands on his leggings, and took deep breaths to crush the panic that threatened to overwhelm him as his cheeks were pushed toward his ears.

The *Winter Song* banked slightly, making a minute adjustment, and Karl looked out the window at mountains to the north, glaciers marching down to the lake, while to the south the desert stretched away to infinity. He felt an unexpected pang at leaving Isheimur, which he crushed, ruthlessly and quickly.

Streams of ice shards flew earthward past the window.

I'll ease back on the thrust now, Loki said. The ship gradually flattened its angle from a seventy-five-degree climb to thirty degrees, and Loki throttled back to about a half of one standard gee.

Karl exhaled a slow breath, clearing out his lungs. The jack prevented him from moving more than a couple of metres from the seat, so he twisted around, looking down the corridor at where Ragnar's men had been thrown by the take-off, and were now clambering to their feet. They shook their heads, trying to clear them.

Ragnar looked up, his face a warring battleground of fear, wonder and delight. "Nowhere to run now, utlander!" Behind him, the others looked more scared than gleeful. Ragnar tottered toward the bridge, leaning into the slope exactly as he would in climbing a steep hill. His left hand was a bandaged mess, the cloth soaked with blood from amputated fingers.

Karl grinned at the evidence of Bera's knife-work, but thought, The urge to impose his will has so narrowed his mind that he can't see the wonder in this. Even Karl – to whom the *Winter Song* was as archaic as a medieval sailing ship – was awed by her sheer brute power. Then Karl saw the look of wonder sweep across Ragnar's face and knew that he'd misjudged the man.

With no physical means to steer the *Winter Song*, Karl thought, Bank to port, Loki. The ship tilted through ninety degrees, but still climbed, even on her side. The manoeuvre hurled Ragnar's men against the wall – now their floor – knocking them senseless.

"That should quieten them for a few minutes!" Karl straightened the ship again. Bera nodded, beads of sweat glistening on her forehead, a tic in her cheek pulsing. "Are you coping?" Karl asked, and she nodded again. "It's a bit scary, the first take-off," Karl said. "But don't worry; after the thousandth time, it's as dull as doing the laundry."

Bera smiled dutifully at the feeble joke.

"I'm keeping the acceleration slow so as not to do anyone any damage," Karl said.

"Never mind us, what about the ship?" Bera said. "It feels like it'll fall apart at any minute!"

"It won't," Karl said. Inside he was terrified, but he thought, If I stay calm, they will as well. He hoped his theory was right. "We should pass fourteen thousand metres in a few seconds. The slow rate of climb should enable us to move around if we're careful."

"What about them?" Bera jerked her head at Ragnar's men.

"See if they can fly," Coeo growled. The humanoid had clearly grasped the idea that the ship was no longer a stationary shrine, although the way he hunched as though expecting a blow hinted at deeply rooted anxiety.

"Show them how merciful you are," Karl said. "That you are a civilised man."

Coeo shrugged as if washing his hands of the whole problem, but when Karl passed him several lengths of cable, he duly trussed the prisoners.

Karl realised that he'd forgotten to check the screens. Fat lot of good it'll do to reach orbit if Mizar B's glare blinds us. But the metal screens slid down to cover the windows, though they groaned and rattled and one stuck for a heart-stopping couple of seconds, and one of the four monitors still worked – Karl wondered why it hadn't been removed by the crew. Maybe they had no use for it, he thought, though it begs the question what they used other monitors for. He had a mental vision of a tribe of humanoids sitting watching a blank screen.

Karl ran through which shipboard cameras were working, showing the pictures from each one in turn. Most were damaged beyond repair, but the fore and aft cameras both worked, as did one of the belly cameras. "Here's a picture of the *Winter Song*," Karl said as an image of the ship appeared on the monitor. Needle-thin central spine, two halves of a globe separated by a five-hundred metre-long lateral lattice. The engine pod is two hundred and ten metres in diameter, the crew pod is one hundred and forty metres across, half that in height.

As the *Winter Song* crawled up through the atmosphere, their prisoners slowly regained consciousness, Arnbjorn first. He watched Karl the whole time, but said nothing.

Thorir cursed and threatened them, until Bera crouched and held her knife to his throat. "Nothing would give me greater pleasure than to use this. So be quiet." Thorir glared, but obeyed.

Orn was also quiet when he came round, but he looked panicked, and Karl worried how the settler would cope with their new environment – particularly weightlessness.

Ragnar was last to recover, and looked confused, but Karl decided that he would make no concessions to Ragnar's age. He's only himself to thank for whatever state he's in, Karl thought.

The *Winter Song* continued her steady climb through Isheimur's atmosphere, the world's curvature now obvious on the viewscreen. Karl sub-vocalised, How are the seals holding up?

Loki came back: *We're about thirty kilometres up, and the air pressure's only a quarter of what it was on the ground, but there are no leaks – and we'd know by now. The airlock to the hangar has held, no matter how primitive it might have appeared, and we seem to be maintaining our integrity.*

"Good," Karl muttered.

But the datarealm is now fighting my instructions.

Can you lock it off? Karl asked.

I'll do my best, but I'm not certain that it will be possible.

Nonetheless, Karl felt the connection go dead – either Loki had locked it away, or for some other reason – the core itself may have decided to go off-line.

When Karl looked around again, Ragnar was studying him. "What are you, utlander, that you alone can do something that no one else has ever managed?"

Bera said, "What he is, is a man you shouldn't have tried to kidnap and hold to ransom."

Ragnar scowled. "Are you a traitor, or simply bewitched by him, girl? I had my reasons."

"Be quiet, the pair of you!" Karl snapped. At Bera's hurt look, he patted her hand. "I don't answer to you, Ragnar." He leaned forward. "You keep trying to make this about you. You're missing the point. This ship goes way, way beyond a feud about hospitality, or horse theft. Listen to me now…"

Ragnar nodded, eyes blazing. "Say your piece, All-man."

"You need me alive, to fly this ship home. Kill me, Ragnar, and you can forget about ever seeing Skorradalur again."

"He's right," Arnbjorn said. He looked up at Karl. "But if we worked with you, you could help us, use this ship right and we could use it to push the Formers' policies on."

"And exterminate Coeo's people in the process?" Karl said, refusing to use the settler's word "troll" in front of them, legitimise it. "The adapted are just that: adapted so that they can live on this world as it is. Raise the temperature much further and change the nitrogen-oxygen-CO_2 mix, and you add genocide to your treatment of them."

"That's our decision to make!" Ragnar said.

"No it isn't," Karl said. "Not in isolation. You're subject to the laws of humanity, whether you like it or not, once a second sentient race is concerned." Karl wondered what their reaction would be if he mentioned the possibility that there might actually be shapeshifters, and who were sentient. He decided to say nothing, though. They have enough to contend with, just assimilating all this, he thought with a trace of pity.

"He's right, Pappi," Arnbjorn said, and added, to both of them: "Forget about who owes what to whom. This ship changes everything. Maybe it could be used in ways that don't harm the…" Arnbjorn groped for a name, "adapted."

Karl, Loki said quietly, *the ship's datarealm has started counter-measures that will eject me from control if we cannot circumvent them. I have no idea what the ship would do in that event.*

Keep working at it, Karl sub-vocalised. We can't allow it to regain control, at least until we've sent the message off, and then only if it doesn't threaten our safety.

Karl turned his attention back to the others. Orn and Thorir sat with bowed heads, too over-awed it seemed to look up at the viewscreen that now showed Isheimur in all her white speckled with green and blue glory. Ragnar and Arnbjorn continued to talk about the various uses the ship could be put to use, from carrying supplies and orbital surveys, to cannibalising it for parts.

Karl found it hard to pay attention to the others. He was more interested in the mission. Ship mentioned the Hangzhou Relay, he sub-vocalised. Can you locate it for us to send a second Mayday?

Loki said, *I'll study the available data, see if I can locate it.*

Karl saw Coeo watching Arnbjorn and Ragnar

intently, and nudged him. Coeo said, "There is much talking. What of?"

Karl explained and Coeo said, "If it's anyone's it is ours. Not theirs to take, especially to make our world unliveable. The old one is like all the others of their kind, preferring to kill us all than share the land. And I do not have trust for the younger one, though I may misjudge him…"

"It doesn't matter, anyway," Karl said. "We have the ship. They don't."

"And it should stay that way," Coeo said. "Surely your people will agree when they come?"

"Of course." Karl decided that now was not the time to explain fractious humanity's fragmented politics.

I've been analysing Isheimur's atmosphere, Loki said. *Comparing it with the readings that the Formers took before they left, and with what I was able to learn from the datarealm before it went off-line. The trends are worrying to anyone invested in the planet's viability. I have no idea whether these are recent developments, or have been occurring since the Formers left.*

Tell me.

Atmospheric pressure is fractionally reduced, although that's expected. The atmosphere will slowly leak into space, partly through too-low gravity, partly through the Mizar solar wind stripping the magnetic field. At point six-seven standard gravities, Isheimur is just below what is considered viable to retain atmosphere against leakage.

But that's not the whole problem?

No. What is truly worrying is what's happened to the ozone layer. I'd discount the readings I'm getting now, were it not that I've got access to the – admittedly limited – scans that Ship ran. They all show that the planetary ozone layer has been reduced by forty per cent in total, and the polar ozone layer has been depleted by eighty per cent.

Are the settlers at risk? Karl said.

Perhaps, Loki said. An image appeared in Karl's peripheral vision. *The first point, with the red square, is the mean average temperature at the time of the Winter Song's crash. Compare it with mean average temperatures when the Formers started their project…*

About the same.

Exactly. This is how much they raised it by – a third triangle flashed up – and this is where it should be – a fourth triangle appeared with a new line joining it to the graph – is what latest readings indicate that it is.

"But that's impossible!"

The others turned to stare at Karl, and he realised that he'd spoken out loud. He continued, sotto voce, "That's several Kelvin below what it should be."

Seven point one, to be precise: I have no logical theory – or solution – at this point in time. Let me work on it.

Agreed. There isn't time to tease through all the implications now. It's more important that we set off a signal that will be noticed by others, rather than relying on just the Hangzhou Relay. However long it takes, outsiders have to be brought to Isheimur. Then we can act on your findings.

Karl noticed that Bera was trying to get his attention. The ship was reaching the planet's Karman-line, where space effectively began.

Bera watched Karl re-focus, wishing he would pay closer attention to their captives. Thorir had that shifty look that he got when he thought he was being clever.

She needed a break badly. She beckoned Coeo and indicated the prisoners. "Can you guard them, for five minutes?" She had no idea how much of her slow, precisely enunciated – but murmured – question he understood but he nodded, taking the sword.

Bera tapped Karl on the shoulder. "Back in five minutes."

"Hmm," he said, eyes glazed again.

"Karl, what is the matter with you?"

He blinked, seeming to see her for the first time. "Loki's struggling with the datarealm."

"I need to piss," Bera said. "I'll be back as soon as possible – but I have to go."

Karl nodded and she fled, acutely conscious of the pressure on her bladder.

It took her a couple of minutes to find the cubicle, which almost proved to be too long, but she just made it. When she returned, Karl seemed to be his old self again, for he winked at her. "Problem solved?" she asked.

"We think so," Karl said, turning back to Ragnar.

"Assuming what you say is true," Ragnar said, "you still have no right to decide the ship's fate, or hold us captive."

"I have every right." Karl beamed. "I'll use the same logic that you've always used, namely, I have the advantage, and Might is Right. One of the things that you'll accept if you wish to negotiate access to a starship is that your son-in-law stands trial for rape – assuming that you recognise such an enlightened concept."

"Karl, no!" Bera cried.

"What?" He gazed at her, bemused. "You don't want this bastard brought to trial?"

"This stays here," Bera said. "I can't face reliving all that."

"That's because it wasn't rape." Thorir smirked. "She came after me."

"You lying bastard!" Bera slapped Thorir. Straining every sinew, she at least had the pleasure of watching his head rock back.

"You see, spaceman," Thorir said. "She's unstable. No kind of witness." He suddenly seemed to remember that Ragnar was present, and adopted a look of injured innocence. "I was in my cups, I admit it. I'm sorry, Ragnar, it was a foolish thing to do."

"You bastard," Bera spat. It was hard to know which was worse – that it was in the open, but Thorir still seemed to be getting away with it, the look of doubt on Karl's face, or Ragnar's ashen visage.

"*You?*" Ragnar whispered, his whole attention fixed on Thorir.

"I'm sorry, Pappi, but–"

"I'm not your father, you maggot! Drunk or not, willing or not, you raped a girl?"

"I was not willing!" Bera shouted.

Thorir swallowed, seeming to realise for the first time that he might not be able to talk his way out of it. "Don't let them distract you from the ship. That's what this little diversion's about. Not a silly mistake I made last summer."

"A silly mistake?" Bera bellowed at Ragnar, her calm finally, belatedly, deserting her. "You were supposed to protect me, to look after me." She poked him in the chest to punctuate each word: "And. You. Did. Nothing! Nothing. Ragnar!"

Ragnar bowed his head.

Karl said, breaking the silence. "I think, deep down inside, Ragnar guessed."

He perfectly articulated her own thoughts. It would explain why you've been so angry, Pappi, and with Karl, who has never done anything to cause you harm.

The bridge suddenly seemed very small, very hot. The ship was climbing in a very shallow trajectory now, accelerating at barely a third of Isheimur's gravity so she could pace the bridge. One, two, three, four steps and she was most of the way across it.

She'd never spoken of the rape for precisely this reason. Any accusation would tear Skorradalur apart. Even if she were believed – and she wouldn't be. She must have done something to lead the bastard on, mustn't she?

Bera thought of all the times she'd laughed with Thorir when younger, never believing what he was possible of. But when she'd started to bleed, her breasts to bud, he'd cuddled her a second too long, or too closely, though it was so subtle she hadn't realised the first few times. When she'd looked uncomfortable he'd backed away, looking hurt, and she'd rushed to reassure him that she did still like him.

She meant as a friend or brother. He'd obviously thought that she meant something else.

Then there'd been that awful night. She still couldn't bear to think about it too much, had resolved instead to block it out, irrespective of the sleepless nights and panic attacks that followed.

But she hadn't expected that she would be so desperately, desperately lonely, nor had she expected the unrelenting ferocity of their condemnation when she had missed her period, and the realisation came that she was pregnant.

It all made sense now. They knew, maybe they didn't know that they knew, but deep down inside they had an inkling and to cover their guilt they made me the scapegoat.

Confronting it, she felt the blister of pain that she had borne for so long split and ooze, and wished that she could take Karl somewhere and show him that she was healing – that she was a woman where it counted – in the only way that she knew how. Her only experience was of humiliation and hurt, but she was sure that there had to be more to love than that. She looked away from Karl's long, slender fingers and the memory of him naked, sure that everyone saw the flush rising up her face.

To distract her from such thoughts she stared around at the others, who had fallen silent in the face of her fury. Their discomfort made her feel better as well.

Arnbjorn cleared his throat. "Loath though I am to agree with Thorir," Arnbjorn said, "now's not the time or place for this. We should defer it until we return to Skorradalur–"

Bera felt her weight abruptly leave her, and grabbed the nearest object, a strut to which a seat had once been attached. For all Arnbjorn's hi-jacking of her life – typical of them! – she wanted to sing out loud at this dizzying new sensation of freedom. I'm flying!

"We've achieved escape velocity, and cut the acceleration," Karl said. "But we should be able to simulate a little gravity by rotating the ship."

Bera wanted to laugh out loud at the way Coeo's fur corona-ed out, though he looked as inscrutable as ever. She quietly enjoyed the panic written across the captive's faces. She kept quiet, instead wondering how it would feel to cuddle Karl without weight holding them in thrall.

She was almost sad when gravity returned a few moments later.

Ragnar's men all breathed a heavy sigh of relief.

I get the distinct impression, Karl sub-vocalised, that once the novelty wears off, our passengers are going to find this voyage tedious, which may encourage them to mischief. I'm not sure that I entirely believe this new milk-and-water Ragnar.

Then it's a shame that they can't see the carnage in cyberspace, you replied. That would entertain them. The ship's datarealm had launched wave after wave of counter-attack to seize control of the power, the helm, even life support, directly or through back door channels such as the sprinkler and other fire-retardant systems. Fortunately you'd been alert enough to slam every door shut before it could gain a foothold, but the battle – a lethal version of three-dimensional chess – tied up more and more of your resources.

During a lull while the datarealm retreated off-line like a predator returning to its lair and you shored up your defences, you swept the Mizar B system with the spectographs and other external systems. There are signs of a recent conflict in the inner Mizar B system, you told Karl. The weapons signatures are identical to those that attacked Ship. But there's also debris which looks as if it's wreckage from them. It's a guesstimate based on the various pieces drifting around, but by assembling them into a cyber-jigsaw, I've established that it's possible, verging on probable that all or all but one of your attackers were destroyed.

That might be what those lights in the sky were a few nights ago, Karl said. Is there anything to confirm the timescale?

Nothing definitive, you said. There are also traces of plastic, metal and other wreckage that look artificial, but don't fit that pattern. If you give me some time, I'll correlate the scatter back to a common origin point and extrapolate. The hours that passed in cyberspace as you fitted, took away and reassembled again and again the billions of pieces of debris into a starship-shaped jigsaw puzzle took mere micro-seconds in real-time, but even so, you noticed Karl become aware of a growing tension among their captives.

It looks, you said, as if the ships like those that attacked you were destroyed in turn, either by Aye ships, or by an unknown third party – more likely the former option. In turn based on one scatter point and the flotsam, there is an eighty-six per cent possibility that one or more of the Aye ships was destroyed.

So hypothesise, Karl said. Could Ship's mayday have led to the skirmish?

Possible. Perhaps some other factor was involved, but Occam's Scalpel suggests excluding any possibility other than that human and Aye ships fought and destroyed each other.

How does this affect the possibility that Ship's Mayday might be answered? Karl asked.

It makes it more likely that it will attract attention, you answered. But those receiving Ship's Mayday may assume that it was generated by one of the combatants recently destroyed.

Leading them to assume that there's nothing left to search for? Karl said.

Exactly, you replied.

In which case, we need to send another message. I think that I have an idea. Get me the reactor schematics.

Not now, you said. The datarealm has just launched another incursion, this time through the life-support back-up objects, which it's just taken off-line. Fortunately the main activity is unaffected.

You paused. You may wish to give Bera and the others your attention. Something is developing.

Bera was worried. Ragnar had barely spoken since she had accused him of failing her. That wasn't unusual. What was unique was that the revelation that Thorir had fathered Palli had seemed to knock the fight out of him. Such a collapse was something she'd never witnessed in all her time at Skorradalur.

The others were also silent but watchful, as if waiting for something. Only Thorir kept up a staccato barrage of comments for Ragnar and Arnbjorn's benefit, denials and justifications alternated with digs at Bera.

Finally Arnbjorn snapped, "Be silent. I want to see this world of ours."

Once they had watched the screen for a few seconds, there was little to see. A white globe, slowly rotating, marked by the mountains and lakes of the single world-encircling continent. It was almost hypnotic. So effective was the distraction that when it ended, Bera took a moment to realise what was happening.

She had been so lulled by the conversation and the view of Isheimur that she had forgotten to re-check their captives' bonds. So when Thorir's hands appeared from behind his back, one clutching an extending sword drawn dragon-swift from his leggings, she could only stare open-mouthed.

Coeo was on the other side of the bridge, and Karl – still jacked into the controls – was deep in thought. So Bera yelled as Thorir cut the other's bonds. His freeing them gave her time to draw her sword, but even so, she only just had time to parry his first wild slash.

Luckily his blade was thin to allow it to partially retract into the hilt – An assassin's weapon, she thought, how appropriate – so that when it clanged on her own short blade the jolt of the impact wasn't quite enough to make her drop it. Instead she juggled it into her left hand, and managed to keep one of the seats between her and Thorir.

In the momentary respite that the move gained her, Bera glimpsed Karl freeing the jack to take on Orn, who stood looking bewildered, while Coeo engaged

Arnbjorn and Ragnar, who seemed equally nonplussed. All of them had drawn concealed swords similar to Thorir's, but looked as though they were being swept along by events beyond their control.

"Come on!" Thorir roared. "We take her, and the boy will do as we say, won't you, Allman?" When they didn't move, Thorir roared, "Has the utlander taken your balls?"

Belatedly, reluctantly it appeared to Bera, the others joined the fight.

"First you have to take me alive, Thorir," Bera gasped, lunging at him left-handed from behind the chair.

But he was alive to that and danced back in the low gravity. "Uh-oh, naughty girl!"

She retreated again, keeping the chair between them, trying desperately to shake the feeling back in her right arm, while fending off his counter-attacks with her left, but each subsequent clang of his sword on hers took another bite from the blade, while the shock stole another bit of feeling from her left arm, to go with her numbed right.

Her only hope was that they needed her alive. She could always fall on her own blade if need be – it wasn't as if anyone would miss her. Karl would be sad for a while, but it would pass.

But there was a stubbornness in her that refused the coward's way out. That and the fact that Thorir was concentrating on disarming her gave her a glimmer of hope.

They danced from side to side, the chair always between them, Thorir grinning, Bera panting, the others yelling, blades clanging. The bridge stank of sweat and the tang of blood from nicks that all the fighters had taken.

As another blow on the blade almost dashed her sword from her hand, Bera felt the tingle in her right as the numbness passed. She gasped and winced.

Thorir's grin grew wider. "Give it up, girly!" It was the same grin as when he'd held her down on her bed at Skorradalur and torn her leggings off.

Furious, she fumbled in her pocket with her other hand and almost dropped the short paring knife that she'd stashed there in the desert. Somehow she got her fingers around the handle. *Clang!* Another blow and she felt the fingers of her left hand loosening.

There was only Thorir and her in the whole universe now. His tongue lolled like a spaniel on a hot day. One more parry of his sword, and she would drop her own.

So she did, as he drew his arm back, and stabbed him right-handed in the heart with the paring knife.

TWENTY

For a moment, Bera wasn't sure that she'd penetrated Thorir's padding all the way through. He wore chest protection like all his comrades, but like them he'd sacrificed battle armour for the lighter padding that they wore when herding near Skorradalur. There attacks were fewer and predators more likely to flee than stand and fight.

Then his eyes widened and he swayed in a phantom breeze that blew all the way from Valhalla. Bera let out a shout, of joy and of rage at his arrogance. He'd been so sure of himself that he'd toyed with her. She unfroze and, putting her boot onto his chest, yanked the knife free. After the sucking sound it made when it finally came free she didn't need to see the blood on the blade.

As if she had turned off a light, life abruptly faded from Thorir's eyes, and a thin trickle of blood ran from his mouth. Bera pushed him, and he fell backward, dead. She felt oddly proud that with such accuracy, one blow had been all that was needed. Almost overwhelmed with relief that he could never hurt her again, she put her hand over her mouth, unsure if she wanted to be sick or sob, or both.

Around her, the others fought on with no indication that they'd heard her. In Ragnar's case he fought Karl only half-heartedly, which was as well. Karl was clearly struggling to cope with Arnbjorn, as the blood running down his arm testified. Coeo and Orn were both covered in blood.

Orn looked so panicked that Bera feared he might berserk at any moment. So picking up a panel about a metre wide that lay against a wall, Bera brought it down on the back of Orn's skull.

"Takk!" Coeo showed his outsize canines in what Bera hoped was a friendly grin.

"Welcome," Bera said, and they advanced on the others.

Ragnar cried out a warning. Arnbjorn half-swung around, saw that he was outflanked and held his sword aloft, point upward. "Truce!"

"For how long?" Karl said. "Until you launch a sneak attack?" But he held back, instead re-inserting the jack into the nape of his neck.

Arnbjorn flipped the sword so that he held the point, and balancing the blade on his other forearm, offered the hilt to Karl. "You can search us, if you wish," he said. "I was surprised you didn't before."

"We're novices," Karl growled. "But we won't make that mistake again. Strip." As Arnbjorn made to take the sword back, inspiration struck. "No, wait!" Karl said. "Will you swear allegiance? I propose myself as your new Gothi."

Ragnar chortled, then stopped. "You're serious?"

"Very," Karl said. "You're in my place now, using my resources."

"Never!" Arnbjorn said.

"Do it," Ragnar said, and knelt. Arnbjorn hesitated, then followed. Orn was coming round, and Ragnar bundled him into position.

"I swear allegiance to my leader. All that I have is yours, and I will follow your lead, wherever you take me. In return, you will give me shelter, succour, honour and trust. On Wotan's name, I swear this."

Bera had stood behind the settlers. She nodded. "It's the proper oath; no crossing of fingers to invalidate it."

With a gesture of resignation, Arnbjorn repeated the oath. For a moment it looked as if Orn might baulk, then he shrugged and did the same.

Ragnar indicated Thorir's corpse. "What did you do?"

Bera shrugged. "It was him or me. Your men attacked us – or have you forgotten?"

Ragnar's eyes narrowed, and Karl said quickly, "The man was a rapist. I passed sentence."

"Accused," Ragnar said, but sounded tired. "Or does-n't your world presume innocence?"

"No," Karl said, "it doesn't. On Avalon we're neither innocent nor guilty until the court hands down a ver-dict. My verdict was that in attacking us, he admitted his guilt."

"I – I still can't believe it," Ragnar said. "He might not have been my ideal son-in-law, but Thorir, a rapist?" He shook his head, as if to clear it of such thoughts.

Bera said, "What if I'd braved his threats when he sobered up the morning after? If I had pressed my case against Thorir, how would you have reacted?" When the men didn't answer, Bera said, "I'll tell you. It would've been, 'What did you do to lead him on?' I'd have been lynched, or it would have been outright civil war if anyone had believed me."

Their silence was eloquent assent.

"When did it happen?" Arnbjorn said.

"The Bride Fair," Bera said. "You left him behind. Hilda was unwell, everyone else was away, he got drunk. That was that." She tried to shut out his crashing open her bedroom door, as if daring Hilda to awake; his bulk in the doorway, teeth gleaming in the midsummer midnight twilight.

"He died in battle against enemy hordes," Ragnar said, "giving his life to buy us time."

"Agreed," Bera said. "No reason Hilda and the children should share his shame."

"Thank you," Ragnar said, eyes shut, hand to his forehead.

"What now?" Coeo said in halting Isheimuri. Ragnar and the others stared, eyes widening.

"You're still denying their sentience?" Karl said. "Because they've chosen a different shape, another way of life from yours?"

"And if we do? Not that I say we will," Ragnar said.

"Then you'll have half the galaxy down on you."

"So they're sentient," Ragnar said. "It will still take some time to persuade Valdimar the Slow out at Skaftafell not to blow his new-found cousin's brains out."

"Then we'll take our victories where we can, and persuading you to accept him will be our first victory for sense," Karl said, grinning at Bera.

You should know that we have a primitive nanoforge aboard, Loki said. *Perhaps the oldest of its kind. We do need raw materials…*

"We'll dispose of the body," Karl said, unjacking again. "No ceremony for this bastard."

Coeo helped him carry out the corpse.

While Karl and the others were fighting and talking, you fought your own rearguard action – worthy of the blood-soaked warrens of Hightshell Five – against the latest incursion of the datarealm's counter-insurgency programmes.

This is pure stupidity, you wanted to tell it, but that was the very point; you weren't in the datarealm's permitted list, so therefore your gaining access meant you had to be removed. It was circular logic and, had the ship's makers had any foresight, they would have provided for the unexpected. But perhaps allowing others to take control of their ship wasn't something that they could ever countenance. The Central Asian Republics of Earth weren't, according to the histories, noted for their enlightenment.

Deep-programmed as you were into your very soul against taking a "life", even that of an obsolete datarealm, you knew you might yet have to overcome that bedrock programming.

Karl changed the monitor from Isheimur-view to maps, but couldn't find anything on the Mizar system to help with the plan that he and Loki had been hatching ever since the download told him of the planet's warming. Then he realised: if the ship was lost, they probably had no maps of the Mizar system!

Sighing, he sub-vocalised, Put the view back. It took several attempts, during which other maps appeared. What's going on?

The datarealm is still trying to retake control, Loki said. *Nothing I can't handle. I could get more data on Isheimur's situation if I use the nanoforge to generate a couple of microprobes, and fire them into Isheimur's atmosphere.*

I have a better idea. Karl beckoned Bera from where she was guarding Ragnar's men, who were still in their underclothes. "I have the impression," Karl murmured, "that Thorir was the one who attacked us, and they followed him like sheep."

"I think so," Bera said. "Maybe they felt some sort of solidarity."

"Probably," Karl said. "They were cornered animals. Panic reaction – fight or flight. They had nowhere to run, so they had to fight together." If he was wrong, it might cost them all their lives, but he had grown used to backing his judgement on little more than instinct these last few weeks, without the benefit of libraries of data download. "Tell me," Karl said, "do you know what frequencies will get us into the Oracle?"

"I don't," Bera said. "But Orn might."

Karl took a deep breath and turned to the others, motioning them to dress. When they had, and sat with varying degrees of caution in the various chairs around the bridge, Karl said, "What do we do with you?" At Ragnar's raised eyebrow, he added, "What would you do, if you were me?"

"Push us out the airlock," Arnbjorn said. "But you're not us, are you?"

Karl smiled. "No. I'm not."

"Why don't you tell us what you want the ship for?" Arnbjorn said. "Are you going to fly her back to your homeworld?"

Karl asked a silent question of Loki and after a few seconds, relayed the answer. "We can't. The ship would take a year to reach the nearest fold-point, and it doesn't have a fold-generator, which we need. Nanofacturing one would require that we stuffed the whole ship into the nanoforge just to make the tools needed to make the fold-generator."

"So what then?" Ragnar said.

"I need to send a Mayday, but beyond that I've no firm plans. I don't deny that I'd have liked to have flown home."

Karl, Loki said. *You should see this.*

Karl held up his hand to the others. "Give me a moment." Yes?

I've found the likely vector for the Hangzhou Relay, and sent a Mayday across as many frequencies as possible. I'll alternate that with sending transmissions directly toward likely rescuers. The problem with those systems is that they're much further away.

Good, Karl said. But you didn't need my attention for that.

No, Loki said. *Also... I fired several clusters of micro-probes into Isheimur's atmosphere, and I've got their readings of the CO_2 levels. They're far, far higher than they should be. But the probes have also confirmed something else – that for some reason, probably due to geodynamic mechanics, the planet's magnetic field strength is diminishing very rapidly – leaving the planet open to devastating effects on the volatile gases. What should have been global warming has given way to global cooling. Unless we can find a way to stop it, the settlers will die.*

I don't believe in coincidences that big, Karl said. Find the smoking gun. How long do the settlers have?

I estimate ten to thirty years, depending on the rate of cooling and precisely when it began. Loki flashed up an image of Bera as an old woman, huddled in vain against the cold.

Karl wondered again at the Aye ships' presence, and tried to block out the image of Bera dying. He turned back to the others. "Something's arisen, involving Isheimur." He asked Orn, "If Loki can find the frequencies, can you access the Oracle?"

"You want me to break into it?"

"Yes."

"Why?"

"We need information." Karl repeated what Loki had said.

Orn looked around, and sweeping the dust off a flat surface that probably acted as a resting place for beverages – it seemed to serve no other purpose – took a marker and scribbled numbers on the surface.

"Can we talk to our wives?" Orn said.

"If we can get access, then yes," Karl said.

Karl stared at the numbers. After a few seconds which probably equated to hours, perhaps days in cyberspace, Loki came back: *I'm in. I'm looking for matches to magnetic fields, climate change, carbon dioxide. Ah, here–*

When Karl emerged from his inner conversation, he became aware that the others were watching him anxiously. "What?"

"Even for you, that was a long, long trance," Bera said. "And while you were talking with your invisible friend, doors started opening and shutting, and lights going on and off."

"Don't worry about it," Karl said, thinking, *Sort that damned datarealm out, Loki!* "Strap yourselves in and get ready to tour the Mizar B inner system. We're going comet-hunting."

"Why?" Arnbjorn said.

"I'll tell you when we get there," Karl said with a huge grin, hand upraised to forestall their protests.

Once Loki had selected their target and everyone had strapped in, Loki ended the *Winter Song*'s spin – to the settlers' consternation.

"Don't worry," Karl said as they grasped at chairs, consoles or anything else that was bolted down, "we'll be under way in a few moments. Once Orn's let go of that panel." The settler had clutched at something that looked secure, but turned out not to be attached, and floated horizontally, with his thrashing feet straight out behind him and his face twisted by terror. Somehow Karl kept his face straight.

"Shame," Bera said, flashing Karl a tremulous smile. "I quite enjoy weightlessness."

"Then we'll do it again," Karl whispered on his way to his chair.

Her smile widened, her eyes glowed, and she bit her lower lip before saying, "Good."

Diagnostics show that we can run for weeks on full power, so we'll have ample time, Loki said. *We'll run out of air before that, even with this ship's archaic CO_2 scrubbers recycling it. They're not the most efficient kit that I've ever encountered.*

"Could we run it through the nanoforge?" Karl muttered.

I doubt it. I've seen more sophisticated tractors than that forge.

Before Karl could reply, a giant fist punched him in the back, and they were under way.

Loki took them up to three gravities for almost an hour, until Karl took pity on the others, particularly Ragnar who breathed like a haddock out of water. Karl told Loki: Drop us back down to one standard g for an hour.

There was a long pause before Loki said, *I am encountering difficulties with this idiot semi-consciousness again.* Then the gravity slowly, steadily dropped. *Executed.*

Karl grinned. "That was said with great emphasis."

Indeed.

After another hour, they dropped back to acceleration at Isheimuri gravity for almost twenty-four hours. Mostly they ate and slept in the chairs they sat in, then stretched and paced the kinks out of their backs, before visiting the facilities.

During a lull in the internecine strife with the datarealm, Karl led a scavenger hunt through the ship; Coeo found some interactive holo-discs in Kazakh that had dropped down behind a chair in the crew quarters. He interrogated them for hours on end, devouring Terran history, astronomy, anything that he could access. Arnbjorn and Orn played cards with a pack that they'd found in the back of a cupboard, while Ragnar sat and brooded, staring into space.

Bera hunted and gathered ragged remnants of fabrics, furnishings and equipment. "Are you nesting?" Karl joked.

She gazed at him with eyes that never blinked. "I'm planning for what happens when – if – we return to Isheimur. Remember our leaving Skorradalur?"

Karl nodded with a little smile. "I'll consider myself suitably rebuked for not thinking ahead."

"Quite right," Bera said, and then she slowly smiled. "You thinking at all is an improvement."

It was, Karl decided, the nicest smile he'd ever seen, but said nothing.

The rest of the time, Bera spent sleeping in the chair next to Karl, curled up in the crook of his arm. No matter how cramped, he rarely moved, for fear of disturbing her.

Loki said, *We're just past the mid-way point, about thirty-seven million kilometres to destination. Do you want me to mirror the acceleration – Isheimuri, standard, then three standard for the last hour?*

"No," Karl said. "Reverse thrust at Isheimuri standard for as long as possible. Let's keep it simple. It strikes me that the fewer changes we make, the less the Idiot fights us." Loki had christened the datarealm thus after one of its sporadic attempts to regain control.

That would seem to be the case, Loki said. *Perhaps now that we're leaving Isheimur it believes we're returning to its*

343

original mission protocol. Our taking what would be the right
course or simply reaching escape velocity has fooled it.

Or maybe, Karl thought, it's just biding its time.

During the deceleration, the others again probed Karl relentlessly about his plans. He remained close-mouthed, partly because data was still pouring in, both from the first micro-probes that Loki had launched and from another subsequent batch.

So to distract as many of them as possible, Karl had Orn and Arnbjorn cut up the cockpit door that they'd blown in; he felt a little uneasy allowing them a laser-saw, but almost anything else aboard could be turned into a weapon, and his gamble had been vindicated. Given a practical task and when his world shrank to the nanoforge in the foundry, Orn forgot his fear, losing himself in reducing the door to forge-fodder. Given raw materials, the forge could produce pretty much any-thing not on the proscribed list, which precluded weapons and explosives. He even ceased pestering them for updates on communicating with the Oracle – Loki had had about seven seconds worth of access be-fore the Oracle. Unable to reconcile his actual location with the Skorradalur co-ordinates embedded in Orn's access codes, he had slammed a metaphorical door on any further communication.

Bera used the forge to "cook", duplicating the sam-ples of various meats and fruit that she'd carried aboard the ship. It seemed strange to Karl that the forge could manufacture complex micro-probes, but was incapable of producing lamb that didn't taste like rock-eater meat, and vice versa.

Karl also didn't want to answer the other's questions because until Loki had a chance to examine their des-tination in minute detail, he had become imbued with a superstitious dread that talking about the plan might jinx it somehow. He would have laughed at such pre-historic ideas back on Avalon, but Isheimur had changed him in many ways.

So when the others tried to get him to talk, Karl instead encouraged the settlers to talk to Coeo, and vice versa. Isheimuri proved easier for Coeo to learn – for all that he had to remember to pitch his voice within certain narrow frequencies – than mutated Kazakh was for the settlers to pick up. Coeo's rudimentary Isheimuri soon improved markedly.

"Where did you think that the original Formers came from?" Arnbjorn asked.

"From hell," Coeo answered. "We thought the old stories passed down from mother to baby, that hell was beneath us, were wrong. We knew where we had come from – that our grandfathers had fallen from the sky and shaped the mud and the rain to make us. But when the sky opened and vomited forth your people, we thought that perhaps hell – as well as heaven – was above us." The adapted man paused. "Every day, every night, rocks rained down on us, screaming across the sky. Some of our people hid in caves, some beneath outcrops and overhangs. Most simply perished in the open, though. Then, when we tried to communicate, we were slaughtered. We were prevented from following our animals on their migrations."

Karl was privately sceptical that the comet-rains had been so concentrated in a short time, but kept silent. Arnbjorn and Ragnar said little during such revisions of their histories except once, when Arnbjorn said, "I'm sorry." After that, the tension eased a little.

As they neared their destination, it became harder and harder for Karl to fend off questions. "Yes, it's a comet," he admitted.

I've fired the last micro-probes at it, Loki said. *Analysis indicates that it's ninety-seven point seven per cent water by mass, about as pure as we could reasonably have wished for. That should make our task easier.* Then the download added, *We're going to overshoot slightly.*

"We need to strap in," Karl said, ignoring the continuing questions of the others.

"It's beautiful," Bera said. She leaned around, craning her neck to see out of the other windows. "Can we see the other worlds?" she said, and the wonder in her voice made Karl's heart turn over. He had Loki pull up a display on one of the monitors, and zoom in on Asagarth and its forty moons, the world itself half-hidden by the Bifrost asteroid belt.

"You never said it was so lovely," Bera whispered, her eyes misting up.

Karl shrugged. "I'm just too used to it most of the time, I guess."

When Loki applied the retros and they decelerated at three gees, it soon became apparent that Ragnar particularly would not stand up to two hours of triple gravity. "OK, we'll stay at two gees for as long as Ragnar can handle it."

Finally the *Winter Song* was travelling alongside the muddy ball of ice that was their destination, and Loki again spun the ship to generate a half standard gravity. It was, Karl guesstimated, no bigger than ten or fifteen kilometres across its main body, although its corona was streaming out for over two hundred and fifty kilometres, and a few wispy strands went even further – perhaps stretching for over four hundred kilometres.

The others looked at Karl expectantly. It was Arnbjorn who ended the silence. "So what's the plan, spaceman?" The title was accompanied by a smile.

Karl took a deep breath. "The Formers came about four hundred years ago, and left about two centuries ago." Karl had Loki replay the charts that the download had showed Karl. "CO_2 has been building up much, much faster than the Formers planned. They may have decided to speed things up and reverse it when they came back – not intending to be gone so long; they may have thought that they could take a short-cut; or they may just have missed something." Karl suspected that there had been some kind of scam, or perhaps that Sigurdsson had hoped for someone to come along in the future with a solution, in the same way that terminal cases had been putting themselves into stasis for almost a millennia, waiting for a cure.

"But that's good, isn't it?" Arnbjorn said. "It'll warm the atmosphere, surely?"

"Some CO_2 can be good, but not always," Karl said. "And something has happened that complicates matters enormously." He continued, "Loki has analysed trace composites in the Isheimuri atmosphere – from the exosphere, right down to the troposphere – that indicate that about a hundred and fifty years ago Isheimur passed through a vast molecular cloud." He gazed at Ragnar. "The vineyards that failed, that shouldn't have? The worsening weather, year on year, decade on decade?"

"Aye," Ragnar growled. "That was the dust cloud?"

"The first part was," Karl agreed. "The traces contain elements barely present in the Mizar quartet. Loki's sensors have just – barely – detected such a cloud way out toward Mizar B's Kuiper Belt. Anyway, the cloud is only part of the problem."

"I sense a 'but' coming," Arnbjorn said.

"Exactly," Karl said. "The 'but' is that the cloud didn't just block out some sunlight. Molecules in the cloud reacted with hydrogen in Mizar B's heliosphere – which extends way past Isheimur – and cascaded vast quantities of electrically charged cosmic rays into Isheimur's atmosphere, stripping away large parts of the ozone layer."

"Whatever the reason, it happened," Bera said, clearly growing bored with the lecture, or impatient for the conclusion.

"So much so," Karl said with a grin at his heckler, "that with some stripping away of the planet's ozone layer, the cloud is about to donate a nasty little leaving present."

"How so?" asked Orn.

If you'd let me speak, I'd bloody well tell you! Karl thought. He took a deep breath. "The magnetic field has just 'flipped' from warming to cooling, which will have catastrophic results."

"What can we do about it?" Ragnar asked.

"That's why we're here," Karl said. "We're going to steer the comet toward Isheimur, then, as we're approaching the planet, dump the ship's reactor into the comet, smashing it to fragments."

"You're what?"

"You'll kill everyone on the planet!"

"That's crazy!"

"How the fuck are we going to get home?"

Coeo was the only one not shouting, but he clearly understood from the others' reactions that there was something going on. Karl took another deep breath and translated into Kazakh.

Coeo seemed unimpressed. "Why should we care about the fake-furs?" he said. "We'll survive. We were made for the cold."

"Not for this cold," Karl said. "In this everyone dies – everyone and everything."

That is incorrect, Karl, Loki said. *It's very likely that the adapted can survive.*

But then he has no reason to help us, Karl sub-vo-calised, and thought of Bera huddled, dying of cold.

"Then we must do it," Coeo said. "Though surely throwing down this icy spear will kill many, many people?"

"We'll keep deaths to a minimum," Karl said. "If we crash the core of the comet down onto the south polar ice-cap, we avoid everything but a few straggling rock-eaters, as most of the adapted will have migrated northward."

"So this comet...?" Bera prompted. It was hardest of all to meet her gaze. The others had barged into his mission, but she'd accompanied him in good faith. Now that might be her death warrant, although if she survived, it would paradoxically be her salvation.

"We push it toward Isheimur, then dump the reactor and detonate it to break the comet up," Karl said, "and ride the biggest fragment all the way down, using emergency power to jump off when we hit the atmosphere."

"What?" Arnbjorn yelped.

"Are you scared?" Karl said, with a grin.

"No!"

"Then trust me – I have no desire to die, either," Karl said.

"What good does one comet do?" Orn said.

"It'll blast carbon dioxide and water vapour into the atmosphere," Karl said, "which will form a protective cloud and seed the ozone layer with water and debris, thereby raising the temperature and moisture. It's only a stop-gap, but it will buy another decade or two, while someone comes along, or until the magnetic field reverses again. Someone will come along to investigate," Karl said. "There's been enough chatter coming out of a supposedly deserted system to attract their attention." He hoped that he was right, but in all likelihood, he wouldn't be around to worry about it.

He explained it all to Coeo, who said, "But it will kill our people! They'll boil or suffocate!"

"No," Karl said. "It will only be temporary." Karl wished that he could be honest, could tell them about the harmonic tremors oscillating through Isheimur's lithosphere, but that would raise too many questions. "By breaking the comet up on the way down, we'll avoid the worst of the fall-out from one huge impact. Larger chunks will still fall to earth, but most will evaporate in the upper mesosphere, like handfuls of glittering dust thrown into the air."

"That's beautiful," Bera said. The others nodded.

Karl sub-vocalised, *You have the flight trajectory? And you've calculated the point where we jettison the reactor?*

You should be aware that even running simulations of these plans has raised the Idiot's levels of activity to unprecedented levels. I hesitate to anthropomorphise it, but the nearest analogy would be to say that it's going frantic. It's testing my control of every sub-routine. It seems intent on gaining control of the reactor in case we dump it into space.

Can you keep it out?

If I can't, Loki said, *you'll learn of it at the same time as I do.*

Karl looked up to find the others studying him. "OK," he said. "We'll need to sit down again." More groans met the statement. "So we'll take just a few minutes while you stretch your legs, urinate or pray." Blank looks greeted his feeble humour. "Sorry, the jokes are due to nerves. I'll shut up."

"You're nervous?" Bera said. "How do you think we feel?"

Karl said, "Yes, you're right." He grinned. "I thought that you were all Viking warriors?" He raised his hands to fend off Bera's rain of playful slaps. "I surrender!"

He turned to the men. Arnbjorn was impassive. Orn looked as scared as ever, while Ragnar seemed lost in thought.

Karl was the last to visit the urinal. Then he retook what had become the captain's seat.

"Start the landing," he told Loki in a loud voice for the others' benefit. The engines fired a short burst, and they drifted toward the comet's ragged, battered surface.

The Idiot's reacting, Loki said. *So far I am able to repel its attempts to seize control of the lateral vents.*

They eased toward a wall of white. Loki fired the forward thrusters as they drifted gently, lazily toward the surface.

It's provoked a counter-attack on all fronts. Karl, it's trying to regain con– Loki went silent. Karl saw the construct's view of cyberspace, with jagged mountains of data hurtling across black, silent voids.

There was a bang from behind them, and all heads swung to look toward the corridor.

"What the hell was that?" Karl forgot to subvocalise, and simply asked it aloud.

Loki was silent, and Karl had the mental image of someone concentrating, with no time to answer. There was another bang, and Arnbjorn, face drawn, began unbuckling his restraints. Karl heard a distant whistle.

"Stay where you are!" Karl said.

Uh-oh, Loki said.

What? Karl sub-vocalised.

The Idiot isn't such an Idiot, Loki said. *It's not after the reactor controls at all. It's fooled me. It wanted the access codes – it's blown the hatch on the roof of the corridor.*

The whistling grew louder, and turned into a roaring wind.

TWENTY-ONE

The gale howled, tugging at them with greedy fingers, almost paralysing Karl with its insistence. The nanophytes would – by switching to emergency mode and pumping blood to his brain and limbs – give him two or three minutes of exposure to vacuum. But to stay where he was meant a swift and inevitable death.

Maintain position but tilt left ninety degrees, he told Loki. The *Winter Song* responded.

Karl emptied his lungs as much as he could and, releasing the catch on his harness, dropped to what was now the floor. The howling storm pulled him along, and out of the corner of his eye he saw the others unbuckling. "Stay there!" he yelled, emptying his lungs still further, but it came out as only a croak.

He ran through the vacant doorway and careered along the corridor toward the next door, the wind pulling him along so that he almost toppled over. That door was blown outward into the corridor, presumably by the *Winter Song*'s idiot datarealm detonating catches in the door-frame, and too late as he hurtled past, he realised that he could have held on to it and used it to patch the gaping hatchway through which the air howled. His skin already felt cool, where whatever moisture had been on it evaporated. Two doors passed, one – maybe two if you're lucky – left. He got ready.

He leaned into a crouch as he rushed toward the next doorway, and hooked his fingers around the prone door's edge, stubbing them hard enough to draw blood, but he screened out the flaring agony and concentrated on tightening his grip. Had he not, someone thudding into his back would have knocked him loose.

It was Coeo. Fortunately Karl had slowed the adapted man's headlong flight, and Coeo flailed, grabbed and hung onto a metre-long projecting handle in the wall that was fixed at both ends.

Moments later, Ragnar in turn bumped into Coeo, almost jarring the adapted man loose. Coeo released one hand, and Karl saw the muscle-snapping effort that Coeo needed to hold on while clutching Ragnar in the crook of the adapted man's free arm.

"Told you! Stay behind!" Karl gasped.

"Others have!" Ragnar replied, equally breathless, then coughed. Blood trickled from his nostril. He looked pale and his eyes bulged.

Karl guessed that Ragnar had less than half his lung capacity. You have maybe a minute before it's too late for him, Karl thought.

Coeo nudged Ragnar into a position where the settler could grab and hold on to the bar. Coeo looked to Karl who beckoned him. Coeo dived for the door to which Karl was still grimly clinging, and with a whirlwind of scrabbling fingers, gained a purchase on it against the howling gale tugging at his back.

Karl was lucky – with his enhanced lungs he still had maybe a minute left, but he was unsure how much longer Coeo could last. Fortunately when Karl gasped, "Lift!" Coeo reacted immediately. Even so, it took everything he had to get the door to chest, then to shoulder height.

Ragnar squeezed between them, and Karl and Coeo lifted again with the old man's help. Karl felt the spasm of a muscle-strain in his back, Coeo grunted and Ragnar moaned softly, but they levered the door upright and pushed it over the gaping hatchway.

The wind dropped immediately, the howl fading to a whine, and no longer sucked along by the miniature hurricane, weightlessness again exerted its influence. Ragnar ripped a piece of his tunic off and stuffed it into the main gap. The whine quietened, and Coeo slouched, drawing a bushel of air into his lungs. Ragnar drifted against the wall, gasping.

Karl took a deep rasping breath until he felt giddy. Mustn't hyperventilate, he thought. "OK." He wiped a trickle of blood from his nose. "Need to get back, stop this happening again."

He helped Coeo to his feet, and turned to Ragnar, whose face had turned a muddy, ashen colour, but who shook off any offers of help, and bumped and barged back against them as they swaggered slo-mo through the snowstorm of debris that had swept out the bridge, toward where the others waited in the doorway.

Arnbjorn and Orn pushed themselves to his father's side. "You stubborn old bugger," Arnbjorn said. "I told you to let me take care of it."

Ragnar shook his head. "You're needed to run the farm. Yngi's not up to it, much though I love the boy. Orn will help you as well."

"No need for talk like that," Orn said.

Bera took Karl's arm. "Are you OK?"

Karl smiled. "I was about to ask you the same question." She looked unaffected by the experience, apart from being slightly pop-eyed from higher blood pressure. Karl pressed the small of his back where the muscle had torn, and winced.

"What now?" Bera said. "It seems to have gone quiet."

"That's because the Idiot thinks we're dead," Karl said grimly. "That changes now."

Are you sure you wish me to do this? Loki said. It was an all but rhetorical question – they had discussed it already on the way back.

Positive, Karl sub-vocalised. We've lost too much time already. But only if you're sure that you can do it. A botched attempt will be worse than no attempt at all.

I'm certain, Loki said. *And content to do it now. As soon as the Idiot made an attempt on our lives, it legitimised any response.*

Then let's stop talking and start doing. With his usual grimace, Karl plugged the jack into the nape of his neck and sitting down, said to Bera: "I'll seem to go out for a few seconds. Don't worry about it." He slumped.

You ran down the vast corridor that was no corridor at all, but a representation of the connection.

Karl was far behind you, at the mouth of the corridor, arms folded. "Good hunting!" His voice echoed down the corridor. A breeze blew softly from ahead of you. You lifted a hand in acknowledgement.

It felt strange, as if you were part of conjoined twins suddenly split asunder by a surgeon's laspel. But there was no going back, and you knew that being back in this sort of environment – even one whose setting was as impoverished as this one – was really, secretly, what you'd been waiting all these weeks of confinement for.

You hefted the plasma-carbine one-handed, feeling its balance. It was symbolic of course – no more real than your lean, muscular body, but it was a potent symbol, which made it in many ways as real as you were. As real as the little canvas bag that you'd visualised into existence that was slung crossways over your shoulder, and which bumped against your opposite hip.

You turned, leaving the corridor and entering the tunnel into the city.

Karl returned to consciousness like a drowning man clutching at a rope.

"I thought you said catatonic," Bera snarled tearfully, tugging at his earlobe. "You didn't say anything about dying!"

He gave her a broken grin. "Mere details," he said, rubbing his head. "Ach, no Loki lurking at the back of my mind. It's weird to feel empty-headed again, if you know what I mean."

"Your head *is* empty, judging by that folly," Bera said. "What's happened to him?"

Karl indicated the console. "Downloaded. He's gone hunting the datarealm. Even if they just keep each other occupied, it'll give us a chance to get on with dumping the reactor." Karl clutched at her for support. "Still a bit unsteady," he said. "The world keeps moving around."

The viewscreen showed the comet ahead of them, vapour boiling from it in the glare of Gama and Delta-sol, rising in wraiths of steam.

Come on, stop daydreaming, he thought, rubbing his head. He had once placed an antique reality patch on his head, to see how the thing worked. It had been a memory of a visit to a tooth repairist – a dentist, that was the word – back when teeth either wore or fell out.

The subject had actually had a tooth knocked out, and kept probing the gap where it had been, feeling the roughness of the surrounding molars. It was that feeling of emptiness that Loki's absence reminded Karl of. The feeling that something, no matter how reluctantly accepted it had been, was no longer there, leaving only a phantom of memory. Karl shook his head, and releasing his harness, drifted around the cabin with a small sack in hand, stuffing items of debris into it. All Bera's patient gathering of materials for their eventual return to the surface had been undone in a matter of seconds. For some reason that made Karl angrier than anything else.

Leaning on the console, Karl began to flick switches; slowly, then a flurry as he understood a sequence, then slowing again. He swore. "That thruster firing wasn't supposed to happen. Oh, I think it's Loki and the Idiot, fighting."

The lights suddenly dimmed, then returned to full intensity. "That wasn't me," Karl said.

"Karl!" Bera said.

"Not right now, unless it's really urgent, Bera," Karl murmured.

"It depends if you consider Ragnar's having some sort of seizure is urgent!" she snapped.

You emerged from the tunnel not inside the cityscape as you had expected, but on the wrong side of a mesh-fence several metres high. As a deterrent, it was pretty feeble, you decided, visualising a rabbit hole at the base of the fence, and when it appeared, rolling under the fence through the gap it created.

The skyscrapers were a little blurred around the edges, like a picture magnified so that the pixels show. Huge flying ziggurats that you suspected were data objects floated serenely across a lemon and grey sky that you recognised as Isheimur; it was, after all, even though you had only witnessed it through Karl's eyes, the only sky you had ever seen. Shuttle-type shapes comprised of pockets of data flitted like little fishes from ziggurat to ziggurat. And vast columns of numbers rose high into the sky, all the way up to orbit.

Of people, of course, there was no sign. You weren't surprised. There would, after all, be only one inhabitant of this city.

The others gathered around Ragnar's prone body, Arnbjorn kneeling, clutching a box. The container was open, showing bottles and phials scattered. Arnbjorn's face was ashen, and a solitary tear track glistened on one cheek. "I can't read any of these things!" he said and, leaning back on his haunches, shot Karl an imploring look.

"Let me," Karl said, although he had little hope of understanding the labels. He ran his finger over each in turn and listened to the instructions that each label recited. Smart labels, he thought, these bottles must date from when people were just starting to lose archaic skills like reading. But although drug names and ingredients were similar across languages, he didn't know enough to know what the drugs did. Some labels recited what sounded like instructions, but his Kazakh wasn't adequate to translate more than simple phrases.

Karl gazed at the torn-open shirt and the network of scars criss-crossing Ragnar's exposed chest. Ragnar's face drooped on one side, and drool trickled down his face.

Arnbjorn wiped the spittle away. "Help us," he begged.

"I don't know what to do," Karl admitted. "Without access to the medical programme, I don't even know what it is."

"It's a stroke," Bera said. "My grandmother had one. There are drugs that can thin the blood, and–" Her eyes widened. "Would your nanophytes fix him?"

Karl thought, You idiot! Panic in the face of an archaic medical condition with no access to proper intel had frozen his brain. "They might," he admitted, and rummaging in the box, pulled out a knife sheathed in sterile wrapping. He willed clusters of nanophytes to his hand, felt the slight tingling in his arms that spoke of their movement, and after a few seconds, made an incision. "There won't be enough to completely fix him, but they may alleviate the worst effects."

Taking a syringe from its sterile wrapper, Bera drew back the plunger and slowly filled it with blood from the cut. "Inject this into his carotid artery," Bera said, passing the syringe to Arnbjorn, who took it as if it were a poisonous snake.

Arnbjorn fumbled it, so Orn snatched it, and plunged it into Ragnar's neck. "Don't worry," Orn said. "Some of us react better to these situations than others." Arnbjorn didn't answer, preoccupied with his own private hell.

Bera sniffed at a jar and wrinkled her nose. "I think these have gone off." Instead she simply wrapped bandages around the wounded hand.

Ragnar's eyelids fixed on Karl, and he tried to speak, but it came out as a drunken-sounding mumble that Karl couldn't make out.

"If Loki can take control of the ship," Karl said to Bera, "then we should be able to access the medical records."

"You should concentrate on the ship," Bera said. "Leave me to tend to Ragnar." She added, "The first twenty-four hours are key to any recovery, but until the nanophytes have had time to work, we can't do too much apart from keep him comfortable. Go on, leave us to it."

Stamping on any guilt that seeped into his thoughts, Karl returned to the console, and cursed as the *Winter Song* lurched.

Not now, Loki! he sub-vocalised – then remembered that the construct wasn't there to hear him. Sort that Idiot out.

For the longest time you thought that you were alone, as you wandered the city streets looking for the One.

When you saw him on the skyline, you thought at first that he was astride a horse. As you drew closer, step by step down the avenue lined with trees whose leaves were lined with crystalline veins, you realised that the mounted horseman was actually a centaur, his face bearing the cruel look of a Kazakh warrior. "What are you, interloper?" the centaur said, the Kazakh words turning into Standard a micro-second after his lips moved; the faintest of lags, but still visible.

"A construct, the same as you." You made yourself grow bigger, so that you were the same two-and-a-half metres tall as him; no medieval program was going to psych you out.

From nowhere, it seemed, the *Winter Song*'s datarealm drew a bow and turned and fired an arrow at your heart in one smooth motion.

But you stepped to the left so that it sailed harmlessly past you. You pointed the gun at him left-handed but as his lips curled in a sneer, instead took a phial right-handed from the little canvas sack. "Tailored virus," you said, and threw the phial, whose contents were suspended in a solution, at the centaur. "No cure for this," you said. "It's pure germ warfare, as a billion people on New Ithaca learned."

Moments later, the centaur screamed.

"It's the viral equivalent of an old, prehistoric neutron bomb," you said to the twitching, dissolving mess. "Kills the enemy but leaves the buildings intact."

It seemed to take forever, but even in cyber-time it was probably only a minute or so, in outside time perhaps a half-second, and nothing remained of the datarealm but a bubbling pool.

In the moments when you were sure that it was dead, but before entropy could send the systems crashing to the ground, you reached out with arms quickly grown infinitely long. You caught the first struggling ziggurat as it wobbled in its path, and pushed it on its way as before.

More and more, as a juggler will catch balls tossed to him, you manipulated the data structures, wherever possible keeping them going as before, at least until you could work what each one of them did. It took hours of subjective time, but then you realised what bothered you about this faux-world – there were no suns in here, so it was impossible to sense the passage of time.

Then you saw that one of the vast columns of numbers was changing. It was a clock, a mission clock counting off the gigaseconds since the start of the mission.

For a long time, you concentrated on keeping the myriad systems going, learning how things worked one object at a time. Only when you were sure of what you were doing, did you start to actually change arrangements, gradually taking control of the *Winter Song*.

Soon, you forgot all about the passage of time. The data was just so fascinating. This was what you were made for, you belatedly realised.

It took a voice to interrupt your reverie. A familiar voice.

Too many of the protocols needed to complete the operation were either activated by parts of the instrumentation that had been cannibalised on the ground, or worse by the datarealm, Karl finally realised.

Dreading what he might find, he re-inserted the jack.

The cyberscape seemed much as it had before, insofar as one databerg looked just like another, and infostreams were as indistinguishable to him as faces to a blind man.

"Loki!" Karl called, the name a symbol hurtling into the void, shrinking with distance, smoke streaming from them. "Loki!" He cast another copy of the symbol, and then new ones: "Where are you?"

"Here!" came an answering shout, and a sigil loomed out of the void, hurtling at Karl so quickly that he had to duck, but luckily it flashed past him. He breathed a sigh of relief. "I need to be able to communicate with you without jacking in. Any suggestions?"

"There's a speaker on the console for radio messages," Loki said. "Have Orn re-wire it so that it hacks into the jack connection, and it'll pass as a voice-comm."

Karl put Orn to work, removing the jack first.

After a few minutes Orn pronounced the work done. A flat, metallic voice echoed from the speaker: "Finally."

Karl said, "Do you have control of this bloody thing, or is there another ambush waiting just around the corner?"

"I've got control," Loki said, voice echoing through the cabin, metallic and harsh and nothing like the voice that had been in Karl's head these last months. Still, the

implications were such that Karl exhaled with sheer relief, and silently clenched his fist.

"Then let's make up for lost time, and push this rock
to Isheimur," Karl said. The ship rotated through ninety
degrees and nudged forward on thrusters. Then the engines kicked in, gradually growing in volume.

Karl felt the tiniest push of acceleration against his
back, and closed his eyes, trying to achieve some mental equilibrium. The acceleration wasn't anywhere near
strong enough to require him to sit, but he needed to
gather his wits; he seemed to have been in perpetual
motion for hours without a break, but he realised that
it had actually only been minutes, and he was suffering
from a weird sense of temporal displacement. Now he
needed to be absolutely focused upon the task, if they
were to have any chance of survival.

"Ice weighs slightly less than one kilogram per cubic
metre at standard gravity," Loki said. "So a cubic kilometre masses one megatonne. This comet's diameter at
twelve point five eight kilometres means that it masses
almost two thousand megatonnes…"

"How much does the *Winter Song* mass?"

"Just under a megatonne," Loki said.

Orn, still loitering nearby, whistled. "It'll be like an
ant pushing an elephant!"

"Not quite so bad," Karl said. "We're not pushing it
from a standing start, just nudging it to alter its course.
Even at a fiftieth of a gee, which is about all we can
manage for more than a few minutes, we'd have a lateral velocity of sixty metres a second after five minutes.
In the time we have to planetfall, we should have
enough time to correct the course divergence."

He wasn't as sure as he was making out. There was a
margin of error of only a few hundred metres for the
launch co-ordinates. More than that, and by the time

it had travelled several million kilometres, the comet would fly harmlessly by Isheimur. Even more important was that the trajectory was accurate to within a fraction of a degree or they were doomed.

"How long until we need to fire the engines?" "Forty-eight minutes," Loki said, raven's caw voice still grating. "I assume that we don't need the odd few seconds, which have in any event almost elapsed now."

It took Karl a moment to realise that the construct was joking. "Humour from a machine," he murmured.

"Actually, I was serious," Loki said. "You don't call up every result of a search, do you?"

"Hmmph."

"I am concerned about one of the lateral thrusters," Loki said. "It's working, but only intermittently, and when it does it's only at barely forty per cent efficiency."

"It'll have to do," Karl said.

"It sounds odd actually hearing his voice." Bera stood beside Karl, resting her hand on his shoulder.

"Did you think he was a figment of my imagination?" Karl said, laughing.

"Only in the very, very small hours, when sleep didn't come easy. Then you start to doubt everything, even yourself." For the first time Karl realised what a colossal investment of faith Bera had made in him. He must have looked upset, for she squeezed his shoulder and said, "Do you think I could tell just anyone something like that? Take it as a very indirect measure of how much I think of you."

Karl patted her hand. "I will."

The view of the comet in the monitor, though impressive – steam boiled from it – had quickly become stale. On an impulse, Karl said, "Loki, open the shutter covering the side window – the one leeward from the suns."

"Neither side is properly leeward," Loki said, "but I'll open the one away from Gamasol, as it's the more powerful star." The shutter slid up, and the edges of the corona slid past the side window, streamers of ice boiling in the vacuum, forming eerie, spectral banners.

"The comet should have a name," Karl said. "It's not just a comet any longer."

"*Fenris.*" The name was two distinct syllables, the voice coming from behind Karl. He turned and stared at Ragnar, who was sitting, propped up by Coeo, of all people. The former Gothi looked old, and worn to only the nub of the once-vital man he'd been until recently. One side of his face was frozen into immobility.

"The destroyer of worlds?" Bera's scepticism was obvious in her voice.

"It might be," Arnbjorn said. "We hope not, but..."

"It's a risk," Karl agreed. "But if we do nothing, your people will slowly die. If we can add a decade or so to the colony's time, it may allow your people and Coeo's time to negotiate some sort of peace settlement. Because whether or not I'm there," Karl added, "you need to have reached a settlement to avoid dragging those who answer the beacon into one side or the other of a dirty little local war."

"I agree," Ragnar said. His speech was slow and hesitant, but it was already stronger than the time he'd spoken before. But each sentence was still molasses slow, each syllable separated by silent effort before and after it. "What is the troll-speak for 'we want peace', utlander?" His mouth formed a twisted half-grin as he said the last word.

Karl didn't say what he was thinking. Decades, perhaps even centuries will have to pass before your great-great-grandchildren and those of the adapted men will be able to fully trust each other – if ever.

Still, at least it's a start. Instead he said, "Nice to see you've not given up the habit of living." Oddly enough, Karl meant it. The old man had tried to kill him and hunted him across half a world. But he had also twice saved Karl's life, and the crucible of vacuum all around them had burnt off much of what had happened below.

Ragnar tried to speak, but his words were now too slurred to understand. Arnbjorn hushed him. "Rest, Pappi, you've done enough, mighty warrior." As if obeying him, Ragnar closed his eyes, and his head slid sideways.

Karl covered Bera's hand, which still rested on his shoulder, with his opposite hand. "I don't know quite how to say this—"

"Try opening your mouth," Bera said, and laughed. She sobered. "What?"

"I'd quite like to get things in order," Karl said. "I'm sure that everything will be all right, but just in case anything goes wrong... thank you. I mean it."

Bera's eyes widened. "You're not sure that this will work, are you?"

"I'm sure it will," Karl said, thinking, If you offered me odds of a thousand to one, I'd consider them generous. But he had to appear confident, or risk panic.

"What about your family?" Bera said. "Karla and Lisane and Jarl? All this way, and you change your mind?"

"Do you know," Karl said, swallowing the emotion that was threatening to overcome him, "I can barely remember their faces."

"Still," Bera said. "To risk never seeing them again, for what – a world of strangers who won't thank you?"

Karl shrugged. "I'm not doing it for their thanks."

"Why, then?"

Karl didn't answer straight away. He tried to find words that didn't sound pompous, but finally gave up worrying.

"Because it's right," he said. "And I'm not prepared to abandon you. This mad idea will probably kill us all, but if I do nothing the odds are immeasurably greater that you'll die, and I'm not going to let that happen."

They were silent, alone with their thoughts.

Bera said, "If we're putting things in order, I have something to say as well." She looked down, licked her lips, then blurted, "Do you know, that I'm actually a virgin?" Karl was silent, unsure of her point. "I've had sex, but no man has ever made love to me."

"I suppose not." Karl touched her cheek.

She pressed her face against his hand. "I'd like... I... there's one man, I really, really want..."

Karl looked across, but the others were preoccupied. He leaned toward Bera, who lifted her chin. He kissed her. She closed her eyes and kissed him back, and slid her arms around his neck.

Moving them was easy in zero-gravity – he kicked off from a chair and drifted through the doorway, into the corridor. He slid a hand under her blouse, and ran his fingers up her spine.

Bera groaned, and arched her back so that she pressed into him, changing their axis of rotation. Karl ended the kiss, and as they drifted, moved down to her chin, then her cheek, tracing a line of little kisses so minute that they barely touched her skin for more than a micro-second, down the side of her neck and into her clavicle. She pulled open her blouse and cupping her breast pushed the nipple toward him. Karl traced the areola with his tongue, swirling around and around in a clockwise direction.

Bera gripped his ear and between moans ground out, "I wish... that you'd... grow... some bloody hair... to hold on to." She scraped her nails down his back, pushing her hands away.

Karl kicked against a wall, and shoved them into a room off the corridor. It was the room in which Bera had stacked her impromptu nest of items for use on the ground.

As they sailed slowly toward the pile of objects, he lifted her up so that his face was pressed against the base of her breasts, and then moved down her stomach, still tracing the line of kisses, sliding his hands rhythmically up and down her back.

Bera pushed down her leggings, and Karl slid them to around her ankles. With a kick she removed first one foot, then the other, the motion sending her and Karl spinning across the room. As they were about to hit the wall, Karl put out a hand to absorb the impact, and they hovered in mid-air, rotating around an axis that ran down an invisible line between them. Karl's tongue continued to kiss Bera's stomach, and then he moved lower, rubbing his lower lip against her bush.

She pushed his head down, and Karl's lower lip felt moistness. Bera groaned and parted her legs, and his tongue entered her, tasting her saltiness, feeling the richness of her fill his nostrils. She ground against his face, beginning to buck and writhe, sending them back across the room, end over end. Just as her shivers grew to spasms Karl stopped and eeled up the length of her body, her hands tearing off his furs as he did so, so that he too was naked.

He slid into her, felt her quiver as he did so, and gripping a bracket that had once held a shelf, thrust long and hard and slow, feeling her react in time. He gasped, "I can... have the nanophytes–" Bera put a finger to his lips and he was silent.

"Don't hold back," she said, then let out a long, low moan and wriggled to let him in deeper. She lifted her bottom so that he could cup her buttocks, and then, still clutching the bracket, he drove with long, slow thrusts, trying to blank his mind so that he wouldn't climax too early. Bera raked his back with her nails and whimpered, and Karl felt his control begin to fail as he pumped harder and harder and he lost himself in her, and in the moment.

They lay against one another. He could feel her heart fluttering like a butterfly. He stroked her back, breathed in the scent of their sex, and wished that they never had to move, that it never had to end.

But of course, it had to.

"We should go back," Bera said. "They'll miss us."

"Mmm," Karl replied, knowing it was true. He gathered his clothes.

They fell silent, alone with their thoughts.

Karl felt the gentlest tug of gravity. "It's started."

TWENTY-TWO

Afterward – as they prepared to blow Fenris to pieces – Karl was to think of the nineteen-day voyage as the Age of Waiting. That he had time to spend together with Bera, with little else to do but make love and get to know one another, was the only good thing to come out of it.

Karl was still suffused with a post-coital glow, and halfway through pulling his clothes on when the *Winter Song* shoved its colossal cargo toward Isheimur. The faint pull of gravity was no more than a ghost child's tug on the sleeve but still, they drifted to the floor, Karl spinning so that he landed feet first, Bera in an untidy heap. "We're on our way." Karl felt the need to say something, no matter how self-evident.

Bera nodded, flashing him a fleeting smile, dressing with more speed than tidiness.

Walking hand-in-hand onto the bridge with the curious bouncing gait that low gravity induced, Karl was sure that the others would notice a difference somehow, but on one side of the bridge Coeo stared into the steam boiling off the comet, while on the other Arnbjorn and Orn fussed over the still-prone Ragnar. All of them in their own way looked too preoccupied to even notice the lovers' absence.

Karl took his seat and looked around the bridge. Everything looked the same as before, yet subtly different. It's you that's changed. "Loki, give the others the timetable – as we discussed," he said aloud. That was their personal code for, *Don't give them any bad news.*

"Our journey will last nineteen standard days," Loki said, voice crackling over the antique speakers. "The first nine and a third days we'll accelerate at a hundredth of a standard gravity, which is about half-thrust. That's as much as we think the engines will take."

"Basically," Karl interrupted, "we're using the *Winter Song* as a million-tonne tugboat. The thing's built like a tractor anyway." He added, in an aside to Coeo, "I'll explain concepts like tugboats and tractors later."

"No need," Coeo answered, indicating the speaker. "I'm sure that I can learn from our invisible friend in the box."

"What happens at the end of nine days?" Arnbjorn said.

"We spend two hours manoeuvring around to the other side of Fenris, where we'll decelerate at the same rate for another nine and a third days, so that when we get to within a couple of hundred thousand kilometres of Isheimur, we've reverted to our current velocity."

"The faster we go, the sooner we get there," Karl said. "But the harder we'll hit – and the greater the energy that we'll release in the form of an explosion. Imagine the biggest blast you've ever seen, and multiply it by…" Karl shrugged. "I have no idea of what number to magnify it by – but if we release too much energy…"

"Boom?" Bera said.

"Boom," Karl agreed. "So we need to slow down. We could have shaved six days off the journey, but then we'd go in so hard and so fast that the debris thrown up by the blast would kill half the species on the planet."

"Why couldn't we accelerate at full thrust?" Arnbjorn said. "We could be home in half the time, then?"

"Not so," Loki said. "We would still need to decelerate, and while it would knock four days off the voyage, there is an eighty-six per cent probability that the engines would overheat."

"If you're worried about Ragnar's condition," Karl said, "Loki will give you the formula to synthesise anticoagulants in the nanoforge." He waved at the other seats. "So given that we have a few weeks to go, you might as well make yourselves comfortable, lady and gentlemen."

Karl had Loki activate a counter on the monitor screen, one whose red digits showed the four hundred and seventy-seven hours, eighteen minutes and rapidly decreasing seconds to planetfall.

Only later would Karl realise what a mistake that was.

Soon after starting, Orn said, "I'll go and see what drugs I can get out of this nanoforge to help treat Ragnar."

Arnbjorn had helped Ragnar to a seat, and as Orn left, the younger man looked up. "Looks like Orn's got a new toy," he said with a grin. "You won't see him for the rest of the voyage."

On the second day with time already hanging heavy, Karl drew up a watch, ensuring that he and Bera were on different shifts. "We still get to spend eight hours a day together off-duty," he said to her disappointed look, although she voiced no complaint. "You'll be on midnight to eight, the first half with Ragnar, the second with Coeo. Though time's nearly meaningless on board." Assigning the crew to watches gave the day structure and them responsibility – even if Loki was capable of running the ship on his own.

"What shift will you take, Gothi?" Arnbjorn said.

Karl searched the honorific for traces of irony, but could find none. "Sixteen hundred to midnight," he said, and caught their approving nods. Little by little, they'd shown that they knew about his changed relationship with Bera; not toward him – his position was unambiguous – but by their sudden deference to her. At times he could almost sense them thinking. *Do we joke with her? Call her Gothi-kona, as if she's his wife?* But his keeping Bera on a separate watch showed them that he would treat her like any other crew-member.

Even with the new schedule, time dragged for people who were used to working, or lately walking, from dawn to nightfall. So while Bera was on watch, Karl rose early and scoured the eleven decks. To his delight he found a small gym in the ship's cavernous bowels.

"You are joking?" Orn said later, when Karl told them his new idea. "Do I look as if I need exercise?" The devil's ride that Ragnar had led them on had all but melted the flesh from Orn's frame, left him a wasted shadow of the once-bulky man Karl had known.

"You do," Karl said. "To stop muscle wastage in micro-gravity. Or do you fancy hiking across country carrying ten men on your shoulders with your legs buckling under the strain?"

"It can't be that bad!" Orn said. Arnbjorn and Ragnar looked on, grinning.

"Oh, but it can," Karl said. "You want to suffer a heart attack? Cramps? Brittle bones? And why should the others have to do it, but you don't?"

"Why should they?" Orn said.

Karl belatedly realised that he'd made it a test of his own authority, but couldn't be bothered to play games. "OK," he said. "You're on your own. We'll take longer watches to cover your absence, and when you're hurting on the ground we'll leave you to die, like we would a stranger." He turned and walked away, ignoring Orn's protesting shouts.

The next day Karl paced the inside of an exercise wheel when Orn accompanied Ragnar into the gym. Orn helped Ragnar into a walking frame, setting it to the minimum level, then climbed aboard an exercise bike, all while studiously avoiding Karl's gaze.

When he had finished, and was on his way out, Karl stopped by the bike. "Thank you," he said to Orn, and nodded to Ragnar.

The old man's face still drooped on one side, and his words were so slurred they were barely intelligible. "You play a dangerous game, Gothi," he growled, giving Karl a lopsided grin.

"I don't play games," Karl said. "I meant what I said. I'm not a man who can throw dissenters out of the airlock, so if a man refuses my order, all I can do is walk away."

"Making him outlaw," Ragnar said. "Sooner or later, it's a tactic that will backfire."

"Maybe."

On the fifth day, Loki said, "I've found the crew records."

"What took you so long?" Karl said. He was only half-joking.

"There is a lot of corrupted data. I'm not sure whether it led to the datarealm's attacks, or whether it's a result of the Idiot wiping a lot of the memory banks to stop us accessing them."

"Why?"

"I'm assuming that it was some sort of electronic scorched-earth policy. If it couldn't stop us taking over the ship, it would leave us without information."

"So what have you learned?"

"They originally hoped that the *Sardar* – as they called the *Winter Song* – would fly again. So while the lake was still melted, they filled the fuel tanks with water, and decreed that nothing essential to space-flight was to be stripped."

"Hah," Karl grunted, in acknowledgement and surprise. "That's it?"

"There is considerably more," Loki said. "When they realised how unlikely it was that they would be able to get back to civilisation – for that was the problem, not that they couldn't take off, but that they were light-years off-course and hopelessly lost.

"The decision was made to adapt Coeo's ancestors to make them as self-sufficient as possible, while never sacrificing the ship – so the veneration of it began. Do you want to hear the rest? The personal testimony of the captain and crew, as they slowly froze, starved, or choked to death on the thin air, one after the other of them taking what they called The Long Walk?"

"No thanks," Karl said. "How long did they last?"

"Long enough to speed-grow the first generation, and teach them what they could. Four years, the last survivor held out before taking The Long Walk into the snow."

Karl breathed out slowly, trying to imagine how that last Kazakh must have felt, his colleagues dead, his children alien. "Add their records to the mayday loop," he said. "They shouldn't be forgotten."

"Agreed," Loki said. "The records also explain an oddity about the nanoforge."

"Oh?"

"It's configured so that organic and inorganic materials are classed separately, and one can't be remade into the other. It's a constraint hardwired into it, so it explains why the crew left much of the ship unstripped. And why Orn is having trouble getting the forge to respond to particular commands."

"You mean it won't make a door into a steak, or vice versa?"

"Exactly – which limits your food stocks post-landing, should you wish to factor that in."

Karl looked around for Arnbjorn, and saw that he was on the other side of the bridge with a speaker in one ear, concentrating on listening to an audio tape. "You think that there'll *be* a post-landing?"

"I would estimate the odds of the ship surviving the landing as approximately three thousand to one, but I am taking my lead from you."

"As you should," Karl said. "We work on the principle that we'll survive the landing."

Karl turned and waved at Arnbjorn to attract his attention, and after several failed attempts called, "We should get Bera making us garments from any spare spacesuits, or other synthetic clothing." At Arnbjorn's puzzled look, Karl explained the problem with the nanoforge.

"So that's why it refuses Orn's instructions so often," Arnbjorn said. "But why do you want us to make new clothes?"

"The furs are organic," Karl explained. "We can use them to forge food from the patterns we've saved already."

"I'll talk to them when I finish my shift," Arnbjorn said. On his way back to his seat, the settler paused.

"What is it?" Karl said.

"What are your plans when we land?" Arnbjorn said.

To stay alive... somehow, Karl thought. "I don't know," he admitted aloud. "I wasn't planning on staying as Gothi, if that's what you're worried about."

Arnbjorn looked sheepish. "I did wonder," he said. "Not that you've done a bad job."

"It's my environment," Karl said. "But I know that Isheimur is yours. I'd be a fool to set myself up as leader down there."

Arnbjorn nodded, deep in thought. "Aye."

The next days passed in a dull haze of make-work and trying not to think of what lay ahead, a prospect made grimmer by lack of sleep – Karl's dreams were haunted by a vast, crushing object bearing down on him or by nightmares of being burned in a vast conflagration, so that he awoke leaden-limbed and sluggish of thought.

Karl worried especially about Coeo. At least the settlers kept each other company, and he had Bera, but the young adapted man had followed Karl blindly and was alone. Without the benefit of constant activity he seemed to draw in on himself, although Karl made a point of talking to and involving him as much as possible.

Bera too increasingly withdrew to "their" room, losing herself in adapting the clothing they had scavenged from around the ship to replace their furs, while humming along to music from antique discs and a player scavenged from around the ship. Guilty at sitting watching her work, Karl helped as best he could, but most of his attempts at sewing pieces of fabric together were at best rickety, at worst they came apart, so Bera took them from him. "Stick to what you're good at," she said.

"Which is?" he teased. "Bossing people around?"

As she struggled with one particularly tough seam, she poked her tongue out and rested it on her philtrum. He thought, How did you ever think her plain?

She looked up. "What?"

"Nothing," he said, failing to smother a smile.

"I suppose you're good at one thing." She raised an eyebrow.

"Oh." He took the sewing from her and put it down. "In some ways," he said, "micro-gravity's better than weightlessness. You get almost all the benefits, like not weighing as much, but you still come to ground in the end."

He kissed her and they made love, slowly.

But afterward, he saw her gaze unblinking at the wall. "What's wrong?" he said.

"Do you miss them?" Bera said.

Karl didn't answer for almost a minute. When she opened her mouth to speak, he held a finger to her lips. "Every day," he said. "Just as, if you and I were separated, I'd move worlds and more to get back to you. Would you want me to be the man who forgets those who are important to him when they're out of sight?"

Bera shook her head, and smiled tremulously. "I... no, of course not. But it's hard, sometimes, living with ghosts. Sometimes it feels like they're all around me."

"How do you think it feels for me?" Karl said. He turned and returned the wan smile she flashed at him, and images of Karla, Lisane, Jarl – even the baby, though he'd never seen him or her – flooded his mind.

"Tell me what you're thinking," Bera said.

"I'm not sure that's wise," Karl said.

"No, I want you to."

"I was..." Karl started. "I was trying to work out how long it'll be before the birth; it's scheduled for about now." The menage had deliberately decided against learning the baby's gender, with the dissenting Karla accepting the majority view. If we don't survive, is this the universe's way of keeping the numbers balanced, my death for the baby's life? If so, whose death will Bera and the others offset?

He wondered whether his family would have understood what he was doing, assuming they ever learned his fate. He wasn't sure that he fully comprehended himself. Somewhere along the journey, perhaps meeting Coeo, perhaps their all saving each other's lives, he had assumed responsibility for them all.

"You have too much time to think," Karl said, conscious that it applied to him as well. "But that won't last for long. Enjoy it while it does."

The next day, for the first time in nine days, the faint pull of gravity ended. It was as abrupt as if it had been switched off, the only harbinger the klaxon warning of the planned mid-point manoeuvre braying throughout the ship. Karl headed for the bridge, though it wasn't his watch. Orn and Arnbjorn turned as he bounced through the doorway.

"I'm going to fire us away from Fenris," Loki announced. "We'll be under one gee for twenty seconds, flattening our trajectory to a circumpolar orbit and coming down the other side." Loki paused before adding, "If I can persuade this recalcitrant thruster to behave."

"Still having problems with it?" Karl said.

"Yes... but considering how long the ship was buried beneath a frozen lake, it's a miracle that it's the biggest problem the ship is presenting us with. It's a testament to how robust the ship was."

"Agreed," Karl said.

"You should hear the rattles and creaks and groans down in the lower decks," Orn said. "Deck eleven sounds as if the rivets are going to pop out of the walls at any moment."

"Rattles and creaks just mean loose fittings," Karl said with a grin. "And if you took a spacewalk down to the engines, and went inside to the little emergency control hut, you'd hear a lot worse – except that the noise would blow your eardrums in about fifteen seconds flat."

Loki said, "I'm lowering the screens, as we're about to emerge into sunlight."

On the monitor Karl watched mountain ranges and abysses in miniature pass by, and then fall away as they cleared the comet's summit. "We'll no longer be able to transmit to the Hangzhou Relay," Loki said.

For the last ten days the *Winter Song* had beamed their Mayday to that site, in the hope that a distress call with a second signature might achieve more than Ship's original message on its own. "Make 'em think there's some sort of ships' graveyard in this system," Karl had said with a grin.

"Isn't there?" Coeo had replied. "How many of those – what were they called – Aye ships and the raiders were destroyed?"

Karl nodded acknowledgement and said to Loki, "You've allowed two hours to change position?"

"Two hours forty-five," Loki said. "If Fenris is like most other comets – and early indications are that this is so – then the sunward side will be considerably less regular than the lee side. We'll need most of that time to find a flat, regular secure plateau to land on."

Loki was correct. After two false attempts, with one of the ledges collapsing beneath the ship, Loki finally found a third plateau which held, but it took more than half an hour of jockeying the *Winter Song*, trying to offset the intermittent loss of thrust from one corner, before the ship settled, and Loki announced, "We're in position."

Loki raised the shadowside blinds on the sight of Fenris filling every window with a wall of dirty white. Ahead of them, the miniature mountains and valleys of their sanctuary surrounded tiny peaks that could have been kilometres high, but in reality were probably little taller than he was. Karl wiped the sweat from his forehead, and breathed a long sigh of relief. "It's time to resume our tugboat act, then?"

Loki said, "If we decelerate too quickly, the voyage will take much longer. Every minute we start early here adds seven minutes at the other end. But I suggest that we start thirty minutes earlier than originally planned, to allow us a margin of error. I am becoming concerned at the build-up of heat in one of the exhausts."

"Can we do anything to reduce the temperature?" Karl said.

"The best way is to let the engine rest for a while, but we have little time to spare. I will keep monitoring it."

"In that case," Karl said. "I'm going back to bed for an hour."

"Enjoy," Arnbjorn said with a grin.

Karl didn't answer, but bounced down the corridor to his room, where Bera sat on their bed. She looked up from working on the clothing. "Try this on." She threw a shirt at him, picking up a flexible tape measure. "Hold still, while I measure your leg length."

The ship suddenly bucked and heaved. "Quake," Karl said, changing into the new shirt. "Ugh, it's scratchy as anything. Not like the furs." He shrugged. "Still, they'll make an extra meal or so."

"Get used to it," Bera said. "There's not much I can do to make it less scratchy. You've grown used to wearing natural fabrics."

The ship shook again, more violently this time. "Is this going to keep happening?" Bera said. "The quakes, I mean."

"Get used to it," Karl said, echoing her phrase. He laughed as Bera poked out her tongue.

For the next three days the quakes grew ever worse, while chunks of ice flew off from the comet's surface as the twin suns' relentless heat worked away at the wall of ice on which the ship hung.

On the morning of the thirteenth day, Karl awoke to silence.

The engines had stopped.

TWENTY-THREE

Karl pulled clothes on and yomped to the bridge. "What's happening?"

Bera twisted in the command chair. "Loki's stopped the engines."

Static crackling from the speakers, Loki said: "A quake has shaken us loose of the plateau, and we have slid around and are resting at an angle. Our exhaust vent has jammed into a crevasse. I'm worried about damage, plus venting is unsafe."

"We can't just melt the ice?" Karl said.

"Possibly," Loki said. "But I'd like someone to assess the damage first."

"Maybe we can dig it out?" Orn said. "We could go out the lateral side airlock." He had found a second lock, on deck nine, which would have been beneath the frozen surface of Jokullag. "And we could use those spacesuits you found down on de:k six."

"The ones I've been busily cutting up to make into shirts?" Bera said.

"You weren't given all of them," Karl said. "There's one left for each of us." Karl turned to Coeo, "Will you go with Orn, and help him?"

Coeo didn't answer immediately. "I will," he said at last.

Karl knew how difficult it was for the adapted man to fit into something that must have seemed suffocating. "Thanks," he said.

The next fifteen minutes were tense ones, Karl staring at the ticking counter, which now read one hundred and fifty-eight hours to planetfall. They could loop around, in theory, but Karl was acutely conscious of time passing. But a worse scenario was that they couldn't restart the engines at all, and would sail serenely past Isheimur.

"We're here," Orn said. "The view's beautiful."

Never mind that, Karl thought. "Can you see the vent?"

"Yeah," Orn said. "The weight of the ship jamming it onto about the only bloody rock on this ice-ball has buckled it. Coeo has a small blowlamp, which he's turned onto the ice just *below* the rock."

Fifteen, then twenty, then twenty-five more tense minutes passed. Orn muttered occasionally, but otherwise the men worked in silence. Karl resisted the urge to ask questions, instead letting them work undisturbed.

Orn said, "We've cleared the rock. Loki should be able to melt the ice safely, but the vent itself is buckled. We can't fix it without equipment we don't have."

"OK," Karl said. "Get back in." He said to Loki, "As soon as the airlock cycles, re-start the engines."

"Understood," Loki said.

When the engines fired, there were a few minutes' further delay as Loki melted the last of the ice away, and returned the *Winter Song* to its position of almost drilling into the comet, but then they were under way, with their usual hundredth of a gee deceleration.

Karl bounded down the stairs to the lock to greet the returnees. As he had feared, Coeo was shaking with either fatigue or nerves – or both. "You did a wonderful job," Karl said as the adapted shucked himself out of his suit, and tried not to wrinkle his nose at the rank smell of panic-sweat. Poor bugger must be claustrophobic in that suit, he thought.

He still worried about Coeo throughout the day. The adapted man spent most of his time on his own, either in the gym, or in one of the seats, talking to Loki. Karl knew the folly of trying to overcome centuries of bitterness on both sides and make him one of a virtual family, but he was equally worried that Coeo might become so isolated that the adapted man deteriorated mentally.

"What does he talk to you about?" Karl asked Loki. The counter read a hundred and forty-two hours, he noted absently.

"He questions me," Loki said. "He's like a sponge, soaking up knowledge. He asks about Isheimur as it was before the settlers arrived, as it is now, and how it might change. I have been perfectly truthful on the first two, but exaggerated the effects of the blast."

"What else?" Karl said.

"The current situation in human-space – about which I have been perfectly honest, since you did not tell me to lie – and human history."

At the end of his shift, Bera took over the watch, oozing into her seat. "I've got my sewing," she said dryly. "Like a good little seamstress."

"Should I do the sewing?" Karl said, and was rewarded with a sardonic glint.

"You know the answer to that."

"How about Ragnar?" Karl ignored the snort from the old man, who watched them. Karl glimpsed Ragnar opening his mouth, and held up a warning finger.

"You know that that isn't going to happen in our life-times," Bera said.

"I'm willing to learn," Karl said. "Honestly."

"I know you are," Bera said. "But it's faster for me to do it. So I do."

"So it's not that you're the only one sewing?" Karl said. "That's making you unhappy?"

"Not just that," Bera said. "But it's all I seem to do."

"What would you like to do?" Karl said.

"I don't know!" Bera growled, but her voice rising with each word. "That's just it!" She drew in a lungful of air, and some calm with it. "I'd like to walk under the twin suns again, Karl. I know that it's unreasonable, but I just can't help it."

"I understand," Karl said. He wanted to hold her, and comfort her, but with Ragnar there, that was impossible. "I'm used to sailing on my own, but sometimes even I get cabin-fever. Sometimes there's nothing for it but to tough it out."

Ragnar cleared his throat. "You know," he snarled, and held up a quivering hand, "some of us would sell our soul to be able to hold a needle and thread."

Karl had no answer to that, but instead left the bridge, and walked down the stairs to the gym. As he half-expected, Coeo was in one of the exercise wheels striding from step to step. "You're setting a fast pace," Karl said. "Good to see you're staying in shape."

"I should," Coeo said between breaths, "be fitter... than... before we... took off."

"You're expecting to have to run when we land?" Karl said.

"Perhaps." Coeo pressed a button on the wheel rim, and it slowed slightly. "It helps me to think, this machine," he said, breathing a little more freely.

386

"You don't have enough time to think?" Karl entered the other wheel, next to Coeo.

"Lots of time, but much noise and..." Coeo waved a hand in the air as if to conjure the word. "Distractions."

"Ah," Karl said. "Deep thought." He wasn't sure whether Coeo would understand the concept, but the adapted man nodded. "Exactly."

"Why do..." Karl hesitated, unsure whether he was going to offend Coeo, then pressed on: "You ask Loki lots of questions. Why?"

"To learn," Coeo said, as if it were obvious.

"But why?" Karl said. "Simply for something to do?"

"Partly," Coeo said. "But we have lost too much knowledge, my people. After we fall again, when we go home, I want to be a seer for my people. I want to be like you, to know everything."

Tick. The timer had counted down to one hundred and nineteen hours when Loki stopped the engines again. "We're overheating," Loki said. "I think that the damaged vent is causing heat build-up."

Karl felt his thoughts close up, as if the panic was squeezing the oxygen supply to his brain. "Can we fix it?"

"Unlikely," Orn said. He had been visiting Ragnar on the bridge, just chatting – but he had been the one who had examined the vent. "It needs heavier tools than we have available. We need a portable version of the forge."

"The fastest way is to let the engines cool down a little, and accelerate harder. And we have a little spare time. I originally allocated us seven hours, and even with the time we lost, we still have most of that."

Tick. The timer passed a hundred hours to planetfall mark. It reached ninety-five, just as Karl handed over to Bera, when the engines died again.

"Still overheating?" Karl said. An antique line of a song ran through his head, Hello panic my old friend, and he felt that familiar squeeze of his mind shutting down.

"It will get worse, I'm afraid," Loki said. "I will need to take them off-line, for longer periods of time. But we still have that spare time, albeit less of it."

"Good," Karl said.

Tick. The timer read seventy-three hours to planet-fall.

"I will need to take the engines down for twenty minutes, and resume on fifty-three per cent, rather than fifty per cent of full thrust. Of course, that means that the heat will build up faster. But if we do not, we will pass the point at which we need to detonate the reactor and break Fenris up."

"What would happen?" Ragnar said. "No," the old man added, shaking his head. While one side of his face still drooped, he moved more freely and spoke more clearly than before, but he was still only a shadow of the man he'd once been.

"What?" Karl said.

"Just thinking the unthinkable," Ragnar said, looking sheepish. "Sometimes as leader, you have to ask the stupid questions."

Karl wanted to scream that he didn't want to be leader, he'd only ever wanted to go home, not end up in a box stuck to the face of an iceberg hurtling at a rock. His voice betrayed none of that when he said, "Ask."

Ragnar said, "What would happen if we didn't vent the heat, but kept running the engines?"

Loki said, "The engines would overheat and either burn out or blow up the reactor."

"Ah." Ragnar gave an embarrassed shrug.

"Sometimes the unthinkable really is the unthinkable," Karl said, with a smile. "Worth asking, though."

"So we have a stark choice," Loki said. "If I do not run the engines, we overshoot. If I do run the engines they overheat, and we may overshoot unless I run them harder, in which case we overheat faster."

Tick; and the timer read fifty-eight hours. This time the engines were off for twenty minutes. The time before they had been off-line for fifteen, the time before twelve, the first only ten minutes.

Tick; forty-six hours.

Karl said, "Are we still within the safe range to break Fenris up?"

"It's diminishing," Loki said, "but we are still within range."

"Good," Karl said, and a thought struck him. He looked around, but Arnbjorn was busy on the other side of the deck, hopefully out of earshot. "You wouldn't lie to me, would you?" The download had, after all, lied to the others at Karl's instigation, selected half-truths admittedly, but still not the whole truth.

"I would not," Loki said. "What purpose would it serve?"

"If you tell me that we still have time, then I agree to you taking the engines down so they don't blow. From your point of view, better we sail past the point at which we have to brake than perish in a fireball, surely?"

"I hadn't thought of that," Loki said. "We could of course, loop back around to Isheimur. In theory."

"Assuming we don't run out of air or fuel," Karl said. Got to stop this paranoia.

"If I lied to you and said that I wasn't, would you know?" Loki added, "That way lies insanity, Karl. I assure you we are within parameters for jettisoning the reactor. I will tell you when we are not."

Tick; thirty-six hours. The engines were silent for thirty minutes. Karl had barely slept for the last three nights, and his gut stabbed with invisible knife-wounds. Either his circulatory and digestive nanophytes had died, or had simply been overwhelmed by the stress he was under.

Tick; the timer read twenty-seven hours, and was followed by thirty minutes' silence. Our velocity has dropped to just over twenty kilometres a second," Loki said. "Each individual second is less crucial than when we were at peak velocity."

But not much less crucial, Karl thought.

Tick; eighteen and a half hours. This time they were off-line for forty minutes. "We are approaching the point at which we have very little time to jettison the reactor and get around to the other side safely," Loki said.

"What happens if we blow the comet within a hundred thousand kilometres of Isheimur?" Orn said. He, like the others, was spending more and more time on the bridge, even when it wasn't his watch. It had become like a black hole, sucking them toward it and the view of the monitor and the un-shuttered window with its monotonous wall of white.

Tick; the timer passed the ten-hour countdown. When it changed to nine hours fifty-nine minutes and fifty-nine seconds, Karl breathed a sigh of relief. Another milestone passed.

His relief was short-lived. The engines quietened minutes later. Karl said, "What happens if you keep them running for just a few more hours?"

"We're already at risk of them seizing," Loki said. "I would rather they seized while closed than at full thrust."

Twenty minutes later Loki fired the engines, and micro-gravity again replaced the near-weightlessness of Fenris.

The next five hours stretched like toffee.

Bera was the last person to arrive on the bridge. Her face was thin and drawn, and dark circles beneath her eyes showed how little she had slept the last few nights. Even their desperate love-making failed to give her more than temporary solace.

She took a seat beside Karl, and he felt a hand slide tremulously into his.

"OK?" he whispered.

Her head dipped quickly twice. "I'll be glad when the waiting is over."

"It nearly is," he said. "What's our velocity?" he asked Loki, for the other's benefit.

"It has just dipped under thirteen kilometres per second," Loki replied. "We are just under two hundred and thirty four thousand kilometres from Isheimur, close enough that we should begin jettisoning the reactor."

"Agreed," Karl said.

The roar of the engines died away and for a few seconds silence hung over them all like a shroud. The thrusters whooshed, their tone higher than that of the main engines. For a horrible moment nothing happened, and Karl thought, We're stuck fast! Then they lurched clear of whatever obstruction had snagged them.

They flew south this time, completing another quarter of an anti-clockwise orbit started when they began deceleration. At the pole they slowed, and Loki nudged the *Winter Song* back down to where they hovered centimetres above the surface, before nudging the comet with the ship's crown. Loki fired the main engines again, and a slightly straining whine denoted that they were on full power.

"That's the last time we'll hear them," Karl said. "Strange. I'd begun to hate the sound of those engines, and now I'm almost sad to think that."

"I'm bloody not," Bera said. "Don't be so sentimental, you old fool." She grinned, and he smiled back.

Karl hadn't noted when Loki had started, but after several minutes he said, "How long do you intend to keep this up?"

Loki said, "Seven point six zero one minutes."

The time dragged – then, without warning, the ship slid sideways across the comet's ragged surface, the scraping so loud they had to cover their ears. "What are you doing?" Karl yelled.

"We have completed the course adjustment," Loki said. "We'd wandered slightly as a result of the changes to our braking programme, and would have sailed through Isheimur's upper atmosphere. Now the comet should score a direct hit on the pole, and puncture the underground reservoir to one edge of the cap." It added, "I am now firing the right lateral rear thruster, and left lateral forward, in effect turning us. The main engines have seized while on, as I feared."

Karl swallowed, his mouth dry, and wiped his palms on the legs of his suit. "Arnbjorn, you, Coeo and Orn suit up, and bring ours back, please."

"Helmets as well?" Arnbjorn said.

"Bring them, but no need to put them on," Karl said. "Yet."

When the others returned, Arnbjorn helped Ragnar into his suit while the others changed quickly. The cockpit had held, but to the scraping noises were added ominous cracking sounds. Sooner or later we're going to hit a shard that'll punch a hole in the cockpit. Shit, shit, shit! What do I do now? "Loki, how long will it take to dump the reactor?"

"It will take about two to three minutes to unlock all the bolts, then a few seconds to dump it."

With a lurch, the *Winter Song* broke through a ridge, but even as the other crew members cheered, the ship crunched into the next one and held for a fraction of a second, before breaking free, and in the process slamming them back into their seats. The *Winter Song* flashed across the ragged polar icecaps of Fenris, so close to the micro-peaks that Karl could see every ridge, every striation in the icy surface.

If we hit the surface full frontal at this speed, there'll be nothing left of us, however reinforced the hull is, he thought.

"I will take us out for about fifteen minutes," Loki said.

"We'll never stand it," Karl said. "We must be doing four or five gees."

"Six point three seven seven," Loki said. "In sixteen seconds we have gained a kilometre a second away from the comet."

"Then... turn... us... around," Karl grated. The pressure was crushing, and he feared for the others, especially Ragnar.

"I have put us into a parabola," Loki said. "We need to initially head away from Fenris, to give us time to jettison the core and move as far around the comet as possible. If we do not put up with this discomfort–"

"Discomfort!" Arnbjorn yelled, the effort making the tendons on his neck distend. "It's killing my father!"

If we do not put up with this discomfort," Loki crackled again, "we'll slam into Fenris so hard none of us will survive." Arnbjorn screeched and Loki said, "I am truly sorry for the strain this is putting Ragnar under, but I see no way to avoid it."

A minute or so later, Karl felt the ship turn in a wide circle, and then Fenris filled the monitor, which was on forward view. The ship plunged toward it.

TWENTY-FOUR

Loki's systems raised the lee-side shutter to reveal a half-shadowed white ball from which banners of water vapour streamed out the four thousand kilometres to them, before passing them by. "Have you started the reactor dump?"

"I have," Loki said. "I have set the fuel rods to degrade so that the material all flows together within an hour and a quarter. By then we must be in position on the far side from here so that we're sheltered from the blast. This will be a far bigger explosion than that which destroyed Ship – assuming that the reactor doesn't explode when it hits Fenris."

After about a minute Loki said, "The safety protocols have been overridden."

The ship reverberated with the clang of the explosive bolts jettisoning the reactor toward Fenris' shadowed side and the engines, deprived of power, died. Karl leaned back in his seat and exhaled. He then leaned forward at the acceleration – a tenth of a g – from the thrusters.

They passed the reactor at a tangent, but so close that Karl fancied that he could read the manufacturer's warning printed on the side of one of the pipes. As he watched the five-metre-square block slowly fall away behind them, he breathed a sigh of relief. They were still almost three thousand kilometres away from the comet, but closing on it at over nine hundred a minute.

The others had stayed silent while the *Winter Song* careered around the sky over Fenris, but now they cried, clapped, laughed, or – in Arnbjorn's case – leaned over Ragnar.

The construct said, "I estimate that if the reactor survives the impact, it will take approximately seventy-eight minutes for it to become critical and detonate."

The thrusters slowly pushed the ship northward, away from the slowly rotating, ungainly block of pipes and metal hurtling toward Fenris. Loki fired the forward thrusters again and again to slow the ship's headlong rush, but it was a futile battle – they had less than a sixtieth of the thrust available from the main engines, and had been travelling at more than sixteen kilometres a second faster than the comet when they had dumped the reactor.

"This is going to sound stupid…" Bera said.

"But?" Karl prompted.

"We need to slow down, and be on the far side…"

"And?" Karl said.

"What if we just scraped along Fenris?" Bera said. "Used it as a brake?" She pantomimed sliding one palm over the back of her other hand.

"It would smash us to pieces." Orn had leaned closer to listen.

"Do the two halves of ship separate?" Coeo said. "The part we're in, and the part the engines were in?"

Karl looked ahead, to where a faint puff was the only sign of the reactor crashing into the ice with almost unimaginable force. That's just a taster of what awaits Isheimur, he thought.

"Loki?" he said.

"We have no use for the engine pod," Loki said. "Without a reactor it is just dead weight. As an alternative, I could – if I spun us right around, void one of the pod's water tanks and the reaction from that would slow us slightly. It would leave us critically short of raw material for the hydrogen for the thrusters, but…"

"Do it," Karl said. He turned to where Ragnar had been lowered to the floor by his son. "How is he?" Karl said. Arnbjorn shook his head and resumed tending his patient, who lay still but for his chest, which rose and fell. "Don't quit now," Karl muttered. "Hang on a while longer, Ragnar."

Bera squeezed his hand on her way past to help Arnbjorn.

On the monitor, ghostly giant fingers of steam writhed and plucked at the ship, which now sailed through the thick of the comet's tail.

A judder marked the venting of much of the several thousand tons of water they had carried from all the way from Jokullag. Soon after they began passing the tiny ball of ice. "You're getting very close," Karl said, as Fenris loomed nearer and nearer.

"You implied that my urge for self-preservation might outweigh my loyalty," Loki said. "I do not feel emotion any longer, but I still have some vestiges of the time I spent in your skull. The echo of the emotion that I feel is resentment at such an implication. So I am endangering myself as well as you, in the name of the greater good."

A range of microcosmic mountains barely a hundred metres high loomed. The base of the engine pod scraped the peak, hurling a skittering Arnbjorn across

the deck where he collided with a panel and lay still –
luckily everyone else was strapped in.

As the ship tilted downward, Loki fired the engine
pod's ventral thruster to lift it, and the crew-pod's
dorsal thruster to press that end down, lifting the engine pod further. Somehow the ship missed plunging
rear-first into the next mountain; instead they careered toward the peak beyond, hitting it hard
enough to rip the latticed gantry connecting the pods
loose, and again needing the now-leaking thruster to
fire another burst. A third such scrape loosened the
gantry further, and moments later, the ventral
thruster exploded, blowing much of the pod to
pieces. A fourth such scrape wrenched the entire re-
mainder of the pod and the gantry free of the
command pod. Loki fired the dorsal and left lateral
thruster and missed the bulk of the wreckage by a
whisker.

Alarms buzzed and honked across the command
deck, until ceasing abruptly. "I have turned them off,"
Loki said. "The situation is that we are holed on decks
three, six and seven, and losing air badly on decks five,
seven and eight. Seals on the stairwell doors will keep
the air on this deck secure."

"Bera, check on Arnbjorn, would you?" Karl said.
"Coeo, Orn, with me. We'll patch the holes as best we
can." They ran down the corridor to the stairwell, and
leaning into the doors, squeezed through the constrict-
ing exits.

Karl toggled the radio on his suit as he exited onto
deck three; "Loki, what did all that do to our velocity?
And what air, water and fuel for the thrusters do we
have to get us through the next, what, four hours?" He
grabbed pieces of panel, a plastic bag, anything that
would fit flat over the holes in the hull.

"Three hours forty-two minutes, Karl," Loki answered. "We can use the water tanks on decks ten and eleven, and split them into hydrogen for the thrusters, and fresh oxygen for us. Where you are patching the minor holes, those decks should still be habitable, but I fear that the decks with significant breaches are now vacuum."

"Velocity?" Karl repeated, grabbing a desk, and tipping it over against a wall where tiny fragments were hurtling through gaps.

Still fourteen kilometres per second faster than Fenris, although the explosion will accelerate the fragments. But we do not need to ride your comet down, we are re-entering under our own impetus."

"Trajectory?" Karl said.

"I will keep working to flatten it, Karl."

"Shit," Karl said, realising that if it needed flattening, they were in too steep a trajectory.

"Indeed."

They gathered on the bridge, a weary, bedraggled collection. Karl's head was bowed, and his shoulders slouched. Bera gripped his arm, wincing and touching her clavicle with her free hand. "The belt cut into me when the ship whiplashed us," she said to his raised eyebrow. "But we're still alive," she added fiercely. Coeo's right hand hung at an awkward angle.

The pitted hulk that had been the *Winter Song* sailed on, facing frontward, forward thrusters firing constantly. The timer counted down the seconds, showing two thousand left to detonation, then a thousand, still counting down, the comet falling away at a rate of fourteen kilometres per second, until it was barely visible even on the monitor and the counter read seven hundred. Then when it was over fifty thousand kilometres away a white, blinding pulse overloaded the screen so that it blanked momentarily.

When it reset, the comet was shearing apart in a glittering chrysanthemum of shards.

The watched its shattering silently until Loki said, "The core detonated seven hundred seconds early. Clearly its collision with Fenris damaged it." It added, "But it could have exploded much sooner."

No longer falling away, the largest fragment closed the gap on the racing ship so slowly that it was almost imperceptible. Smaller pieces moved faster; minutes after the explosion the *Winter Song* juddered under a hail of pellets. Then larger pieces rocked it violently, and finally a giant invisible hand seemed to take the ship and shake them, trying to tip them out. Just when Karl thought that the hull must crack under the strain, the shaking subsided.

They were weightless, only their harnesses holding them in place. Karl unclipped his. "Time to check for damage," he said. A clamour of voices volunteered to accompany him. "Orn," said Karl. "The rest stay." The clamour resumed. "Oi!" Karl bellowed, and they fell silent again. Karl held up his forefinger: "Ragnar's too frail," he said and held up his index finger: "Arnbjorn's needed to ensure succession." Ring finger: "Coeo's required to spread the word to his people that peace has broken out." Little finger: "Bera stays here to provide first aid."

Ignoring her hissed "First aid? What am I, Nursemaid Bera?" Karl joined Orn who was waiting in the doorway to the corridor, which they had never replaced.

They bounced feather-light out of the cabin and Orn muttered, "I think they're just a little annoyed with you."

Karl laughed. "That was the idea. Gives them something to complain about, rather than just brooding."

"That was rubbish, wasn't it?" Orn said. "All that talk of succession, and spreading the word among Coeo's people – we're dead, aren't we?"

Karl ignored him. "We need to find materials to plug the holes with."

They bumped down the littered corridor under the dim emergency lighting, and checked the rooms, finding enough suitable pieces of plastic and metal for their purposes. With a few almost empty sealant tubes from which they squeezed the last drops, a thirty-centimetre-square metal plate was converted into a makeshift tray. Repeating the operation over a dozen times gradually reduced and then finally ended the hiss of air rushing through the cracks and holes. "Karl," Bera called from the bridge doorway. "We're getting close now, you'd better finish up."

Returning to the bridge, the white globe of Isheimur completely filled the lee-side front window, and individual mountain ranges and lakes were clearly visible. "How far away are we?" Karl said.

"Less than eighteen thousand kilometres," Loki said. "Just over ten minutes to planetfall." Karl noticed that Loki had turned off the counter, and realised he should have done that days ago. Damned thing's become an obsession.

Bera passed strips of rock-eater meat to Karl. "You must be hungry."

Even now Karl wasn't sure that he was quite hungry enough to eat rock-eater, but he ate it, trying not to think of condemned men eating their last meal. "Tastes as good as always," he said, and Bera giggled.

"Give the worker some smoked lamb," Arnbjorn said, offering some to Orn, who took a handful into his vast paw. Karl also took some with a grateful nod. "Pappi?"

Arnbjorn said, offering his father the lamb. Ragnar shook his head slowly. At some point they had helped him into a seat, but he looked worse than ever with his head lolling to one side.

Karl thought, He seems to have aged a decade or more since the stroke. I wonder how much he held age at bay before by sheer willpower alone.

"I must admit, utlander," Ragnar said slowly, fighting to shape the words clearly, "I misjudged you. But for all that, I regret nothing. If I hadn't had you nursed back to health, and then chased you, we wouldn't be sitting here now, having this marvellous adventure. I'd never have seen the stars." He sighed, seeming exhausted by his speech, but then continued, "If you can buy us time, we'll make peace, even if I have to bang heads together." A thin line of drool had escaped the stricken side of his mouth, and as he slapped away Arnbjorn's attempt to wipe it for him, Karl pitied those stuck at Skorradalur with an infirm Gothi. Ragnar continued, "And our new friend Coeo has offered to share cold-weather survival techniques."

Karl stared, lost for words.

"We've been trying to work out what the effects will be on the adapted men of Fenris slamming into the South Pole," Bera said. "Luckily, there will be no more than a handful that far south, but there's bound to be some fallout."

Karl thought that the understatement of the century, remembering the antique video of Thorshammer slamming into Earth seven centuries before. A three kilometre-wide rock weighing forty billion tonnes smashed into the Mediterranean twenty times faster than a bullet, creating an inferno of vaporised rock and super-heated wind that incinerated most of Italy, Tunisia and Libya.

Karl nodded. "How does he think that they can ride it out?" He and Coeo had already discussed it while he was conjoined with Loki, but it wouldn't hurt to go over it again.

Loki translated the question for Coeo, who picked rock-eater from between his vast canine and the next tooth, and stared at it for inspiration, before answering. "Heading for higher ground will offset the higher temperatures and air pressure. It should be OK."

Karl nodded. Should be OK? he thought. Coeo, you're gambling with your people's future; I'm not sure that it's something that I could do. But then Coeo was adapted – who knew what changing the body did to the mind?

Karl thought of what was likely to really happen and wished he could tell them that when the comet landed it would throw up enough water vapour and debris to occlude the suns' light for weeks, perhaps months. That the ensuing winter would stretch into spring, maybe even into the Isheimuri summer, a full standard year away. This might be Isheimur's year without a summer. Crops would fail, even the grass might die back, and millions of animals, settler stock and native fauna alike would die. Famine would follow.

Karl hoped that he was being pessimistic, but he wasn't sure.

"Look." Beside him, Bera pointed to the windscreen where Isheimur's atmosphere lit up with dozens, scores, even hundreds of tiny flashes popping off all across the hemisphere. Her arm hooked through the strap on the other side, she wrapped her nearest arm around him. "It's beautiful," Bera said as a smudge that was a bigger piece of debris streaked across Isheimur's sky.

"Like you," Karl said.

"Flatterer." Bera snuggled closer. "I want to be near

you… in case, well you know." She looked down. In case we're killed, she meant.

"Fenris is still gaining on us," Coeo said, looking up from the monitor. "Will it hit us?"

"Negative," Loki said. "It will be close, but it will hit the atmosphere ninety seconds behind us."

"Tell us again, Gothi," Arnbjorn said, "What will happen if someone answers all these messages that you've been sending about?"

"Hard to tell," Karl said. "If they're Formers, we'll be reliant on you to argue the case for Coeo's people. If they're Tropists, we'll need to make them aware of the adapted men, and convince them that you've worked out how to co-exist." He didn't add that in all likelihood, one side would probably need to be re-settled, voluntarily or not. It seemed to him that long-term co-existence was unlikely at best, but Karl was used to thinking in decades or even centuries. He said, "The worst alternative is that we might draw the group who originally ambushed me.

"Although," he added, "two sets of colonists may distract them from any thoughts of finishing me off. And of course, no one may come at all." It seemed the least likely outcome to Karl, but it had to be faced.

The ship groaned and shook. Loki crackled, "We've just hit the edge of Isheimur's exosphere. The ride is about to get very, very rough."

"Buckle up, everyone," Karl said, and Arnbjorn helped Ragnar.

"Karl Allman," Ragnar called, voice quavering.

"Yes?"

Ragnar cursed. "You and our friend Loki will have to learn to recite my words for me." He took a deep breath, and when he spoke, his voice had grown stronger, fighting the dull roaring outside.

> *"And when the Gods left Isheimur,*
> *They cast a bolt from the sky…"*

"Oh, no," Karl whispered, trying to keep his face straight. "Not epic verse, please!"

"Hush!" Bera poked him in the ribs. "Show some respect." She bit her lower lip, and let out a small snort of laughter, which she quickly stifled.

Ragnar paused and Karl thought he had stopped, but the old man was merely drawing breath.

> *"Years crawled by with old truths forgot,*
> *Until a man fell from the sky, lived 'spite*
> *   all the odds,*
> *He saw the truth, espied the chance,*
> *To fling the bolt back at the Gods!"*

Ragnar finally finished – or his voice gave up against the steadily increasing roars and rattles from inside and outside the ship – Karl couldn't be sure which. Ragnar said something and Coeo began speaking in a regular cadence that implied that it too was a poem.

When he finished, Coeo unclipped his harness and staggering toward Ragnar, offered the settler his hands. Ragnar hesitated, but then held his out. The two men slowly clasped hands. The moment over, Coeo fell into his seat.

The gradually thickening air outside glowed orange, then red, finally white, and Coeo and Ragnar covered their ears – even Karl's were hurting. The deceleration tugged at his cheeks, muscles and joints. Karl took deep breaths, trying to calm his racing heart, failing miserably. He noticed Bera doing the same and gave her a smile which she returned.

The juddering grew worse, and to the accompanying roar of the onrushing atmosphere the thrusters added their whine. "That thruster is misfiring again," Loki said, static blurring his voice. "I'm attempting to compensate, but I fear that we are struggling to achieve a shallow enough angle. I've no desire to plunge into a steep dive into the ground."

"What's the target?" Karl said.

Loki flashed a map up onto the monitor. "This equatorial sea I have marked, which has not yet frozen."

"Surtuvatn!" Bera cried. "Where I was born – we're going home!"

Karl squeezed her hand.

Loki said, "Fenris is hitting the exosphere." It changed the monitor to show the aft view, where a third sun lit up the sky with an angry orange glow, searing through the atmosphere like an incendiary snowplough.

The whining of the thrusters increased to a shriek, and a piece of metal *spanged* out of a side console and flew across the room, fortunately missing everyone. Loki said, "I have increased power to the other thrusters, to compensate for one that has failed."

"Void all decks except ours of air!" Karl called. "Loki, dump the water and anything and everything else that you can either drop or fire out to act as thrust."

"Proceeding." The roaring outside increased until it hurt the ears. "We're flattening out," Loki said.

Bera took Karl's hand. It felt like holding hands on the mile-high funfair on Avalon. Bera said, "If we live–"

"We will live," Karl said.

"If we live," Bera said, flashing him a tearful smile, "I want your children. I still miss him." Karl thought of a small cairn, back at Skorradalur. "I want him to have brothers and sisters," Bera said.

"I want it, as well," Karl said. "But I can't live on two worlds at once." He thought of Maydays, and oncoming fleets.

"Better still," Bera said. "If they come, if your people come for you, we'll bring them with us."

"You want to come?" Karl felt the stupid grin all over his face. But the shaking's so bad that she probably can't see it anyway, he thought.

"That is one stupid grin, Karl Allman," Bera said, nailing that idea. "Yes, I want to come. Would your family accept me?"

"We'll work something out," Karl said. The juddering grew worse, even rattling his teeth.

"That child we talked about," Bera said, her words juddering out of her.

"Yes?"

"It may be sooner than you think."

"What?" Karl yelled. Heads swivelled around.

"Of course, I may just be late because of stress or something, but if I'm not, you're going to be a father... Pappi."

She burst out laughing. "If you could see your face..." she sobered. "Are you... is it OK?"

"Yes!" Karl cried, feeling the smile across his face. "Yes, yes! Very OK!" He fought the shaking and rattling to throw his arms around her.

"I want," Bera shouted, when he let her go.

"Yes?"

"I want to see the stars with you!" Bera shouted above the noise.

And then, all at once the shuddering eased.

They sat in silence stained by the ringing in Karl's ears.

On the screen the falling sun slammed into the polar ice cap and an inferno of dust and fire formed a pillar rising high into the cloudy sky in an evil blossoming.

"Brace for the shockwave," Loki said. Seconds later an invisible fist punched them in the back, turning them end over end, a tiny leaf in a gargantuan storm.

When the ship finally stopped spinning, Loki opened the screen, and a great white carpeted land lay out below them, stretching as far as the eye could see to the North Pole. The only break was the blue of Saltuvatn, peppered with black rocky outcrops, rushing up toward them.

Karl took Bera's hand as the *Winter Song* fell toward the sea.

ACKNOWLEDGMENTS

Many people helped with this book, and my thanks go especially to Skorri and Haraldur Aikman, Mike Brotherton, Mike Carroll, Roy Grey, Michael Lucas, Josh Peterson, Sharon Reamer, Rob Rowntree, Bernard Scudder and Nik Whitehead. Praise is due to them, but any mistakes are mine.

ABOUT THE AUTHOR

Colin Harvey lives in Bristol in the south-west of England, with his wife Kate and spaniel Alice. His first fiction was published in 2001, since when he has written novels, short stories and reviews, edited anthologies. He has judged the Speculative Literature Foundation's annual Gulliver Travel Research Grant for five years. His next novel, *Damage Time*, is also due to be published by Angry Robot.

www.colin-harvey.com

DAMAGE TIME
by Colin Harvey

Coming soon
from Angry Robot

Shah sighed and closed the feed.

"Anything?" Marietetski said. The light glistened off his shaven scalp, which was so black it looked blue.

"Maybe," Shah tried to suppress an ache at leaving those searing blue skies behind for the sooty rain of New York. "The memory's from Arizona, and it's a boy, which fits our amnesiac. It's fresh too, no softening of the images like you'd expect with old memories – no imprinting what we'd have liked to have happen, over what did."

"Arizona would fit the soil type taken from the vic's fingernails," Marietetski said. "He's got Hopi tattoos on his forearm. Did you say that there was a cistern with Hopi style designs?"

"Yep," Shah said, running thumb and forefinger down an invisible beard on either side of his mouth. "I think we've got enough to farm it out to Neuvo Mexico. 'Bout time they started running decent ID files on their new citizens, isn't it? They wanna buy the state, they should take responsibility for their new citizens."

Marietetski's laugh was more of a grunt. "Too busy building their new border," he said. "Besides, most people want to go the other way nowadays. Maybe their Missing

Persons people can turn up some long lost relatives here? Had to be a reason he ended up in New York."

"I think they aren't too bothered about talking to any of the Displaced about whether any of their relatives are missing," Shah said. "Besides, if that memory was him, and his family couldn't support the kid while he was fit – that was why he left – what chance will they have of taking back a vegetable? The bastards that did thi… ripping almost all his memories and posting them, for what, for a few calories?"

"Easy, easy," Marietetski said, patting his shoulder before walking away.

Shah hunched over his desk, surrounded by metre-high mountains of clear plastic folders each bulging with paper. Around him, the ten by ten metre-square room was packed with desks at which uniformed and plain-clothed men and women sat and worked quietly.

"Doodling?' Captain van Doorn's quiet voice cut through what noise there was.

"The psych analysts like to call them 'thought representation graphics'," Shah said without looking up. The thoughts they represented were primeval – anger, sadness, fear – but his voice was level.

"I've heard you say you grew up calling them doodles. You gonna clear some of these?" Van Doorn slapped his hand on one of the miniature mountain ranges on the desk.

Shah stared up at the seamed face. "Better we don't have 'em at all. Heaven knows, we shouldn't save the last of our trees if it means we can't find a file for two seconds."

"That's right," van Doorn said, ignoring Shah's sarcasm.

Shah continued as if van Doorn hadn't spoken, "My old man used to talk 'bout how a hundred years ago the futurologists claimed there'd be paperless offices. Hah. Turn of the Millennium they gengineered parasites, auditors, who made everyone afraid about everything.

They scared our bosses 'bout seventeen different types of backups all crashing at once and how if we couldn't find a tiny piece of paper that it'd send us all to hell that they reckon it's better we spend our time shuffling papers than catching perps."

"You finished ranting, dinosaur?" Van Doorn added, "Paper isn't made from trees anymore. Everyone knows that."

He didn't wait for an answer, so Shah had to settle for glaring at his broad back and muttering, "Yeah, pseudo-yeast. I know that's where it comes from, helmet-head." He tore a corner off and chewed it, then spat it out. "Don't taste any better than it ever did, though." He stood up, and placing one hand on the top of the nearest pile to hold it in place, pushed the bottom six inches of the pile off his desk and into the garbage can.

Shah returned to his doodles. His stylo gouged deep holes in the scrap 'paper' that he used up faster than any-one else in the office.

"Got you a coffee." Marietetski placed the cardboard cup with its steaming inky contents beside his pad. "NoCal okay?"

"Thanks," Shah said without looking up. Then he straightened, for even the thirty-seven calories of the murky sewage would go onto Marietetski's account, and count toward his young partner's government-approved fifteen hundred-calorie basic allowance. "NoCal's just fine. Thanks for remembering it." Kids of Marietetski's age had long ago had any kind of sweet tooth ripped from them by a world of shortages.

Marietetski shrugged. He had as many cases as Shah, but far fewer folders, and they were anorexic by compar-ison. He picked up a particularly thin folder and replaced one piece of paper with another. "Couldn't have you spit-ting coffee all over me." When Shah didn't rise to his provocation, he added, "Bitch, huh?"

"I got nine-hundred-ninety-seven on-going cases." Shah poked the stylo savagely through the paper. "You know, I know most of them lead back to a single source. Arson, burglary, petty theft, prostitution, memory-ripping: their common denominator's called Kotian. And can we prove it?"

He glared at the windows, which for all their self-cleaning implants, seemed to accumulate grime in the way New York's windows had always picked it up. Then he turned that glare on Marietetski. He said three words: "Five more weeks."

Marietetski made a *what-can-I-say* gesture.

"Five more fricking weeks and I could have, should have been sleeping late, strolling down to Manny's for breakfast, then working out how I was going to spend all of that free time that retirees earn." The words spilled from him now, a white-hot lava-flow of accumulated resentment and frustration. "Van Doorn just comes out with 'SuperAnn Fund Deficit' like it's a traffic report. No frickin' 'sorry, we're raising the retirement age by another five years, and you've got to work till you drop'."

He stopped abruptly. Took deep breaths, and visualized a beach, waves breaking on tropical golden sands. Gradually, his heart-rate slowed, and he opened his eyes. Marietetski's patrician features were carefully blank, composed into their usual impassive mask. Only his eyes gave him away. But instead of their usual distant contempt, Shah had caught a flicker of sympathy.

Then Marietetski grinned. "Walk down to Manny's? You'd die of boredom in a month with no Kotian to bitch about!"

"I'm a dino, all right," Shah said. "I arrest perps, not make up shit about why our clean-up rate for hour-old crimes has dropped from seventeen-point-three per cent, to seventeen-point-two."

"Hey, Triceratops, it's up to seventeen-point-five. Climbed point-three of a base point over that bust of Jeffreys yesterday. The perp owned up to eight more dockets."

"Well, hallelujah," Shah raised his cup in a mock-salute. "It might even get us off the bottom of the league, but hijo, I gotta tell you, while you're yoked to me, you ain't going to get that Cop of the Month award."

Marietetski shrugged. "Who wants to go to the Micronesian Enclave anyways? I went there on my honeymoon. And Beijing? Big deal. No, I'm just happy being a dino-sitter."

The sheer outlandishness of the claim made Shah burst out laughing, and his partner grinned.

Both men sipped at their coffee, staring into space. Then Shah strolled across to the recycler, and stared out of the window at Ellis Island and the radioactive stump that was all that was left of the Statute of Liberty, bathed in the watery sunshine that separated several bands of showers.

A woman's voice called from the partition separating the front of desk from the office, "Excuse me... sir? Sir, you there with the dark grey suit? Could you help me? Please?"

Shah looked over. It had been on the tip of his tongue to tell her to talk to Hampson, who was staffing the front desk. Then he saw the line of people, and let out a low whistle, before double-taking on the woman herself. Shah turned to see Marietetski's raised eyebrows, and caught his partner's nod toward the desk. He noticed that almost all of the men had stopped working to stare, and that Marietetski was grinning."Your treat," the young man mouthed.

"What's the problem, ma'am?" Shah said. Hampson hadn't even looked over, but was trying to calm a couple of irate Chinese down.

"I've lost my ID – or it's been lifted," the woman said in an accent that smacked of money. She was jaw-droppingly beautiful, probably – Shah guessed – cosmetically enhanced, and any of her clothes probably cost more than what he made in a month . She glanced round at the people around her as if she had awoken in the midst of a pack of hungry feral dogs. She looked close to tears. "I've been waiting for almost an hour and this, ah, gentleman–" she nodded at Hampson, "well, he's clearly very busy, but I don't even have enough credit for a glass of water. Please?" Her voice rose on the last word, but she subsided at Shah's outstretched hand, palm down in a *stay calm* gesture.

"It's okay, ma'am" Shah said. "I'll get you a glass of water. You just have a seat, and take a few deep breaths, and I'll be back in a few seconds." On the way to the cooler, Shah passed Hampson and hissed in the duty officer's ear, "What the hell's going on? She's been waiting an hour."

"No she hasn't," Hampson said without taking his eyes off the Chinese tourist, nor without allowing his fixed smile to waver as he answered the Mandarin tirade in a loud, slow voice; "I understand your frustration, sir, but until we can get an interpreter – and we can't get one for another hour – we're just going to have to try one another."

Shah reached the water cooler. "Fine looking woman," Detective Stickel said. The vertical line between her eyebrows deepened. "Course you'd help just as much if it were a guy, wouldn't you?"

Shah filled two cups. "Course I would. Good Samaritan and all."

"A what?" Stickel's head retreated an inch, as it often did when she was surprised.

"Read your Bible," Shah said.

This time Stickel's head recoiled a full three inches, and her eyebrows shot up. "You? Telling me to read that old book-thing? Ha, that's a good one!"

Does she know I'm a musselman-boy? Shah wondered. Is that what she means by the 'You?' He kept his face dead-pan though, letting none of his thoughts show. "Oh, I'll quote any old bit of religion." Shah raised one cup. "L'chaim!" He tossed it down and refilled it, slowly, all to irritate the waiting Stickel who was a royal pain in the ass. "See, Hebrew too! I'm covering all the bases, just in case God turns out be real, and he's affiliated."

"Yeah," Stickel said to his retreating back, then removing any doubt, "Salaam."

As Shah passed again, cups of water in hand, Hampson turned from the Chinese tirade for a moment. "Can ya take care of her? Please?"

Shah almost said, "Loss of ID, while it's serious, only needs the counter-sig of one of the Duty Officers." But it had already been a long day, and he had five more years of long days. "Ah, fuck it," he muttered, and kicked open the partition door. "Ma'am? Follow me to one of the interview rooms. We"ll sort this out now."

"Thank you," she said, her voice wavering momentarily.

Shah waited, then walked alongside her, listening to the clack of her heels on the floor tiles, breathing in her faint perfume and studying her out of the corner of his eye. Tumbling blonde hair, tip-tilted nose almost too perfect, and he'd already noticed the wide but rosebud mouth and cornflower blue eyes. That she was half a head taller than him in her heels was all that marred her perfection – and oddly enough, that made her human.

"That a mark on your temple?" he said when he sensed that she was about to make a smartass comment about him looking her over.

"This?" She pointed at the faint pink scarring on her skin, but didn't touch it, which impressed him more. "Where they caught me when they lifted my eyepiece." She grimaced. "I am such an idiot. You hear stories about the street-gangs mugging people for their pieces, but you never think it'll happen to you. They left my purse, which only makes it more galling."

Shah held the door to the interview suite open for her. "Thank you." She shot him a dazzling smile, and he stood in the doorway collecting his thoughts and enjoying watching the play of her ass beneath her expensive skirt.

He strode in and waved to the visitor's chair. "Take a seat, Ms…" and wondered idly whether everyone knew and shared Marietetski's pity over his bad news; Anything to stop staring.

"Debonis." She sat and crossed an elegant leg. He guessed that just her pointed-toed stilettos cost a few thousand bucks, or duty-free rupees, as seemed more likely. "Aurora Debonis. The little bastards skinned me while I was out shopping,"

She held up a tiny paper tote bag, no doubt containing her equally tiny but expensive purchases. "My friends all work the dayshift, so there was no one I could call. I thought that I might as well report it straight away. And see if I could beg the cab fare to a friend's place. Please don't suggest the subway."

Shah bridled, but then laughed silently at himself. Of course she wouldn't want to ride the subway; you might be okay, but her clothes would scream target louder than a damn siren.

"I'll just call up some details," Shah said. " Social security number?"

She rattled off a string of digits which Shah repeated, the tiny sensors in the eyepiece picking up the movements in his jaw, although as often happened, the numbers that appeared in front of his vision included an incorrect five instead of the correct nine. He repeated the number, mentally cursing, and this time the number came up true. While his eyepiece responded, he took a retinal scan. Within seconds, her face stared back at him

from his lens. No criminal record, he noted." You're a..."
He almost said *hooker*, but suspecting that it would be inappropriate, changed it to, "companion?"

"I am." The crispness of her answer endorsed his guess. "All licenses and taxes paid up. Does my profession change anything? Perhaps you'd have left me waiting where I was?"

Shah tried to keep his face straight, and gave up, allowing a small smile to creep across it. "Not a darn thing, ma'am. As long as you're legal, I've got no issues at all." Many of his colleagues were still old-fashioned enough that they would have left her in the line, but the thought of ducking his outstandings to help a hooker made him feel as if he'd really flipped the Mayor the bird. He checked his eyepiece and checked the whistle that he almost made. "You live in Llewellyn? Business must be good – think I should change careers?"

She took in his rumpled suit, the faded coffee stain on his tie that wouldn't come out, and his mournful face and grinned back. "You'd clean up in no time, officer. I think the house next door's for sale."

Shah grunted. "How many millions?"

Aurora made a moue. "You know the old saying – if you have to ask..."

"You can't afford it. Yep."

"Do you foresee a problem with issuing a replacement card?"

"No more than you would expect from the FBI," he said with a smile that she didn't return this time. "I'll call the attorney you have listed as your contact." He rattled the number off to the meeting-phone that sat on the desk.

Moments later an androgynous voice echoed round the room: "Harcourt and Robinson. How may we help you today?"

"I'd like to speak to Stephen Harcourt, please," Shah said. "I'm Officer Pervez Shah of the NYPD, calling about Ms Aurora Debonis."

Faster than any human could have managed, a fractionally more masculine voice said, "Officer Shah? This is Stephen Harcourt. What's this about Ms Debonis?"

"I have a lady with me who's been mugged and lost her ID," Shah said. "If I turn the cam on her, and she says a few words, can you provisionally confirm her ID pending DNA verification? It'll only cut a day or two off her waiting time for a replacement ID, but every little bit helps." Shah swiveled the cam.

"Of course," Harcourt said. "Hello, Aurora."

"Hello ,Stephen. Yes, it's me. That'll teach me to be casual in NYC, won't it?"

"I'll need you to answer some security questions. You have a memory copied to me for identification. What is it?"

"A tennis tournament I played in when I was fifteen. I won when my opponent back-handed into the net."

"Great. Please provide the police officer with a DNA swab."

Shah took a tiny scraping from the inside of her cheek and inserted it into the analyzer. After a few seconds' delay, Harcourt said, "I provisionally confirm the voiceprint as Ms Aurora Debonis," and repeated her social security number. "Thank you, officer."

The line went dead, saving Shah the job of wondering about the etiquette of how to say goodbye to an AI on the Micronesian fleet. He called the DHS number, recited the coded instructions, and hung up. "They're not good with routine requests – too many emergencies – and making you sweat a couple of days gives them time to nose through your trash. But you should have it in a few days."

"Oh." She sat blinking through the implications. "That means no travel, no–"

"Shopping. Yeah," he said sympathetically, standing up. "I can loan you cash to buy food, maybe at a corner Mashriq. I'll call you a cab, and put it on my card."

"Thank you. I've been worried sick," she explained with a little laugh, her eyes glinting." I walked all the way here." She showed him blistered heels, and echoed his thoughts. "And in these shoes!"

He walked her down to the pick-up point. Although it was six floors down, he had the native New Yorker's aversion to riding in elevators since continual brownouts had started with the power rationing and multi-sourcing of energy, and waited with her for one of the rare and hideously expensive little yellow pods. She turned as she climbed in. "You've been a great help. Thanks."

"My pleasure."

"See you soon, I hope." She flashed him a smile. He was sure it was purely professional, but was still surprised at its warmth.

"Who knows?" He smiled back.

"When you said 'see you soon' I didn't think you meant this soon," Shah said.

Aurora smiled.

"Can I get you something else?" Karl shouted over the background noise of the bar.

At Shah's enquiring look, Aurora shook her head. "I've had enough for now." She glanced him a momentary smile he almost missed. "To drink."

"Ah." Shah kept his voice carefully neutral. He had found over the years when lost for words that "ah" was a good expression. He also found it useful sometimes to stay silent, and let the silence squeeze the next answer from the other person. If Aurora had shown any signs of wanting to leave he might have said more, but she looked as if she was settled.

The lengthening silence repaid his faith. Aurora stared at the counter and said, "You know–", then stopped again. She looked up at him. "You're not making this easy." Her nervous little smile robbed the words of any rebuke.

"Making what easy?" He knew now where the conversation was going, but he wasn't sure why.

"I was going to repay you with your own cash," she said. "If I can't do that, I have only one thing that I can offer. But normally, I don't have to work quite so hard to sell it."

"Well," he said, nodding slowly, gravely, to show his sympathy." That must be very difficult for you. Having to work quite so hard at whatever it is that I'm not making easy."

Her laugh was an explosion of air that ended as abruptly as it started. "You're very funny," she said, tone belying her words. "Are you fully partnered, or just as slow as you make out?"

"Partnered? Yeah, I have one, though she's mostly on a different shift from me. We overlap slightly, occasionally."

"Ah." She tilted her head back, and her little smile suggested she was deliberately mocking his earlier non-commitment. "So… complicated, huh?"

He laughed staccato, betraying a slight attack of nerves. "If we lived out in the boonies, it wouldn't be an issue. Everyone's reverted back to working daylight time only, to save on the power bills."

"Not everywhere. We live shifts in Llewellyn." She ran her finger around the rim of her glass and studied him. "Stop changing the subject, Officer Shah. Is your name Persian, by the way?"

That she recognized its ethnicity warmed him inside. "It is. And I'm not changing it so much as trying to work out what the subject is." He looked straight into her eyes, and held her gaze until she looked away. "I'm an old man–"

"Middle-aged–"

"I'm an old man," he insisted. "I'm not young enough, or ruggedly-handsome enough in an old-man kind of way to be remotely attractive to a woman like you. Nor rich enough to afford your rates."

"Do you know?" She snapped, "That's the first sweeping generalization you've made since we met."

She tapped her finger on the bar, and he guessed it was to help her think of what to say next. "Why do you think my clients come to me?" She asked, flushing slightly. "Apart from the obvious."

He puffed his cheeks out. "Dunno."

"Good answer," she said sarcastically. "There's as many reasons as clients. Some come for sex, no two ways about it. Others book me for a massage. Sometimes they'd rather talk – they just need someone to unload onto, because they're lonely, or they have friends, but they think those friends aren't interested in their problems." She stared at him and tipped the dregs of her glass down her throat, but when he reached out to signal Karl, she put her hand on his arm. "And you think you know why I want to go back to your place!"

"Sorry." Shah held his hands up in surrender.

Aurora took a deep breath, then grinned. "Even whores have feelings." Adding quickly, "Not that I consider myself a whore." She leaned closer to him and whispered in his ear. "There's one other reason."

"Yes?"

Aurora straightened so that the gap between them was again a meter or so. She tipped the salt shaker up and sprinkled grains of sand on the counter, and licking her finger, dabbed it on the micro-mountain she'd made. Then she sucked her finger and when she'd finished said, not loudly but clear enough to carry: "I like to fuck."

Shah sat, his face burning and thought It's so quiet in here they must all be able to hear my heart racing. "Oh."

"Oh," Aurora echoed, her face straight, but he could hear the not quite suppressed laughter in her voice. "I'm here, you're here. I like you. Do we really need to complicate it with our motives?" She sprayed perfume from a tiny atomizer and held out her wrist. "Like it?"

It wasn't strong, but the perfume seemed to poke him between the eyes. Wow, must be some powerful pheromones in that. "Yeah, very nice."

Aurora stood up. "Come on. Let's go back to my place."

Shah stood too. "I'm not going all the way to Llewellyn tonight. My place is three blocks away."

Aurora took his hand and led him to the doorway. Shah felt every pair of eyes in the place tracking him. One of the construction workers grinned at him, and Shah winked. He couldn't ever remember feeling so good, or so young.

Outside the rain had slackened off and was barely worthy of the name any longer. Men and women still strained between the shafts of their harnesses as they hauled their cabs along, while the clop of a few horse-drawn hansoms echoed along the street, interspersed with the beeping horns of the even rarer yellow cabs. One chugged past, bloated hydrogen bag on its roof now almost empty and drooping, spilling over the sides of the roof onto the tops of the windows.

Aurora took his arm and led Shah to the curb. "Nah, it's okay," he said, suddenly feeling very lethargic, and determined for some reason to fight it "We'll walk to my place. Three blocks."

"Let's get a cab," Aurora said. "I've a town house a mile or two away."

Shah took a great lungful of air and with a huge effort hauled himself upright. It was the hardest thing he'd ever had to do, though not quite as hard as what he did next.

Somehow it seemed important, though he couldn't quite fathom why. "No," he said. "I have to go to work tomorrow. Not until late, but I have to work. My place – or nowhere. Sorry, Aurora, but that's the deal. And I can't afford cab fares."

"Then let's compromise. If they'll take this C-note of yours, we'll see whether it'll carry us to your place. Okay?"

"Okay," Shah sighed.

He was acutely aware of her hip pressing into his as they sat scrunched close together in the back of the pedi-cab, the fragrance of her perfume tickling his nose, and the warmth of her breath on the side of his neck.

The cabbie, a muscle-bound giant who probably ate every calorie he got in fares just to stay alive, grunted with exertion.

"See." Aurora sprayed her wrist again. "I said we should get a cab."

"But that note of yours wouldn't have got us to your place, even the one in town." Instead he'd run his credit down that little bit more. He shifted slightly, hoping she wouldn't feel how much he wanted her, but she ran her hand over his erection, stopping his breath.

"We could always go onto my place afterwards," she crooned. "I've got something that'll keep you going all night, my fine stallion." She nibbled his ear.

"We're here," he croaked, running his card through the cab's scanner, and hearing the clunk of the doors unlocking as it successfully validated the payment.

She held onto his arm as they ran through the rain to the lobby, stopping to wipe their feet on the mat. "We'll break our necks on the floor if we're not careful," he explained.

"It doesn't absorb the water?" Aurora sounded shocked.

He sniggered. "The landlord would put another thousand a month on the rent if it did."

Too tired to walk, they took the elevator for once. He caught her chewing her lip slightly as she straightened her hair in the mirror. He looked up at her, and touched her arm. "Leslyn and Doug will be asleep." He added, "But they have their own room."

"Leslyn switches?"

"Yeah, our shifts intersect once a month or so."

"Doug 's fully hetero, then?"

"Both of us are." He smiled slightly. "Our generation weren't quite as, um, flexible as yours. It's Leslyn and me, or Leslyn and Doug." He added, "Do you know, I had only one set of parents." He laughed at her shocked look. "They called it a nuclear family."

"They were toxic?" She leaned her shoulder into his.

"Boom boom," he said, adding an equally ancient punch line.

She seemed to understand, for she said, "It's the way I tell 'em," a line almost as old as her previous joke.

"Hard as may be for a young lady like you to believe," he said, straightfaced, "but it worked perfectly well for thousands of years."

"Yeah," she drawled as the elevator juddered to a halt on fifty-four, "but we don't live on raw meat nowadays, or club each other unconscious as a pick-up line."

"It only broke down in the end because so many people worked all around the clock, and partnerships split up all the time. It was pressure that broke it, not inherent flaws in the idea."

She shuddered theatrically. "Imagine it: only one set of parents, and just blood-brothers and sisters."

They emerged from the elevator into the thickly-carpeted corridor. "Hush now," he said. "This is a respectable building."

427

She snorted. "You just want the last word. No one in New York goes to bed before three am."

Shah awoke muddled, the room swimming. An image, of him naked and her head moving down his torso, past his waist…

The thunderous pounding that had dragged him from sleep resumed, and a male voice shouted something that Shah didn't catch. The room seemed to wobble and waver.

"Whuh? Aurora?" Shah peered blank-eyed, head tilting one way then another, to offset the wobbling of the room.

The door crashed in and a man's voice shouted, "NYPD! Flat on your face! I said *flat*! NOW!"

DAMAGE TIME
by Colin Harvey

Coming soon
from Angry Robot

**ANGRY
ROBOT**

Teenage serial killers
Zombie detectives
The grim reaper in love
Howling axes **Vampire
hordes**   Dead men's clones
The Black Hand
Death by cellphone
Gangster shamen
Steampunk swordfights
Sex-crazed bloodsuckers
Murderous gods
Riots **Quests** Discovery
Death

Prepare to welcome
your new
Robot overlords.

angryrobotbooks.com